STORMFRONTS

AN ALPHA BILLIONAIRE ROMANCE

MICHELLE LOVE

CONTENTS

Made in "The United States" by:

Michelle Love

© Copyright 2021

ISBN: 978-1-64808-833-9

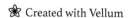 Created with Vellum

When billionaire property mogul Theo Storm gives the Commencement address at her college, grad student Jess Wood initially dismisses him as a rich, bland businessman. When he notices her in the audience however, his blatant admiration for her attracts whispers amongst her friends and colleagues and an embarrassed Jess escapes from the throng, only to find herself unable to stop thinking about him.

Storm tracks her down to her tiny apartment and persuades her to have dinner with him. The incredible attraction between them becomes almost unbearable. Theo takes Jess back to his luxurious penthouse and going against all her self-made rules, Jess goes to bed with him. Instead of breaking the tension between them, their tempestuous, uninhabited sexual chemistry awakens something almost feral inside of her, leaving her craving more and more of this incredible man.

1

COME WITH ME PART ONE

I t might have been the fourth glass of bourbon, or the fifth or the sixth. Theo Storm wasn't sure. All he remembered was making a dumb bet with Max who, with mischief in his eyes, shook Theo's hand, muttering 'Good luck with that' under his breath.

Theo opened his eyes and stared up at the ceiling of the hotel room. God, why was it every time he went drinking with Max, he turned into a loud mouthed asshole who thought that he ruled the world? The trip to Vegas had been to celebrate the opening of their latest boutique apartment building – and to thank Max for working every hour of every day to get it done. Theo had promised himself that he wouldn't get trashed. He never came out on top when drinking with Max. The guy had hollow legs, for Christ's sake.

'Jesus.' A headache shrieked around his skull and Theo groaned. He rolled out of bed onto the floor and briefly considered staying there for the rest of his life. Reluctantly he staggered to his feet and into the bathroom, stepping under a too-hot shower and sighing with relief as the water hit his tired body. After he'd dried himself, he wrapped a towel around his waist and stood at the small sink to brush his teeth, studying himself in the mirror. Almost forty years old and he still acted like a twenty-year-old college kid, partying nearly every night. He knew what his dad would say, with disappointment in his eyes. Settle down, son. Grow roots. Make a home, a family. Theo sighed. It wasn't enough for his dad that he was the head of StormFronts, the company that Theo had built from literally nothing. That he'd been top of his class at MIT or that he'd designed, built and paid for his dad's retirement home in the Florida Everglades (thankfully a continent away from his own Seattle penthouse).

Theo rinsed his mouth and then threw back a couple of glasses of tap water to combat his hangover. He'd been moaning about his Dad's attitude last night at a staggeringly unsympathetic Max, who merely rolled his eyes and called him a poor little rich boy. Max was right, he knew. He just had to ignore the parental pressure but still... it was probably why he'd made that ridiculous bet with Max.

I will find the love of my life within three months.

Theo shook his head at the thought of it. Why the hell had he made that bet? Hubris and hyperbole. He shrugged – it wasn't as if Max would hold him to it in the cold light of day.

'I AM ABSOLUTELY GOING to hold you to it,' Max told him on the plane back to Seattle. Theo groaned and slumped back in his seat. His hangover wasn't abating at all and now he was on the way to give the Commencement speech at Seattle's most prodigious college. Theo was used to public speaking in his job, not that it was his favourite thing to do, but he'd agreed to it back when he'd been dating a girl from Tacoma – whose name he couldn't remember, he thought now with a jolt of shame – whose cousin was part of the graduating class. The speech was written, his custom-made Armani three piece pressed and waiting. He'd even managed to shave this morning. Outwardly, he'd look the part of the billionaire mogul but inside... he swallowed a wave of nausea. Idiot. Why get hammered the night before the speech?

· · ·

THEO DEFINITELY WASN'T in the mood for another grilling from his best friend. Max fixed him with a serious glare.

'You promised me you'd find the one. I want you to, at the very least; try to have a social life. You haven't dated anyone since Lorelei.'

Theo grimaced and Max sniggered. Lorelei had been a sweet girl but her obsession with the healing power of crystals had doomed that relationship very, very quickly. Theo chuckled at the memory.

'Yeah, see? '

Max rolled his eyes. 'That's not a reason to avoid the whole dating thing. You can't write off the whole thing just because your last girlfriend thought she could talk to the spirit world. It's an important part of life and besides, you're not getting any younger.'

'Thanks, dude.'

Max grinned at Theo's sarcastic tone. 'I'm serious. I want you to meet someone who'll make you happy.'

Theo studied his friend. 'You say that with all the smug complacency of the happily settled.'

Max flashed him his cheesiest grin. 'What can I say? I got lucky with Joel. Now if only you'd embrace your inner gay guy, I've got a hundred friends panting to meet you.'

Theo grinned. 'Ah, your ongoing campaign to turn me. Sorry, dude, I appreciate it but...'

'You worship at the Alter of Vadge, I know.'

Theo sniggered. 'Charmingly put.'

Max sighed dramatically. 'Well, a guy can dream. How long has it been since you were serious about someone?'

Theo didn't answer – mostly because he couldn't remember ever being serious about anyone. 'Can we drop this?'

'Nope,' Max was grinning wildly, 'I tell you what, I'll make this interesting. You get married before Christmas – I'll work for you for a year for free.'

Theo's eyebrows shot up. 'You're serious? Married? Not going to happen.'

Max nodded, leaning forward in his chair. 'Dude... you're my best friend and I just want you to slow down. You work, work, work, which is all good but you're missing out on so much. Meet someone, fall in love, and get married. Hell, I'd be happy if you just dated someone. Come on, help an old romantic out. Besides...' he sniffed huffily, 'I really don't want to find you dead of a stress-related heart attack at your desk. We'd never get the smell out of the carpet.'

Theo grinned at his friend but as Max pulled a blanket over himself and turned away to take a nap, Theo stared out of the window of the plane at the sparkling blue waters of the Pacific, the craggy beauty of the West Coast and wondered if Max was right. Maybe it was time for something more, something real. Thing was... he didn't even know where to start, what he was looking for, or who he wanted as his partner in life.

He glanced over to his sleeping friend and knew his friend was right. Theo grinned to himself and settled back into his seat to enjoy the rest of the flight.

'I hate to ask.'

Jessica Wood narrowed her eyes at her boss. Professor Gerry Land grinned sheepishly and shrugged as they sat together in the college's refectory, empty coffee cups in front of them. Jess sighed. She knew this wheedling tone of old. Gerry had been her mentor, her champion for four years through college and when she'd applied to be his research fellow to pursue a Ph.D., he'd pulled strings to make sure that she'd gotten the position.

Occasionally though, like now, he'd call in the favor.

'Yeah, yeah, what now?'

Gerry smirked, knowing that he had her. 'Commencement.'

Jess made a face. 'Oh, no way...I did it last time.' Their Art department was supposed to send a representative to the ceremony and while they both appreciated the true meaning of the tradition, it was deathly boring – sitting for hours, applauding everyone, listening to some celebrity rambling on about how the graduating students should 'reach for the stars'. They actually had a tally on how many of the illustrious guests used clichés like that.

'PLEASE? I just have so much work to do....and this funding application isn't going to write itself.'

Jess made a face at him, knowing that he'd won. If she didn't go to the ceremony, Gerry would dump the application process on her and no way – no freaking way – she was getting into that.

'Fine.'

Gerry nudged her shoulder with his. 'I owe you one.'

'YOU OWE ME MANY.' But she smiled. At twenty-four, Jessica Wood was exactly where she wanted to be – immersed in a world of art and study. She wasn't rich. That world belonged to her step-brother, Jules. Her mom had married Jules' French millionaire father but now, after they'd both died, it was just her, Jules – and Jules' never ending puppet strings. That was the one thing wrong with her life. She worked for Gerry and part-time in a one of Seattle's artisan coffee houses and still only managed to make enough to cover her rent and food. She was okay with that but Jules still managed to exert his influence over her life in so many different ways.

She pushed the thought of him away now, and fought the heavy dread that always followed when she thought of her step-brother and went to get changed for the ceremony.

HER APARTMENT WAS LESS than a block from the college and she quickly showered and slipped into her go-to dress; a dark burgundy silk sheath that shimmered down and hugged her curves. At five foot four, she wasn't the tallest woman, but the dress flared out at her waist, showing off her surprisingly long legs. Her dark mahogany hair fell almost to her waist and she pulled it up over one shoulder. The lightest of make-up was put on, then she added a delicate gold chain which lay against her dusky skin and fell into the valley of her full breasts. Glancing in the mirror, Jess nodded once. She knew people considered her attractive but... 'They can't see the damage within', she thought. She dismissed the thought and scooted out of the door.

BACK AT COLLEGE, she made her way to the ceremony, held in the wide courtyard. She glanced at her watch and saw that she was early. She grinned to herself and decided to call Gerry to pass the time. She ducked into a quiet corridor and pulled out her cell phone.

'I'm calling to issue you an official death threat.'

Gerry chuckled. 'Hey look, at least you get to hear about how the world is indeed a shellfish-based opportunity for our students.'

'About how this is 'only the beginning of the adventure?''

'Yep and of course, and how they are all astronauts.'

'Huh?'

Gerry sighed. ''Reaching for the stars'?'

Jess laughed. 'Oh of course, sorry. God, would it kill one of these people to quote some Eudora Welty? Some Dorothy Parker? Even some Bill and Ted would be nice.'

'Snob.'

'You bet. I'll see you later – and I'll be armed.'

Gerry laughed loudly. 'I'll buy you dinner to make up for it.'

'You bet you will.'

SHE HUNG up and turned to walk out to the courtyard. She stopped, a small gasp escaping her. At the end of the corridor, watching her, a man was stood half in shadow. Jess's heart began to thud as the man's gaze locked with hers, burning into hers. He was tall – very, very tall, at least six five, and his huge body was expensively clad in an exquisite three piece suit. With his dark curls close-cropped and his face angular, he looked sculpted to perfection.

THEY STARED at each other for a long moment then the Dean appeared and bore the man away. Jess let out her breath out in a rush. What the hell was that? She felt the blood burn hot through her body, a pulse beat between her legs. Jesus... The way he had been looking at her – as if he wanted to tear off her clothes, possess her... Jess turned and leaned her burning forehead against the cool stone wall. For a second, she closed her eyes and imagined what would have happened if the Dean hadn't interrupted the moment. Would the man have come closer, pushed her against the wall, kissed her? The tension had crackled along the distance between them and now she fantasised that he'd lifted her up, tugged her panties aside and fucked her hard, right then, right there. She gave a small groan at the thought then pushed the thought away she stumbled out into the courtyard and found her seat amongst the other faculty and representatives.

WHAT THE HELL'S the matter with me? She shook her head as the thought ripped through her. Was she that bereft of a sex life that she was imagining rough sex with a total stranger? Ummm yes. She sighed, shaking her head. The woman next to her gave her a strange look and Jess smiled sheepishly at her. The Dean was at the podium now and talking, and Jess tried to concentrate on what he was saying.

'...HEAD of the multinational property corporation that has not only specialised in high-end properties but also worked closely with Habitat for Humanity to bring much need shelter to those in need around the world. I'm pleased to introduce to you, Theodore Storm.'

. . .

JESS FELT her heart flutter as the guy from the corridor stepped up and shook hands with the dean. Her first glimpse of him had not done him justice. He was gorgeous, a Greek god amongst his serfs. His expression serious but kind, and there was a smile on his full mouth. Looking at him was like staring at the sun, Jess decided, dangerous, risky, a threat to sanity but she tried to look away and couldn't. As he began to speak, his low, melodic tone made his speech even more compelling and Jess was gratified to hear him speak of opportunity, and of hard work.

'YOU'LL HEAR a lot from other about how this is your time...,' Theo Storm fixed his audience with a confident and authoritative stare, '... and maybe it will be. What they won't tell you is just how hard you will have to work if you want to achieve even one per cent of your 'dreams'. Nothing – nothing – will be handed to you in this world. I say this as someone who grew up in a poor family. Yes, now I can live comfortably as anyone – but it took every ounce of everything I had to get there. Determination, willingness to work every minute of every hour. There was a point when I lived in my car to save on rent money.' There was a murmur in the crowd and Theo grinned, shrugging good-naturedly. 'I know, a property mogul living in his car. But,' – his face turned serious again – 'that's what it takes. That kind of sacrifice. If you're just interested in the latest iPhone, the latest cool sneakers as soon as you graduate then...go work for someone else, do the nine-to-five. There are some among you who will do that – and believe me, there's nothing wrong with it if that's all you're looking for. Me, no. I couldn't. I believe in going after what I want.'

AND HE LOOKED DIRECTLY at Jess, caught and held her stare... and held it.... and held it. Jess felt her heart falter then quicken, her cheeks flame scarlet as they gazed at each other. The crowd, silent, now started to murmur and Jess was aware of the people turning to gaze at her. A minute turned to two, then Theo cleared his throat and smiled at her.

'THERE ARE ALWAYS things beyond our reach seemingly,' he spoke again, his even tone belying nothing of the fire burning in his eyes, 'But the best way to combat that is this – pretend that it isn't. Pretend you can have anyone – anything, I'm sorry, anything you want and you're halfway there. So there it is. Thank you, Dean, for inviting me to speak and finally, my last words of advice are these...' Storm grinned them and the sharp angles of his face softened, became boyish. He laughed briefly, still gazing at Jess, who couldn't help returning his infectious smile. Theo nodded at her slightly then leaning into the mic, he spoke his final words. "Be excellent to each other... and party on, dudes."

JESS WAS STILL GIGGLING as she made her way back to the art department. Theo Storm was rich, gorgeous and as funny as hell. The whole package, she sighed, almost with longing. She relayed what had happened to an appreciative Gerry.

'Well, you got your wish,' he said before returning to his work. Jess sighed, flushing slightly. Almost. Her mind flittered back to that moment in the corridor, that feral need inside of her for Storm to take her in his arms and...

'An Art Department with its own living, breathing work of art.'

His voice made her start, spin around. Theo Storm was leaning on the doorframe, grinning at her.

'HEY,' Theo couldn't help from chuckling at her pained expression.

'Um....hi.' She had a low voice, almost a purr and it made his pulse quicken and his groin tighten. She was achingly beautiful: big brown eyes, long dark hair, and a curvy figure but it wasn't that which drew Theo to this young stranger. It was her sense of humor, and her obvious intelligence.

HE WAS aware he was staring and her face was becoming redder and redder from his intense scrutiny. He stepped towards her and saw her quiver, glancing into an office at the side of the big room. He saw a middle-aged man bent over his desk. Theo looked back at the girl and held out his hand.

'COME WITH ME.' He was gratified when, despite a little hesitation, she slid her little hand into his and allowed him to lead her out of the room

JESS HAD no idea where he was taking her. All she knew was she would follow him anywhere. He led her outside to a waiting limo, opened the door for him and she slid into the back seat as if in a daze. He got in beside her and spoke to the driver, who nodded then put up the privacy screen. Theo smiled at her, touching his finger to her cheek.

'HEY THERE, I'M THEO.'

She swallowed, wanting to lean into his touch. 'Jess...I'm Jess.'

Next to him, she felt tiny, dwarfed as he moved his body closer, his palm cradling her face.

'Hi Jess...' he whispered, his face close to hers and then his mouth was on hers. She sank into the kiss, his soft lips moving against hers tenderly, his tongue gently exploring hers. She moaned softly and his kiss grew rougher, his breathing as laboured as hers. He pulled her onto his lap and she curved her arms around his neck as his hands slid around her waist, his big thumbs stroking her belly in a way that made her weak.

. . .

'CHRIST, YOU'RE BEAUTIFUL,' he murmured against her mouth. She opened her eyes to find him gazing at her with clear green eyes. She gasped slightly as his hand slid between her legs, caressed her through the cotton of her panties.

'I WANT YOU,' Theo Storm told her and every cell in her body melted at his words. She nodded, wanting him to tell her more.

'We're going to my apartment, Jess, and when we get there, I'm going to peel that dress from your glorious body and fuck you all night long. You are mine now, understand?'

She nodded, breathless, speechless. Was this really happening? If it was a dream, then she didn't want it to end. She wanted this man to possess her completely, to never wake up from it. He kissed her again, a long, intoxicating kiss that made her head spin and then the limo was stopping.

SHE DIDN'T REMEMBER how they got from the car to the elevator, all she knew was that once inside, Theo drew the spaghetti strap of her dress down and exposed her left breast, catching the nipple in his mouth and sucking on it. She gasped at the feeling and felt her legs quiver. She tentatively slid her hand down to his groin, the feel of his thick heavy cock huge against her hand and the hot length of it thrilling her. Theo moaned at her touch and smiled down at her.

'IT WILL BE inside you very, very soon, Jessica.' His hand, stroking her already wet panties, slipped inside the cotton and his fingers started to rub her clit, sliding along her cleft to her sex. He slid two fingers into her, moving them in and out of her. Jess's head was swimming now and she barely heard the elevator stop. Theo swung her up into his arms and kissed her as he carried to her towards what she

supposed was his bedroom. He set her on her feet and true to his
word, he unhooked the dress from her shoulders and let it slither to
the floor. He dropped to his knees, burying his face in her soft belly
and she felt his tongue circle and dipped into her navel, his lips
against her skin. God, she wanted him so badly. She tugged at him
and he laughed at her impatience, sweeping her onto the bed. He
stroked her face tenderly.

'OKAY, but this is the last time you get to set the rules, my Jess.' She
heard him unzip his fly, heard the condom snap on then he was
pushing her legs apart and he plunged his huge cock into her. Jess
almost screamed with pleasure as he fucked her harder and harder,
her legs curling around him as she rode him. He pinned her hands
above her head, his hips grinding into hers so roughly she felt pain
but she didn't care, she wanted to take all of him in, feeling him
pounding her into otherworldly pleasure. She came again and again,
but he kept on, his massive cock driving into her deeper and deeper
until she was crying with pleasure. She felt him come, finally, his
amazing body jerking and shuddering with the force of his climax.
He stayed inside her as he shivered to a stop and then kissed her so
passionately that it made her head swim.

'JESSIE, JESSIE, JESSIE...' The way he spoke her name, a name no-one
else called her, in a way was so intimate, so tender that she wanted to
cry. He buried his face in her full breasts, breathing her in, catching
his own breath. She cradled his head for a moment then as he shifted
so he could look at her, she placed her palms flat against his
immense, hard chest, marvelling at the feel of his solid body. His face
had softened from the sharp angles of his arousal now and he smiled
down at her.

'Well, hello.'

She chuckled. 'Hello,' she suddenly felt shy, ridiculously, incon-
gruously. Theo brushed her lips with his.

'Jessica... I wanted you from the minute I saw you in that hallway. This morning I had a wicked hangover and a speech to give. I didn't expect to find a goddess.'

SHE BLUSHED FURIOUSLY at his words and suddenly felt vulnerable. Was he giving her a line? Why bother now he'd already had her?

Theo was studying her expression and he stroked her face with his big thumbs. 'No bullshit, I swear. But I did, I had to have you.'

He touched the pad of his thumb to her bottom lip then drew it down the centre of her body. Her belly quivered as he splayed his big hand across it. Jess couldn't look away from his gaze and she reached up tentatively to brush her fingers along the dark circles under his eyes. He smiled as she did.

'HARD NIGHT, LAST NIGHT', he explained. 'If I'd known, I'd have gotten more rest so I was ready...'

'Ready for what?' Her heart was beating fast, her voice barely a whisper. Theo Storm kissed her again, a deep throaty chuckle rumbling through his body.

'To fuck you all night long, beautiful Jess, all... night... long.'

JESS WOKE in the middle of the night, thirsty. Beside her, Theo slept, his handsome face relaxed and sleeping. He looked much younger, almost boyish. He was on his side, facing her, his hand splayed across her belly protectively, his lips pressed against her shoulder. '*Wow*', Jess mouthed to herself, grinning. She couldn't really believe what had happened in just a few hours. Feeling her throat protest, she slid carefully from under his grip and out of bed.

THE NIGHT WAS cool on her skin and she shivered. Snagging his shirt from the floor, she wrapped it around her body: it was so big it fell almost to her knees and wrapped around her petite body nearly twice. She grinned, burying her face in the fabric to catch his scent. Fresh and woodsy, clean linen. She padded into the kitchen and grabbed a glass from the sink, rinsing it and filling it with water. She drank an entire glass then refilled it, wandering out into the living room. Three walls were made entirely of glass and now she wandered over and looked down to the streets below, leaning her hot forehead against the cool glass.

THEO HAD KEPT his word and had thoroughly and expertly fucked her until she was exhausted, his complete domination over her body making her limbs liquefy and her senses explode.

NOW, here in the silence of the night, Jess wondered how she'd gotten here – how his sheer machismo and dangerous charm had overcome the rules she had set up for herself. Don't let anyone get too close.

SHE REASONED that sex wasn't the same as emotional closeness but then again... something told her Theo wasn't one of those hit-and-run guys.

'You should always be lit by the moonlight.'

She turned at the sound of his voice and grinned at him. He was leaning against the doorway, the way he had earlier, watching her. He smiled as she chuckled, and went to her. He slid his arms around as she smiled up at him.

'That was so cheesy,' she murmured and he laughed, kissing her. He pulled the shirt open to reveal her body and she watched him as he admired the full breasts, the slight outward curve of her belly. He touched his fingertips to her cheek and she leaned into his touch, her gaze locked with his. He bent his head and kissed her slowly, taking the glass from her hand, and pulling the shirt from her body. Lifting her up, he pressed her back against the cold glass and she gasped at the icy feel against her skin. She could feel his cock, so ram-rod hard as it nudged against her sex and she moaned with longing, the honey flowing from her to cover his shaft.

HIS EXPRESSION WAS SO FIERCE, so focused on her that she felt a thrill of adrenaline spike through her. No-one had looked at her like that before, as if he wanted to own her, worship her. She wrapped her legs around his back as he supported her with his big hands, pressing her hard into the glass as he thrust into her. His immense strength made her feel as if she would rip in two as he drove relentlessly into her, his mouth grinding down onto her lips hungrily. He was so strong that he could hold her up with one arm, the free hand tangling in her dark hair, bunching it in his fist, holding her head still.

'Jessica.... say my name.'

She gasped it out, barely able to catch her breath. 'Theo...'

'Again.'

'Theo...'

He rammed his cock so deep into her that she screamed his name out again and again. Bright lights exploded in her vision as she came but he was unrelenting and Jess felt as if she were going to pass out. By the time he lowered her, gasping for air, she felt as high as if she'd mainlined heroin. Theo stretched out beside her, head propped up on his elbow, watching the rise and fall of her breasts as she caught her breath, his hand stroking lazily over her belly. Eventually, she grinned up at him and he bent his head to kiss her. She stroked the hard lines of his cheekbones. His eyes were soft and, looking into them, she felt as if she'd known him forever. He smiled, seeming to read her mind.

'JESSICA WOOD,' he spoke softly - she thrilled at the melodic low growl of his voice, 'You are the best reason to stay awake all night long. I'd like to see you again... to show you more of my world, learn about yours'. He bent his lips to hers and then locked his gaze onto hers. 'I want to teach you about a world of pleasure that you've never even dreamed of.'

HER BREATH CAUGHT in her throat and a thrill of fear and pleasure mingled in her senses. His eyes were dark, dangerous, the sharp angles of his face even more defined by the darkness and the moonlight. He kissed her throat, then took each nipple into his mouth in turn and teased them until they were so hard they throbbed with pain. He pressed his lips against her belly then looked up at her.

'A PREVIEW. I promised you I was going to taste every inch of your skin. I'm going to fuck you hard, Jessica Wood, so fucking hard. My tongue is going to go deep inside you, and you're going to scream my name, and beg me to fuck you. Are you on birth control, Jessica?'

Breathless, she nodded. He smiled. 'Good. Because I want to feel your sweet cunt on my cock, Jessie, flesh on flesh. I want to fill you with my cum.'

His words were making her so wet she could barely speak but she managed to gasp out 'I want to suck you.'

Theo grinned and flipped her so she straddled him. She moved down his glorious body, kissing his hard chest, the rippling stomach, taking his cock, so rigid and huge in her small hand, gliding her lips over the wide crest of it, feeling his body tense as she began to draw on it, her tongue teasing the tip. She could taste the sweet, clean skin, the saltiness of his pre-cum. She felt him tangle his fingers in her hair, the pads of his thumbs massaging her scalp. She dug her fingernails into the skin of his hips, heard his sharp intake of breath, his low, triumphant 'Yes!'. His hips began to shudder as he neared his peak, and Jess felt his cock grow harder and then pulse as he shot into her mouth over and over.

. . .

JUST AS QUICKLY, he moved her onto her back and pushed her legs apart, his mouth hungrily clamping onto her sex, his tongue lashing around her clit, his teeth grazing the sensitive bud, the folds of her labia swelling and pulsing with arousal. She reached for his head but he grabbed her hands and held them at her sides. His tongue swept along her cleft and delved deeply into her and she nearly screamed at the feel of it. Her entire skin vibrated with ecstasy, almost unbearable pleasure and when she came, she let herself go, forgot everything else but his touch, his mouth on her. She had no time to recover before he plunged his cock into her again, roughly pressing her legs further apart, making her hips ache. He kissed her and she wrapped her arms around his neck, never wanting to let go, never ever ever...

THE SUN WAS STREAMING through the bedroom windows when she opened her eyes. She glanced over to the clock on the nightstand. Eleven-thirty. Shit. She bolted upright then remembered – it was Saturday. She heard a commotion from the kitchen and got up, snagging Theo's shirt again. She padded through the apartment, following the scent of food.

BARE-CHESTED and wearing some grey jogging pants, Theo had his back turned to her as he flipped pancakes onto a plate and she slid her arms around his back. He started a little, then pushed the frying pan to the back of the stove and turned the gas off.

'Hey! You're up.' He turned in her arms and kissed her, obviously delighted at seeing her. 'I missed you. How did you sleep?'

She pressed her mouth against his. 'Wonderfully, thank you.'

It was true: the first time in months, maybe even a couple of years that she had actually slept right through. Usually, she woke every half-hour or so, listening for any noises, any intruder. Jules was to thank for that: the night he'd broken into her apartment and beaten her badly, and had broken her ribs.

· · ·

BUT LAST NIGHT, wrapped in Theo's big arms, she had felt safe. She knew it was ridiculous but she felt she had known him forever, not just the few hours she had. She smiled up at him now and he smoothed the hair away from her face.

'Good.' He bent his head to kiss her slowly, deeply and she sighed, her body relaxing into his. 'Mmmm. I made you breakfast, but now I'm thinking I should maybe help you work up an appetite.'

Her smile widened, and she arched an eyebrow at him. 'And how will you do that, sir?'

He laughed, cocking his eyebrow up. 'I can tell you but I'd rather just show you.'

She kissed him. 'What did you mean last night.... a new world of pleasure?'

He smiled. 'Forgive my assumption but something tells me you've never been made love to the way a beautiful, exciting woman like you should be. Am I wrong?'

She smiled slightly. 'Until last night.'

He chuckled, kissing her to thank her for the compliment. His lips moved to her ear. 'That was nothing compared to what I'm going to do to you, my beautiful Jess.'

SHARP SPIKES of pleasure jagged through her at his words, her breath catching in her throat as she gazed up at him, into those gorgeous green eyes. She touched his face gently, noticing the strong jaw, the aquiline nose, the dark, thick eyelashes. His expression, she realised, could look so hard, almost dangerous but when he looked at her...

THEO SLID his arms under her and lifted her onto the counter, his lips seeking hers. Jess wrapped her legs around his waist as he slid the shirt from her shoulders. Reaching down, she cupped the hard length of his cock through the jogging pants – Christ, he was so big, and under her touch, he growing bigger and harder every moment. He grinned at her, a lazy, love-drunk look in his eyes as she slipped her hands inside his pants and freed his cock, her hands working up and down it. Theo nipped her earlobe with his teeth.

'LAY BACK FOR ME, BEAUTIFUL...'

She did as he asked and felt him push her legs apart, his big fingers spread the lips of her sex, tease her with the tip of his cock. Theo pressed his lips against her belly, his tongue tracing circles around her navel, making her moan with pleasure. She heard his low chuckle.

'SENSITIVE BELLY, HUH?'

She nodded, too lost in desire to speak. Theo buried his face in her belly again, just briefly, before pushing her legs open as wide they would go. He slid his cock into her slowly – too slowly – grinning as she gasped with anticipation. He pushed himself into her until their hips ground together and as he began to thrust, he kissed her.

'I love your belly,' he told her, 'it's the softest, most sensual, most fuckable belly in the world.'

HIS THUMB STROKED her belly then dipped into the hollow of her navel and began to mimic the thrust of his cock, finger-fucking her belly-button. Jess groaned at the sweet pain of his thumb pressing into her flesh and Theo smiled triumphant.

'That's it, Jessie, let go now... let yourself go.'

He was fucking her so hard that it shook a glass from the counter but neither of them paid any heed to the glass shattering on the floor. Theo groaned as he neared his peak, burying his face in her neck.

'I'm going to come on that beautiful belly of yours,' he whispered and she moaned so beautifully that he laughed aloud. 'You like that, don't you?'

. . .

SHE NODDED and then her body tensed and jerked with her orgasm. Theo pulled out and came, shooting thick streams of cum onto her belly, groaning with his own climax. Not letting her catch her breath – he was getting good at that – he swept her from the counter and carried her back into the bedroom. He lay her on her stomach and covered her body with his. He took her buttocks in his hands, parting them gently. Jess was gasping, shaking, still trying to catch her breath when he whispered in her ear, his voice a sensual purr.

'May I?'

Breathless, she nodded then moaned as he slowly pushed into her ass. Pain shot through her but unexpected pleasure, a new kind of thrill. Theo moved, slowly, expertly as yet another orgasm shivered through her body and finally he came too, collapsing down on top of her, panting, his body weight heavy on her.

'GOD, I could fuck you forever, Jessie,' he murmured into her ear and deftly flipped her onto her back so he could look at her. Her skin was flushed pink, her dark hair matted to her skin with sweat. Theo looked down at her. 'Are you in this with me, Jessie?'

Staring up into his eyes, Jessica Wood could do nothing but nod. Yes. Yes. Yes.

MUCH LATER, famished, they ate the cold pancakes and took a long, hot shower together. Jess bunched up her underwear and stuffed it in her bag, slipping her dress back on. Theo, dressing, watched her amused. 'So I'm supposed to think about anything else but the fact you're naked under there?'

She grinned and flashed him, making him laugh and reach for her. She skipped out of his way and darted into the living room, giggling. Theo, with his pants halfway up his legs stumbled after her, arms outstretched, moaning like a zombie. He caught her and tumbled with her onto the sofa. Jess was laughing uncontrollably, the tears pouring down her face, and he kissed them away.

.   .   .

JESS CAUGHT HER BREATH. 'You are a CEO, Mr Storm, such behaviour is frowned upon.' Theo grinned, his hands sliding under her dress and she smacked them away playfully. 'And you are insatiable.'

A cell-phone started squawking from the bedroom, and reluctantly, they both got up to check.

'Mine,' said Jess and Theo watched as her lovely face clouded as she noted who was calling. She glanced at him apologetically. 'I have to take this, it is family.'

Theo nodded. 'Of course.' He left the bedroom to her to give her privacy. Whoever it was on the phone – she didn't really want to talk to them, he guessed. The stricken look on her face when she'd registered who was calling... hell, if anyone dared upset his girl...

Wow. His girl. Theo went into the kitchen and poured himself a glass of water. Really, man, your girl? This fast? Theo clenched his jaw, trying to think straight. She had completely enraptured him; all of his focus in the last – he checked his watch – eighteen hours had been on her and now, yeah, he couldn't imagine his life without her.

And yet, he knew next to nothing about her except she worked or studied at the college and that she was, without a doubt, the most beautiful woman that he'd ever laid his eyes on. That soft honey-colored skin, those deep, deep brown eyes, that full, blush-pink mouth, her low throaty voice...damn.

HE HEARD HER TALKING NOW, her voice raised and he edge closer to the door, unable to stop himself snooping.

'No, no, fuck you. You don't get to run my life, Jules. No...' She sounded upset now, her voice breaking a little. Theo went to the door of the bedroom. She was turned away from him and he could see her shoulders shaking, her head bent low.

.   .   .

'IT's none of your business where I am. How the hell did you even know I wasn't at home? Jesus, why can't you leave me alone?'

A sob now and her entire body slumped. Theo marched into the room and with one arm, swept her into a hug and with his free hand, took the phone from her.

'Call her again and I'll end you, motherfucker.' Theo shut off the phone and held the trembling Jess in his arms. He heard her sob twice then stop, taking in deep breaths. She pulled away, turning to wipe her face with her hands.

'I'm so sorry about that,' she said, her voice trembling.

'Who was that?'

She tried to smile. 'My step-brother. He's... a little bit of a control freak.'

Theo had the feeling that she wasn't telling him the whole story but studying her, he knew if he pressed her at this moment, she would clam up. There was plenty of time, he decided. She would tell him what she needed to when she needed to and when she did, he would do everything in his powerful to make things right for her.

IT WAS THEN Theo Storm realised that he'd fallen for this tiny, beautiful mystery of a woman. It took his breath away. **She** took his breath away.

He stroked the back of his hand down her face. 'Jessie...would you spend the day with me?'

She hesitated, gazing up at him, the looked away. 'I would honestly love to but I have to get back to my apartment.'

Theo swallowed his disappointment. 'Your step-brother?'

She made a disgusted noise. 'Regardless of what Jules thinks, I'm not at his beck and call. No, I have someone at home I have to care for.'

'KID?'

She smiled, shaking her head, amused at the worried look on his face. 'Dog.'

His expression cleared and he smiled. 'Please don't judge me for that. But hey, look, I'll drive you home. We can still hang out, right?'

Jess smiled but glanced around her surroundings. Her tiny studio was a world away from this place. Theo saw her expression and took her in his arms.

'Whatever it is that concerns you, please don't give it another thought. All this is just window dressing. Really, it's the company's apartment really. I just use it when I stay in the city. I have a much, much smaller home out on Bainbridge Island.'

Jess nodded. That explained the lack of home comforts, she thought, but still... her place was clean, tidy and as comfortable as she could afford to make it but...

Theo kissed her forehead. 'Jessie, you could live in a cardboard box with a tin can for a shower and I'd still want to hang out with you.'

She kept her expression blank and said in a monotone. 'I actually live under a bridge.'

Theo pretended to consider then held out his hand. 'Well, it's been good to meet you but this is goodbye.' He smiled before he reached the end of the sentence and Jess giggled, punching his arm. He pulled her into his arms, kissed her until her head swam. Theo gave a deep sigh and rested his head on the top of hers. 'Could your dog wait a half hour?'

She giggled and extracted herself, tugging him to his feet. 'Come on, Casanova, take me home.'

BACK IN HER APARTMENT, Theo had greeted her German Shepard, Stan, like an old friend and was, even now, play-wrestling with the dog on the floor of her tiny studio. She watched them both, grinning widely as they played like puppies. An overexcited Stan backed into the small table holding her some of her books and knocked them over. Theo stopped and both he and the dog looked so guilty that she burst out laughing.

SHE TUGGED Theo to his feet and moved to pick her books up. He helped her, reading through the titles as he did, commenting. 'Loved this. And this. Couldn't get to grips with this, though,' he said, holding up a book by the latest literary phenomenon, 'How about you?'

SHE SHOOK HER HEAD. 'Turgid. I've tried twice now and just...nope.'

Theo smiled and sat down on the sofa bed that took up a great deal of the room. He looked around the small living area, dominated by books and art prints, paper, soft pastels and watercolors in small tubes spread across the table, pencil sketches Jess had been toying around with. He picked up a couple and studied them. Jess watched him nervously. He smiled at her.

'These are incredibly good. Do you sell your art?'

She shook her head. 'I just play around, really. My work is mostly in art restoration; not that I've been working on anything big, just a few minor pieces at the university. But no, to answer your question, I'm not nearly good enough to sell.' She patted Stan as she spoke, suddenly shy.

'I disagree,' Theo said softly and she flushed.

'Thank you.'

He took her in his arms. 'And I love your place. Reminds me of mine on Bainbridge.'

Jess looked askance, disbelieving. 'Uh-huh okay.'

Theo laughed. 'I will take you there and you'll see what I mean. You and Stan. There's a good-sized garden he can run around to his heart's content – and he'll have a pal. I have an English Cocker spaniel. She's called Monty.'

'She's called Monty?'

'Blame my four-year-old nephew.' It was the first time he'd

mentioned any of his family and Jess wanted to ask him more but then he kissed her, sliding his arms around her waist and pulling her down onto the sofa and she forgot everything else.

THIS TIME she didn't stop his hands as they slid under her dress but just as he began to slide two fingers in and out of her, her gasps of pleasure brought a bout of barking from Stan which made them both collapse into laughter but when he'd calmed down, they tried again Instantly the dog started barking. Jess sighed.

'MOMENT'S OVER,' she giggled as Theo defeated, sat up, shaking his head in mock disgust. Stan, unrepentant, and triumphant went to curl up in his basket, a huge doggy grin on his face. Theo swept a finger down Jess's cheek.

'So, you know how I was telling you about my place on Bainbridge... yeah, the bedrooms have doors.' He pretended to scowl at Stan, which made Jess giggle again. She wrapped her arms around him.

'Well, Mr Billionaire, if you have fancy things like doors, how can I resist?'

He caught her lips with his, kissing her until her head spun. 'And when we get there, Miss Wood, I'm going to begin your education in love-making the Storm way...'

She moaned with pleasure as he kissed her throat and Theo chuckled. 'The sooner we get to my place and I'm inside you the better as far as I'm concerned...'

She gave a breathless laugh. 'You are a machine, Theodore Storm...'

He sat in the car parked across the street from her apartment and watched her leave with a tall guy he didn't recognise. Jealousy, rage curled in his gut as Julién Gachet watched his step-sister, his Jessica, as she talked and laughed with this stranger. When the man bent his head to kiss her, Jules's hands tightened on the steering wheel.

Whore. She knew what happened when she dared to defy him, betray him. Jessica had belonged to him the moment that his father had introduced him to her and her mother, back when Jessie was a kid, just a teenager. Jules always got what he wanted and he had wanted her from the start. Her frightened eyes when he crept into her room at night and put a hand over her mouth. Shhh shhh, little Jess...

Now, watching her kiss this other man, this stranger, this bastard, her glorious body against his, Jules's anger consumed him. She would be reminded, he decided, reminded who she belonged to, who owned every cell in her beautiful body.

AND IF SHE would not fall in line, then she would have to die...

2

PLAY WITH ME PART TWO

Theo watched her from the door. Christ, she was so beautiful, he couldn't get enough of just looking at her. There were the times when her hair brushed his arm, or she'd reach up for something and her t-shirt would ride up, revealing a long expanse of her soft belly. His cock would harden and it would all that he could do to stop himself taking her there and then.

Now, though - and he grinned to himself - the other patrons of the coffee house where Jess Wood worked might object to the live sex show.

'HEY AGAIN.' Her voice broke through his reverie and he realised he had been blocking the door of the coffee shop. He stepped aside to let an elderly couple in. They smiled and nodded their thanks.

Jess smiled at him from behind the counter. She was already fixing his coffee the way she knew he liked it – Americano with an extra shot.

. . .

'HELLO TO YOU, BEAUTIFUL. THANK YOU.' He leaned over the counter to kiss her as she slid the cup over to him. He took a sip, the hot liquid burning his tongue. He enjoyed the quick wash of pain. He put the cup down. 'As always, perfect.' He smiled. 'How are you today?'

'Much the same as yesterday,' she grinned. 'Can I persuade you to try a muffin today?' She always asked and he always politely refused. He liked the fact she was trying to make a joke between them, it felt strangely intimate, even if it was just about baked goods. It was their 'thing'. Theo chuckled at the thought and told her.

'FUNNY,' she murmured and leaned over to whisper in his ear,' I thought our thing was fucking each other senseless.'

Theo laughed, caught her mouth with his. 'You shouldn't say stuff like that when we're not alone.'

Jess glanced up at the clock on the wall. Ten of seven. The coffee house would close at seven and then they could go back to his place or her place and get very, very naked.

Theo was watching her, a knowing look in his eyes. For a long moment, their eyes locked, a silent communication.

'You have no idea what I'm going to do to you tonight, Jessica.' Theo's voice was low, steady and he watched as her cheeks grew pink, her eyes wide and excited.

TEN MINUTES LATER, she locked the door and pulled down the shades. Theo stood in the middle of the room, watching her. She lowered the shades on all of the windows and turned off all the lamps so that only the glow from the coffee machines lit the room.

'STAY WHERE YOU ARE,' Theo ordered as she started to move toward him. She did as she was told, smiling, her eyes soft with desire as he stalked around slowly. He circled her once then nodded toward her.

'Take your shirt off – slowly. Then your bra.'

. . .

SHE PULLED the shirt over her head, unhook her bra, dropping them both to the floor, and stood waiting, her hair tumbling over her shoulders. Theo moved to face her, tracing the shape of her lips with the pad of his thumb then running it gently down her body, between her breasts, over her stomach until it rested in her navel. Jess was trembling now and Theo grinned as he saw the arousal in her eyes. His hand drifted down under her denim skirt, brushing her inner thigh. He was gratified at her sharp intake of breath but took his hand away, moving to unbuckle his belt and removed it. He pulled her hands behind her back and bound them with the leather, his lips against her soft throat.

'JESSIE,' he murmured, 'If you want me to stop...'

'No,' she interrupted him and he chuckled, straightening so he could into her eyes.

'Let me finish, beautiful,' he said gently, his clear green eyes locked onto hers. 'We are going to do some things you might find.... challenging. I'll promise you two things – I will not hurt you unless you want me to...and if you say stop, we stop. No questions, no guilt. I want you to enjoy what I'm going to do to you.'

SHE NODDED, breathless and he stood back for a moment, admiring her in the soft light, then pulled his own shirt off and dropped to his knees in front of her. Sliding her skirt down, he buried his face in her belly as his fingers wound around the sides of her panties and pulled them down. Jess gave a small moan as Theo's tongue traced down the midline of her belly and dipped into the hollow of her sex. His tongue lashed around her clit, priming it, the bud hardening and becoming so sensitive that Jess thought that she might explode. Theo gently parted her legs and then his tongue was deep inside her, exploring, tasting. Jess gasped, wanting desperately to touch him but unable to, her bound hands straining against the leather. She heard him chuckle and he stood, kissing her deeply, sliding his hands around her waist to link his fingers into hers. His eyes burned with an intensity that thrilled and scared her in equal measure.

'Jessica,' he murmured, rubbing his nose gently against hers, 'I'm going to fuck you now.'

SHE BARELY HAD time to respond before he swept her onto one of the tables and pressed her body down with his own, her tied hands digging into the small of her back as Theo's fingers parted the soft lips of her sex and his cock, so thick, so long, thrust into her. Theo hitched her legs around his hips as he fucked her, his strokes rough and deep, almost violent with his desire for her.

JESS LOST herself into the delirium of being so expertly screwed by this gorgeous, virile man, not wanting it to ever end. She gasped his name and was rewarded by his triumphant smile.

'Are you mine?' He asked and his green eyes seemed darker, more otherworldly than ever as she nodded, breathlessly. 'Good, because I am yours, my beautiful Jessie...'

THE SIMPLE DECLARATION made her heart swell and she bucked against him, straining to take him deeper, deeper, and deeper. Theo was merciless, smiling at her gasps of pleasure and pain. She came so hard she thought she might die, lights exploding in her vision, her body liquefying and when, a moment later, Theo pulled out from her and came on her belly, she realised that she could die in this moment and not care.

THEO WASN'T DONE with her and lifting her to her feet. He pressed her against the wall and took her from behind, his still diamond-hard cock thrusting deep into the slick wetness of her cunt. The wall was cold against her breasts and belly, providing some relief from the inferno raging on her skin. Theo's lips were at her ear.

'Do you like to be fucked hard, Jessie?'

'Yes...'

Say it.'

'I want to be fucked hard, Theo.'

'Call me Mr Storm.'

'Mr Storm, fuck me hard, please...' she shuddered as an orgasm ripped through her, the pressure of his cock inside her overwhelming. Theo chuckled and pulled out, parting her buttocks and pushing into her ass. Jess groaned, letting her head drop back against his shoulder. His fingers were on her belly, stroking a pattern around her navel that was driving her crazy. She really was his, she realised, all his, forever...

LATER, when they'd reluctantly dressed and calmed down, he drove her back to her apartment and they shared a beer on the little balcony overlooking the Seattle streets. Theo sat against the wall, with Jess settled between his legs, his arm wrapped around her, pulling her back against his chest. He was such a huge man, tall and wide, that Jess always felt tiny but safe with him. He nuzzled into her hair, pressing his lips against her temple.

'YOU'RE QUIET,' he said and although his tone was without reproach, she could sense he was probing her. She waited, a small smile playing around her mouth.

'Are you okay with what we did?' He asked finally and she grinned, turning her head so she could kiss him.

'Very. Very, very okay.' She studied the relief in his eyes. 'In fact... if you want to do... more, I would be open to it.'

His surprise was mixed with desire. 'I'm glad. I want to experience every pleasure with you, Jessie.'

She loved the way he said her name, so tenderly, so intimately. 'Is there anything you really don't want to try?' he continued, stroking a finger down her cheek.

Jess looked away from him and took a long swig of beer before answering. 'Nothing with knives.' She hated the way her voice broke when she said it and she felt Theo's arm tighten around her. When he spoke, there was a note of anger in his voice.

'I WOULD NEVER... JESSIE?'

Dammit. Hot tears started to pour down her cheeks. Oh dammit. She didn't want to think about what Jules had done to her and she really didn't want to talk about, not with Theo. She didn't want any second of her time with him spoiled by her past.

'Jessica?'

No. No. She couldn't do this. She pushed away from him and scrambled to her feet, stepping back into the apartment. Theo followed her, his handsome face creased with concern.

'Was it something I said?'

SHE SHOOK her head not trusting herself to speak. Theo came to her and pulled her into his arms and held her tightly. She buried her head in his chest, breathing in his clean smell, fresh laundry and man. Theo's hand stroked her hair gently.

'Do you want to talk about it?'

She looked up at him. 'No. I'm sorry...please, let's change the subject.'

HIS EYES WERE STILL troubled but he nodded. They stood there for a long minute in silence then Theo kissed the top of her head.

'I'll never let anyone hurt you, Jessie.'

And in that moment, she desperately wanted to believe him.

. . .

FRESHMAN YEAR. Jess had saved every last penny from her job at the coffee house to get a small studio apartment in St Anne's, not wanting to take anything more from Jules than she had to. Her tuition was covered by the provision in her step-father's will but Jules still held the purse strings. She hated it but worse was the thought of hundreds of dollars of student debt hanging over her forever. Now, though, she thought she'd found a way out. A scholarship. Well, she reminded herself, a possible scholarship. The company offering it had strict guidelines on who could apply for it – only those students with the most pressing need. Trouble was, her family name was well known in Seattle and her step-brother Jules was known to be one of the richest men in the city. Just because she got nothing from him other than her tuition wouldn't be enough to convince the board she needed that funding – mostly to escape him. Jules had done interviews lately in his position as a handsome eligible millionaire, raving about his 'close relationship' with his step-sister. The interviews had made Jess sick to her stomach. If they only knew...

All which meant she couldn't plead poverty to the board – unless Jules publicly and notably cut her off.

He was coming over later to discuss it with her – had even been genial about the idea over the phone. She would frame it as a bonus for him. He would save the few hundred thousand dollars that her degree and her masters would cost. She told herself that would be enough.

IT WASN'T. Of course, it wasn't.

Jules listened to her reasoning politely, a supercilious smile on his face and she knew immediately it was no good.

'WELL,' he said, standing and pacing around the room – between her and the door, she noted uneasily as he turned to smile at her. 'Obviously, I have no intention of...'disowning' you, Jessica. Why would I?'

· · ·

HE STOOD in front of her then, hands deep in his pockets and she could see him stroking himself through the thin material, putting on an exhibition for her. Nausea swept over her and she stood, wanting to push past him.

BUT THEN HIS hand was on her throat, squeezing hard. He grabbed her and slammed her back down on the couch. Jess struggled against him but knew of old, she had no chance against his strength. They'd been in this situation so many times... except this time, Jules' eyes glowed with malice. He ground his mouth down on hers, his hand burrowing under her skirt.

'No... no... please st-...'

His hand clamped over her mouth as he tore her panties from her. Jess bucked frantically trying to push him away but then, grinning, Jules had shown her what he had in his hand. She froze.

A knife. Oh god, no...

'Stop fighting me, Jessica, or I'll put this into you. I'll gut you, Princess, without a second thought. You belong to me, Jessica. I say what you do, where you go. Whether you live or die. Do you understand?'

TERRIFIED, she could do nothing but nod, tears streaming down her face, as Jules, triumphant, took her with his knife to her throat.

Jess woke up, panting, trying not to scream. Beside her, Theo slept soundly, his big frame making her bed seem tiny. Jess edged out of the bed and padded silently to the kitchen, grabbing a glass and filling it with water. She drained the glass and refilled it. Her body was trembling from the nightmare – the memory – of Jules that night.

IT HADN'T BEEN the first time he'd raped her, just the first time he'd threatened to kill her and Jess had no doubt he was capable.

. . .

SHE SAT down at the kitchen table and laid her head against the cool wood. She hated that he held this power over her. She'd told him she was going to the police, defiant at last, but he'd gotten to them first with his expensive lawyers and limitless influence. She was unstable, he'd told them; her mother had been committed several times in her life before her suicide. Using her mother's mental illness against her was both evil and genius. However much she protested after that, she could see it in their eyes: Nut job. Attention seeker. Hysteric. As if this was the eighteen hundreds and not the twenty-first century. Jesus.

JULES HAD PUNISHED her of course. Breaking into her apartment and beating her – only where it couldn't be seen in public, of course. She'd stayed away from college for a week, unable to stand because of her bruised abdomen where he'd kicked her so viciously she couldn't stand up straight for two days.

AFTER THAT, she'd almost given up. Buried herself in studying, letting Jules continue to pay for everything, control everything she couldn't. She moved apartments frequently, whenever her lease was up and never took apartments with longer than a six-month tenure. Jules always, always found her.

THE ASSAULTS CAME LESS and less as long as she obeyed him and she clung to that. She rarely went out, and she never, ever dated. And each year she squirrelled away money so that one day she could just run. Another country, changing identity, to get away from Jules. That had been her plan.

UNTIL SHE MET THEO. Until she remembered what affection felt like. What love felt like.

. . .

SHE WALKED SILENTLY BACK to the bedroom and lay down beside him. In sleep, the harsh angles of his beautiful face softened, his full mouth curved up slightly in a smile. She pressed her lips gently to kiss and then stroked his face. She studied him for a long minute before closing her own eyes.

Before she fell back to sleep, she kissed him once more and whispered 'I love you'.

A MOMENT LATER, Theo opened his eyes and smiled. 'I love you too, beautiful one.' But she was already asleep.

NEITHER OF THEM heard the door to the apartment door creak open. Jules Gachet sneaked through the room until he stood at her bedroom door, staring down at them. The way Jessica was curved around the big man's body, the protective arm he had wrapped around her. Jules' gut churned with jealousy, with anger. Fucking whore. He fantasised about having this bastard wake up to find her dead beside him, covered in her blood. Jules grinned nastily to himself. If he could have gotten away with it... but no. Not yet, at least. He moved silently to her side and brushed a fingertip down her soft cheek, pushing a lock of dark brown hair away from her lovely face. If he ended up killing her, he wanted it to be an intimate, unrushed time. He wanted her to die slowly, painfully, looking into his eyes and begging him to spare her life.

HE TURNED his attention to the man sleepily beside her. He was vaguely familiar but Jules couldn't place him. Never mind, he didn't matter. Just the thought of this man inside his Jessica made him want to roar, rage and to implode with malevolence.

. . .

AN IDEA CAME to him then and he smiled to himself. If Jessica thought she could be happy with this man... Jules almost laughed aloud. Yes, he was going to enjoy destroying her piece of mind, her security, her new love.

He'd consider it an appetiser to her murder.

THEO STORM GLANCED up as Max came into his office, grinning. 'Where have you been and what is her name?' His best friend had raised eyebrows and amused look on his chubby face.

Theo smiled. 'Max, buddy...you've already lost your dumb bet and you don't even know it.'

Max started to scoff then, as he saw how serious Theo was.

'Really?' He looked sceptical. 'No. No way, I know you too well. You're yanking me.'

Theo barked out a laugh. 'Projecting as usual. No, I'm serious, Max. Here...'

He pulled out his cell phone which already had a ton of photos of Jess. He flicked to them and handed it to Max.

'Her name is Jessica – Jess. She's a Ph.D. graduate at UW. Art restoration.'

Max whistled. 'She's a beauty, alright. Where'd you meet her?'

Theo told him about the commencement speech then gave him a cleaned up version of the last few days. 'I really want you to meet her. She's going to be around a long time.'

Max blinked. 'Wow. Never seen you like this before. '

Theo grinned a little smugly. 'Now about that bet...'

Max scoffed. 'Bet schmet. When am I going to meet her?'

JESS CHOKED ON HER DRINK – which was a shame because the cocktail was utterly delicious and very expensive – but Theo's best friend Max was just too funny. He was in the middle of regaling her with stories of his and Theo's childhood, growing up together, going to an exclusive private school for boys and not behaving as 'young gentlemen should' in any way or form.

MAX GRINNED as she wiped her mouth and tried to stop laughing. Theo was shaking his head good-naturedly, pretending to be disgusted with Max's loose tongue.

'SERIOUSLY, dude, stop trying to kill my girlfriend. Breathe, Jess.'

Jess sucked in a few deep breaths, trying not to be over-excited about the fact Theo had just called her his girlfriend. She felt like a freakin' teenager but there was no denying the warmth flooding her every nerve and cell when he called her that. Theo chuckled at her and leaned over to kiss her briefly.

'THAT'S my cue to get more drinks,' Max disappeared off to the bar. Theo kissed her again, slower, deeper, his hands cradling her face, his tongue caressing hers. Jess melted into the embrace, sliding her hands around his waist, feeling his muscular body under her fingers. God, she had never wanted anyone this much in her life, wanting to be naked with him all day and all night. Well, she thought a little smugly, she had been for the past few days but tomorrow, she had to get back to work, back to reality. Theo had gone into the office today for an hour or so but had returned just after lunch. She'd been naked and ready for him when he walked into the door – they hadn't made it to the bedroom before they were tangled in each other and sweating.

AFTER AN AFTERNOON OF SCREWING, she could still feel the ache of him, her vagina pulsed with a pleasant soreness, her thighs stretched and her hips felt like liquid still. His lips were on her throat now and she closed her eyes, concentrating on the sensation.

. . .

'AT THE END OF THIS EVENING,' Theo spoke in a low, deep murmur, 'we'll say goodnight to Max and then I'm going to take you into the alley around the back of this place and fuck you so hard, Jessie, so very hard. Then we'll go back to my place and do it all over again until you're helpless in my arms.'

JESS SUPPRESSED her moan of desire but her body trembled and she heard him laugh softly. She buried her face in his neck.

'I want you now.' She whispered and, moving quickly, he pulled her onto his lap so she was straddling him. Their eyes locked and a silent assent passed between them. Theo reached down and unzipped his fly, freed his already stiffening cock, and pushing her panties to one side, slid into her. She nearly gave them away as she felt his cock fill her, giving a moan which he quickly smothered with a kiss. Rocking gently as if only moving with the kiss, she felt his free hand caressing her sensitive clit, sending shivers of delight through her body. His lips moved against hers as they kissed, tender but firm and Jess wondered how she ever lived before this kind of pleasure. She was glad that they were sitting in a private, secluded booth, that the rest of the club couldn't see that they were screwing and when Theo started to move in and out of her, the fact they had to be discreet, had to keep the frenzy within was so incredibly erotic, she came quickly. He followed her and for a moment, they stayed connected, breathing hard, gaze locked on the others. Theo looked around then.

'Max is coming back.'

She slid from his lap and sat, shoving her legs together as Theo tidied himself.

''JEEZ, you'd think there was a world shortage of bar staff,' Max was moaning, dispersing their drinks to them, completely unaware that

Theo's semen was still inside her. Jess tried not to giggle at the thought and Theo shot her an amused, conspiratorial look. It had been a quick, dirty, thrilling fuck with adrenaline coursing through them at the fear of being caught and she grinned back at him. God, she would do anything for this man. She wondered what else he had planned for their lovemaking. Being tied up, losing part of the control of the situation had been, ironically, more liberating than she had expected and now there was little she would contemplate letting him do.

THEO WATCHED as Jess and Max fell easily back into conversation. He slid his hand onto the back of Jess's neck, caressed the muscles there and he was gratified when she squeezed his knee. He let his gaze wander lazily over her body, the full breasts, the slim waist, the almost-flat belly and then her thighs which he noticed she had rammed together, keeping his seed inside of her. She was so beautiful, he could hardly believe it.

'YO, THEO? HEY, SPACE CADET!' Max prodded his shoulder and Theo shook himself. Max grinned at him. 'I gotta go. You –' he grabbed Jess's hand, 'are a freaking princess. If I wasn't gay, I'd be fighting Theo for your hand.'

Jess flushed but Theo noticed the tiniest wince when Max had said 'princess.' When Max had gone, Jess leaned back into him and he tipped her chin up so he could kiss her.

'THERE'S a lot about you I don't know yet,' he murmured, brushing his lips against hers, enjoying the sensation of her soft skin against his mouth.

. . .

'THERE'S plenty of time for that... our sordid histories.' She laughed but again, he detected something else, a hesitance, a wound but he decided tonight wasn't the right time to pursue it. He stroked her face gently.

'Ready to go?'

On the way out, he nodded to the security man who led them out of the back door. Outside, rain was plummeting down from the storm that rages overhead – Seattle always knew exactly the best time to throw down with the weather. Theo glanced up then shook his head.

'A literal rain check for our alleyway shenanigan?'

Jess grinned wickedly and shook her head, skipping past him into the darkest part of the alleyway. Theo followed her then watched in amazement as she slipped out of her clothes and stood before him, naked, rain pouring down her glorious curves. She smiled at him and held out her hand.

'Fuck me, Theo...'

He didn't need to be told twice. In two strides he was over to her, pulling at his clothes, almost in a frenzy. She helped him, freeing his ramrod cock from his pants then laughing wildly as he picked her up, pushing her back against the cold, wet wall. He thrust into her hard and she moaned, kissing his fiercely.

'FUCK ME HARD, THEO ...'

Her eyes were alive and his breath quickened in excitement. He rammed himself into her as hard as he could, slamming against the wall so hard he heard her gasp a 'yes, yes!'. The rain was a monsoon now, covering their hot bodies as they moved together. The feel of being inside her, her softness, her sweet, sweet sex was something he could take anytime, anywhere, even in this filthy weather. He loved that she wanted to fuck in the rain. It spoke to her innate sense of humour, of the sense of adventure he thought that she hid most of the time. It meant she trusted him and that – he thought now as he shuddered to a climax - meant the world to him because he knew,

knew that something was broken inside this beautiful girl and he desperately wanted to be the one to fix it.

JESS MANAGED to straighten her soaking wet dress over her body enough so she looked decent. Her skin, her mind felt frenzied with excitement and desire. She was astonished at herself, at the certainty that she wouldn't have let Theo call off their promised alleyway tryst. She wanted it. Bad. She wanted to do every mad thing with him, experience everything. Everything.

THEO TOOK her hand now and they walked down the alleyway to where his car was parked. As they rounded the corner, suddenly there were flashes of light and people yelling his name, jostling them. Theo cursed and curved his arms protectively around Jess as he hustled them to his car. Inside, Jess turned away from the windows as the paparazzi crowded around the windows and Theo pulled the car away from the curb.

AFTER A MINUTE, they both breathed a sigh of relief as the car sped through the night. Theo turned the heat in the car to high and Jess gave an involuntary shiver as the warm air hit her cold body. Theo looked over at her, gave her a grin.

'YOU OKAY, BEAUTY?'

Jess smiled and nodded, let her hand rest on his thigh. Her clothes – and his – were soaked through but she didn't care. Theo concentrated on the road for a second before shooting her a curious look.

'Jessie, last night I told you something and I'm not sure you heard me. So I wanted to say it now, again, when I'll be sure you'll hear me.'

Jess's eyebrows shot up. 'What's that?'

Theo smiled. 'I'm in love with you, Jessica Wood, and I know it's batshit crazy fast and I'm aware I'm putting it out there when we don't really know each other as well as I'd like. But I have to be honest here. I love you.'

Jess's heart swelled in her chest and tears sprang into her eyes. 'I love you too.'

She watched as Theo's shoulders relaxed and she heard him exhale slowly. He pulled the car over to the side of the road, released his belt and took her face in his hands. His lips pressed against hers softly, as if for the first time.

'YOU ARE MY WORLD,' he murmured and Jess's stomach dropped with desire and love. His tongue was exploring hers, caressing and massaging. Jess closed her eyes so she could concentrate on the explosion of sensations his kiss created in her. She felt it all over her body; her belly quivered, a frantic pulse beat between her legs and she moaned as his fingers tangled in her hair.

'GOD, Jessie, when you make that sound... we need to get home now.'

They both laughed as they disengaged and Theo started the car. Jess was sure they broke all sorts of laws as Theo drove the car back to her apartment.

THEY'D BARELY GOT in the door before Theo started to peel her dress from her. Jess turned to kiss him, gasping as he pulled her roughly to him, grinding his mouth down on hers with a frenzied need.

'Theo...'

She gasped his name as he slid two fingers inside of her, grinning wickedly. Barely able to concentrate she stripped him and they tumbled onto her bed, his hand still caressing her, making her wet and unbearable excited.

. . .

'I WANT TO TASTE YOU,' she said and was rewarded by his kiss.

'Want to try doing it at the same time?' Theo's eyes were excited, sultry with his desire for her. She nodded, smiling and he manoeuvred her so he could bury his face in her sex as she took him into her mouth. She heard him moan as her tongue teased the tip of his cock, could feel it jerk. God, he tasted so good, clean and salty and the silky softness of his skin belied the diamond-hard stiffness of him. She felt his tongue sweeping along her cleft, circling her sensitive clit.

BEFORE LONG, Theo was desperate to be inside of her and he shifted her so she straddled him. He slid into her velvety slickness, his fingers digging into the soft flesh of her hips as she moved on top of his, rocking her hips to take him in as far as he would go. She gazed down at him, as they moved, her long hair tumbling in damp strands across her shoulders. Theo cupped her breasts in his hands, teasing the hard nipples with his thumbs, letting his fingers drift down her stomach, stroking her belly with his thumbs. The way he looked at her in these moments was addictive, thrilling and she found herself telling him she loved him over and over and over...

THE BUBBLE BURST in the morning. The paparazzi had done their job thoroughly and their photo was splashed over the morning's tabloid – local and national. A billionaire mogul like Theo Storm having a new girlfriend was big news in the gossip columns and the business world.

Jess read the write-ups silently. They'd done their homework and found out who she was – lord knows how but there it was. They'd gone public.

'You okay?' Theo had presented her with the papers earlier without comment and now he studied her with a wary look in his eyes.

Jess tried to smile, shrugging her shoulders. 'Well, we knew it wouldn't be long before it got out. Shame. I liked it when it was just ours to enjoy.'

She sighed and Theo took her in his arms. 'I'm sorry but yeah, it was only a matter of time. Doesn't change anything between us – at least not for me.'

Jess kissed him. 'Me either.'

He hugged her to him. 'Still want to go back to work today?'

Jess nodded, smuggling into his big chest. 'Yeah, I have to. We've got big projects coming up and I've already stretched Gerry's good-will. Not that it wasn't totally worth it.'

She grinned up at him and Theo smiled.

'Anyone tell you, you have the most beautiful little face?' He said and she giggled, flushing.

'No, you the pretty one,' she singed at him and he laughed.

'No you is a purty girl,' he replied, mimicking her tone then kissed her. 'How about I come pick you up after work? I could meet your boss, your friends.'

She considered for a moment. 'That would be good. I'd better get going.'

THEO DROPPED her off at work – after kissing her thoroughly – and she drifted into her department with a happily dazed smile on her face. Gerry was waiting for her, his arms crossed. She knew from the look on his face he was trying to look stern but she gave him a wide, cheesy grin and he crumpled.

'You stood me up for dinner,' he accused as she dumped her bag on the desk and shrugged out of her coat. She smiled at him. He looked like he'd dressed in the dark as always; bedraggled beard, smeary spectacles, food-stained clothes. Jess hugged him fondly.

'I know. I'll make it up to you, I promise but I did have a good reason.'

'I know.' He waved a copy of the paper. 'By my reckoning, since I asked you to go to the speech instead of me... you owe me two dinners.'

'Fair enough.'

Gerry went back to work with a satisfied harrumph and Jess sat down to go through the work piled up on her desk. The morning passed quickly as she deftly dealt with paperwork, delivery notes and emails.

THEO CALLED HER AT LUNCHTIME. 'Hey, beautiful.'

Jess smiled down the phone. 'I missed you.'

'Me too. Any trouble at work?'

'None. Gerry's very easy-going and as yet I've not had time to see anyone else. You?'

'Only Max's less than subtle jokes. He wants to double-date, by the way. I think you have another admirer. I might get jealous.'

She laughed and as they said goodbye, she felt a warmth settle in her stomach. The fact Theo wanted to involve her as much as he could with their family made her feel good, that she belonged. It was an oddly new feeling.

'HEY...' Gerry had stuck his head out of the office. 'You wanna grab some lunch? We've got a whole afternoon of restoration; the museum is sending over 'Luna Soleil'.'

Jess smiled. 'Wow. Yes, let's go grab something, I'm starving.'

JULES STARED at the paper's front page, fury roiling inside him. Fucking, fucking whore. And that rich bastard with her. Now he knew who had threatened him. Theo Storm. A fucking billionaire. So much for Jessica's holier-than-thou attitude. She'd been screwing a freaking billionaire.

JULES GACHET HAD NEVER KNOWN such anger. After all her crap about money meaning nothing, she'd betrayed him for a fucking meal ticket. He couldn't – he wouldn't – let her get away with that, by god, he would make her pay.

He slammed the door on his way out.

At a quarter of six, Jess stood upright and stretched. Working on the painting had been all-consuming, inspiring and now she had an evening of food and sex and love and Theo to look forward to. Yes.

Gerry had disappeared somewhere so she was alone in the studio. The main lights were off; only her work lamp, concentrated on the painting was on and she flicked it off and blinked, her eyes adjusting to the dark. She flexed the muscles in her back, her shoulders, let out a long breath, glancing at the lock. Her stomach gave a little flutter as she realised that Theo would be here very soon.

She grabbed her bag and headed to the ladies bathroom to freshen up. There was a shower cubicle and she quickly stripped and let the hot spray of water relax her tired body. After, she dressed, not bothering to slip her panties back on. Theo was in the habit, when they were in his car, of running his hand up her thigh. Today, she almost purred at the idea, his fingers would find her ready for him. Damn, you are turning into a wanton woman, she grinned to herself. The thought of him touching her made a pulse between her legs and she squeezed her thighs together hard to control herself.

She went back to her office and was gathering her things when she felt two hands slide around her waist.

'How did you manage to slink in so quietly, sir?' She said, grinning but as she turned she gasped with shock, shoving herself backwards, away. Jules smiled, and it was not a pleasant smile.

'Waiting for your billionaire, Jessica?'

Her heart beating furiously, Jess's eyes narrowed. 'Get out or I'll call security.'

Jules, in a quick movement, cuffed her so viciously around the face, she tumbled over her desk. He pushed the phone from the table then grabbed Jess, forcing her onto the table. She cast around for anything to help her fight him off, but Jules was stronger, had her at a disadvantage, pressing his forearm against her throat, choking her.

'Fucking hypocritical little bitch. Why don't you share the good fortune, huh? Maybe I should take you with me, see how much your rich fuck will pay to get you back alive? Because now Jessica, right now, all I wanna do is break you.'

JESS, barely able to breathe, was losing consciousness, Jules's arm was cutting off her oxygen supply. Jules smiled and with his free hand, he pried her legs apart. As his hand moved towards her naked sex, Jess summoned all the strength she had left and jerked her knee upwards, hard, into his groin. Jules howled with agonised rage and jerked away from her. She scrambled up and darted towards the door, but he grabbed her hair and threw her to the floor. His face was a mask of uncontrollable rage, and he grabbed something from the desk as he dropped to his knees, straddling her. Jess's blood froze when she saw it was her paper-knife.

OH GOD, no...

Jules put his face next to hers, so angry was he, he spoke and fleck of spittle flew out. 'Don't ever forget who you belong to, little girl. Next time he's fucking you, remember, my cock was in your sweet little cunt first, my hands were on your tits before you even knew him.' He was pressing the blunt tip of the paperknife hard into the soft flesh of her belly but then he released his grip, pulling her to her feet by bunching his fist in the hair at the nape of her neck. He pulled her against him, put his lips to her ear.

. . .

'I'LL KILL YOU. I'll fucking kill you, Jessica. Break it off with him or next time...' He pressed the knife to her belly again.

Jess felt herself shrinking back into the terrified young girl she had been the first time Jules had assaulted her. Destroying her peace of mind. Humiliating Her. Hurting her.

Jules smirked nastily and let her go. 'I mean it, Jessica. End it with him. You belong to me.'

He flung her paperknife back on her desk and stalked out.

Jess's legs gave way then and she sank to the floor, hyperventilating, trying to stop the jagged sobs which were forcing themselves out of her. Her mind screamed with pain, terror, heartbreak, fear... shame. Who was she kidding? She must have known that Jules would spoil it, ruin her happiness. Jess curled up into a ball and sat there for she didn't know how long until she heard footsteps.

OH GOD, Theo... She wanted to get up, straighten out her clothes, dry her cheeks but she found she was paralysed, unable to move. Broken.

THEO PEERED into the dusky light of the room. The security guard, with a knowing smile, had directed him up to the art department, to where he knew Jess worked but now he wasn't sure he'd found the right place. He had turned to leave, retrace his steps when he heard it. A sob. He darted back into the room and saw her, curled up in a ball on the floor, her hands over her face. His heart began to beat a frenetic, panicked beat.

'SWEETHEART! WHAT IS IT, WHAT HAPPENED?' He dropped to his knees beside her and gathered her to him. For a moment, she resisted then let him pull her tightly against his chest. His mind whirled with fear and worry. Instinctively – desperately – he knew it had something to do with them – and something to do with the controlling step-brother. Asshole.

HE LET her cry herself out then just held her as she caught her breath. Eventually, she moved away from him, brushing her tears away with the back of her hand. She gave him a watery smile.

'I'm so sorry, Theo. You didn't need to see that.' She scrambled to her feet and held out her hand to him. He stood, his brows knitted together, the angles of his face sharpened with tension. He watched as she sucked in a couple of deep breaths and let them out.

'What happened?'

'Just a row with Jules – that's my step-brother. He's not too wild about the idea of you and me.'

Theo made a disgusted noise. 'What the hell business is it of his?' Her face was in shadow and he could not read her expression. He reached over her desk and flicked the lamp on. He looked back at her – and his stomach disappeared. Across her throat were dark red welts and bruises.

'JESUS CHRIST…'

She looked away and he realised that, unbelievably, she was ashamed. His heart thudded with pain and love for her. Gently, he took her face in his hands, tipping it up so he could kiss her gently. He swept his thumbs over the plains of her cheeks, wiping the moisture from her eyes. Her lovely dark eyes were red and full of pain, and she wouldn't look at him. For a moment, he didn't know what to say.

'What did he do to you?' His voice was soft but she winced and pulled away from him.

'Like I said, an argument. Please, Theo, for me, don't push this. I'm not ready for you to be dragged into my ridiculous family drama.'

That stung but he nodded, acquiescing. He held his arm out to her. 'Want to go home?'

She hesitated then nodded, taking his arm. They hadn't got a few steps, though, before he stopped her.

'I just want to say: whatever it is, whatever he's doing to you, it isn't right. You only have to say the word, Jessie, and I'll make it all go away.'

Jess closed her eyes and he saw the conflict raging inside her. Finally, she spoke and her voice was a broken thing, low and gruff.

'Please Theo... I just want to forget.'

He nodded, once, stiffly, and led her down to the car.

'Easy now, careful.'

Theo guided her carefully into the house. She suppressed a smile, ignoring the small tug of irritation.

'I'm not made of glass, Theo,' she chided gently. His face was tense and she reached up to smooth the small crease between his eyes. He leaned his face into her hand. 'You look so tired.'

He sighed. 'I'm not the one who got assaulted.'

'I'm fine.' She pulled away from him and went into the kitchen. Stan trotted up to her and, despite his size, she scooped the dog into her arms, kissing his furry head and burying her face in his fur. 'He's growing by the second, I swear.'

'I hope not, he's already Godzilla.' Theo's tone was fond as he scratched the dog's ears.

'He's still my baby.'

Theo smiled and reached for the kettle. They stood in silence while he prepared the tea, Jess hugging the dog to her for comfort.

The atmosphere was heavy, leaden. The light coming in from the window was a pale blue, ghostly, cold. It leeched the colours from the room.

Jess swallowed and found her throat closed, sore. The adrenaline that raced through her earlier has dissipated and now all she wanted to do was sleep. Fucking Jules. He was a monster but Jess was more disgusted with herself. She didn't believe Jules would go through with his threat to kill her – he was too much of a coward – but he could make her life very, very difficult. And if he hurt Theo...

She felt tears pricking her eyes. She was lost. Jules's threats had brought her to the edge – and Theo's kindness despite his confusion– had pushed her over the edge. She simply could not take it anymore. She was broken.

SHE DROPPED the dog gently on the floor and rushed upstairs. In the bathroom, she threw up, great rasping sobs wrenching from her uncontrollably.

DOWNSTAIRS, Theo listened to her heartbreak with his head in his hands. His chest thumped with despair, with the desperation of a man who didn't know what to do, how to help, how to reach her. The bruises on her throat would fade soon, horrific as they were but they were simply physical wounds, not these deep chasms of hurt.

There was a knock and he dragged himself up to open the door. Max. He'd called him as soon as they'd gotten back to his place, when Jess had been in the bathroom. He wanted to know everything about Jules Gachet and he knew Max would be a tenacious private detective and besides Jess, Max was the only person he trusted implicitly.

THEO KNEW despair was etched on his face when he saw Max's expression.

'Jesus, you look...' He stopped when he heard the sobs from upstairs. 'Row?'

Theo gave short, humourless laugh. 'I wish, buddy, I really do.' He stood aside to let Max in and told Max what had happened Max frowned.

'You got there in time to stop him?'

Theo shook his head. 'No. I was too late. She was just sitting there, in a ball on the floor. God, you should have seen her, Max, she was terrified. I've never seen anyone that... traumatised.' His shoulders slumped.

Max was silently for a long moment. 'Theo...I'm going to say this and remember, I adore Jess but you've known her what? A week?'

Theo's face was hard. 'I love her, Max, I'm in this.'

Max held up his hands in conciliation. 'Okay, fine by me. So, what's next?'

'I need to know everything about this asshole. Stuff Jess won't or can't tell me.' He looked up at Max and his eyes were filled with grief. 'I never want her to have to feel like she does right now, Max. ever.'

He sighed. 'She's pretty beat up emotionally. I hope she can come back from this.' He winced at the words.

Max shook his head. 'She just needs time. It's the violence she'll have the most problem with coming to terms with. She'll go through the stages, denial, grief, anger. But she will come out the other side. You both will.'

Theo smiled sadly at him. 'They teach you that little speech at Harvard?'

Max grinned self-consciously. 'Something like that.' They both listened to the sound of the bath being run upstairs. He patted his friend's shoulder. 'Anyway, I'm on it now, man.'

'Yeah.'

Later, when Max had left, Theo took some tea up to Jess. She was wrapped in a towel drying her hair. Theo sucked in a breath at the sight of her bruised neck. She saw him looking at her and wouldn't meet his eyes. He put the tea down in front of her.

'THANK YOU.' Her voice was soft. He braved trailing a finger along her cheekbone and was gratified when she didn't pull away.

'You're welcome.' They stayed like that for a few minutes. Theo noticed how wan she looked, her skin, usually so glowing, was yellow and grey. There were deep, navy blue lines under her eyes.

'I think you should sleep, now, rest a little.' He cupped her face with his hand, she leaned into his touch.

'I don't want to be alone.'

'NEVER.' Theo was surprised though when she pulled him down on the bed next to her, nuzzled his neck. Her arms wound around his neck and her mouth came up to cover his. Theo kissed her deeply, tenderly, pulling at the towel around her. She pulled his t-shirt up over his head and he laid her back on the bed. He stroked her body gently, feeling the soft curves swell under his touch.

HE WAS hesitant at first but when she took his hand and placed it between her legs, he covered her body with his. She fumbled with his belt and zipper before he kicked his pants off and for the first time that night, she gave him a genuine smile. He looked down at her, the long dark lashes sweeping over the pink cheeks, her dark eyes liquid and soft.

'GOD, YOU'RE SO, SO BEAUTIFUL,' he murmured and grinned as she reached down to stroke his cock, feeling himself becoming hard as she caressed him. She wrapped her legs around his waist as he guided himself into her, hearing her gasp as he thrust all the way in.

'Can we just stay like this forever?' She whispered as they moved together and Theo kissed her, pouring all his love for her into the kiss.

'For all time, my Jessie...'

LATER WHEN THEO WAS ASLEEP, Jessie slid from the bed and wrapped Theo's robe around her. She went to the window and looked out over the garden, drenched in darkness and silent. They'd made love long into the night and although she was exhausted, she couldn't sleep, just knowing Jules was out there. She looked back at Theo's sleeping form. Could she really end things with him? The thought crippled her but if it meant keeping him safe from Jules' psychotic nature.

SHE THOUGHT back to the moment he had held that knife to her. That was nothing new but today there had been a frenzy in him, a blood-lust. He wanted to hurt her, maybe even kill her. Searching her feeling, she realised she had always known this, that her obvious love for Theo – or for anyone that had come along – would set him off. Could she go to the police now? Would the fact she was with Theo – and boy, would the feminist in her loathe that she need a man, even Theo, to give her credibility – would Theo's position help convince the police she was telling the truth?

JESS SLUMPED AGAINST THE WALL. She had no proof and Jules would use the best lawyers, use his money to paint her once again as no more than an attention seeker.

She looked back at Theo. There was no doubt in her mind that she loved this man, loved him completely and unconditionally. But did that mean she'd risk her life – and worse, his life – to keep what she wanted?

She imagined losing Theo forever. She knew which one she'd rather take Jules's violence over and over than risk it. She couldn't end things with Theo.

She drew in a long shaky breath and closed her eyes. A moment later she felt Theo slid his arms around her waist and felt his kiss on the back of her neck.

'Can't sleep?'

She shook her head and turned around to face him. She ran her fingertips over his cheekbones, feeling the tension in his muscles. 'I love you, Theo Storm, so, so much.'

'As I love you, Jessie.'

He kissed her then and led her back to bed. 'I can relax you if you'd like?' He had a small but teasing smile on his face and she sighed and nodded.

'Please...'

They made love slowly, their gaze locked on the other's until both of them were moaning and vibrating with pleasure.

JULES GACHET, sitting in his exclusive private men's club, was at the point of being too drunk. He didn't often lose control, didn't allow himself to but tonight he was celebrating. She was his again, his Jessica. Yeah, she might, even now, be fucking that bastard Storm, but Jules knew, she'd be thinking of him, of that knife pressed against her vulnerable skin.

YES, he knew he'd gotten to her, unleashed that same terror that bound her to him when she was younger. She'd got revoltingly independent, less afraid of him as she grew up, and that had enraged him.

JULES GACHET HAD REACHED his late thirties without ever forming a serious romantic attachment. Why would he? With his French good looks, dark eyes, dark hair, olive skin, he was considered one of the world's most eligible bachelors. He'd fucked around, taking his pick of supermodels, actresses, socialites, each one thinking they'd won the lottery when they'd met him. He let them think that, for a time, before cutting them dead with an almost gleeful finality. He enjoyed the mind games, the confusion and the humiliation.

BECAUSE NO-ONE, no-one, compared to Jessica. That tumbling dark hair, those wide brown eyes, that honey-coloured skin. He got hard now thinking about it. And today, he'd reduced her back to the terrified teenager that she'd been the first time he'd taken her, in the room next to their parents, late at night.

. . .

YES, today she became his Jess and again and not only that, he'd had a revelation, an epiphany. What he really wanted, what he most desired, what his endgame had always been whether he knew it or not.

HER BLOOD ON HIS HANDS. He was going to kill Jessica one day. He wanted to kill her.

Then he really would possess her entirely.

A brunette wandered into his eye-line. She didn't compare to Jessica of course, but she was an adequate substitute. He beckoned her over with two fingers and she smiled, drifting over to him through the busy club.

He fucked her in the ladies bathroom, not even bothering to learn her name. She was the usual type, good-looking with that hungry, eager look in her eyes.

'I've seen you here before,' she said, smiling as he led her to the bathrooms. I was wondering when I'd see you again.'

'Shh.'

HE LIFTED her up and thrust into her. She winced, not ready for him but stayed silent, enjoying his brutality, his clinical sexuality. She tried to kiss him but he turned his head away. Afterwards, after they dressed, they walked out of the club towards his car. She slipped her hand into his. He dropped it almost immediately. She had trouble keeping up with his stride.

'WAIT.' She said finally. He stopped and when he turned to look at her, it was with a blank stare, as if he'd only just noticed she was there.

'Can I come back to your place?'

He laughed in her face. 'Why the fuck would I want that?'

She baulked and he realised that under that slutty façade, she was just a kid. It made no difference to him.

Amateur. He turned on his heel with a disgusted look on his face and got into his car.

PROFESSOR GERRY LAND noticed Jess's pale face and exhausted eyes but discreetly said nothing. For a change, he swept all of the usual paperwork from her desk and told her to concentrate on the 'Luna Soleil'. Jess was grateful for his kindness.

SHE WAS glad to be away from her desk. Every time she looked over at that side of the room, she saw Jules – felt Jules – with his hands on her. She'd thrown her paperknife away, dumping it in one of the cafeteria's bins. It didn't make sense but it made her feel better to know it was gone, that it couldn't be used on her.

Theo had called her every hour, on the hour, just to check in and as soon as she heard his voice, she felt warmth flood through her. How could she give this up? Give him up?

As she worked on the painting, she lost track of all time, lost in what she was doing, lost in dreaming about Theo. She put all thoughts of Jules out of her mind.

The light was already fading by the time she walked out in the cool evening air. She knew Theo had a late meeting so she was surprised when his Mercedes pulled up beside her. Max leaned over and grinned at her.

'I'M YOUR RIDE TONIGHT, LADY.'

She giggled and got in the car. Max pulled the car around and drove out of the campus. Jess studied him as he drove.

'It's nice to see you again, Max,' she began, 'but you really didn't need to do this.'

Max shrugged good-naturedly. 'Did Theo mention I came over last night?'

She shook her head and he sighed. 'Okay, well, he told me what happened with your step-brother – or rather that you and he had an argument. Both he and I don't believe that's all, by the way,' – and he grinned over at her to soften his words. 'Let Theo help you, whatever it is. You won't betray the sisterhood, I promise.'

His tone was light and she smiled at his words but she could sense his seriousness.

She sighed. 'Max. It's not fair to Theo or you. My history with Jules is complicated.'

They drove in silence for a while then Max pulled the car over to the side of the road.

Jess took a deep breath in. 'Max...'

'Do you love Theo?' The question took her by surprise and she realised then that to her and Theo, in their little bubble, their love was overwhelming but to others looking in – especially a concerned best friend, it must seem...

'Max, I love him more than anyone else in this world. I know you must be concerned, especially given Theo's position, his wealth. If I were you, I'd be looking at me thinking 'is she looking for a white knight? Is she here just for his money, his influence? But I don't care about all of that. I love Theo for him. Nothing more. I just don't want past horrors to affect our life together.'

Max was studying her intently, listening to every word carefully. There was a long silence then he leaned over and kissed her cheek.

'I'm sorry, I had to ask. I just don't like secrets. For the record, I've never seen Theo like this. He's fallen hard.'

Joy rushed through Jess. She poked Max's shoulder, grinning wickedly. 'What a sap.'

'Complete wuss.' He joined in with her joke and they both laughed. Max shook his head.

'Man, when you think this all started with a dumb bet...'

Jess smiled, confused. 'A bet?'

Max laughed. 'He bet me he would find the love of his life within three months. That was less than a month ago. Quick work even for him.'

Jess's chest felt tight. 'A bet?'

Max sensed the change in her tone and looked over at her, a frown on his face. 'Hey wait, I...'

'Could you take me home, please, Max?'

'No, Jess, I didn't mean... god, it was a stupid joke, I didn't mean. He...'

'Please, Max, take me home.'

Theo looked up at Max, as his best friend burst into the room, and his heart began to thud unpleasantly at Max's expression.

'Where's Jess?'

But looking at Max's stricken face, suddenly Theo didn't think he wanted the answer...

3

SLEEP WITH ME PART THREE

J ess opened her eyes and stared up at the ceiling. How many times in her life had she woken up in this bed, sick to her stomach with nausea and fear? Crippled by guilt. Waiting to face her tormentor over the breakfast table as their parents ate and chatted obliviously.

And yet, last night, she'd come here after Max had dropped her off, wanting to be somewhere familiar. Camilla, the housekeeper, told her Jules was away for the night and the relief she felt was over-whelming. She'd sat with Camilla, shared a supper with her old friend, not wanting to talk or think about Theo Storm.

SHE WAS A WINNING BET. A winning bet, for Christ's sake. She wondered how long Theo would have to pretend that he loved her before Max would concede defeat. She should have known better than to trust a rich man – after all, didn't she know that they always got what they wanted? Damn you, Theodore Storm. But the pain in her stomach ripped through her when she thought of him. She'd turned her cell phone off so he couldn't reach her couldn't talk or kiss his way out of it.

Jess sighed. She needed to get her life back on track which meant getting up, getting showered and getting to work. She swung her legs over the side of the bed and hoisted herself into a standing position. Grabbing her robe, she opened the door and froze. She could hear Jules' low accented drawl from the end of the hallway.

Shit.

Jess closed her door quietly and scooted back to bed. She rolled onto her side, curling herself up into the foetal position. She tugged the sheet over her shoulders and, closing her eyes, made her breathing steady, regular. She tensed as she heard the door open.

For a few minutes, she stayed still. He must have gone by now, she thought and she let her body relax.

'I know you're awake.'

Shock drilled through her at the sound of his voice. She felt her body jerk and silently cursed herself again. She kept up the pretence of being asleep. She heard him laugh softly and she gritted her teeth. Bastard. She felt his body heat then as he leaned over her, she heard him breathing, an inch from her skin. She trembled and he laughed again, soft, intimate. She abandoned the pretence of sleep and looked at him, her eyes hard.

'Leave me alone.'

Jules smiled and leaned into kiss her. 'Never.' His voice was a whisper but it sent blank terror through her body.

He reached down and cupped her breast.

'So pretty, pretty.'

She hit his hand away and he grabbed her wrist. For a moment, she could see nothing but murder in his eyes. Then he smiled, turned her hand over and kissed it. He dropped her hand and walked out.

Trembling, Jess got up and threw her clothes on, grabbing her purse, skittering down the grand staircase and out to her ancient Gremlin. What the hell had she been thinking? She had to get out of here.

Now.

. . .

THEO HAD SLEPT in his car outside her apartment when it became clear she wasn't in. He'd left a thousand messages on her voicemail. Her silence was the loudest thing in his life. He woke now, stiff and aching. He opened the door and almost rolled his huge frame out of the car. He stretched and rubbed his hands through his short dark curls. His chest hurt with the fear that he'd lost Jess and for what? A stupid misunderstanding. He didn't blame Max, it had been a 'funny story' to tell, he would have had no way of knowing she would react the way she did. Theo could not get it straight in his head. Why the hell would she think that he had been lying to her all this time? He gave a short bark of laughter. All of this time. What was it, a month?

HE SIGHED AND TURNED, leaning against the car, was about to call her again when a movement caught his eye. He turned his head and saw her, at the end of the street getting out of her car. She looked exhausted. She saw him and froze, her eyes wide and wary. He hesitated for a brief second then walked towards her, afraid she was would skitter away from him.

'Please. Please, Jess, wait...'

Jess wavered but stayed still and as he reached her, he was shocked by the distress in her eyes, the thick violet circles under her eyes. He reached out to touch her face. She ducked away at first but when he caught her face in his hands, she stiffened and relaxed, seeming to slump into his touch. He tipped her chin up so he could look into those beautiful eyes.

'JESS... what Max told you, it was a joke. A coincidence. A drunken bet which has nothing, nothing to do with us. Nothing. I love you. I could lose every penny I have, every home or ridiculous extravagance I surround myself with and I'll still be the richest man on the planet because I had you.'

He stroked her cheek with the back of his hand. 'You are my world, Jessica Wood. I would die for you.'

That got her. She exhaled shakily and leaned against his chest. He wrapped his arms around her tightly for a second then she pulled away. He bent his head to kiss her but she shook her head.

Stung, he drew back but she smiled then. 'I haven't brushed my teeth yet.'

He laughed, relieved, and she took his hand and led him into her apartment.

JESS BRUSHED her teeth the minute she got the apartment, with Theo stripping her even as she brushed. She rinsed, reaching in to crank the shower on as Theo shed his own clothes then pulled him under the spray with her. He kissed her finally, his mouth fierce against hers, his fingers tangled in her hair. She pressed her body against his, feeling the hard chest against her nipples, his already stiffening cock against her thigh. God, this is all she wanted, his skin on hers, his mouth against her lips. Theo swept his hands under her buttock and lifted her so he could plunge his cock deep into her and she cried out as the force of his thrust slammed her back against the wall.

'I'm sorry...'

But she shook her head. 'No... harder... Theo... please...'

THEY FUCKED ALMOST VIOLENTLY, clawing at each other, biting, scratching, wanting consume the other. Theo manoeuvred her so they lay on the bathroom floor, her legs hitched high around his waist, his hips ramming against hers as he drove deeper into her, his lips against her throat, kissing and murmuring his love for her over and over. Jess squeezed her thighs, locking him inside her and Theo trapped her hands under his, forcing them above her head.

Jess felt totally naked and open and vulnerable and she loved every minute, delicious delirium screaming through her brain, through her body. She tilted her hips so he could slam into her as deep as he could and cried out her excitement as he bit down on her shoulder. Her orgasm made her almost demented with passion.

Afterwards, they lay, their limbs entangled, breathless and sated. Theo smoothed the damp hair from her forehead and smiled down at her.

'DON'T EVER RUN from me again, my Jessie.'

She brushed her lips against his. 'I promise. I'm sorry that I didn't give you the chance to explain. I just...I don't find it easy to trust, especially...' – and she grinned ruefully – 'very rich and handsome young men. I'm sorry if that offends you.'

SHE SAW the hurt in his eyes but he nodded. 'Understood. Then it's up to me to prove you can trust this one.'

She stroked his cheek. 'We have time to work this all out. Unless – ' and she stuck her tongue into her cheek and grinned, '-of course, you need to get married by Christmas, save yourself some money.'

Theo rolled his eyes. 'Neither Max or I were serious when we made that bet. He just thought I was working too hard.'

'Were you?'

Theo considered. 'Maybe – although I've certainly made up for that this last month.' He moved his body on top of hers and she revelled in the weight of him, chest to chest, belly to belly. Her legs, with a mind of their own, twined around his hips. Theo looked down at her, his eyes suddenly serious.

'Jess...you're not the only one who's overwhelmed. I've never felt like this before, I didn't even know it could be like this. We fit so perfectly, it seems, but yeah, we're gonna find some obstacles, have some misunderstanding, going to disagree on stuff. If you're not ready to share certain things yet, that's fine. Let's just promise to be open, honest. Please just don't run away without giving me the opportunity to make it right.'

. . .

JESS NODDED, tears glistening in her eyes. He always seemed to know exactly what to say, she thought and as he kissed her, she found herself with an undefinable ache in the centre of her chest. She wanted to tell him about Jules, what he had done to her, what he still might do to her, feel the protection of Theo's arms, know it was over forever and she was safe.

But not today. Today she wanted to forget that last night ever happened. She knitted her fingers into Theo's hair and kissed him back, wanting to taste every part of him. Theo shifted his weight and she drew in a deep, shaky breath as his cock, diamond hard and huge, pushed into her slowly.

THEO'S green eyes burned into hers as he began to move and in and out of her, thrusting harder each time. She lost herself in his gaze, every nerve ending on her skin on fire.

'Is there something – oh god, that's good – is there something you want me to do?' Her voice was low but steady, 'or something you want to try with me? To me?'

He smiled knowing exactly what she meant. 'You liked being bound, didn't you?'

She nodded.

'Would you like to go further?'

She smiled up at him. 'I would do anything for you, with you.'

Theo thrust harder and she moaned, heard his low chuckle. 'You might regret saying that, Jessie...I'm going to fuck you in so many different ways, you'll beg for more...'

AND FROM HIM, in this moment, it didn't sound like a threat.

Despite the warm, safe feeling that lingered after he'd dropped her off at work and gone to his office, Jess felt on edge as she walked into her department. She was the first in and she moved around the room, flicking lights on as she went, illuminating ever dark corner. Jules had tainted this place for her now as he'd tainted the family home for so many years. She still remembered the excitement she'd felt when her mother had brought her to the big house when she was nine, that first couple of years when it was just Ma, Erich – her affectionate but stern step-father - and the friendly staff, especially Camilla, housekeeper, nanny and playmate all in one. Camilla was the only reason she ever went back there now, that one last link to her mother.

SHE'D BEEN twelve when Julien, Erich's only son had come home from Oxford University. She'd been wary of him straight away, the way that his dark eyes had run all over her fledgling curves, the small buds of her breasts which as yet didn't need a bra. It was a look of ownership, of possession and it hadn't been long before Jules started to 'visit' her at night. At first, she fought but Jules, with his immense strength honed by racing crew at Oxford, overpowered her easily.

Jess swallowed and pushed the thought away. She knew where this brooding would take her – the first time Jules had raped her.

Jess closed her eyes and started to sing loudly, anything, to distract her mind. It was a technique she'd perfected.

'BON JOVI?'

Jess's eyes flew open and she saw Gerry standing in the doorway, grinning at her. 'That's a new one,' he said, shuffling an arm full of papers down onto her desk. 'Morning.'

Jess relaxed. Gerry was used to her tuneless singing by now – although he had no idea why she would suddenly burst into song. 'Heard it on the radio on the way in,' she said now.

Gerry snickered. 'Crazy girl. I thought you were warning me I was 'living on a prayer' if I gave you this paperwork.'

Jess punched his shoulder lightly. 'Well, that too.' She squinted at the stack and quelled a little. 'Is that all for me?'

Gerry had the grace to look sheepish. 'Sorry. But seeing as I'm letting you have Luna Soleil all to yourself...'

'God, okay, okay.' But she grinned and took the paperwork from him.

It was late morning before her cell phone beeped and she took a moment to re-orientate herself after concentrating on her work before she took the call. She didn't bother glancing at the caller i.d. then swore silently as Jules' clipped French accent greeted her. Her stomach dropped and she gritted her teeth.

'What do you want?' She didn't bother to return his faux-friendly greeting. It made her skin crawl.

Jules laughed. 'Always such civility. As it happens it isn't something I want, rather, William has asked us to meet him to discuss the estate. You'll be twenty-five this year.'

'I'm aware, thank you.'

'Then you'll remember the logistics of our arrangement will change. Your allowance will increase - along with your family duties, of course.'

Jess rolled her shoulders, tension and irritation making the muscle cramp painfully. 'What if I don't want your money?'

Jules laughed again and she fought the temptation to hang up on him. 'Jessica, if you weren't interested in money or status, why are you opening your legs for one of the world's most eligible, most powerful billionaires? Let's be adults. William wants us to meet him for dinner next week. You will be there.' He named the most expensive restaurant in the city.

JESS WAS SILENT, seething over what he'd said and Jules sighed impatiently.

'Tuesday. Eight thirty. Don't be late and don't let me down. Your department gets a very generous bursary from this estate, don't forget. It could easily get cancelled.'

The phone went dead and Jess growled and cussed softly under her breath.

. . .

SHE WAS TIED SECURELY to the chair. The blindfold was as he'd promised, so inky black that no light penetrated and she was utterly blind. With her hands pulled tightly behind her, soft leather wound tightly around her fragile wrists, another band of leather under her breasts to keep her torso from slumping in the chair.

SHE WAS NAKED. Helpless. His.

THEO PULLED the clip that held her gorgeous dark hair in a chignon and let the long, long waves tumble down her back. Her skin, in the dim light, was luminous, gold and amber and pink. Her breasts rose and fell with her breath, full and ripe, the dark nipples hardened with her arousal. Theo crouched in front of her. He was fully dressed, an impeccable Saville row suit. He bent his head and pressed his mouth against her belly, smiling when he heard her sharp intake of breath.

'QUIET.'

JESS CLOSED her perfect rosebud mouth then, utterly submissive to him. He trailed a fingertip across her skin, around her navel and down, stopping just before her sex. She shivered.

'Open your legs for me.'

Jess did as he asked and he could see the beauty of her sex, already glistening with her honey.

'Wider.'

She pressed her legs further apart and he sank to his knees between them. He bent his head and ran his tongue along the length of her folds, tasting the sweetness of the soft peachy labia, curling his tongue around the clitoris. Her whole body trembled as he tasted and teased her until she couldn't help but moan.

Theo stood and bent her head back so he could grind his mouth down on hers, his tongue lashing against hers.

'Can you taste yourself, Jessica?'

She nodded and he stroked back her hair. 'Good. I want you to taste me now. What do you say?'

'PLEASE...'

HE SMILED and rewarded her by tracing his fingertips across her stomach, cupping each breast, grazing the nipples with his thumbs. He stepped back and freed his cock – already so hard, pulsating and weighty. He traced the outline of her lips with the tip then as she opened her mouth to take him in, he sighed at the feel of her tongue on him, flicking around the tip, drawing him in. Her pretty cheeks hollowed as she sucked at him, the smooth motion of her lips along the shaft making his head swim with desire. She traced the vein with her tongue, grazing him gently with her teeth. God, the feel of her, the sight of her, her flushed face, head thrown back, the long dark mane sweeping along the floor.

'YOU HAVE no right to be so fucking beautiful,' he said, his breath ragged as he neared climax. Her lips curved up around his cock in a smile and he came, shooting violently into her mouth. She swallowed him down, taking his seed deep into her. Theo pushed the blindfold from her eyes and she smiled up at him as he caught his breath.

'God, I love you,' he said and with one move, freed the strap under her breasts and pulled her down on top of him so she straddled him. He moved to untie her hands but she shook her head emphatically.

Theo smiled and without a word, spread her labia wide and impaled her onto his cock, rigid and throbbing with desire for her. As she began to ride him, he gripped her hips, digging his fingers deep into the soft flesh there. Jess's eyes came alive at the pain and he increased his grip until he heard her moan.

'You like me hurting you, don't you?'

She nodded and he took her nipples between his finger and thumbs and pinched hard. Hard. She gasped and he felt her honey, hot and slick, cover his cock as he bucked under her. He pressed his finger hard into her navel and she came, throwing her head back and gasping for air.

Theo swiftly moved so he was on top, pressing her hard into the floor, tugging her legs over his shoulders, and ploughing into her roughly, harder and harder until he too climaxed, utterly abandoned and spent.

They caught their breath and then he freed her hands, gently massaging her sore shoulders and wrists. She still hadn't spoken and he grinned at her.

'You can speak now, you know.'

She smiled gently at him. 'I don't know if I can. That was...' and she was silent for so long he started to get worried. He propped himself up on his elbow and stroked her face, still damp with sweat.

'Hey...was that too much? You know, if it ever got too much, you know the safe word right?'

She nodded and placed her hand against his chest. 'I do. But Theo, damn, that was so intense – in a very, very good way. I love being under your control. Love it.'

He gathered her to him. 'I know,' he murmured, his lips to her ear, trailing his lips down her neck. 'I know what it took you to even consent to this. Even if you won't tell me everything, I can see it in your eyes. Thank you for trusting me.'

Jess wound her arm around his neck and gave him such a sweet smile, he had to have her again right there, on the floor again and again....

MAX WAS WILDLY relieved when he got a call from Theo – and he heard Jess call out 'Love you Max!' over the phone. To think his big mouth nearly cost Theo the best thing that had ever happened to him. Max had needed no more convincing of Jess's feelings for his best friend than the heartbreak in her eyes when she thought she was just the punchline of their joke. Max would never forget it. He'd scrambled to make it better and when he couldn't, he had told Theo everything. Max drained his drink. The bar on 9th was one of his and Josh's favourites – in fact, it had been exactly six years to the day they had met here, both then with other partners. He'd seen the tall Mexican laughing with his friends and fallen, right there. During the night, he'd manoeuvred and networked so hard they'd ended up talking in the same group. Joshua Ruiz was funny, gorgeous and erudite – and by the end of the night, he had Max's number. Ten days later, they moved in together.

Josh was making his way back to the bar from the restrooms now, stopping to say hi to friends as he went. Max marvelled again at his husband's lithe body, weaving so gracefully towards him. Max himself was prone to weight gain – just enough that a few extra pounds added back the puppy fat he'd worked so hard to remove. Josh didn't care at any rate. Max had never doubted his love for a second, such was their connection.

SO HE COULDN'T REALLY BLAME Theo for falling so hard, so fast. Max got it. The only thing he took pause over was what Theo had said the day he'd nearly wrecked it for him.

'I think she's been damaged, Max. I think it's why at any sign or perceived slight, Jess's default reaction is mistrust. She runs.' Theo had been quiet for a while then had said, almost to himself, 'I need to put this right.' He turned to Max. 'How quietly can we hire an investigator – a discreet one – to look into Jess's family? Not Jess, you must stress that, under no circumstances must she be followed or investigated – just her family. Especially her step-brother. The story's there, I'm sure of it.'

Max had assured him he could set it up but when he'd told Josh, his husband had raised an eyebrow.

'NOT SURE THAT'S going to do anything but make matters worse. If he is mistreating Jess, Theo might rush in. Things could get very nasty and that girl could be caught in the crosshairs.'

But Max had done as he asked and now, burning hot in his bag – well, that's what it felt like – was the investigator's preliminary report. Max had glanced at it quickly and had not liked what he'd read.

The investigator had talked to people from where Jules had gone to school, his college tutors. All of them were reticent to speak about Jules – no-one had a bad word to say about him – but neither did they say anything good. They were scared, the investigator had surmised. Frustrated, he'd finally been put in contact with a local police chief, Bud Clermont, who'd had plenty to say on the subject of Julien Gachet.

'Is he in trouble with the law?'

The investigator assured him he wasn't.

Clermont gave a frustrated hiss. 'Damn, I was hoping you were gonna tell me he fucked up. Finally got what was coming to him. Well, I can't tell you anything that'll hold up in a court of law, just that he's a piece of work. '

'I can tell you what I saw, what I think. Knew it from the second I met him, something wrong in that kid's eyes. They were dead, blank. First and only time a kid scared the shit out of me. Kept an eye on him as he got older, seems to me, someone like that, they're gonna escalate from petty crime. Of course, his family's money made that all go away. Something big happened too, only it was all hushed up and grunts like me never got to know what. Something to do with the step-sister. He was obsessed with her. Pretty disgusting – she was only twelve, I believe. Julien liked to play with knives, loved the sight of blood. I believe he was kept away from home as much as possible. I kept my eye on him. There were complaints from some of the female students – girls who looked just like the sister. Like I said – obsessed.'

Max felt another wave of nausea flood through him. He hadn't told Theo anything yet and he thought again about Josh's words of caution. The last thing he wanted was to put Jess in more danger – if that was what she was in.

Josh headed back then and started to talk to him but Max barely listened. He couldn't shake the feeling that something bad was coming, something very bad indeed...

Theo hooked a leg around Jess's hips and pulled her back down onto the bed. She protested, giggling, but as soon as he started to kiss her stomach, she gave up.

'I have to go soon,' she said gently, stroking her fingers through his dark curls. Theo, his lips against her belly, shook her head and she laughed. 'That tickles.'

He lifted his head and grinned. 'Why is this dinner so important?'

Jess sighed and sat up. 'It's to do with the estate. If it were just me that was affected by the changes in the estate, I'd tell Jules to go to hell but...'

'But?'

She rubbed her face roughly. 'When I was younger – and so freaking naive that I believed Jules – he set up several trusts for projects I cared about. Called it an eighteenth birthday present. He's managed to make it so that if he withdraws that funding – like from my art department – the project will suffer, or even have to close.'

Theo was appalled. 'Jess... that's blackmail.'

She nodded. 'I know. But what can I do? Tell him to screw it, I don't want his money anymore so screw everyone else? Not an option.'

She climbed off the bed and started to dress. 'It's not as if he's...' and she swallowed hard before looking away from him '...using it to do anything untoward to me. He just wants me to be a part of his family.'

'Paying you to be his sister?' Theo's voice was harsh and she winced.

'If you want to put it like that. Makes him sound pathetic when you say it like that.' She considered and a small smile played around her mouth. 'Actually, he is pathetic.' She turned and leaning over, kiss Theo on the mouth. 'And he's not your problem.'

Theo caught her face between his hands. 'Let me come with you.'

Jess shook her head. 'It's an hour, or two, and it's not even as if it's at the house. It's a restaurant with people, he can't...' She broke off, realising she'd said too much. She grabbed her clothes as Theo stood, tugging his jeans on.

'He can't what, Jessica?' Theo's voice was hard.

She could look at him. 'I have to get dressed.'

'Jess...'

'No. No, Theo. I have to get dressed.' She turned and walked out of the room, leaving Theo to stare after her.

JESS WALKED into the restaurant at precisely eight-twenty-nine to find Malcolm, Jules's bodyguard and driver waiting for her. He said nothing but handed her a cell-phone.

'Jessica, change of plan. William has come to the house instead. Malcolm will bring you here.'

SON-OF-A-BITCH. Jess handed Malcolm the phone, and he guided her out to the car. She couldn't believe she'd been conned by Jules again. Asshole asshole asshole. She couldn't protest, not without making a scene and she wouldn't put it past Malcolm to drag her by the hair to the waiting limo. He'd always scared her, his smug expression, the way he looked he looked at her make her feel sick. He was perfect for Jules, she thought, grimly, settling in the back seat, as far away from the driver as possible.

They drove through the rain-slicked streets and out of the city, towards the place she dreaded. Jess pulled her cell phone from her bag and flicked to Theo's number – and stopped. No. She wasn't the little princess in need of a white knight. She would handle this herself. She glanced up to find Malcolm smirking at her in the rear view mirror. She narrowed her eyes at him and he chuckled darkly and looked away. Why must everything in her life be filled with dread and menace? Jess sighed and leaned her forehead against the cold glass of the car window.

Everything except for Theo. He made everything okay. She glanced back down at her phone then, on impulse, sent him a message.

'Mr Storm, later this evening, I have a feeling I may need disciplining.'

Her phone bleeped straight away. 'Miss Wood, I concur. Present yourself to my room, stripped and ready to be chastised. Thoroughly.'

She giggled, a hot rush of desire flooding through her, a pulse beating between her legs. God, he could make her wet just by thinking about him. She closed her eyes and visualised trailing her lips against his strong jaw, pressing them into the hollow behind his earlobe, breathing him in.

THEN THE CAR stopped and reality came screeching back. Jules opened the car door and smiled down at her coldly. 'Jessica, my darling. Welcome home.'

MAX WAITED until Josh was asleep before sliding out of bed and into the living room. He grabbed his phone and called Theo.

'Yup?'

'It's me.'

Theo laughed softly. 'I guessed that from the caller i.d., buddy.'

Max was silent for a beat and Theo cleared his throat. 'You okay, Max?'

Max drew in a long breath. 'I got the preliminary report on Jules Gachet. It's not good, Theo.'

It was Theo's turn to be silent for a moment. 'Tell me.'

Max related everything to him, including what Bud Clermont had told him. When he was finished he waited, listening to Theo cuss softly.

'What do you think he's doing to her?' Theo's voice broke.

Max really – really – didn't want to answer that, didn't want to speculate. 'I don't know.'

Theo sighed heavily and told him what Jess had relayed earlier to him.

'Fucking manipulative creep.'

'I pray that's all he's...' But Theo couldn't finish the sentence and both men knew without a doubt, that it wasn't the full story.

'What do you want me to do, Theo?'

Silence. 'Nothing. Jess would freak if I told her what we'd done. I realised today, our relationship is balanced on a tightrope. Until we both can entirely be honest with each other... god.' Theo sighed. 'I'll just have to protect her as much as I can until she's ready to confide in me.'

AFTER MAX HAD HUNG UP, he sat in the cool darkness of his apartment for a while then went back to bed. As he slid into bed next to his sleeping love, he felt a weight pressing down on him. Guilt. His love was here, safe in his arms, absolutely no secrets between them, complete love, complete trust.

Max prayed that Theo and Jess would one day get there. He prayed they would be free to love without limits, without the threat that hung over them.

Because Max had no trouble believing that Jules Gachet was, if nothing else, evil.

JESS REASONED THAT AT LEAST, Jules had only partially lied to her about the evening. William Corcoran, the kindly family lawyer was waiting for them at the house, and over dinner, discussed the financial status of their family estate. Jess didn't listen to most of it, certainly she had no idea that William was discussing her until Jules tapped her shoulder rudely and nodded at William.

'I'm sorry, William, what did you say?' She liked the old man very much and smiled at him now.

He flushed with pleasure. 'Jessica, you are twenty-five in October and as you know, you are due to receive the balance of your trust fund your father set up.'

Step-father, she corrected silently but nodded. 'Yes. I already discussed with you what I want to do with the bulk of it. The projects, the college, the art societies. You still have my outline for how to split the money, correct?'

William looked embarrassed and glanced at Jules. Jess looked between the two of them, her heart sinking. What now?

'Jessica, Julien has informed me that he wishes to continue funding your projects indefinitely. In fact, the trust board had indicated that this is the only way they will agree to disperse the money. They feel that if you were given such a large amount, that, due to the history of mental illness in your family lineage, that you could be a danger to yourself. Drugs. Alcohol. Jules has informed me of your... episodes.'

JESS WAS SPEECHLESS. More than that, she was sure she was having a nightmare. 'What episodes? What the hell, Jules?'

Her step-brother put his hands on her shoulders. A warning. 'You know how you can get, Jessica. It's just better this way.'

She couldn't believe what she was hearing. 'Are you insane? That money is legally mine...'

'If –' Jules smiled widely, 'you remain under the conservatorship of the Trust. Father was very clear. After your mother's suicide, he made sure that if you were to suffer a breakdown like her, then you would be cared for.'

He had her. With a few simple lies to the police all those years ago, her 'hysteria' was on record and if she tried to run, everything she cared about would be gone. The art department would close, a women's shelter...

Jess felt if she would scream. She stood, unsteadily. 'I need to use the bathroom.'

In the restroom, she sank to the floor, dragging deep breaths into her lungs. She would never be free of him. He owned her. Jess muffled the sobs that forced themselves out of her throat.

She had to get out of here. Too late, she realised she had left her cell phone in her bag in the drawing room.

She clambered to her feet. She would ask William to drop her home but when she got back to the drawing room, Jules was alone. He smiled without warmth, offering her a glass of scotch. She shook her head.

'William had to leave suddenly,' Jules explained and Jess knew he had asked the older man to go so they could be alone.

There was a long silence then Jules smirked. 'So it just leaves us, Jessica.' His meaning was revolting clear and Jess lost her temper.

'There is no 'us' Jules!' Anger rippled through her, overwhelming the fear. 'Why don't you get that? Stop trying to tell me what to do with my life.'

SHE GOT up but he was beside her immediately, gripping her arms and pulling him to her. 'Fucking ungrateful little whore.'

She wrenched her arm from his grip. 'I'm sick of people trying to tell me what they think I should do with my life, especially you.'

'If I was Theo Storm, it would be a different story. You let him climb all over that beautiful body of yours, fuck you senseless. Do you think I can't see it on you? Smell him on you?' Jules's voice was bitter but underneath that there was something else, something that made her blood pump. A menace. She turned to face him, wary now.

'I love him. He loves me. He knows me, Jules, he wants to know me. He doesn't just take and take. We're not even blood, me and you. Who do you think you are?'

JULES'S EYES narrowed and he stepped towards her. 'I'm your family, Jessica. Your only family. Don't you have any loyalty?'

'Loyalty to whom?' Jess laughed without humour. 'You? The man who molested me constantly before I was able to get away? When I was a child? The man who continues to threaten and control my life.'

Jules put his head on the side, a small smile playing around his mouth. 'Did I threaten you, Jess? Or was it just your imagination? Or your desire?'

Jess sighed. 'I'm not playing these games anymore, Jules. I'm tired.'

'I'm the only family you have now, Jessica.'

Jess's chin lifted. 'It doesn't give you the right to lay claim to me. Let me just go home, Jules. Please. I have to get back.'

'What if I won't?'

Her gaze was cold. 'Won't what?'

'LET YOU GO HOME.' The terror came screeching back. His smile was humourless, his eyes fixed on hers. Jess's hands flexed, she took a deep breath, trying to stop the fear from overwhelming her. In its place was a fire, something burning inside of her, something that overpowered everything else. Anger. Suddenly, she wanted to goad him, pick a fight. Adrenaline surge through her, she could taste metal in her mouth. Reckless. She ignored that thought and returned his cold smile.

'What do you imagine will happen if you don't? What do you

have planned, Jules? More knife games? More threats?' She got into his face, ignoring the fear that spiked in her gut. 'More rape?' Her voice was a whisper but she hissed the word at him.

HE MOVED TOO QUICKLY THEN, slamming her back against the wall. She yelped in pain and he covered her mouth with his hand. 'If you like, Jessica,' he hissed, his mouth an inch from her face. He tugged up her skirt and desperate, she struggled with him. She managed to drive her knee into his groin and as hr groaned, she darted away. He grabbed her by the hair and threw her to the ground, spread-eagling himself over her.

The knife in his hand seemed to come from nowhere. Jess felt him press the tip against the thin cotton of her dress and for once, she was furious rather than scared. She looked him straight in the eye, a grim smile on her face.

'Do it,' she said, challenging him, 'Kill me. Run me through. Stab me to death. I'd rather that a million times over than your revolting prick inside me ever again.'

THE PRESSURE INCREASED and she felt the nick of steel in her skin. Jules was breathing heavily, his eyes crazed, sweat pouring down his contorted face. Time stopped for a long moment then with a roar, Jules cast the knife aside and started to push her dress up past her hips, tugging at her panties. Jess screamed – no, no, no, no – but Jules was unrelenting.

Then someone else screamed. Jules stopped and Jess, sobbing, pushed him away and clambered over to the shell-shocked, deathly pale Camilla, who stood in the doorway. The older woman enveloped Jess in her arms, staring at Jules as if he was the devil.

'YOU WILL NEVER, ever, touch her again or I'll go to the police, I swear to God, I will.'

Jules wiped his mouth, smirking. 'Get out. Take that whore with you and get out.'

Camilla raised herself up to her full height and stared him down. 'Your father would be ashamed of you, boy.'

JESS WAS ASTONISHED to see Jules's armour crack a little at the housekeeper's words and the little boy beneath show in his eyes. Camilla had been with the family since before Jules had been born and her words carried weight. Jules turned away from them and Camilla half carried Jess out of the room.

THEO RE-DIALLED HER NUMBER AGAIN. 'Pick up Jess. Pick up, please.' He half expected the same voicemail message he'd gotten the previous seven times but when it was picked up and a strange voice greeted him, his heart seized. The woman sounded older, kind but tired.

'Jess's fine, she's okay but...hang on...' There was a rustling then his heart leapt as Jess spoke.

'Hello my love, I'm fine. Just the...usual crap. I'm getting a cab to yours now.'

He suddenly felt dumb.

'Theo?'

'I'm here, honey. Just get here as soon as you – scrub that, I'm coming to get you.'

'No, no, please, Theo, the cab is already here. Honestly – ' and she lowered her voice, 'I'm really fine. Just tired.'

'Come home to me.'

'I am. I'm on my way.'

JULES KICKED his way back into his bedroom, picked up the nearest object, a book, and threw it across the room, opened his mouth and screamed his frustration, a primal sound. The rage burned through him. Fucking bitch. He walked to the bathroom, stripping, leaving his clothes where they dropped and cranked the shower onto the coolest setting. He stood under the water, letting it prick his skin, his eyes wide and staring. It was coming, the end, he could feel it, it was time.

JULES REACHED DOWN and began to masturbate. He leaned his head against the cold tile as he thought about the day. He'd been so close to killing her. When she'd called his bluff, he'd wanted to drive the knife into her again and again, feel the blessed, blessed relief, the sensation of her warm, viscous blood on his hands, the pain, the horror, the life in her eyes fading away, the feel of her last breath on his face. Jules came, shouting and grunting as he imagined Jessica's life slipping away.

JESS WENT into work the next day as if nothing had happened. Lying in Theo's arms that night – their schedule of S&M put on hold for the night – she'd spent a sleepless night going over everything in her mind. She couldn't allow Jules to continue to control her life this way. Theo had grilled her and she'd fudged the details, telling him about the 'inheritance with conditions' and he'd been suitably outraged.

'I'll fund your projects. We've been thinking about setting up a foundation just for this – you could run it.'

She'd protested but the offer was so tempting, so full of love she'd promised she would consider it. It was a way out. An easy fix. But something didn't sit right with her – bailed out by another rich man? It made her uneasy, even if she did trust Theo meant well.

By the time she got to work, the exhaustion had caught up with her and she didn't see the figure waiting in the corner of her office until it was too late. Jess suddenly looked around and gasped in shock.

.   .   .

JULES SAID nothing but stalked across the room and ground his mouth onto hers. Jess squirmed away from him but his hand was tight around her throat, squeezing, squeezing hard and she began to gasp for air as Jules started to strangle her. His face was a red mask of hatred and lust.

'You don't get to go home to him again. This way, you're mine forever.'

Theo's blood ran cold when he saw them and in a blur, he dragged Jules from Jess, throwing the smaller man across the room. He bent to pick up his stricken love, his heart thumping at the terrified expression on her lovely face but then Jules launched himself into them. Jess was thrown from his arms and Theo slammed into the wall. Jules was a feral whirlwind of rage, raining blows down on his. His fist caught Theo a glancing blow across the temple and he reeled, black spots crowding into his sight. He staggered back but then saw Jess behind Jules, coming at him with a heavy box file. She crashed it over Jules's head but he turned and drove his fist into her stomach, making her double up. Adrenaline coursed through Theo then and he grabbed Jules, throwing him into the other room.

'You'll never ever fucking touch her again,' he growled, following his quarry. Jules, clambering to his feet, sneering.

'She belongs to me, Storm, she always has, she always will.'

Theo charged at him and grabbed him throwing him across the room just as Jess, staggering and breathless, screamed 'No!'

Jules's whole body slammed into and destroyed The Luna Soleil.

THEO OPENED the door and stood aside to let her in. She moved slowly, almost catatonic, into his apartment. He locked the door behind them, double locked it. After Jules – after they – had destroyed the painting, he and Jess had stood frozen while Jules scrambled up and disappeared. The noise of the fight had brought others who got there in time to see Jules clambering from the wreckage of The Luna Soleil. Theo, in disbelief, had turned to see Jess, shell-shocked, staring at the remains of the priceless artwork.

Her knees had given out and he caught her as she collapsed. Every-thing after that was a blur of police interviews, photographs. Gerry had been there, and the dean and after the police had finished, the dean took Jess into his office and shut the door. Theo and Gerry waited anxiously but when Jess came out, she said nothing, just gathered her things, kissed Gerry's cheek and walked out, Theo following. In the car she had been silent, just stared out of the window but now she looked at him, and he saw the depth of her pain.

'I RESIGNED,' she said softly. 'There was nothing else to do. The Dean accepted it, he would've had to fire me anyway. This way, at least, I get to keep my dignity...except not really...' and she started to sob. Theo took her in her arms, letting her cry herself out. He carried her to the bedroom and lay down beside her, stroking her face, kissing her tears away. As her tears shuddered to a stop, she fell into an uneasy sleep.

THEO PULLED the comforter over her and went into the living room. The dean answered the phone on the first ring. Theo apologised for the late hour.

'I wanted to say, let me have the details of the owner and I'll pay for the damage.'

The dean was silent for a beat. 'Mr Storm.... the painting was destroyed.'

Theo cleared his throat. 'I know. I'll pay for it. Dean Roberts...he was trying to kill her. Something infinitely more precious than a painting would have been destroyed. What happened was the result of Gachet's violent behaviour. Please don't punish Jess – she was the victim here.'

The dean sighed. 'I do know that, Mr Storm. Look.... I can't say what is going to happen except this will be big news. I don't know how we can keep your name out of it.'

'That's fine, I don't expect miracles but tell the truth. Don't let them crucify Jess.'

He ended the call and rubbed his hands over his face.

'Thank you.'

He looked up at the sound of her voice. She was standing in the doorway, barefoot, her hair tumbling down her back. Her beautiful face was drawn, her eyes tired but she had the sweetest smile on her face.

He got up and went to her, sliding his arms around her, kissing her softly. 'You don't need to thank me for anything.'

'You saved my life.'

He stroked her face. 'I love you. I'd never let anything happen to you.' She leaned into his touch.

He looked into her eyes and saw a lifetime of hurt and abuse and fear.

'I want to take care of you – as long as you want me to.' He kissed her again. 'So I'm going to ask you this and I want you to think about seriously. Move in with me. Let me look after you. In exchange, you can look after me. A partnership, a forever thing. Live with me, Jessie...'

4

LIVE WITH ME PART FOUR

Jess pulled her clothes from her drawers and shoved them into her old and battered suitcase. She looked around her bedroom, with its now bare walls and stripped down queen-sized bed. A palpable sadness had settled in her chest but she knew now she couldn't stay here. Jules was out of control and Theo had offered her safe harbor. She'd be a fool to turn that down.

Theo poked his head into the bedroom and smiled at her. 'That ready to go?' He nodded at her suitcase.

'I'll be just a minute.'

Theo came into the room then, took her shoulders and made her look at him. She knew what he was seeing; wounded eyes, black and purple marks on her neck, defeat. She moved to hold him, wanting to reassure him.

She looked at Theo's anxious face. 'I'm okay.' He smiled at her but she could see he wasn't convinced. She let him go and he watched as she walked over to the suitcase and locking it.

'Thanks for doing all this,' she smiled at him. 'I don't know where I'd be without you. Probably dead.' She tried to smile but regretted

her words when she saw the pain in his face. 'Sorry. It's just everything is... I'm finding it difficult to believe any of this is real. At the
same time...' She touched her bruised throat and gave a short laugh.

Theo stayed silent. Jess sighed.

'Come on, baby. Let's get out of here.'

She moved into the living room, towards the door but, as she
passed him, she stumbled a little. Theo saw her legs give way and
caught her. She was shaking badly but dry-eyed as he held her.

'Jesus, Jesus...' she whispered. Theo buried his face in her hair
but she pulled away and looked up at him.

For a moment, she thought about the attack and a brief flash of
fear cross her face. Theo saw it.

He bent down and kissed her gently.

'I won't let him anywhere near you, don't worry.'

'It's not just me I'm worried about.'

He frowned. Jess smiled at him but her eyes were serious.

'He hates you, Theo, if he hurt you...'

Theo turned his nose up. 'He's a coward, Jess. And a misogynist.
He sees women as inferior, weaker, easily manipulated.'

She nodded, her face somber. Theo smoothed her hair back from
her face.

'You okay?'

SHE NODDED but her face was tight and she suddenly pulled away
from him, her face flushing a deep scarlet. Angry.

'I'm mad, Theo. Just mad. Who the hell does that bastard think he
is telling me who I can love, deciding whether I live or die? Asshole.
Who the fuck gave him the right?'

Her voice was rising with each word and her eyes were wild. She
moved away from him, casting around for something, anything that
would help her feel better. She gave a short laugh. She picked up a
mug; a nondescript red coffee cup shoved into a cardboard box and
showed it to Theo.

'He drank from this.' She hurled the cup at the wall, her face set in a grim smile as the ceramic smashed. She whirled around and scooped up a plate.

'Call me a whore, motherfucker?' And she flung the plate against the wall.

'This is for every time he hurt me.' Her hair flew around as she grabbed more and more plates and launched them at the wall.

Theo sat, a smile spreading across his face as he watched her smash her way through an entire cupboard of crockery, yelling, cussing, screaming all her anger, her rage. Theo started to smile. By the time she had finished, out of breath, they were both laughing helplessly.

'Feel better?'

SHE GRINNED AT HIM, tears of laughter in her eyes. 'So much better.'

He stood and slid his arms around her waist. 'Good.' He kissed her and she sighed happily.

'Okay then. Let's get out of here and start our new life together.'

HE NEEDED to back away for a while, to stay away from her. Jules Gachet's cheek muscles hurt from being clenched in anger and he stretched out his mouth to loosen them. He dragged his hand through his hair, long overdue for a cut, and glanced at his reflection in the mirror. Hard-bodied and fit, but he'd stood no chance against Theo Storm's huge strength and now Jess was under Storm's protection.

No. He had to be careful, plan his next movement, and be patient. Jessica would pay for her betrayal of him, would suffer the worst of his fantasies before he killed her. Attacking her at the college had been a mistake: too many witnesses. He'd been expecting a visit from the police since that day but nothing. She hadn't pressed charges. *Maybe she thinks I should be grateful enough for that*, he mused, smirking. Not a chance, bitch.

·   ·   ·

HE DRESSED QUICKLY and strode down the hallway. Camilla was talking to a delivery man at the front door and Jules rolled his eyes as he pushed past her. He'd only been half-serious when he'd told her to get out the other day; anger made him forget just how well she ran the estate, took most of the toil from him so he could continue playing the way he wanted to. He knew she thought he was disgusting; what on earth would she say if she ever found out what he used to do to Jessica when she was a kid? Jules smirked as he jumped into his car. Who cared what that old spinster thought? Jessica was his, had always been his and would always be his.

Even after she was dead.

HER POSSESSIONS LOOKED pathetic next to the opulence of Theo's home and she felt somewhat ashamed of what her life added up to. Few clothes, more books, and art supplies. Theo had unpacked her books and had lined up the battered paperbacks and textbooks next to his on his shelves and now she was in his bedroom – their bedroom, she supposed now – procrastinating over unpacking her clothes.

She didn't hear Theo come into the bedroom behind her and started as he slid his arms around her waist and pressed his lips to her neck.

'Hey, beautiful...'

SHE TURNED in his arms and tilted her head up so he could kiss her mouth. Theo moaned slightly as his lips moved against hers. 'God, you taste so good.' His hold on her tightened and Jess felt her pulse quicken. God, would she ever not want this man?

Theo slowly drew the straps of her dress down her shoulders, trailing his lips across her skin. The dress fell to the floor and she sighed as he picked her and laid her down on the bed, stripping off his sweater. Her hands went to the zipper on his pants and soon they were both naked, kissing, caressing. Theo moved down her body, the tip of his tongue circling her nipples, dipping into the deep hollow of her navel. Jess gasped as his teeth grazed her clit, his strong fingers spread the folds of her labia apart so he could taste her. She closed her eyes as he bit the tender flesh of her inner thighs, and his fingers slid inside her, one by one until only his thumb remained to stroke her clitoris with increasing pressure. Theo shifted so that he could kiss her mouth as he penetrated her, his fingers probing and stroking her until she was shivering with pleasure.

'YOU LIKE THAT?' Theo asked her softly but his eyes were intense on hers and she nodded, unable to speak, her fingernails digging into the smooth hard skin of his back. He chuckled softly, dipping his head to take her nipple into his mouth, flicking the tongue around the sensitive nub before gently biting down on it. Jess gasped out 'This is too much, too much...' But she pressed herself into his touch, grinding herself down onto his hand, still buried deep in her. Theo teased her nipples with his mouth then pressed his lips into the valley between her breasts.

'COME FOR ME, Jessie.... that's it, give yourself to me...' The pressure on her clit became almost unbearable and her back arched upwards violently as she climaxed, only Theo's sheer weight keeping her from bucking herself off the bed. Theo didn't give her time to recover before plowing his diamond hard cock into her and Jess thought she might die from the explosion of sensations ripping through her body. Theo clamped her hands above her head and began to thrust mercilessly, fucking her hard, ever thrust going deeper and deeper. Her hips screeched with pain and Theo forced them wider to gain access to her. Their eyes locked on the others as they slammed against each other and she was coming again and again as she felt Theo shudder and spasm, his cum shooting hard into her. Jess was on the verge of passing out but she never wanted it to stop.

Theo flipped her over and before she could catch her breath, his cock was pushing deep into her ass, so slowly and deliciously that she gave a long, delirious moan.

'GOD, when you make that sound, Jessie... you make a man almost want to...' Theo didn't finish his sentence but she felt him bite down hard on her shoulder and she cried out with pleasure. His lips were at her ear then. 'You like it when I hurt you, don't you?'

She nodded and shivered through another orgasm as Theo gave a low, almost dangerous chuckle.

'JESSIE... I'm going to take you away somewhere, somewhere private and we're going to try some things that you'll like, and I'm going to have complete command over your glorious body.'

He pulled out and turned her to face him. His green eyes were dark with passion and danger and her breath quickened under his gaze. He bent his head to kiss her neck, her breasts before shifting to bury his face in her belly. For a second she just felt his hot breath on her skin then he looked up at her, a wicked grin on his face.

'I'm going to fuck you in so many different ways, Jessica Wood, until you beg me to stop.'

She smiled, her skin damp with sweat and glowing. 'I'll never want to stop.'

Theo smiled. 'Good. Because this body is mine. These breasts –' He nipped at her nipples with his teeth making her squirm with pleasure, 'this belly...' He traced a circle around her navel and she felt her eyes roll back into their sockets from the sensation.

'Theo...' Her words were a sigh and then he was kissing her mouth tenderly, lovingly.

'You are my life,' he said and the softness, the truth in his voice made tears roll down her cheeks and she pulled his head down to kiss him.

. . .

JESS LOOKED out of the small airplane window down at the island. Theo's island, she thought to herself and shook her head, grinning. My boyfriend owns an island. She didn't know why this shocked her but because she had always insisted on going Dutch with him when they went out, and of course, from the obvious opulence of his homes, she'd never been this aware of his great wealth until now. Something about it bothered her, she could feel it but she pushed that thought away. For once, just don't overanalyze, just enjoy, sister. She smiled and turned to Theo. She took a moment to take him in as he tapped away on his laptop next to her. That face – all fierce angles that were so quickly softened by his boyish smile, the way his eyes would almost disappear when he laughed. She loved it all, the way his dark hair curled slightly around his ears, the hint of five o'clock shadow.

THEO SENSED her scrutiny and looked up with a smile. 'Okay, baby?'

'Very, very okay. I love you, Theodore Storm.'

Theo smiled and closed his laptop, shoving it to one side. In one movement he had pulled her onto his lap, winding his arms around her waist, pressing his lips to hers. 'And I you, beautiful. Excited?'

There was something burning in his eyes and she smiled enjoying the double meaning in his words. She nuzzled his neck. 'God, yes...' she whispered and felt his chuckle rumble through his chest.

'Not long now...'

Jess stroked his face and then glanced around the private jet's cabin. 'We're all alone now...'

Theo said nothing, but a small smile played on his mouth. Jess slid from his lap and knelt between his legs. She reached for his fly, freeing his cock and stroking it gently.

'Put your head back, Theo, relax...'

She took him in her mouth, her soft lips parting and gliding over the wide crest of him, the soft skin of his cock feeling like silk against her tongue. She traced the delicate veins with her tongue and traced tiny circles around the tip, feeling it harden and Theo drew in a sharp breath. Jess moved slowly, drawing the shaft in and out of her mouth, teasing him. Theo closed his eyes and leaned his head back, sucking in air between his teeth as she worked.

'Jessie...' He tangled his fingers in her hair and began to massage her scalp, sending shivers of pleasure down her body. She hollowed her cheeks, sucking gently on him, feeling his cock quiver and swell. Theo groaned and she could taste salty pre-cum. She smiled – quite a feat considering his cock was now so huge in her mouth she had to stretch it so wide it started to hurt.

Then he was groaning and coming, shooting into her mouth over and over and he collapsed back into his seat, pulling her into his arms.

'Do it. Kill me. Run me through. Stab me to death. I'd rather that a million times over than your revolting prick inside me ever again.' Jules sighed. She was calling his bluff. Wrong move, Jessica. Very, very wrong. 'Oh, why must you make me do this?' He turned and thrust the blade into her belly. She gasped, shock, terror. He stabbed her again. 'Ungrateful little bitch. Don't you know what I've done for you?' He twisted the blade, feeling her hot blood pumping over his skin. 'This could have all been so different.' Jules smiled, caught her as she fell, laid her on the floor. 'No, no, please...' She was staring at him, her beautiful eyes wide with disbelief as he brought the knife down again and again and again...

Jules's fingers twitched on the steering wheel as he drove towards the city. The consuming rage when Jess had challenged him still flowed through his body, making his skin itch, his fingers pulse with every heartbeat. Disobedience, the ingratitude. It always started like that, the resistance, the arguments until he was forced into disciplining her. Sometimes he had dealt with her quickly, taken her violently, letting her know he was, in every way, her superior. He had decided, however, he would try again with her. She was special. He would give her one more chance to come to him and be his forever. But if she resisted, he decided, he would devise a punishment for her that would be beyond comprehension, something unimaginable.

BUT FIRST, he wanted to know everything about the prick that had his hands on her now, Theo Storm. He imagined the devastation on that bastard's handsome face when he found the love of his life stabbed to death, slaughtered by her one true master. Maybe he would make him watch her die. Whatever, he would destroy both of them, psychologically and emotionally before finally killing Jessica. He would make them learn about loss. *I will give them a world beyond pain*, he thought and with a grim smile, he hit the gas and sped into the city.

THEO DROVE the hire car along the island's coast road. Jess was already overawed with the beauty of the island, heavy with colorful and fragrant flora; hibiscus, bougainvillea, mandevilla as well as lush green grasses. The air was heavy with heat but along the road, through the open windows, Jess could feel a cool breeze coming from the salt water.

THEO LOOKED over at her and she smiled at him. He grinned, sliding his free hand onto her belly. 'Not far now, gorgeous.'

She put her hand over his, enjoying the feel of his skin on hers. Theo turned down a sandy track, almost overgrown with vines and creepers. A ways down the track, he nodded in front of them. A sprawling single level home lay in front of them, wood and glass, the windows wall to ceiling.

They got out of the car and Theo opened the door for her. He led her hand-in-hand through the silent house, pulling open the large glass doors and now she could see that outside the largest, outside the living room was the beach, silky white sand and the azure, teal, turquoise ocean crashing waves gently onto it.

Jess realized she had been holding her breath. 'I think I'm in a dream,' she breathed and Theo laughed, wrapping his arms around her.

'All very real, my love, and we have it all to ourselves as long as we want it.' He brushed his lips against hers. 'Are you tired?'

She shook her head, meeting his gaze. 'No...'

He grinned, kissed her and then said, 'I bet you're hungry, though...'

Jess groaned and laughed. 'Well, now I am...'

In the kitchen, they found the refrigerator almost overflowing with good food and soon they were enjoying soft bread and fresh cream cheese, succulent peaches which dripped juice down their fingers. Theo opened a bottle of champagne and Jess swooned at the heavenly taste of their feast.

'I COULD GET USED TO THIS.' She caught a dribble of juice that ran down her hand and Theo leaned over to kiss the juice from her mouth.

'Tastes like you,' he murmured then took another peach from the bowl, splitting it into two with his long fingers. Keeping his eyes on her, he ran his tongue along the soft flesh and Jess's stomach dissolved with desire. Theo knew exactly what he was doing, she knew, but she didn't care.

THEO CASUALLY REACHED over to her and started to unbutton the bodice of her dress. She watched him lazily, spaced out with desire. He ran the peach down her skin, leaving a trail of juice down her belly then followed it with his tongue. Jess felt drunk and she was floppy in his arms as he picked her up and carried her into the bedroom. He stripped her of the rest of her clothes then stood.

. . .

'ONE SECOND,' he said before disappearing. He was back in an instant with the half empty bottle of champagne. 'Lie still for me, beautiful.'

She gasped at the cold liquid as he poured champagne into her navel and then she giggled as he chased it with his tongue .as it dripped down her sides. Theo put his mouth over her navel and drank the champagne from it, his tongue delving deeply into the hollow of her belly. He took a swig from the bottle then and pushed her legs apart. Jess gasped as he took her clit into his mouth, the champagne bubbles bursting against it. She moaned at the feel of it, and of him as he traced every part of her sex as if it were that same peach, biting gently down on the soft folds of her labia then his tongue was deep inside of her. Theo poured more champagne onto her skin as he pleasured her and Jess knew she would do anything for this incredible man, her insatiable, skilled lover...

JULES TIED her to the chair, the bindings biting into her skin. Jess knew now it was hopeless. Jules was going to kill her, now, today, in the next few minutes and she would never see Theo again. Was it really only hours ago they had been in his bed, delirious with happiness, making love with careless abandon?

And now she was about to be murdered. Stabbed to death by her own step-brother. Her tormentor. Her rapist. Now he was about to become her killer.

Jules smiled down at her as he cut her thin shirt away from her body. 'You can scream if you like. No-one will hear you here.' He threw the scraps of material away then ran his fingers down her belly.

'Christ, you are perfect,' he said, almost tenderly. He leaned over and kissed her and she felt the cold steel against her. 'Oh, Jessica...my love, my love...'

The blade slid through her flesh like butter.

JESS SCREAMED – not the sudden awakening from sleep in a shock type of scream, but a deeply visceral, desiccating howl of agonizing terror. She felt hands on her and incredibly the panic increased, a berserk fear ripping through her.

'Sweetheart, sweetheart it's me...'

Jess struggled to regain her countenance, make sense of the world she had awoken to.

'Theo?' Her voice cracked.

'Yes, darling, it's me, it's me...you're okay, you're okay. You just had a nightmare...'

All the adrenaline left her body and she slumped into his arms, weeping. 'Sorrysorrysorry...' she was babbling she knew but the dream had so real. She still felt the pain of the knife, of her skin being torn open, her insides cut to pieces, her blood gushing out of her...

'Sssh.' Theo was rocking her and for the next few minutes, he just held her while she calmed down. Eventually, she wiped her eyes and smiled weakly at him.

'Sorry. Stupid dream.'

His eyes were concerned as he brushed the damp hair away from her forehead. 'Tell me.'

Jess drew in a couple of lungfuls of breath. 'He had a knife.'

She knew she didn't have to say any more than that. Theo's arms tightened around her and he pressed his lips to her temple.

'I will never, ever, let him hurt you again.'

She so desperately wanted to believe him.

MAX HAD dinner done ready for when Josh came home – it was his turn and he'd missed the last few. So it was his turn and lord knew he wanted a quiet evening in with Josh after the day he'd just had. He poured himself a glass of wine, checking the chili was bubbling away nicely and headed into the living room. He flicked on the television, putting a comedy show on for background noise.

Max watched it for a couple of minutes, knowing he wasn't taking it in then, sighing, he lifted the heavy file from his bag. The file on Julien Gachet. Since he heard what the old cop had said about Jules' history, he hadn't been able to get it out of his head. Max wasn't stupid – he'd guessed that Gachet's preoccupation with Jess hid something far more insidious, far more disturbing. He'd talked a psychologist friend of his who had run several ideas past him. The one he couldn't get out of his head was that Jules had made Jess his sexual obsession.

'NOT WHEN SHE WAS A KID?' Max had asked his friend, appalled. His friend had nodded, his eyes angry and sad.

'Probably. Has she said anything of the kind to you or Theo?'

But he couldn't ask Theo. Theo had expressly forbidden him to look into Jess's background but without doing so, he wouldn't have found out so much about that son-of-a-bitch Gachet. Max felt a roiling hatred inside of him for the Frenchman. How dare he treat Jess like that? He had to find out their family dynamic before he would risk going to Theo. He opened his laptop and found the map to Jules' home. The house where Jess grew up.

Max decided then and there to go there – and find out just what sort of childhood his friend had... and what Jules had done to her.

THE ROOM WAS DARK, just lit by the warm, flickering candlelight. The glass doors to the beach were open and a hot breeze blew the delicate white drapes into the room. Soft music played in the background, Lana Del Rey playing her Video Games and Theo and Jess danced slowly to the slow, sensual tune. Jess's head was on Theo's shoulder, his arm wrapped securely around her, his other hand in hers as they moved. A day of sightseeing, glorious sunshine and sea and delicious food and now the inky night outside had lulled them both into a sensuous fog of desire. Theo stepped away from her for a moment and picked up his tie. He wound it around her eyes gently.

· · ·

'READY?' He whispered and she nodded and smiled. He ran his tongue gently along her lush bottom lip then kissed her. He stepped away from her and she continued to sway gently to the beat.

Theo watched her, his eyes blazing with desire. The red silk shift dress she was wearing clung to every curve of her, and as she moved, the silk embraced the full breasts, her soft belly, the long strands of the pearl necklace she was wearing moving counter wise to her dancing.

'Jessie...'

'Yes?' Her voice was soft, dreamy, waiting to be commanded.

'Jessie, run your fingers up the inside of your thighs for me and touch yourself. Let me see you.'

STILL DANCING, she did as he asked, sweeping his hands gracefully under the hem of her dress, pushing it up, tracing her fingers over the soft skin of her thighs. Theo watched as she stroked her hand into her sex, her movements rhythmic with the music. He watched her masturbate herself and thought it the most beautiful thing he'd ever seen. His cock strained against the fabric of his pants and silently, he stripped off, moving so he could cup her buttocks his hand. Blind-fold, she started slightly at his touch but then started to grind gently back into his hands. He let her push herself against him, his cock ramrod erect. He let it lay on her skin and she moaned at the feel of its warm length. Theo took the strands of pearls from her neck and wound it around her hands, binding them behind her. He pressed his lips down onto her shoulder.

'Are you mine?' He whispered, his lips at her ear, his teeth nipping gently on her ear lobe.

'Yes, sir.'

A THRILL WENT through him but he kept his stern tone. 'Correct answer, woman. But still I think you need to be punished.'

He heard her breath quicken, watched a scarlet flush cross her cheeks. He tightened the binding on her hands until he could see it was uncomfortable. He stood behind her, reaching around to run his fingers up and down her belly as he moved her towards the sofa.

'Bend over and open your legs, girl...'

She did so and he thrust into her sharply from behind, feeling the soft moistness of her stretch and envelop his cock, which by now was so diamond hard he thought he might explode. Jess gasped at his force and he smiled.

'ASK ME...'

'Fuck me, please sir, fuck me...'

He slammed into her, hearing her moan. He gripped her hips, digging his fingers deep into the soft flesh of them.

'Ask me again.'

'Please, sir, fuck me, fuck me harder...yes...god...'

THEO DID AS SHE ASKED, ramming his cock as hard as he could into her deliciously wet cunt. Jess moaned and he could feel her whole body trembling. He pulled out, flipped her and pushed her down onto the couch. He wanted to look at her... her lips, her breasts, her belly... as he fucked her. Her golden skin shimmered with sweat and heat as he plunged into her again. He lifted her legs over his shoulders and pushed the blindfold from her eyes. He had to see the love in her eyes and now there was a fire too, a new fire, one of being possessed and wanting to be possessed. By him alone. She was his.

THEO CAME, his cum pumping into her so forcefully he shuddered at the release. Jess was panting beneath him and he lifted her into his arms. She leaned into his embrace and they were kissing. He released her hands and she wound her arms around his neck. Neither of them spoke – there was no need for words. Their kissing was tender, loving, tasting each other. Jess gathered her necklace into her hands and cupped his cock, running the pearls over his skin, stroking them against his sac until he was half-crazed with arousal. Jess straddled him and guided him into her, riding him slowly, teasingly, taking more of him into her every time she moved until their bellies touched. He felt himself swell and fill her entirely and then she was trailing her fingernails up and down his back. God, he wanted to consume her, be inside every part of her. He reached over to where he'd left the toys they had bought with them and grabbed a dildo, some lube. He covered the toy and his hands with lube and reached around her to part her buttocks gently. Looking into his eyes, Jess nodded, smiling and he began to push the dildo slowly into her ass as she rode him. Soon their rhythm matched and Theo felt an elation he'd never felt before. They were one person now.

'I love you...' He whispered and felt her clench her vaginal muscles around him. She was moaning now, and he felt the hot rush of her orgasm flood over his cock. He swiftly moved so that she was under him, pulling out and ejaculating on her belly.

Finally, near exhaustion, they lay on the couch, wrapped in each other. Skin on skin, sated and delirious, they fell asleep in the others' arms.

MAX SAT in his car outside the big house, waiting for any sign that Jules Gachet would be leaving for the day. He didn't have to wait long. Jules' gray Audi R8 sped out of the gates just after nine a.m. and Max wasted no time.

The woman at the door had a kind face and a rounded, well-fed body. Max wanted to hug her immediately. He told her he was a friend of Jess' from college. The woman – Camilla – had squinted at him doubtfully but invited him in anyway. He soon found he couldn't lie to her for long, and gave a shrug of his shoulders.

'I'm Theo Storm's best friend – so that makes me a good friend of Jess too.' He gave her the woman a grin and she smiled back, won over.

'That's better. There're too many lies in the world and definitely too many in this house.'

She ushered him into the kitchen. 'Have you had breakfast?'

She made him a huge stack of the most heavenly blueberry pancakes and sat down with him, a huge cup of coffee in her hand. 'So, Mr...?'

'Max. To tell you the truth, I'm not supposed to be here. Well, Theo would kill me. But he's worried. We both are. There have been incidents between your employer and Jess that have left her scared and bruised. It has to stop but she won't press charges. It would help to know how to help her if I knew something of her upbringing... what the dynamic here was.'

CAMILLA WAS SILENT FOR A MOMENT, looking out of the window, then she sighed. 'Jess came here fifteen years ago when Mr. Gachet Sr. married her mother. Julien was away then but he came back a couple of years later. He claimed Jess straight away, was possessive, drove her friends away, was always with her. We just didn't realize how bad his fixation was. When the parents died and Jules was left to run the estate, that's when things got really bad. He tried to control every part of her life and she had to move out. He still never leaves her alone. He uses money to control her – which makes it worse and the other day, I found him...'

She fell silent and Max waited, patting her hand. The woman struggled to speak for a time.

'Camilla?' Max's voice was gentle. 'Do you think he abused her? Sexually? Physically?'

Camilla burst into tears. 'I should have protected her... I should have...' She was sobbing now and Max put his arms around her to comfort her.

DRIVING AWAY from the house a short time later, Max's heart was thumping unpleasantly against his ribs and he felt guilty about invading Jess' privacy. But Julien Gachet was a sick and twisted fuck that she'd been forced to live with and who was still trying to control her. Max was betting that once Theo Storm – international billionaire came along – Jules had panicked at the thought of losing Jess to someone who could help her gain freedom from him. He smirked humorlessly. Jules was exactly the kind of misogynistic asshole who would think Jess would find 'someone better' just for the money. Max may not have known her long but he knew for sure that Jess loved Theo despite his great wealth.

MAX DECIDED he would try and warn Julien Gachet off. If he'd learned anything growing up a fat gay Jewish kid, was that bullies were ultimately the worst kind of coward. Theo's wealth and influence far outstripped this little piece of human crap.

I owe you, Theo, Max thought, *this one's on me.* He pressed his hands-free on the dash. His assistant answered.

'Jenny? I need you to arrange a meeting.'

THEY ATE breakfast in a comfortable silence, Theo lacing his fingers with hers as they sat at a little table on the deck outside. The ocean crashed sedately onto the white sand a few feet away and Jess sat back, shaking her head slightly and smiling.

'What?' Theo grinned at her expression.

She turned to him, her eyes shining. 'This week has been heaven. Actual heaven. You know something? I never wanted money, it wasn't something that we ever had before Mom married my stepfather. She didn't marry him for it, she fell in love and it actually took him three attempts to get her to say yes. She was worried we'd get too attached to the good life, that it would make me lazy and unambitious as far as my education went. It didn't, of course, she'd raised me right and despite our new wealth, we didn't do over-the-top stuff. I mean we got to travel and I'm so grateful for that but today, here with you, I can see how having money can give you little peeks at what the good life could be. Of course, if we came here too often, it would ruin it.' She glanced back at Theo and grinned. 'Sorry, I'm rambling. What I meant to say was thank you. Without you, it would mean nothing.'

THEO WAS MOVED beyond words so he leaned over and kissed her. 'Want to go for a cheesy romantic walk on the beach?'

'Hell yes, I do.'

Theo laughed and stood, offering her his hand. 'Come on then.'

They walked for miles along the bright white sand, Jess taking in the wild beauty of the hills that rose in the center of the island, seeing tiny houses dotted occasionally amidst the palm trees.

'Is there a town here?'

Theo nodded. 'A small one but it's pretty lively. They have a great little music venue of you feel like dancing...again.'

She laughed and hugged him. 'Always...in fact...' She grinned wickedly and skip away from his reach.

Theo gave her a bemused smile. 'What?'

She kissed him. 'Take me dancing tonight and you'll see...'

JULES GACHET WAITED at the restaurant of Theo Storm's new boutique hotel, feeling edgy and irritated. Camilla had given him the message quickly then made herself scarce without explaining who had called and why.

But it piqued his interest. 'Your presence has been requested for lunch at the Stormfront Seattle Private Restaurant at 1pm, Thursday. I look forward to meeting you. Maximillian Zeigler, Vice President, The Stormfront Corporation.' For a second he'd been confused until he remembered it was that bastard's company, the one who was screwing his Jessica. Still, it was free lunch and he'd listen to what-ever empty threats Storm's muscle made and then ignore them. He'd punish Jessica for the threats when she returned from wherever she'd gone with that asshole. Maybe his goon he was meeting would tell him where.

· · ·

MAX ZEIGLER WAS IMPECCABLY DRESSED in a suit that was tailored to fit his slightly rotund body. His face was soft, doughy but there was no mistaking the steel in his dark gray eyes. He shook Jules' hand very briefly then gestured for him to sit.

Jules smirked, picking up the glass of Lagavulin he'd ordered and draining it. 'So, how I can I help you, Mr. Zeigler.'

Max's smile was chilly. 'Mr. Gachet, I'm not one to mince my words so here it is. You will end each and every claim you think you have to Jessica Wood. You will not contact her at any time in the future. You will continue to honor the commitments you have made to Jessica's chosen projects.'

JULES WAS ALMOST SPEECHLESS THEN he burst out laughing. 'Did that actually just happen? Or is this some elaborate joke? What possible business is my relationship with Jessica Wood of yours? I mean, apart from the fact your boss is screwing her. What on earth makes you think you can tell me what to do?'

Max leaned forward and the anger in his face made Jules rock back a little. Max cleared his throat. 'Because, Mr. Gachet, if you don't then I will have no option than to ask the police to investigate you. You, Mr. Gachet, are an abuser, a manipulator and I'm pretty certain you're a pedophile. You have repeatedly assaulted Jessica over God knows how many years. I believe it began when Jessica was twelve years old? Statutory rape would give you twenty-five to life. Attempted murder – sorry, I mean repeated attempted murder, man, you would never see the outside world again.'

Jules stared at the man in front of him, barely believing what was happening. That fucking bitch. He gritted his teeth.

'WHATEVER JESSICA HAS TOLD YOU...'

'She has told me nothing. Mr. Storm asked me to have you investigated after the last time you tried to kill Jess.'

''Jess' now is it? You screwing that whore too?'

Max went dangerously quiet and Jules noticed his fingers tapping the table. For once in his life, Jules was actually scared. 'Fine,' he said, standing. 'You get your way. She's pretty much all used up now anyways,' he added spitefully and was gratified to see Max's expression of disgust.

HE STALKED out of the restaurant, snapped at the valet to bring his car around. He'd never felt this kind of smoldering white hot rage before. Of course Jessica had told Storm everything; she clearly had some sort of death wish. I'm going to help you out with that real soon, Jessica...

Whatever. Right now, he wanted to get trashed and laid and forget everything about this afternoon's humiliation. There would be plenty of time to plan his revenge.

Max needed three showers to get the lunch meeting off of him. He dried himself off, listening to the television from the other room. He'd just grunted at Josh when he got home, his mind still whirling, and now he felt guilty.

His husband was sprawled on the couch and Max bent over and kissed him.

'Sorry.'

'Forget about it. I ordered pizza, come sit with me and chill. You look like Frodo at Mount Doom.'

Max snorted with laughter and slumped into the couch. Josh threw his arm across his shoulders and studied him.

'What's up?'

Max was silent for a minute then grabbed the t.v. remote, muting the sound. 'I need to talk this out with someone but I need to know it won't go any further until I say it can.'

Josh, his usually merry eyes flat and worried, nodded. 'You have my word, babe, always.'

Max drew in a long breath and told him everything from Theo telling him of the attacks on Jess to the meeting with Jules Gachet this afternoon. Josh listened with obvious horror in his expression. When Max finished, he got up and grabbed a bottle of wine from the fridge, pouring them each a glass. After a moment, Josh looked at Max.

'YOU HAVE TO TELL THEO. Even if you did overstep the mark. Jess could be in serious trouble if this asshole decides to punish her for involving you and Theo.'

Max rubbed his hand over his face. 'I know, I know, it's just... crap, Josh, should Theo really be dragged into something for a girl he's known for so little time? No, don't answer that. The bottom line is he loves Jess – hell, I love Jess and unless this asshole is removed from her life once and for all, I can't see them being able to live happily...'

'Ever after...' Josh finished but he wasn't smiling. 'Look, they're still away. Let's give it a few days and see what this jerk does. But, Max, if he's really as dangerous as you say...'

Max leaned back, staring up at the ceiling and wondered what it was he had started.

AS THEY WALKED the mile from town to their little island haven, Theo and Jess were laughing so much they had to keep stopping. The night in the sweaty, sensual club, dancing and drinking and kissing had been an incredible turn on. Jess wore a silky gold dress which ended six inches above her knees and showed off her beautiful tawny skin

IN THE DIMLY LIT CLUB, they'd found an unlocked back room and as soon as they were inside, they were on each other, kissing, biting, clawing at each other. Theo pushed her back against the wall as she freed his diamond-hard cock from his pants and he ripped her panties from her. Jess gasped as he scooped her up and plunged into her, using his entire body to thrust, making her scream. The unlocked door and the thrill of being caught were exhilarating, Theo grinning as Jess entreated him to screw her hard, please. It was a dirty and quick and sweaty white-knuckle fuck and they'd come together and returned to their booth, giggling, kissing.

Theo looked at his love, the pale light of the moon making her flimsy dress almost silver, her skin glow. Jess grinned back at him, pulling him along by the hand, down onto the sand.

'IT WOULD TERRIBLY wrong if we didn't skinny dip at least once.'

She pulled her dress over her head in one quick move and beckoned him on. Theo didn't hesitate, stripping down and chasing her into the warm waters. Jess shrieked with laughter as he caught her around the waist and spun her around in the waves, splashing the waves. They fooled around, kissing until Jess was shivering. Theo wrapped his shirt around her as they hurried home but barely got in the door before he was sweeping her legs from under her. He laid her on the edge of the bed and lifted her ankles over his shoulders.

'Tilt your hips up, baby,' he whispered and she complied, moaning as he slid into her, oh-so-slowly.

'CHRIST, you make me so hard when you make that sound, beautiful...' He thrust deep, rubbing her clit as he did, feeling her damp thighs quiver, her body damp with sweat. So turned on were they both, that they came quickly and collapsed together, dragging great lungfuls of air into their exhausted bodies.

Jess grinned at him. 'Man, you're really good at that.'

Theo laughed. 'I'm only good 'because you make me good, woman.'

Jess rolled onto her side and looked down at him. 'I have a confession.' She tried to keep her voice light but Theo could see something else in her eyes. He reached up to cup her cheek in his palm.

· · ·

'YOU CAN TELL ME ANYTHING.'

Jess hesitated. 'I wasn't a virgin when we met but... I've never had sex with a man I loved... before you.'

That floored and horrified him at the same time. She was telling him what Jules had done to her. She was confirming it. His chest began to hurt.

'I wasn't sure I would ever want to be physical with someone... until that day at Commencement. As soon as I saw you, I got this rush of feelings I never knew I was capable of.'

He studied her face. 'Are you okay?'

She nodded. 'Yeah. I think I am.'

'Don't be scared, baby.'

She smiled at him. 'I'm not. I'm mad. I'm pissed that I was denied this for so long.'

He grinned. 'Good.' He moved his body onto her hers. 'Gotta tell ya, woman, you're hot when you're angry. Sorta like the anti-Hulk.'

'Smooth.'

He laughed and starting kissing her neck. She ran her hands over his arms, down his back, over his buttocks. She tightened her arms around him, wrapped her legs around his hips.

'Theo?'

'Yeah, darlin'?'

In the moonlight he looked so much younger, his big green eyes on hers, his easy smile. She thought he had never been so handsome as he was this night. She smoothed his cheeks with her thumbs.

'I love you.'

He kissed her, crushing his mouth against his. 'I love you too, baby. Just me and you now. For all time.'

SHE SMILED but her eyes were sad. 'Make the world go away, Theo.'

He pressed his lips to her forehead, kissing away the crease and ran his hand down her stomach. 'Anything for you, darlin'. Anything.'

He gathered her to him and they made love for the rest of the night.

The girl he'd picked up at the club unzipped his pants and bent over him.

Jules leaned back and relaxed while she worked on him, touched her red hair as her mouth enveloped his cock. He closed his eyes and imagined darker hair, darker skin, a sweeter touch. When he was almost there, he pushed the girl back to the floor and thrust into her, ignoring her little cry of pain. She had Jessica's face and he was fucking her hard, punishing, a raging hatred and lust inside him. He wanted to kill her for sharing their little secret with that fucker. Scratch that, he just wanted to kill her, period.

But an idea had come to him earlier, as he drank one drink after another, and now he was certain it hadn't been Jessica who blabbed to Storm or Max Zeigler. It was someone else, someone who he'd thought would never betray him or the memory of his father. Someone who should know better.

JULES HAD GOTTEN drunker when he realised what he had to do and now, fucking this girl whose name he hadn't bothered to learn, he forgot about that and instead imagined he was Theo, with Jessica in his arms, and as he imagined her skin against his, he came, grunting and sobbing until he was exhausted.

'I REFUSE TO GO. I say to thee, sir, I refuse.'

Theo started laughing as Jess pouted on as Theo started to pack. It was their last full day before flying back to Seattle at an ungodly hour the next morning. He leaned over and kissed her.

'Beautiful, nothing would make me happier than to stay here forever with you. However, to pay for this haven, I have to work. We still have tonight to enjoy.'

Jess sighed and dragged her case over to the bed. 'And I have to look for another job.'

They packed in silence for a while before Theo, with uncharacteristic shyness, spoke.

'You don't have to. Work, I mean. I'm not trying to be... but, you know, you could finish your Ph.D., concentrate on that, take some time to figure out what you want to do next. You have a big brain, you could do anything.'

Jess's face was blank. 'Theo, I have to pay my way. I love you but unless it is occasional treats like this place, I wouldn't feel right. It's my responsibility, not yours.'

Theo felt stung. 'Jess, I never want you to think I'm trying to run your life for you. I'm not Jules.'

Distress crossed her lovely face and tears sprung to her eyes. She dashed them away impatiently. 'I know that.' Her voice was thick and he wanted to reach for her, but her body had tensed and he felt the distance between them.

'Jess... I'm just saying, take some breathing space. You deserve it.'

'Can we talk about this later?'

Theo sighed inwardly. God, the damage Jules had done to her that she couldn't accept any kindness. 'Sure.'

THEY PACKED A LITTLE MORE, in silence, then Jess slipped from the room.

He found her looking out at the ocean. He slid his arms around her, relieved when she leaned into his embrace.

'I'm sorry,' she said softly, 'I'm an idiot. I know you were trying to help and it's incredibly generous. I just don't want to be one of 'those' women.'

HE TURNED her to him and took her face in his hands. 'You will never be that kind of woman, you will never be the type of woman who sees men like me as a meal ticket. It's not in you. I do get it, you know, I really do. Can we talk about this seriously, as a business venture for both of us, when we get back?'

Jess hesitated then nodded.

'Good.' He pressed his lips to hers. 'Now...let's change the subject.'

He dropped to his knees and pushed her dress up to her waist, bunching the fabric at her hip with one hand, pulling her panties down with the other. He lifted one of her golden brown legs over his shoulder and began to kiss her belly, moving down to her sex. Jess leaned back against the wall and sighed, knotting her fingers in his hair.

He made her come twice before standing, and she reached for him immediately, freeing his cock and dropping gently to her knees. She smiled up at him.

'My turn...and Theo?'

'Yes, baby?'

'I NEED SOME DIRTY TALK...' Theo chuckled at her wicked grin and as she took him into her mouth, the lush velvety softness of her hot mouth, her gentle lips around his cock felt so good that he had no trouble telling her what he wanted.

'You feel so good baby, your beautiful mouth on me, you make me want to come and come, to fill you with my cock....'

She began to stroke her hands up and down his shaft, pulling gently down on the skin so her tongue could get to all the sensitive points on his cock. Theo's eyes closed, experiencing every second of pleasure.

'After I've come, beautiful, I'm going to take you into my bed and fuck you for hours and hours until you're so exhausted, you'll beg me to stop. I'll fuck your angel mouth, your heavenly cunt, so juicy and wet for me...'

He could tell by her breathing that she was hot for him, her breasts heaving. 'God, I want to taste you so bad right now...'

Jess sucked him, her hands on his buttocks, her nails digging into him and he came, shouting his love for her as he pumped into her eager mouth. He scooped her into his arms as he struggled to catch his breath and she kissed him, her eyes wild with arousal.

'Fuck me against the wall... from behind... hard,' she ordered and he almost slammed her against the wall, parting her legs with his foot and thrusting into her ready, sodden cunt, pressing her hands above her against the wall.

'YOU WANNA BE FUCKED all night, pretty girl?' he murmured in her ear as he screwed her almost violently and she nodded, her skin glowing with sweat. His hand reached around to rub her clit, feeling it harden and pulse against his fingertips. 'You're all mine tonight, and I'm going to fuck you mercilessly.'

She came quickly, moaning breathlessly. 'Fuck me in the ass, Theo, please...'

Pushing into her soft, tight ass, Theo struggled to control his own orgasm. His free hand circled her belly. He knew that drove her wild. God, this woman. They were made for each other, he knew that without a shadow of a doubt. She was his and he was hers...

'This is forever, Jessie... you and me...'

Shuddering and vibrating with pleasure they made love for the rest of the day into the early hours of the morning, falling asleep sated and delirious with happiness, and with the certainty that nothing, nothing would touch them now.

A WEEK later and Theo was wondering why Max was avoiding him. He tracked his best friend down to the cafeteria of the Stormfront HQ and cornered him just as Max was attacking a salad and looking very morose about it.

Theo grinned, pulling a chair out opposite his friend. 'Josh put you on another diet?'

Max rolled his eyes. 'He's on it too, and making it look easy. He found my stash of Ding-dongs,' he added with more than a little outrage, 'and threw them out. Threw them out!'

Theo laughed and took a long sip of his coffee. 'Where've you been? I've hardly seen you since Jess and I got back. She wants to double-date and meet Josh, by the way.'

Max nodded. 'Sure, sounds good.' There was a pause. 'How is she?'

Max's question was obviously loaded and Theo squinted at his friend. 'She's good. Why are you asking?'

'Just wondering if she's had any more trouble with that asshole step-brother?'

'NOT THAT I KNOW OF. Max, what are you hiding?'

Max sighed and shrugged. 'I wasn't sure if I should tell you but I met with Gachet.'

Theo's eyebrows shot up. 'What? Max...'

'HE'S TOXIC, Theo, he's dangerous. I spoke to the housekeeper at the Gachet mansion, the place Jess grew up. She more or less told me that Jules had been molesting Jess from when she was young. Very young. I didn't want to ruin your holiday or bring up painful memories for Jess so I arrange to meet him.' The words were flooding out of Max now. 'Something need to be done, something to try and stop what he's doing, something to let him know that Jess is protected now.'

'What happened?'

'When?'

'When you met Gachet.'

Max looked Theo dead in the eye, his gaze confident. 'I threatened him. Told him if he knew what was good for him, he'd renounce all claim on Jess and her rightful inheritance. Told him his manipulation and bullying of her stops now or we would go to the authorities.'

THEO GOT the feeling Max wasn't telling him everything but instead of being angry, he was grateful for his friend. Unbelievably moved that his very best friend would go to bat for the woman he loved. Theo nodded, smiled and could see the relief in Max's eyes.

'Thank you, buddy,' Theo said softly, 'I mean it. Well, we'll see what his next move is. He won't get near Jess again, that's for damn sure.'

'How is she, really?'

Theo hesitated. 'Best if we don't tell her about this. For now. Keep this between the two of us.'

Max nodded. 'Deal.' The two men silent for a long moment then Max shook his head. 'Man, the things men do to women.'

Theo had no answer to that.

CAMILLA TUGGED her coat around her as the Seattle skies opened with a vengeance. The car was parked all the way over on Fifth and now she wished she'd ordered her clothes from the internet rather than go shopping in this monsoon. The evening had crept up on her, her much-longed-for day off was coming to an end and she was exhausted. She walked quickly to the parking garage and got the lift to her level.

He grabbed her as soon as she exited the lift. Camilla felt her body being lifted and slammed down to the hard concrete of the floor and a man bent over her. In the dim light and through her fear, she couldn't make out who it was – until he spoke.

'You shouldn't have opened your big mouth, Camilla. It won't save Jessica and it won't save you.'

Camilla had no time to scream before her killer cut her throat.

JESS WAS WAITING for him when he got back to the apartment and Theo realized how much he loved that she was there. She had an old t-shirt on and raggedy jeans and looked about nineteen.

'Hey pretty girl,' Theo pulled his tie off as she came to him, standing on her tip-toes to kiss him hello.

'Hey, gorgeous. I hope you're hungry, I've been making my signature mac-and-cheese.'

'From the box?'

'You bet your ass,' and she laughed. Theo tightened his arms around her, nuzzling her neck.

'You smell so good,' he murmured and felt her chuckle.

'If cheese sauce is your thing,' she replied but kissed him tenderly. 'Why don't you grab a shower, dinner will be about twenty minutes.'

'Twenty minutes huh?' and she grinned, knowing what he wanted. She pulled her t-shirt over her head.

'Fuck me quick then, soldier,' and she skipped away from him, laughing. Theo shook his head in mock disapproval.

'I've turned you into a wanton woman, Jessica Wood,' but within seconds they were naked in his shower, and he was lifting her so he could plunge inside her.

After, they ate their pasta in front the television with Jess in her underwear, Theo in just a pair of jog pants. Theo grinned over at her as she dropped her food.

'You have mac-and-cheese.on your belly,' he waggled his eyebrows, 'lucky mac-and-cheese.' He leaned over and scooped up the food with his mouth, kissing the soft skin of her stomach, making her giggle.

'Loon,' she swiped her hand at his head then started as her cell-phone rang. She grinned at him as she answered the call.

'Yes? This is she?'

THEO WATCHED the expression on her lovely face changed from happiness to confusion to horror. Jess drew in a shaky breath and she looked away from Theo. He frowned, wondering if Jules was up to his old tricks again. She'd changed her number but who knew how far Jules would go to hound her.

'When?' Jess' voice broke and immediately Theo took her in his arms. Jess was trembling violently.

'Yes. Yes, of course, I'll be here, please come over as soon as you can.'

Not Jules then, Theo realized with relief but the look on Jess's face haunted him. Despair. Disbelief. Grief.

She ended the call and gazed at him with eyes full of bottomless horror and sorrow.

'What is it, love? What's wrong?'

'That was the police. They're coming over to interview me. God, Theo... it's Camilla... they found her in a parking lot on Fifth an hour ago,' she said in a broken voice and Theo's heart broke for her. 'She's dead, Theo. She's been murdered. Oh god, oh god, please, no...'

Theo held her tightly as she sobbed, aching for her but in his head, a voice repeating the same four words over and over. This is your fault.

Oh god, he thought, *Max, what have we done...?*

5

FIGHT WITH ME PART FIVE

J essica Wood nodded once at the medical examiner's aide. 'Yes, that's Camilla Amotte.' She couldn't take her eyes off the dead woman's face, so peaceful and serene showing no signs of the violence of her death. The coroner had deliberately covered her neck, the deep horrific gash, but Jess could still see bruising. She felt numb. After the past few days when she felt like screaming day and night, now she was exhausted, resigned. Camilla, her beloved, lovely Camilla, was gone and Jess knew, without a doubt, that Jules had killed her.

THE POLICE HAD TOLD her there was no physical evidence to go on and Jules had provided them with a seemingly watertight alibi.

'It's my fault,' she'd said to Theo that first night when he'd held her as she sobbed her heart out.

'No, no, no...' He'd rocked her gently as he reassured her but she would not be told otherwise.

Now, as she took a waiting Theo's hand and they walked out of the antiseptic stink of the morgue into bright Seattle sunshine, she turned to him, leaned against him.

'Theo, I feel like I need to go away for a while. Out of the city, clear my head.'

Theo stroked her face. 'We can go anywhere you want, sweetheart. Just ask.'

She pulled away slightly. 'I meant... on my own. No,' she added quickly after seeing the hurt on his face, 'I'm sorry, I don't mean to be hurtful, just for a few days.' She gave him a weak smile. 'I really do need to clear my head and you, Theo Storm, are a big distraction. I need to figure out what to do workwise and how I can go forward. I know you've told me not to worry about money but it wouldn't sit right with me, living off you. It's just not me.'

Theo was silent for a moment, his eyes intense on hers then they softened and he smiled slightly. 'I get it. But look, just so I don't go crazy wondering if you're safe, I have a cabin down in Oregon, on the Santiam River. It's secluded but not isolated. Very chill.'

Jess nodded gratefully. 'That would be heaven, thank you. And maybe after a few days, if you can spare the time...?'

Theo pulled her into his arms. 'Always for you, Jessie.'

AT BREAKFAST, Jules Gachet looked through the resumes of the new housekeeper candidates. He was bored with this process but hey, he realised, it's all of your doing. He could imagine Jessica's grief, her guilt and it made him smile.

THE POLICE HAD COME to question him, no doubt on Jessica's say-so, but he'd had a watertight alibi. Malcolm, his driver, a man as full as special proclivities as himself. They'd covered for each other. He didn't know if the policeman who was investigating the murder entirely believed him but who cared? Without proof, they had nothing. Jules narrowed his eyes – things wouldn't be so simple when he murdered Jessica. Theo Storm, crazed with grief, would make sure of it. Jules shrugged. He'd already decided that once Jessica was dead, he himself would have nothing left and would down a bottle of the best scotch and a handful of pills. He wanted the world – and especially Theo Storm - to know that he was Jessica's killer, that at the end of her life, she had belonged to him entirely. Another idea, another strand of delicious revenge occurred to him then and he grinned to himself. Oh yes, that would be the coup de grace. Jules Gachet flung the resumes down onto the table and headed to the shower where he jerked off and imagined the hot water flooding over his body was Jessica's blood.

JESS GAZED around her at the wood frame cabin, nestled on the river bank, and grinned happily at Theo. He raised his eyebrows and she nodded. 'It's perfect, Theo. Just perfect.'

Her small suitcase, a stack of books and her art materials sat in the corner of the tiny living room. Theo dug out the remote and handed it to her.

'WIFI password's MyJessieLove.' His cheeks flushed a little as she grinned at him.

'Sweet boy.'

He took her in his arms. 'You'll call me every day? Ollie, your nearest neighbor's a good guy, a family friend. If you get scared or lonely, call him. His number's on the breakfast bar. The farmer's market is a mile down the lane and...'

'Theo... stop. I'll be fine. It's just a week and then you'll be here.' She kissed him gently. 'Before you go... wanna give me a tour of the bedroom?'

THEO GRINNED and swept her up the wooden staircase into a room with the softest bed, draped in white mosquito netting. He undid her shirt slowly, kissing the skin he reveal with each button. When his fingers reached the fastening of her jeans, she groaned to hurry him. Theo grinned up at her.

· · ·

'I'LL BE without you for a week, missy, I'm taking my time.' He slid his hand into her panties, felt her body relax as he began to stroke her. He pressed his lips to hers, taking his time to taste her, his tongue gently massaging hers. Jess reached inside his pants for his cock, let her fingertips drift up and down the stiffening shaft.

'Damn, that feels so good,' Theo murmured and the air shifted, became charged as he slipped a finger inside of her, their kiss becoming hungrier, their breathing ragged. Theo kicked off his pants and hitched her legs around his hips. He held her wrists in one hand, forcing them above her head. Jess arched her back so their bellies touched as he drove himself hard into her, slamming his hips against hers. Her lovely face flushed scarlet as he fucked her, a dewy sheen of sweat making her glow. So fucking beautiful, was all he could think now. How could he leave her here alone, how could he be without her for an entire week?

JESS TIGHTENED her legs around his waist, wanting him to plough her hard into the bed, her hips burning with the pain of being forced so rough apart. She clenched her pelvic muscles, grinning as Theo groaned as she gripped him, gave him the tightness, the friction he wanted, that made him shudder with pleasure. Theo's mouth was on her throat, her neck as he thrust, not caring if he hurt her. The intense ache in her back, her legs, her hips twined around the absolute pleasure of him ravaging her body, owning it, leaving her in ruins.

Afterwards, hey lay, their limbs tangled, gazing at the other. Theo let the back of his fingers drift down her face.

'No matter what happens,' he said softly, 'it's you and me forever. Fuck anything and anyone else. Whatever comes our way, as long as we're together, we can beat it.'

She kissed him softly. 'I love you, Theodore Storm.'

He left after supper and she grinned at his chagrin at having to leave her. When he'd gone, she double-locked the door and tugging her hair out of its messy ponytail, went to run a bath. As the tub filled, she made herself some tea and chose a book from the stack she'd brought with her.

For a moment, she stopped and just listened. Aside from the running water upstairs, the evening was utterly silent. It was comforting. Jess slowly went upstairs and undressed, slipping into the hot water with a sigh. It felt an age since she had been alone anywhere - not that she complaining, she loved Theo more than anything but it felt good to clear her head. She had some serious decisions to make, she thought now, letting the hot water soothe her aching body. She wanted Theo to come get her in seven days with her future somewhat planned.

The only thing she was sure of was her future lay with Theo Storm and she would anything to protect that.

Even if it meant breaking free of Jules forever – whatever that took.

Max smiled at Theo as his boss and best friend wandered into his office and flopped into the chair opposite. Max chuckled at his woebegone face.

'Seriously, dude... you're useless without Jess. It's only a week – not even that now – six days. You're letting the 'Bro' crew down.'

Theo laughed then. 'Just can't settle to anything. Oh, except I want to talk to you about setting up a foundation – the Stormfront Foundation for the Arts.'

Max grinned. 'Oh 'for the Arts'? Nothing to do with your girlfriend being an artist, of course.'

'Of course.'

'Joking aside, it's a great idea – I assume you want Jess to run it?'

Theo nodded. 'Well, I'm going to try and persuade her that it isn't a handout, that it's something that we were planning to do anyway.'

Max gave him an amused look. 'Good luck with that. Have you broached the subject at all yet?'

Theo grinned sheepishly. 'She said it was a great idea then when I told her I wanted her to run it she said 'Why yes, of course you want a twenty-four-year-old to run a multi-million dollar charity.''

Max laughed. 'God I love that girl, she has you all figured out.' His smile faded. 'Is she doing okay? Really? I got a call today from the M.E. They're releasing Camilla's body next week.'

Theo nodded. 'Jess told me to let her handle the funeral. Apparently Camilla didn't have any family.'

The men were silent for a long moment. 'What a mess.' Max sighed and leaned back in his chair. 'It's my fault, I shouldn't have....'

'No,' said Theo roughly. 'The killer is to blame. You sound like Jess.'

'She's blaming herself?' Max put his hands on the desk, leaned forward. 'We should tell her, then, tell her what I...'

'No. No way. She'll only feel worse that we were trying to protect her. No. We wait.'

Max nodded unhappily then locked his gaze on his friend. 'You think it was Gachet?'

Theo stared back evenly. 'There's no doubt in my mind.'

JESS OPENED one eye to look at the clock. Seven a.m. And that was definitely someone knocking at the front door. She clambered out of bed and fell over, the duvet tangled around her legs. She cursed and stumbled down the stairs. Pausing at the mirror in the hallway, she took in her ragged appearance, hair sticking up, old t-shirt hanging to just below her knees. She grimaced and opened the door.

A good-looking dark haired man stood outside, smiling at her. For a second she gaped at him, trying to place him and then it clicked. Her neighbor – or rather Theo's neighbor – Ollie.

'Hi.'

'I'm sorry did I wake you?'

She smiled. 'No, I'm sorry. Come in, please.' As he passed her, she rubbed her eyes, trying to wake her brain up. She led him into the kitchen.

'I am sorry for coming so early. You must think me very rude.'

'Not at all, it's really good to see you again' She snagged two coffee cups from the cupboard then realised that the t-shirt she was wearing was riding up her thighs and giving Ollie a free show. She snuck a look at him but he was gazing discreetly out of the window.

'You know... I could make the coffee if you want to...' He said, still not looking at her and Jess smiled gratefully.

'That would be good, thank you, I'll be two seconds.'

She darted upstairs and tugged on a pair of jeans, went to the bathroom to quickly brush her teeth. When she got back downstairs, Ollie was putting two mugs of steaming coffee on the table. He grinned at her and she started laughing, then, shaking her head.

'Sorry again,' he said but she put a hand up to halt his apology.

'Please. You're very kind, my brain's not fully engaged in the mornings. So... hello, I'm Jess.'

Chuckling he shook her hand. 'Ollie Barnes. Theo said you might need a lift to the farmer's market...' He looked down and laughed, once. 'Okay. I'll start again.'

Jess frowned, nonplussed by his seeming confusion. He smiled at her.

'I'm snooping, I admit. I've known Theo for years – since we were kids – but I've never seen him bring anyone out here since Kelly.'

Jess looked up sharply. 'Kelly?'

Ollie nodded, not noticing her tone. 'My sister. Before she died, she and Theo used to come back here to get some space.... Jess, are you okay?'

She could feel the blood drain from her face, her skin cold. For a second she struggled to talk, to form the words then she shook herself. Theo was allowed to have secrets, wasn't he? She had enough of her own. She touched Ollie's arm.

'I'm sorry, Ollie, please go on. I'm so sorry about your sister.'

Ollie was studying her. 'He didn't tell you, did he?'

She shook her head but smiled. 'No, he didn't.'

Ollie's breath hissed out between his teeth and he seemed to be considering something before he gave her a little grin. 'What a jerk wad.'

She laughed, grateful for his saving her – again. 'Total dill hole.'

They both laughed. 'Tell me about Kelly – if it's not too painful.'

Ollie looked out of the window. The sun was streaming in and Jess could see the dust motes swirling in the beams hitting the kitchen floor. 'Feel like a walk?'

They strolled along the riverbank, the air so fresh and with a slight bite still from the early morning.

'KELLY AND THEO were off and on for years in their teens,' Ollie explained. 'When Theo graduated from college, they got back together. About a year later, Theo came home from work one day and she'd slit her wrists in the bath. He couldn't save her. Kelly had always suffered from depression and over the years, she'd become an expert at hiding it. She thought if she told him about it, he'd leave her.' Ollie sighed. 'He wouldn't have, he has a white-knight complex.'

'That I know,' Jess muttered. 'God, Ollie, that's so sad, so – why didn't he tell me?'

'Theo blamed himself for not seeing the signs – we all did but Theo took it the hardest.' Ollie looked at her. 'Should I be telling you this?'

Jess shrugged. 'I don't know, honestly. I won't say anything to Theo if you don't want me to. If he and I go the distance, I'm sure he'll tell me himself eventually.'

SHE WASN'T sure of that at all and later when Ollie had gone, she thought about what he'd said. It made her wonder how much they really knew about each other. Theo knew loss as much she had. It made her sad that he hadn't shared that with her yet. Her thoughts drifted to Camilla and the heavy feeling in her chest came back. Fucking Jules... she wanted to rip him limb from limb for what he'd done. In the days after the murder, she'd considered going to the police but the cops who had visited Theo's apartment had obviously looked back in their files and their attitude to her had been colored by Jules' remarks all those years ago.

'They don't take me seriously,' she'd said bleakly to Theo who couldn't help agree with her. She saw the anger in his eyes and he'd begged her to let him tell them about the attacks on her. She couldn't face it though and there was something else. She wanted to make Jules pay. She wanted him to lose everything. She wanted him to hurt.

She wanted revenge.

He was waiting in the shadow of the alleyway when Jules Gachet walked out of the restaurant. With one hand, he clamped down on the other man's shoulder and pulled him backwards. Max slammed the smaller man against the brick wall of the building, getting in his face, and was gratified to see a flicker of fear in his eyes.

'Get your homo arms off of me,' Jules puffed himself up, a sneer on his face, Max smiled grimly.

'Oh, so you've done your homework, Gachet? Good. Then you know who you're dealing with.' Max searched the other man's face. 'You enjoy hurting women, Gachet?'

The other man chuckled darkly. 'Where'd you get that idea?'

Max looked at him in disgust. 'I won't wait forever, Gachet. Draw up the papers to transfer Jess's inheritance to her by the end of the week.'

Jules nodded once and walked towards his car. Max watched him as he opened the door and then turned, smirking.

'Shame about Camilla...,' his smile widened, '...tell Jess to take extra care, won't you?'

Jess opened the door to the cabin and flew into his arms. Theo, laughing, picked her up and twirled her around joyfully. He pressed his lips to hers. 'It's been a very long week, Miss Wood.'

Jess kissed him, her hands on his face. 'Agreed, way too long. Come inside and say hello properly.'

She opened a bottle of wine she'd bought at the Farmer's Market as she cooked pasta for them and Theo filled her in on his week. When he brought up the idea of the charity again, she smiled at him.

'I've been thinking about that too. I have a proposal for you, something I've been thinking about all week.'

Theo nodded. 'Go on.'

SHE SIPPED her wine before speaking. 'We rushed into everything so fast, you and I. We're living together, you want me to go into business with you and as for sex... I've done things with you, I never imagined I would. But I don't know your mom's name. I don't know why you went into property. Hell, I don't know your shirt size. The minutiae of a person's life – surely these are the things we need to know about each other. You don't know that I can play the piano or that I once went on a date with a man who swore he could 'make me a movie star'.

She pulled a face at that and he laughed. 'Second date?' Theo raised his eyebrows in amusement.

'God no. But do you see what I mean? Your generosity in giving me a home, offering me a huge promotion in terms of my career – don't think I'm not grateful because I am. But all I want is you. If you want me to run this charity, I will, but I don't want any special favors just because we sleep together. I'll take them if we mean something more than that.'

Theo chewed his lip, pondering her words and frowned. 'Jess, surely you know by now... you are the love of my life. Hands down. If what you want to is to know me, then I'll tell you everything you want to know.'

She nodded. 'So I propose... we start over. Now, today. We tell each other everything, we get to know the other as well as possibly could. You are the only person in the world I trust implicitly. I hope I'm right to do so.'

She waited, willing him to tell her about Kelly, about that wound in his past. When he was silent, she felt a little pull in her chest but brushed it aside. There was time.

She leaned over to kiss him and he pulled her into his arms.

'Anything you want, you just have to ask,' he murmured as he kissed her. She kissed him back, melting at his touch then as she pulled back, she gave him a wicked grin.

'Maybe... we should just go to first base, you know if we're starting over.'

Theo chuckled. 'Yeah, good luck with that.' He slid his hands under her t-shirt, stroking her belly, cupping her breasts and she grinned.

'I missed your hands.' She kissed him. Theo smiled lazily at her.

'Oh yeah? Let me show you what they can do.' He slipped his fingers into the back of her jeans and stroked her buttocks. She sighed.

'Yeah, that's the stuff.' She kissed his neck.

Theo grinned. 'You know what else they can do?'

He cradled her in his arms and rolled her onto the floor. She giggled. He undid her jeans and pulled them off.

'I'm quite sure this goes against our new rule.' But she wriggled with pleasure. Theo shook his head, a mock serious expression on his face.

'No, no. We're just making out, that's all like you said. But I should tell you since we last did this,' he kissed her, 'Times have changed. There's a new definition of 'making out'.'

'Is there.... oh lordy...' She gasped as his mouth found her sex, his tongue curling around her clit and lashing against the deep cleft of her. Theo looked up at her.

'Man, you taste so good...'

She sucked in a deep breath as her body began to quiver until Theo brought her to a pitch of excitement she could not hold back and moaned as her orgasm shuddered through her. Theo propped himself up on his elbow and let his fingers drift gently down her body as she caught her breath. He smiled at her shining eyes, so deep and warm and full of love for him.

JESS CHUCKLED at his satisfied smile.. 'Wow. Theo, I think I like your new definition of making out.' She pushed him onto his back and stroked his face. 'I think maybe it's my turn to add a new definition.'

'You do, huh?'

'Oh yeah.' And grinning, she moved down his body.

JULES WATCHED Theo bring her to orgasm and the rage he felt was all consuming. He waited outside Theo's apartment the entire week in the hope he would lead him to wherever Jess had gone but now he wished he hadn't seen them together like this. Defiling her, defiling his Jessica.

He stood at the side of the window, watching them, watching her as she repaid her lover's generosity. Theo had pulled her t-shirt off and Jules admired the smooth skin, the way her back curved. Jules felt in his pocket. The gun. He had never used a gun before, not to deal with any of his... problems. But Jess was special. And having that rich asshole around had presented a whole new set of complications. A gun was necessary.

He felt the cold steel with his fingers. He imagined putting a bullet into that beautiful curve in the small of her back. The thought excited him. Jules grunted and froze. Theo had looked towards the window. He could see him sit up, looking concerned. Jules ducked down and darted back into the trees.

'WHAT IS IT?' Jess looked scared.

'Thought I heard something.' Theo got up and headed towards the door. He looked back at her and smiled. 'Don't worry, I'm just going to check around the house.' He winked at her. 'If you hear anything, lock the door. Don't be scared, baby.' He went out into the night. Jess felt a cold fear settle around her. But seconds later, Theo came back. He grinned wryly. 'Sorry sweetheart, I didn't mean to scare you. Guess I'm just jumpy after everything that's happened.'

He locked the door behind him and took her in his arms. 'I want you to know I heard what you said earlier and I'm on board. Completely. Except for the first base business... I don't think we should deprive ourselves...' He grinned wickedly and she chuckled.

'You may have a point,' and she slid her hand down his groin, cupped the long shape of his cock through the denim of his jeans. She glanced around and then grinned up at him. 'Wanna fuck me on the stairs, soldier?'

Theo growled and scooped her up roughly, and then they were clawing at the remains of the other's clothes. Theo tugged her legs around him, his cock so ramrod hard he had no trouble thrusting deep into her ready sex. He clamped her hands above her head as they fucked, brutally, desperately, their mouths hungry for the others.

They made it to the bedroom and much, much later they fell asleep in the other's arms. Neither of them woke when the door to the cabin creaked open. Jules moved silently through the house, up the stairs.

JESS LAY ON HER BACK, naked, Theo's arm across her stomach, his face buried in the curve of her neck. Her long dark lashes swept down onto the smooth skin of her cheeks, the flush of lovemaking still pink. Christ, she was beautiful. Jules pulled the gun from his jacket and aimed it at her belly. An inch away, just one inch. His finger twitched on the trigger as he imagined the bullet smashing into the soft silky flesh, her gasp of shock and agony, Theo Storm's horror as she bled out in his arms. He'd let him watch her die before he shot him too. Jules smirked to himself. It was a nice fantasy but no...not yet. He pocketed the gun and slipped back down the stairs, through the woods to where he'd left his car. He downed a bottle of water before starting the engine, lost in thought. It was good to know that they had no idea the lengths he would go to – stupid fuckers. Hadn't Camilla been enough to terrify them?

What he'd done to Camilla was nothing to what he would do to Jess. Nothing at all.

The sky was heavy with snow a week later and Seattle was gearing up for a bad winter storm. Camilla was laid to rest in a small cemetery just outside the city and afterwards, Theo held Jess's hand tightly in the car back home. Her head rested on his shoulder but he was surprised she hadn't cried. Instead, he saw a slow burning anger behind her eyes. Good, he thought, that would keep her vigilant, keep her safe. He hadn't told he that he'd found footprints and evidence of an intruder at the cabin that day.

HE KISSED HER TEMPLE. 'Hey, what say we grab some lunch then go over the paperwork Max sent over? Get a jump start on your new job?'

Max had gotten together a bunch of information – in record time, Theo grinned to himself – and if Jess was up for it, then the Stormfront Foundation would soon be a reality.

Jess looked up and smiled gratefully. 'That sounds good to me, I could do with a new focus...apart from you, that is.'

JESS LOOKED around the wide spacious office with views across the city and her jaw dropped. Max smirked at Theo, who put a hand on Jess's shoulder. 'Don't get freaked out. We have a ton of advisors ready to help you. We just thought you could get up to speed at your own pace.'

'And in one of the best offices in the city,' she managed to choke out. Theo laughed and opened his hands in apology.

'I can't help it, I want you to have the best.'

Jess nodded but chewed on her lip. Max cleared his throat. 'We have a press conference coming up – no, don't panic...' He shook his head at the panic on Jess's face. Theo wrapped his arms around her.

'It's just to announce the Foundation's formation – we need to get the word out if we're going to be helping people. I'll be there to do most of the talking, Max too. We'll introduce you as the president of the foundation...'

'Much to the amusement of the local art world,' Jess said. She looked at him evenly. 'Do you honestly think people won't say it's you finding a job for your feckless girlfriend?'

Theo took a deep breath. 'To begin with, maybe. We have to be realistic, they're gonna have their opinions. But when the foundation – when you - start making a real difference to young and exciting artists, they'll change their minds. We just have to ride the wave of skepticism.'

'Including yours,' Max said with a grin and Jess couldn't help but laugh.

'In that case, I think I can handle it.'

THE PRESS CONFERENCE went off without a hitch and suddenly the realization that she was the head of a charity made Jess more determined than ever to prove herself. In the weeks that followed, she worked late into the night with Theo's advisors and even some picks of her own to source the most suitable projects to fund. She called up her old boss Gerry who was delighted to hear from her and she took him to lunch to pick his brains.

GERRY GRINNED HAPPILY AT HER. 'You were always too good to be someone's assistant, anyway, Jess. I was selfish to hold you back.'

She protested but his words meant the world, gave her confidence.

IT WAS A WEDNESDAY NIGHT, towards the end of November when Theo came looking for her in her office. She was sprawled out on the floor in her bare feet, looking through applications and samples, engrossed in her work when he knocked on the doorframe. She looked up and grinned.

'Hey, sexy.'

Theo smiled and lifted her to her feet to kiss her. She wound her arms around his neck and sank into the kiss. 'Man, I needed that... what time is it?'

'Past eleven.'

She looked appalled. 'God, I'm sorry, honey, I just lost track.'

'You never have to apologize for being as committed as you are to this. I hope this doesn't sound patronizing but I'm so proud.'

She kissed him again, a light brush of the lips. 'Not patronizing at all, thank you for believing in me. This can wait until tomorrow.'

'Not tomorrow, Norma Rae. It's Thanksgiving.'

Her eyes opened wide. 'Jeez, I totally forgot. We haven't got any food in the apartment.'

He smiled at her. 'Max and Josh have invited us to go to their place for dinner. Josh is expert in stuffing us to the gills. I honestly think it's why Max married him.'

Jess laughed. 'It's a good as a reason as any, and that sounds good. About time I met Josh.'

Theo felt warmth flood through him. Without saying anything, she had made it sound like a family. His arms tightened around her. 'Wanna go home?'

She hesitated but he saw fire in her eyes. 'Actually...'

He raised his eyebrows. 'What?'

She pulled away from his arms and shut the door behind him, shut off the light. She started to unbutton her shirt. 'I was admiring the view from the windows today. The panoramic views and it occurred to me. I didn't know who could see in here. No-one I think, but what if we gave them something to look at?'

· · ·

SHE STEPPED out of her skirt, unhooked her bra and drew her panties slowly down her legs. Theo's groin was almost painful, watching her sensual striptease. He yanked his own clothes off, grabbing her roughly and ground his mouth down onto hers. She moaned slightly, the soft sound of it making his cock diamond hard, and then he pushed her against the window, her breasts and belly hard against the glass as he stroked her clit, bit down on her neck.

'I'm going to fuck you so hard, beautiful girl, so – he thrust his cock deep inside her and she gasped – 'fucking' – harder – 'hard.'

SHE TURNED her face so her cheek rested against the cool glass and tightened her muscles around his cock as it rammed so brutally into her. Theo's teeth nipped at her earlobe, his fevered breathing. His arms were wrapped around her waist, lifting her so he could fuck her as deeply and as savagely as they both wanted, as she entreated him to. She screamed her orgasm into the glass and he came, pumping hot semen into her ready sex, then, still ramrod stiff, he turned her to face him and entered her again, feeling the damp warmth of her envelope him. This time, they moved slowly, eyes locked, lips brushing. Theo angled her so that he would rub against her clit as he thrust; she cupped his balls gently, massaging them. She bit down on his nipples as they neared the climax and as they came they both tumbled to the floor, moaning their love for each other. As they shuddered to a halt, torchlight swept over the window of the office door and giggling, they hushed each other as the security guard tested the locked door. After a few minutes, they got up and still laughing, dressed.

'Consider this office well and truly christened,' Jess grinned at Theo who nodded.

'Which reminds me. My office needs a good rebirth.'

'Later, babe, if we've got to be social tomorrow, I need some sleep. Well, some, at least.'

. . .

'THAT, YOUNG LADY,' said Josh to her the following day as she sprawled out on his and Max's couch, groaning and holding her belly, 'is a food baby.' He tapped her stomach lightly and she giggled. Max and Theo were washing the dishes from the magnificent Thanksgiving dinner Josh and prepared and now he and Jess had decamped to the couch to gossip. They had gotten along as soon as Max had proudly introduced his husband and now Jess studied the handsome Mexican.

'I keep thinking we should have met before but then I remember, it's only been a couple of months since I met Theo.' Her eyes popped in wonder. 'Wow.'

Josh smiled. 'He's a changed man.'

'Really?'

'Really. He's crazy about you. Never seen him like this.'

Jess glanced over to the kitchen door. 'Not even with Kelly?' She lowered her voice when she asked the question and saw understanding in Josh's eyes. He leaned in and whispered back.

'Not even then. Does he know you know?'

She shook her head – a mistake, she realised. She'd had a couple of glasses of wine which had gone to her head. She felt giddy with food and love and laughter.

'No. I want him to tell me in his own time. So, please don't'...'

'Of course not. But yeah, he's all in, I can promise you that.' He studied her for a second. 'I get the impression that it's a new feeling for you, being loved the right way.'

Jess blinked at him in confusion but Max and Theo came back into the room then and she didn't have the chance to ask Josh what he meant.

LATER JESS and Theo took a cab home, her head resting on his shoulder, His arm tight around her waist. She wanted to ask Theo about what Josh had said but now, in a sleepy haze of love, she didn't want to break the mood.

.   .   .

IN THE BEDROOM, they slowly undressed each other, lingering over the feel of skin on skin as they held each other. The outside world was silent as a blanket of snow fell across the city and in their own little haven, Theo and Jess made love gently until they were both sated. Jess fell asleep in Theo's arms but Theo found himself exhausted but unable to find sleep.

While they were doing the dishes, Max had told him about the second confrontation with Jules and now Theo couldn't stop worrying that his friend had overstepped the mark; angered Gachet to a point where he could hurt someone, hurt Jess. After Camilla's murder, Theo was taking nothing on chance. Carefully, surreptitiously, he'd increased the security around Jess, around Max and Josh, around anyone who could be at risk from Gachet. Not wanting to scare any of them, he'd made sure the protection was discreet and maintained a certain distance but still. The thought of anything happening to Jess now...

THEO SIGHED. The scar, the wound, the hurt of Kelly's suicide had forever marked him and even though Jess had healed his broken heart, the terror of losing her was still palpable. Eventually, he fell into an uneasy sleep, racked with nightmares; knives, blood and a pale and lifeless Jess in his arms.

JESS' head pounded with a headache that had been bugging her all day. Theo had apologized but he'd be at work late so she went home alone, soaked in a bubble bath for an hour before ordering pizza. After a couple of slices, though, she felt sick and curling up on the sofa, closed her eyes. It took the reception two tries before she realised the entrance phone was buzzing.

'Yes?'

'Miss Wood, there's a Julien Gachet here to see you.'

Fuck. She sighed then an idea came to her. She would confront him about Camilla. She would know, for sure, that he had killed her, by his reaction. It was worth a shot.

'Send him up.'

Jules had obviously taken a lot of trouble with his appearance but she stared at him with hatred and impatience.

'What now, Jules? Another murder attempt? More threats?'

He smiled snakily and it made her stomach lurch queasily. He sat down on the couch – their couch, hers and Theo's – without being asked. 'Don't be ridiculous. I just came by to see how you are. After Camilla and everything.'

She stared at him in disbelief. 'After you killed her, you mean?'

Jules smirked. 'As if. Camilla was an important member of our family, I'm as devastated as you are.'

'Funny you missed her funeral then.'

Jules raised an eyebrow at her. 'Well if you're not going to tell me when it is...'

He got up, moved towards her and Jess edged away from him to the other side of Theo's large desk. Her hand went to hover over the small red panic button he'd had installed under it. Jules watched her amused and mocking.

'Something wrong, Jessica?'

She met his gaze. 'Nothing that won't be solved by the two huge security guards I can call in an instant.'

Jules laughed. 'Paranoia doesn't suit you, Jessica. Well, I just wanted to the ivory tower he's got you in. Oh, that reminds me. Congratulations on the new job. I have no doubts as to how you earned it.'

He made a crude gesture with his fingers and Jess, her temper exploding, forgot the panic button, forgot about the threat and stalked over to him. Using all of her strength, she slapped him hard, watching his head snap to the side. 'Get out of my home. Now.'

He grabbed her, his eyes raging, and crushed his lips against hers.

Jess struggled, desperately but she was no match for his strength. Jules pulled her tightly against him, grinding his groin against her.

'Don't let this fool you. You belong to me. Every minute you deny it, someone else could get very hurt. What will happen when you run out of people to protect you?'

'Fuck you,' she hissed, the red mist descending, and spat in his face.

He pushed her away and wiped his face in disgust. 'Stupid whore.'

'Get out.'

'I haven't finished with you yet.'

She walked to the front door and opened it. 'Get. Out. Now.'

He moved as if to leave but paused when he reached her. The simmering violence in the air was making her tremble but she held his gaze. He smirked coldly.

'YOUR CHOICE, Jess. Live with the consequences or should I say...,' he leaned into her and whispered, '...for as long as I allow you to live.' He mimicked stabbing her and she jerked back reflexively. Jules laughed and behind him, Jess saw Theo's security man step into the hall, his eyes fixed on Jules. She held her hand up to him as Jules smirked, and as he left, the security guy, Alan, turned to her.

'You okay, Miss Wood?'

'Call me Jess, would you? And I'm fine, Alan. Do me a favor. Don't tell Theo about this. It really was nothing.'

Alan looked unhappy but nodded.

She closed the door, double locked it and leaned back against it. She recalled what she'd said to Alan. It was nothing. How fucked up was her relationship with Jules that a promise to kill her was nothing? That she took it for granted now? She really had had enough this particular day. In the bathroom, she opened the cabinet above the sink and took out the small bottle of Tylenol PM. She hesitated and then swallowed two with a handful of water from the faucet and fell into an uneasy sleep.

· · ·

THEO LEFT the office just past midnight and had just stepped into his Mercedes to drive home when his cell phone buzzed. Max.

'Hey, buddy.'

There was silence on the end of the phone then he heard a sob. His heart leapt into his chest. Jesus. 'Max, what is it? Are you okay?'

Max sobbed louder now. 'I can't believe it, I can't believe it...'

Theo waited for his sobs to calm before telling him, 'I'm coming over now, Max, right now.'

When he got to Max's apartment, there were cop cars parked outside. He gave his name to the uniform at Max's door and then he was in. Max fell apart when he saw him and Theo looked around for Josh. He had a bad, bad feeling about this.

He grabbed his friend by the shoulders and hugged him. 'What is it, Max? What's wrong?'

He wasn't sure he wanted the answer.

SHE POINTED the gun at Jules and he laughed. 'Really, Jess, do you think you could kill me? Try, go on, baby girl, take your shot.' She pulled the trigger and the bullet smashed into his forehead. He stopped.

Then to her horror, the gaping hole sealed itself up and Jules sneered at her. 'My turn.' He grabbed the gun and although she struggled, he was too strong, unnaturally strong and turned it so the gun was pressed hard into her belly.

'IT'S A SHAME,' he whispered, his voice intimate, 'You really are the most beautiful woman I've ever known. If you'd only realised you belong to me but it's too late now.'

He smiled, kissed her tenderly and pulled the trigger.

· · ·

IT WAS ALMOST dawn when Theo woke her from her nightmare. Groggily she looked up into his drawn face and quelled at the pain in his handsome face.

'What is it? What's wrong?'

Theo gazed down at her, sorrow etched deep in his eyes. 'It's Josh... he's been murdered.'

THE OFFICIAL STORY was that Josh had been hit by a car on his way back from work. It could have so easily been an accident except that the driver had backed up over Josh's prone body – twice. It had all been caught on CCTV but the car, a plain black RV had blacked out windows and no plates. The police had no leads but Jess had an overwhelming sense of foreboding and when finally she, Theo and Max were alone, after Josh's cremation, Max said what they had all been thinking.

'Fucking Gachet did this.'

Max looked terrible as if he'd been smoking six packs a day and drinking straight bourbon. Jess closed her eyes for a moment, trying to quell the nausea that threatened.

'I DON'T UNDERSTAND. Why would Jules kill Josh? How would Jules even know Josh?' Her voice was scratchy and low. Max wouldn't look at her and she felt the heavy weight of guilt settle over her.

Theo and Max exchanged a look then Theo nodded, once, brief, stiff. Max sat down opposite Jess and took her hands. 'We were trying to make things better... for you.... I...'

'I asked Max to look into Jules' background,' Theo interrupted his friend, 'He'd hurt you, had threatened your life. I'm sorry I didn't tell you but there you have it. It was for the best.'

Jess pulled away from Max's hands. 'You were investigating me?'

'Jules, not you. But obviously, there was some overlap. After Max talked to Camilla, we realised exactly what he'd been doing to you. We had to do something/?'

Jess had gone very still. 'You talked to Camilla? Did Jules know?'

The room echoed with their silence. 'Oh Jesus...' Jess sank to the floor, curling her knees up to her chest. Theo bent to touch her but she shied away from him.

For a long time no-one said anything then Theo looked at Max, who nodded and left the room. Jess got up and paced around the room while Theo watched in silence. Finally, she turned to him.

'This is my fault. My fault. He told me he would hurt people I cared about and I dismissed it as...why? It's my fault Camilla and Josh are dead. I should just have let him kill me.'

'STOP IT!' Theo was furious as she had ever seen him. 'None of this is your fault. It's him, it's Gachet.'

'Who is my problem, Theo. I did this. I tried to escape from him and...'

'You shouldn't have had to 'escape' from anyone. What you went through... he's a monster. How old were you when he first raped you?'

The question, so simple, so straightforward, made her crumple. Theo gathered her to him as she sobbed. 'You don't have to tell me if you don't want to,' his voice was gentle,' but please, put it out of your mind that it's your fault. We need to go to the police, tell them everything.'

Her sobs subsided but she sighed, defeated. 'They won't believe me. They didn't then and I got punished.'

Theo was silent for a long moment. 'Then we need to break that cycle.'

Jess was quiet for a long time before she pulled away from him. 'I can stop this by... I can't let anyone else get hurt because I fell in love with you. I need to take responsibility for that. I need to make this right. I need to go.'

Dread was flooding through Theo's body as he took in what she was saying.

'Wait, Jess. You can't be serious? Are you ending this? Us? No, no, we can't let him win, please.'

He reached for her but she ducked away.

'No, Theo please, don't, I can't bear it. I love you, god, so, so much but we need to take so time to figure out everything. People have died, there's so much damage.' She was brushing her tears from her face and it broke his heart. 'Please, just.... let me go. Give me time to figure how I can make it stop, make him stop.'

Theo nodded, trying to hide his heartbreak. He picked up her coat and draped it around her shoulders. Tipping up her face to his, he kissed her tenderly. 'Okay.... okay, Jess you can have all the time you need, all the time. But know this. I'll wait forever. I love you.'

Fresh tears poured her cheeks and he kissed them away. 'I love you too,' she whispered, 'You are my heart.'

His gut twisted as he kissed her mouth then, tasting her lips, lingering, not knowing when he would kiss them again – if he would kiss them again.

Eventually, she broke away from him and picked up her bag. 'I have to go.'

Hand-in-hand, they walked to the door and he opened it for her, and – his heart shattering into a million pieces - watched the love of his life walk out of it.

He called down to the limo driver. 'Make sure she gets where she wants to go safely.'

Then he hung up the phone and as Max came back into the room, he looked at his friend and knew he shared his pain.

'She's gone, Max. I had to let her go.' And he began to sob.

Jules, parked in the shadows away from the gaze of the security guards, sat up as he saw her walk out of Storm's apartment building. He smiled when he saw she was crying.

'Don't worry, my Jessica,' he whispered to himself, 'You'll be dead soon.

So very, very soon.'

6

HURT WITH ME PART SIX

I t was so much worse that she'd imagined. Jess bent over at the waist then when that wouldn't quell the nausea, she darted to the small bathroom in her hotel room and threw up and up. When she finally stood, rinsed her mouth at the sink then went out to the suite, the papers were still there, the television reports were still on the t.v. and the photographs of her and Jules, young and apparently care-free, assaulted her vision.

'THEO STORM'S Girlfriend's Secret Shame'. Every word battered her, the lies, the hideous twisting of facts that made her a temptress who seduced every rich man she could – even her own step-brother, even as she was a young teen. Some asshole in the police department – more than likely with a kick-back from Jules - had leaked the police interviews where she'd been branded a fantasist, a liar. Everything, everything, was twisted and wrong and so evil she could barely breathe. She wanted to feel angry, searched for that feeling in the melee of emotions that overcame her but all she could feel was shame. Humiliation. Hopelessness.

. . .

THE FRANTIC RAPPING at the motel room door made her jump and she quelled, her entire body trembling as she stared at the thin wood frame rattling.

'Jess? It's me, sweetheart.'

She flew to the door, yanking it open and falling, sobbing into Theo's arms. He gathered up into his arms and kicked the door shut behind then. Carrying her, he sat down on the bed and rocked her until her sobs turned into sniffs and shivers. He pressed his lips to her temple.

'I'm so sorry, baby,' he murmured. 'For all of it. I'd ask why Jules would do this but I already know. We'll get through this and I'll make that fucker pay, I promise you I will.'

Jess said nothing but nuzzled closer to him, her lips pressed against his neck. He tilted her chin up and kissed her, his arms tightening around her protectively.

'I miss you,' she whispered and Theo groaned and pulled onto the bed, his hands slipping under her t-shirt and pulling it over her head. Feverishly, Jess kicked her jeans off and unbuttoned Theo's shirt. He'd obviously just come from the office and he was wearing the blue shirt that she loved on him, the one that brought out his green eyes and complimented his dark hair perfectly.

'IT's BEEN hell without you, Jess, actual hell...'

She was straddling him and he gazed up at her, his eyes soft with the relief of being with her. It made her heart jolt to see the hurt on his face. I did this. I hurt him. I'm so sorry, I'm so sorry....

Jess ran her hands over his hard chest and leaned down to press her lips against his. 'For me too. I'm so sorry, Theo.'

With one quick move, he flipped her onto her back and gazed down at her. 'Stop apologizing. You and me, that's all that matters.'

She coiled her legs around his waist and she could feel the hot length of his cock nudging against her damp sex. 'I want you inside me, Theo, now, forever.'

He smiled, though his eyes were still tired and anxious. He trailed his lips along her jaw, pressed them to the hollow of her throat. 'Jess, you are my life...'

His cock slid into her welcoming cunt, filling her, and as he began to slide in and out, she tensed her muscles to grip him, keep him locked inside of her, her body taking control and cleaving to him, skin to skin. She rocked her hips against him as his thrusts became ever harder and faster, gasping out her pleasure, calling his name.

WHAT BEGAN as tender lovemaking suddenly became something else, abandoned, uncontrolled, brutal. Their desperate need to erase everything that had happened lately, just to get back to the feral desire that had driven their entire relationship. Jess begged Theo to please, fuck her harder, harder and Theo responded, his kisses rough and greedy, biting down on her shoulders hard enough to leave teeth marks, his immense strength and size having complete command over her body. They both lost themselves in the storm of sensations that raged through them and when, finally, they both came, crying out and shouting their love over and over, it seemed as if the rest of the world had simply melted away.

Jess lay, locked in Theo's protective arms, stroking his damp face, drinking him in. Neither of them spoke for a long time, not wanting to break the spell.

FINALLY, Theo traced the shape of her lips with his forefinger. 'Jess... my Jessie... I know this is all unbelievably horrific, what Jules has been doing. But I want you to know, there's nothing I won't do to keep you safe, nothing I won't do to make this better for you. I only ask this – please don't shut me out again. Whatever happens from now on, we do together. Promise me.'

She gazed up into his impossibly handsome face and smiled, her body relaxing as she let herself believe that everything would be okay as long as they were together.

'I promise you, Theodore Storm.'

The smiled and took her left hand in his. 'There's just one other thing.'

She smiled and brushed her lips against his. 'What's that?'

'Jessica Wood, would you do me the great honor of marrying me?'

JULES SAT in front of the pile of newspapers running the story and could have laughed. Two birds with one stone – destroy Jess and Storm's reputations. Well, he thought, destroy may be an overstatement. Sullied. That was better, he liked that. I sullied their reputations as sure as I sullied Jessica a long time ago. He could still remember that first time, the complete trust of the naïve, the unlocked bedroom door of the twelve-year-old Jess. Her long dark hair spread across her pillow.

'BOSS?'

Jules looked up. A smug-looking Malcolm stood in the doorway. Jules smiled at him. His partner-in-crime.

'What's up, Malccy? Have a seat, buddy.'

Malcolm grinned at the nickname and sat down opposite Jules, pulling out a sheaf of papers and handing them to him. Jules ran his eyes down the documents and smiled. 'Perfect.'

'Are you sure you want to do this?'

Jules nodded. 'Oh yes. Keep them wrong-footed, confused. Jess won't be alive long enough to enjoy it anyways.'

'I wanted to talk to you about that,' Malcolm took a deep breath in. 'I'm prepared to do Jessica for you, boss, I'm prepared to take the rap. Just say the word and I'll stick my knife in her. It would be my pleasure.'

Jules grinned at Malcolm, gratified that he would do that for him, excited by the other man's bloodlust. He enjoyed killing as much as Jules did – it was what bound them together, what made Malcolm so loyal. He'd killed that homo's husband without being asked twice, came home and they both enjoyed the retelling of it.

'Thank you, Malcolm, but she's mine. I'll be the one to kill Jessica.' He considered for a moment. 'You can kill Storm if you like – but not until he's had time to grieve Jess. I want him to feel that pain, Malccy.'

Malcolm laughed. 'Deal.' Jules could see the calculations begin in his mind, how he would do it, the pleasure he would take.

'Until then, however.... this.' He waved the documents in front of Malcolm. 'I'm going to enjoy this. They'll never see me coming.'

JESS LOOKED up as her assistant Molly tapped on the door. She'd been back at work for weeks now but still came in early so she could miss everybody's curious stares, barricading herself in her office with a pile of paperwork. Occasionally someone would walk past her office and she would look away from their gaze. Now, though, she saw that Molly wore a smile and no pity and she was glad.

'Can I order you some lunch, Jess? I was just going to get a sandwich but I can order out if you'd like?'

Jess smiled at her. 'Thanks, Mols, ham on rye will be fine. Has anyone called?'

Molly rolled her eyes. 'Press, mostly. Don't worry,' she added seeing Jess's face pale, 'I dealt with them.' She pretended to wield a baseball bat, patting it into her palm.

Jess laughed. Molly Che might be five foot nothing and tiny but she could be fierce when it was needed. Jess had liked her immediately when they'd met and when Theo assigned Molly as her assistant, Jess and the young woman quickly became firm friends. Jess realized it had been a while since she'd had a really good girlfriend. The few she'd had always been scared off by Jules's creepy come-ons. Jess was suddenly amused by the thought of Molly 'dealing' with Jules. Hell, she might buy her an assistant a real baseball bat, just in case.

. . .

'YOU ROCK, Mols. When lunch comes, why don't you come in and eat with me? I could do with a good gossip.'

'You're on. Jess?'

'Yes?'

Molly shifted her weight and leaned against the doorframe. 'In case you were worried, no one believes that crap in the papers. Not one person. They're all on your side.'

Jess felt tears prickle in her eyes. 'Thank you, Molly. That means the world to me.'

Molly grinned. 'You're family. No one messes with our family.'

She left Jess alone then. Jess dashed away the tears that had settled on her cheeks. Family. That word had been a source of pain for so long now she hardly recognized it. Grow a thicker skin, she told herself fiercely. Her phone rang then and even without looking at the screen, she knew who it was. She answered the call with a smile in her voice.

'Hello, beautiful man.'

Theo laughed and she enjoyed the rich sound of it. 'That's a nice way to be greeted. How're things, sweetheart?'

He was in New York, a continent away, for a meeting he couldn't reschedule. Anyway, she had told him, they weren't going to be dictated to by anyone else's agenda. She'd insisted he go, telling him she had Max, Molly and Alan and a whole squad of security. Now, though, hearing his voice, she wished she'd gone with him.

'Good, except I miss you.'

'Me too, darling. I'll try to be back as soon as I can but this meeting's running late already. You staying with Max tonight?'

'Sure am – I think he's doing better. At least, that's the impression he's trying to give. God, Theo, I feel so guilty – '

'Stop it. Max doesn't blame you, no-one blames you. You being there is good for him. He loves you, y'know. You're his family now.'

There was that word again. Every time she heard it, it made her a bit braver, hardened her heart against Jules' machinations.

'I love you, Mr. Storm.' Her voice was soft, full of love and she heard him sigh happily.

. . .

'Love you too, almost-Mrs. Storm.'

She smiled. 'Call me later.'

After he'd said goodbye, she held her left hand up, enjoying the glint from the solitaire diamond she now wore on it. Mrs. Storm. She could get used to that. Jessica Storm. She's said yes to Theo without hesitation the day he'd proposed, the day of the scandal, the newspapers. In that hotel room. She didn't have any doubts, even now, a few weeks later. They were meant to be together. *For as long as I allow you to live.* Jules' words came back to her then, a body-slam and she bent over, trying to quell the nausea that hit her.

'You okay?'

Molly was at the door again, her dark eyes filled with concern. Jess tried to smile. 'I'm fine, just a little nausea.'

Molly handed her a brown paper bag with a sandwich in then sat down opposite her. Studying her. 'You're not pregnant, are you?'

Jess shook her head. 'Definitely not.' Then, a wave of amusement came over her. 'Nope, no little gold-digger spawn for me just yet.'

Molly laughed, clearly relieved that she was okay. 'Shame, though. You and Theo will have the most beautiful babies.'

Jess flushed with pleasure. 'Thank you, but woah horsey. We've never talked about kids, let's just be happily engaged for a bit.'

Molly pouted then laughed. They chatted through lunch and by the time Molly went back to her own desk, Jess was feeling good again. She glanced once more at her engagement before shoving everything to the back of her mind and getting on with her work.

Theo shook the hands of his colleagues and went to find an empty office. He switched on his laptop, and as he was waiting for it to fire up, he switched his phone back on. A text from Jess...

Pretty sure Max has soundproof walls... wake me when you get in tonight, I'll make it worth your while. I love you, J xx.

Theo grinned and shot her a reply.

I look forward to it, beautiful. I love you.

Then he flicked through his call log. Three missed calls. Same as yesterday and the day before and the day before that. Theo sighed. Time to bite the bullet. He pressed the call button and let it ring.

She answered on the third ring.

'Theodore Storm, where the hell have you been?'

Theo let a long breath and cleared his throat.

'Hi, Mom, how have you been?'

AT ALMOST FIVE, Molly knocked on her door again. Jess blinked, trying to get her head out of the file she was looking at. Molly was frowning.

'Jess, there's a guy here who says he's your family lawyer. William Corcoran?'

Jess's eyebrows shot up and she got up and walked into the outer office. 'William?'

The older man smiled kindly at her and she embraced him, ushering him into her office. They sat together on one of the long couches. William looked around approvingly. 'This is very impressive, Jessica, your parents would be proud.'

Jess grinned wryly. 'You mean they wouldn't believe I slept my way to the top?'

William frowned, shaking his head. 'No one who matters would believe that. Does believe that.'

Jess thanked him. 'Why are you here, William? Not that isn't always lovely to see you.'

'Sweet girl. Well, I come bearing gifts, though I hardly believe it myself. Julien has released your inheritance. The board has agreed and I have the paperwork here.'

Jess was speechless for a long moment. 'What's the catch?'

William looked at her, understanding in his old eyes. 'None that I can see.'

Another long pause then Jess shook her head. 'I don't understand.

After all this time, Jules would just give in. I don't trust it, I don't trust him.'

'I understand, Jessica, believe me, I do. But, legally, as far as the transfer is concerned, it's all above board.'

No, no. There was something very wrong here. Jules wouldn't just give up his only way to control her, not this easily. She sat back, running through every eventuality in her mind. Did Theo or Max have something to do with this? Did they find evidence of Jules' involvement in Camilla and Josh's deaths? If they did, she would insist they go to the police, not use it to blackmail Jules into releasing her. No, that couldn't be it. No matter how loyal Max was, he'd never let Josh's killer go free to protect Theo, to protect her. Nor would she. Theo...she wasn't sure. He loved her more than life, she knew that. She would have to talk to him.

'JESSICA? JESS?' William was speaking to her and it took a moment before she responded, so lost in thought was she. She smiled at him. He patted her hand.

'Congratulations.' He nodded towards her engagement ring and she smiled.

'We haven't announced it, I'm sorry I didn't tell you before. We just kept it low key.'

'I understand.'

The elderly man stood and kissed her cheek. 'Jessica, marry Storm, he is a good man. It doesn't take much to see that. Julien is nothing more than a spoilt little brat. I think this is his way of admitting defeat.'

Jess wished more than anything she could believe him.

THEO LET himself into Max's apartment a little after one a.m. He glanced at the bottom of Max's bedroom door and saw his light was out. Pushing the door of the guest bedroom open, he stopped in the doorway and just watched her sleep. She lay on her stomach, naked under the sheet, her face turned toward the bedside lamp so the soft glow fell across her honey-colored skin. Her dark hair clouded around her on the pillow, her long dark lashes swept down onto the faintly flushed cheeks. So beautiful. Theo closed the bedroom door and stripped quickly, dropping his clothes onto the floor then slipped under the sheet. Jess murmured and smiled as he pressed his lips to hers. Her body was so warm next to his and he sighed as she reached down for his cock, cupping it in her warm hand. She smiled sleepily at him.

'HEY BABY...'

She moved slowly down the bed, tracing a line down his body with her tongue, grazing his nipples with her teeth. Theo stroked her hair with his big hands gently pulling the soft silky strands through his fingers. As he felt her soft lush mouth envelop his cock, he felt it respond, blood rushing to fill it, her tongue tracing the pulsating veins. He grew harder as she sucked at him, her fingers tracing a line between his balls and his anus, pressing the sweet spot there. Theo's breathing was coming in ragged gasps now as she worked on him, his cock quivering and swelling under her touch.

'Christ....Jessie, I'm going to cum...'

He felt her lips curve up in a smile and then as he shot into her mouth. She swallowed his seed, again and again, massaging his balls, prolonging his pleasure. As soon as he shuddered to a halt, he pulled her up into his arms and kissed her so thoroughly they were both breathless by the time they broke away from it. He hitched her legs around his hips and plunged his titanium-hard cock into her, gratified at the gasp she gave. He molded his hands over her soft breasts, teasing her nipples with his thumbs until they were hard and quivered under his touch. As he thrust, he enjoyed the undulation of her soft belly, the way she flung her head back as she neared her orgasm, the scarlet blush of her skin. He caught her waist with hands and thrust harder, driving her onward. God, he wanted to consume every part of her, bury himself inside her and his head spun as he shot thick creamy semen into her. She tensed and shivered through orgasm after orgasm and eventually, as they collapsed back on the bed, he traced a line between her breasts down to her navel, rimming the deep hollow and making Jess moan with pleasure. He caught her mouth with his, tasting her sweetness alongside his own salty tang.

'HELLO, BEAUTIFUL...'

She smiled up at him, awake now, her hands tracing a pattern on his chest. 'Hey, you. I missed you so much.'

He pulled into the cocoon of his arms. 'A second would be too long without you, lovely one.'

She stroked his face. 'You look exhausted.' He leaned his face into her palm.

'I admit I am...but in a good way.'

'You're home, handsome, sleep.' She pulled his head down to her chest and curled her arms around him. 'Sleep...'

THEO WOKE to an empty bed and the sound of laughter. Pulling on his jeans, he wandered out into the kitchen to find Jess and Max demolishing a stack of blueberry pancakes. His body relaxed at the sight of his two favorite people. Max still looked drawn and thin but at least some of his color had returned and the dark circles under his eyes were starting to fade. Jess was good for him, for them, Theo realized now. For all her dark past, the woman he loved was a light in their lives, someone from whom love shone and warmed everything she touched. She looked up and her face lit up at the sight of him.

'HEY, SLEEPY BOY IS UP.' She hopped off the bar stool and came to him, sliding her arms around his waist, tipping her face up for a kiss. Theo, grinning and obliged until Max protested and they broke off, chuckling at Max's mock-horror. Theo nodded at the remnants of their breakfast. 'Saved any of that for me? I'm starving.'

'Of course...,' Max faked annoyance, '...as if I'd deprive you of my famous pancakes.' He pulled out a stack that he'd kept warming in the oven. Jess grinned at Theo.

'If I'd known those were in there, I would have totally deprived you.'

Theo mussed her hair. 'Food demon.'

Max leaned on the breakfast bar. 'Saturday with my homies,' he said softly. 'Almost perfect.'

Jess squeezed his hand. 'There'll always be four of us here, Maxie. Always.'

Max looked at her gratefully. 'I know.' He was silent for a moment then shook himself. 'I like having you both here. If it doesn't cramp your style.'

Theo and Jess looked at each other, then Theo patted Max on the shoulder. 'We'd be happy to stay as long as you want.'

'Seconded.' Jess grinned at him, nodding her ascent. Max visibly relaxed.

'Thanks, dudes. I appreciate it. I also appreciate that the walls are so thick,' he grinned and waggled his eyebrows suggestively.

'You should be,' Jess dead-panned. 'I'm quite the screamer.'

Theo nearly choked on his coffee as Max laughed out loud.

LATER, they had decamped to their favorite coffee house and Jess told them both about William Corcoran's visit and Jules' seeming relinquishment of his financial control of her. Both Theo and Max were as skeptical as she was.

'It makes no sense,' Theo was scowling, 'Why trash you in the press to just give up like that? I don't trust this.'

'Me either.' Jess looked at Max who nodded his agreement.

'It's a trick, sweetheart. He's an evil motherfucker. If he thought he was losing an inch of control over you...'

'He's fooling himself thinking he has any control over me anyways. Not now, not ever again. As far as I'm concerned he can drop dead. I wish he would.'

The three of them sat for a while, quiet, a silent assessment and the same question on each of their minds. Could I kill another person? When Jess met both their gazes, she knew the answer. Yes, if that person was Jules. They each had reason to end Julien Gachet.

A PART OF HER WANTED JULES' gesture to be genuine contrition so that none of them would have to consider taking drastic action but...

'What are you thinking, Jess?' Theo's voice was low, full of pain and she turned to look at him. His green eyes were troubled. She smiled at him, touched his face.

'Nothing worth saying out loud.' She turned to Max. 'Hey, you, I wanted to ask you something. I've talked to Theo about this and we wanted to run something past you.'

Max sipped his coffee. 'Hit me with it.'

Jess and Theo exchanged a glance. 'Well, it's about our wedding. You're Theo's best man, of course, but we, well, I was, wondering...' She stopped and cleared her throat, feeling tears prickle in her eyes. Theo's arm tightened around her shoulders and he gave her a reassuring nod. Max looked bemused.

'What is it, Jess?'

Jess drew in a breath. 'Max, I wondered if you would mind double-duty. I wonder if you would please walk me down the aisle?'

Max's eyebrows shot up and Jess was amazed to see tears in his eyes. 'Jess, I would be honored. Truly honored.' He stood and pulled Jess into a hug. 'Thank you,' he murmured into her ear, 'thank you.'

OUTSIDE, Jules watched them through the blacked out windows of his car. They looked more relaxed than he'd expected. Good. He wanted them to be as unprepared as possible for his next move.

Jess peeked into Max's room to see him passed out on his bed with an adoring Stan and Monty curled up next to him. The dogs looked up as Jess made a face at them. 'Doggy sluts,' she muttered and blew them a kiss. She pulled the door to and wandered out into the living room. Theo was flicking through the t.v. channels, not even looking up as she curled into his side. His arm looped automatically around her shoulders, pulling her close. She watched the t.v. with him for a few moments before turning her head to kiss his cheek.

'I know this is a weird thing to say, given everything that's happened, but right here, right now, I feel happy. Safe.'

Theo pressed his lips against her temple. 'Damn right you're safe. Always with me, Jessie. Always.' He clicked the television off and pulled her onto her lap, smoothing the hair away from her face, studying it with such a look of love she felt her insides melt. He kissed her, quick, soft as if he was a shy teenager and she smiled.

'Mushy,' she whispered and he grinned – a definitely unshy grin. He maneuvered her onto the floor and lay above her, his fingers knotting in her dark, soft hair.

'Mrs. Storm...'

She grinned but pretended to frown at him. 'Not yet, big boy, don't get cocky.'

Theo snorted with laughter and ground his hips against hers so she would feel the hard length of him. She grinned and lightly nipped his earlobe with her teeth. 'That would be so much better off inside me...'

Theo was already pushing up her dress, his long fingers sliding into her panties and pulling them down. She moaned softly as his tongue found her clit, flicking around it until she was half crazed.

Suddenly he stopped and looked up. 'Shit, my mom.'

For a beat, Jess looked down at him askance. 'If your mom's in my crotch, I think I'd know about it.'

They both lost it. Jess buried her face in her hands to hush her laughter, Theo pressed his face into her belly, his whole body shaking with mirth.

'Sssh, sssshhhhh,' Jess waved her hands towards Max's open bedroom door. She pushed him off of her and hitched her underwear up. 'Moment's over, chuckles.' She pulled him to his feet. 'Let's go get pizza before we wake the kids.'

IN THE RESTAURANT, they shared pizza and beers. 'So, what about your mom?' Jess teased him. 'When she's not hanging out in my groin, that is.'

Theo snorted. 'That's just wrong. She called me. Actually, she stalked me via phone when the news stories came out.'

All trace of humor left Jess's face. 'I see.'

Theo leaned over to touch her cheek. 'Hey, it's okay. She wants to meet you, is all.'

Jess didn't relax and she pushed her pizza away, rubbing her forehead to ease the sudden tension. 'So the fact that she reached out after her son's girlfriend was outed as a nympho gold-digger shouldn't bother me?'

Theo gave her a wry grin. 'Well, when you put it like that...'

'God, Theo.'

'Hey, listen. She and I talked, I told her what a bunch of crap it was. I'm her son, she believes me over some damn tabloid assholes. It is fine, she just thought it was about time she met the love of my life.'

Jess smiled then, stroked his face. 'What did she say when you told her we were engaged?'

Theo's expression gave him away. 'Um...'

'Theo!' The tension was back. 'You didn't tell her?'

He shrugged good-naturedly. 'I thought we were keeping it low key.'

'Not from your family. Jeez.'

'He rubbed his hand up and down her back, trying to relax her. 'We'll tell her together. This weekend.'

She gaped at him and he gave her a cheesy grin. 'Sorry. I meant to tell you earlier.'

Jess sighed and her head slumped onto the table. 'Kill me now.'

Theo winced and she was sorry. Suddenly she realized – meeting her fiancé's mother was nothing to what they had been going through lately. She sat up and kissed him. 'It's okay. It is about time I met your family.'

HE NODDED and she could see he was happy. 'I do have another motive,' he said, '-and it's one you'll like. A few years ago, I bought a house out on Whidbey Island, mostly as an investment. It was far too big for just me so I've been renting it out as a holiday let for the past few years. But now, it's perfect for a family home, Jessie. It's secluded but not isolated and has its own private beach. I want to take you there, see what you think. If you don't like it – or you think it's too close to Mom – then fine, we'll find something else.'

Jess listened to him and couldn't help feeling excited. She suppressed a grin. 'Just how close is your Mom?'

Theo smiled widely. 'Way over on the other side of the island, and it's a big ass island.'

She laughed. 'Then, I can't wait.'

Theo kissed her. 'We can go over on Sunday.'

'We're staying at your mom's all weekend?'

Theo grinned nonchalantly and she swiped his shoulder with her hand. 'There's no way you're getting laid tonight.'

He leaned over and pressed his lips to hers. 'Yes, I am,' he murmured, his green eyes glittering, sliding one hand onto the nape of her neck and the other to her stomach. Jess sank into his embrace and nodded her assent.

'Yeah, you so are...'

THEO GLANCED over at her as they stood on the deck of the ferry out to the island. Jess was dressed in a simple white cotton dress that the breeze from the Sound was whipping up, showing a tempting amount of honey-skinned thigh. Her long hair was pulled into a messy bun at the nape of her neck, and her face, touched by the lightest makeup, was beautiful but a little tense.

.   .   .

STRIKE THAT, Theo corrected himself, a lot tense. He wrapped his arms around her, felt her lean back into him. 'Stop worrying, it's just my mom and maybe a couple of my irritating kid brothers. Nothing to worry about, I promise.'

JESS SMILED AT THAT. Theo had one older sister, Milly, married and living in Portland, and three much younger brothers who adored their older brother. One of them, Alex, was at Harvard, the younger two, Seb and Tom, were identical twins. Theo's mom, Amelia, she didn't know much about, telling Theo that she'd rather not build up a picture of a formidable woman. Theo had rolled his eyes.

'She's just my mom, Jessie.'

But he knew that Jess's own family situation had been tainted so much by Jules that she couldn't reconcile family as being happy with her own experience. He kissed her temple.

'I know a way you could relax...'

She turned in his arms and studied his face, a small smile playing around her lips. 'Do you indeed,' she raised her eyebrows at him. 'This is a public place, you know.'

His eyes were dancing. 'All the better.'

He took her hand and led her along the ferries' deck until they came to a small alcove, hidden away from the sight of the other passengers and the crew. Theo pushed her against the cool steel of the ferry, his gaze intense, burning. He slid his hands under her dress and she gasped at the shock of him yanking her panties from her, ripping the delicate material easily. Theo ground his mouth down onto hers as she reached for his zipper, easing her hand into his pants to free his diamond-hard cock. Theo lifted her and she wrapped her legs around him, perfect trust in him, as he entered her, thrusting with deep, even strokes, kissing her lush mouth as he fucked her. Jess's lips were at his ear, telling him how much she loved him and when he came, so turned on he couldn't wait, he felt the violent furious spasm of his cock inside her, filling her as she buried her head in his shoulder and muffled her cry of ecstasy. They caught their breath, staring at the other, completely oblivious to the cool breeze, the roiling of the dark waters of the Sound, the possibility of being caught. Neither said a word, neither needed to say what they were feeling; it was in the sensation skin-on-skin, the deep, abiding understanding in their eyes. Theo lowered her gently to her feet and straightened out her dress while she ran her hand through his dark curls, tidied him up. Their fingers entwined, they walked slowly back to the passenger lounge, never taking their eyes from each other.

AMELIA STORM OPENED the door to the large house and walked down the stairs, smiling. Jess, her heart hammering frantically, smoothed her dress down and smiled tentatively, looking to Theo to make the introduction. She needn't have worried.

'Jessica, dear, it's wonderful to meet you at last.' The older woman, stately and graceful, her gray hair swept up into a chignon, kissed Jess's cheek and slid a friendly arm around her shoulders. 'I told Theodore that he's very bad, keeping you a secret all this time.' She mock-scowled at her son, who grinned good-naturedly and rounded the car to hug her.

'Don't scare Jess off right away, mom. At least feed us first.'

Amelia looked at Jess and Jess saw she had the same wicked gleam in her eyes as her son. 'Always thinking with his stomach. What about you, Jess? Shall I scare you first or are you hungry?' Her smile was the same as Theo's too and Jess relaxed, grinning back at her.

'It's a tough choice but...'

Amelia laughed. 'Come on in then, both of you. Theo, leave the bags until we've had a drink.'

Theo dutifully followed the women into the house. 'Where are the demon spawn?'

'Down at the beach. I told them a pod of orcas was spotted in the bay.'

Jess grinned excitedly but Theo squinted at his mother suspiciously. 'Were there?'

Amelia grinned wickedly. 'Nope, the suckers. But it's a good way to get rid of them for an hour.'

Jess and Theo laughed. Amelia, smirking, went to the refrigerator and pulled out a jug, waving it at them.

'Iced tea?'

Theo leaned over to Jess, with a stage whisper of 'Don't trust it.' He straightened up and fixed his mother with a stare. 'Iced tea...? Regular or Long Island.'

His mom made a face at him. 'It might have a couple of shots in it. Let's take it out to the deck, shall we?'

AN HOUR AND A HALF LATER, Jess knew two things. One: she was very, very drunk and two: she had fallen madly in love with Theo's mom.

'I'm thinking of leaving you for your mom,' she told a grinning Theo, who was clearly enjoying her drunken state.

'Quite right too,' Amelia toasted her with an empty glass. 'I was thinking of experimenting with my sexuality and you, Jessie, are a very beautiful girl. What say we cuckold Theo here?'

Jess clanked her glass clumsily against Amelia's. 'Ho's before bro's.'

Theo chuckled, shaking his head. 'The state of you both...' Amelia smiled and raised her glass to him.

'Yep, but at least, Jess isn't scared anymore.'

Jess looked between the two of them. 'Oh, so this was a scheme?'

Amelia nodded while Theo tried to look innocent. Jess mumbled to herself and giggled.

'Dude!' Two lanky and impossibly handsome boys appeared from nowhere and threw themselves onto Theo, who wrestled them to the ground easily enough but soon lost out to the puppy-dog strength of his brothers. Jess watched them, grinning while Amelia rolled her eyes.

WWF-session over, Theo extracted himself from the melee and the boys, who Jess could not tell apart, stood and smiled at her. Theo beamed as he introduced them and they stuck out their hands to shake hers.

'I'm Seb,' said one of them, 'you can tell us apart by this mole just under my eye, see?' He stuck his face close to hers and when she leaned in to look, planted a kiss full on her mouth. She burst out laughing as did Amelia, Theo pretended to be enraged and Seb and Tom high-fived each other.

Tom nodded at the now empty jug of alcohol. 'You getting drunk again, mother?'

Amelia peered at him over her spectacles. 'I gave you life, child, I can just as easily beat you senseless.'

The twins started to tease their mother and Jess sat back. This, this was a family, the teasing, the joking around, the lack of judgment, the absence of malice...suddenly she felt tears swept over her vision and realized she felt more at home with these three strangers than she ever had at home once her mother had married Eric. She could feel Theo watching and when his hand covered hers and squeezed it gently, she knew he understood. He bent his head towards hers, his lips at her ear.

'Are you okay?'

Jess nodded, leaning her forehead against his. 'You know what? I really think I am now. Truly.'

And in that moment, she felt like everything would be okay.

AMELIA HAD COOKED a wonderful roast chicken and over dinner she and Theo talked about the house, getting Jess even more excited about seeing it. Later that evening, she and Theo undressed slowly in his old room and made love slowly, quietly and tenderly. Laying wrapped in his arms, Jess was nearly asleep when she heard him whisper. 'Mom really loves you, y'know.'

Jess turned her face up to his. 'And I love her too. I love your brothers, your home, everything about this family. I love you most of all. Thank you for showing me what happiness is.'

She could tell from his expression that her words had gotten to him and it was a moment before he could speak again and when he did, his voice was thick with emotion.

'I want to marry you, Jessica Wood. Soon. Very soon. I need to be your husband, yours and yours alone.'

Tears fell down her cheek and she smiled through them. 'I'll marry you as soon as we can make it happen.'

He kissed her. 'Mom wants me to announce it to the press and tell all those assholes to go to hell. They want the real story, it's there on your finger. It's in that big brain of yours, that heart which holds so much love for everyone.'

It was Jess's turn to be speechless and she kissed him fiercely. 'You and me, forever.'

'Forever,' he agreed and pulled her into his arms.

THEO DUG through his pockets to find the key and opened the door. Jess hopped from foot to foot beside him, like an excited puppy. As they had driven up to the house, she had gasped and covered her mouth. 'God, it's perfect.'

THE LODGE WAS PAINTED a light blue with a porch surrounding the ground floor. Huge picture windows, thick wood walls surrounded by trees. Jess 's eyes were shining as Theo parked the car and she hopped out, running to the edge of the house to look down to the beach. Her eyes were shining as she grinned back at him and he knew she was already won over. A picture came into his mind; Jess, her belly rounded and ripe with pregnancy, holding the hand of a beautiful child with dark curls and her mother's eyes walking along the sandy path to the beach, laughing and singing. The vision made his heart swell with love.

NOW, as he led her into the house, she clutched his hand, trying not to get too overexcited. The lodge was big but homely, the living room cost with large fireplace, the kitchen big enough to fit couches as well as tables, a hub for the family. They moved from room to room and began to talk about their future in each room, how they'd redecorate, which rooms would be reserved for the guests, which for their children.

THEO LED her into a large room at the back of the property, its large arched windows overlooking the blue waters of Puget Sound.

'This is our room,' Theo said and smiled as her face shone with pleasure.

'It is perfect,' she murmured and slid her arms around his waist. Theo kissed her.

'So, I take it...'

'Theo, it's more than I could ever have hoped for. Yes, yes please,' Jess laughed as he picked her up and swung her around. 'Is anyone living here at the moment?'

Theo shook his head. 'I have a confession. The last tenants moved out a couple of months ago and I've been fending off new inquiries ever since I met you because I just had this feeling. This is our place. Yours, mine, our children.'

'Stan and Monty's too,' she reminded him, 'Can't forget our furry kids.'

Theo kissed her then, slowly, his tongue massaging hers. As they kissed, he drew her towards the king-sized bed and pulled her down on top of him. There were no sheets or pillows but they didn't even notice, tearing at the other's clothes. Theo's cock was pulsing, rigid with the need to be inside of her and he tugged her ankles over his shoulders. Jess grinned up at him, a sheen of sweat already sticking her hair to her forehead.

'Nail me to the bed, soldier,' she told him and cried out as he drove his cock so hard, so deep into her that the bed moved with the force of it.

'I'm going fuck you so hard, so long, beautiful,' Theo held her hands above head as he thrust, 'I'm going to fuck you for the rest of my life.'

Their lovemaking was almost savage, brutal, not caring if they hurt or were hurt by the other. The quiet of the big house was broken by their cries, their love, their laughter.

Shattered and sated, they lay together, their naked bodies tangled up, in a pool of sunlight that drenched the afternoon. Jess pressed her lips to his jaw. 'Theo?'

He looked down at her lovely face and smiled. 'Yes?'

'I don't want to leave here. Not ever again.'

THEY MOVED in the next week, hiring movers to take their stuff over to the island as soon as possible while Theo and Jess worked out the logistics of living and working between the island and the city. They decided that Jess should work from the lodge three days a week so she could look after the dogs and Theo would do the rest of the week – or more if he could get away with it. Jess grinned at that, as they were packing the last of their belongings at Theo's apartment.

'Afternoon delights don't make for good work practice,' she said, pretending to disapprove. Theo shrugged, a wicked gleam in his eyes.

'I disagree. How else will I build my porn empire?'

Jess laughed and took his hand, pressing it against her warm sex. 'Start building, Hef...'

The pizza they'd forgotten they'd ordered arrived ten minutes later and Jess shrieked with laughter as Theo, sporting a newspaper and only a newspaper, answered the door to a bemused and embarrassed delivery man.

Finally, surrounded by boxes, Theo locked the door to the lodge and, grabbing a bottle of champagne, went to join Jess in the living room. She was curled up on the couches and as he sat, she moved to tuck herself into his arms. He handed her a flute of champagne.

'To our new home.'

She clinked her glass, took a sip and then kissed him. 'To us.'

Theo smiled. 'To us, baby. I love you.'

. . .

THE ENGAGEMENT IS ANNOUNCED between Miss Jessica Eleanor Wood of King County, Seattle, Washington, and Mr. Theodore Flynn Storm, also of King County, Seattle, Washington. The marriage is expected to take place within the next month and will be a private occasion.

JULES READ THE ANNOUNCEMENT. He'd never felt such anger. Rage. Rage.

THEO PRESSED HIS TEMPLES, trying to ease a headache that was building. The meeting had gone on too late and now he was desperate to get out of there. He glanced at Max who shrugged apologetically and mouthed 'Sorry, boss.'

The investor was too important to the company to blow off so Theo smiled at him. 'I'm so sorry, do you mind if I make a quick call?'

Alone in his office, he called Jess and the tension eased the second he heard her voice. He apologized for being so late.

'I'm going to take the 'copter out the island as soon as I can,' he promised.

'I'll wait up for you and make it worth your while.' He loved the soft tone in her voice. How had he ever existed without this woman?

'I hate leaving you alone at night.'

Jess made a noise. 'I'm not living on tenterhooks anymore, Theo. Besides, I have the dogs.'

'And the gun.'

'And that.'

Theo sighed. 'Okay, well, I'll be home soon.'

He returned to his meeting and with a jolt of annoyance found himself soon dragged back into the dull conversation. At the back of his mind, there was a constant chant, a constant pleading.

Just keep her safe until I get there. Just let her safe, please. Please.

. . .

AT HOME, Jess let Stan and Monty outside to pee. The land behind the house, woodland lit by Theo's floodlights, was an eerie green in the artificial light but she knew, just before midnight, the lights would snap off and the house, the wood, everything would descend into an inky black. Inside, she flitted around tidying, keeping busy, trying not to think about being alone this late. She loved being here, and to her surprise, loved doing the ordinary things a homemaker would do. The sisterhood will have my head, she grinned to herself. In the kitchen, she heard the dryer click off. Folding the clothes, she hugged the warm stack to her as she went upstairs. She put the clothes away and moved over to close the drapes.

SHE JERKED BACK from the window in shock. A figure, silhouetted against the floodlights, was standing at the edge of the woods, watching the house. Jess edged to the window to see if she had been imagining it. No. There was someone there but she couldn't see his – or her - features. As she gazed down, the person lifted their hand and gave a languid wave. Jolted, she went downstairs. She grabbed her phone and went to the front door, peering out, her heart thudding. The dogs started barking and she ran to get the gun Theo had made her practice with before he would leave her alone. Angry now as well as scared, she opened the back door and the dogs skittered in, their tails wagging. That made her feel better at least. She clicked the safety off and stepped onto the porch.

THERE WAS NO ONE THERE. She scanned the trees. Nothing. She blew out her breath, relieved. The fog had started to roll in from the water and it seeped around the house, hanging like gossamer across the floodlit wood. The floodlights clicked off. Midnight.

COME HOME, Theo, she begged silently. She went back inside and turned to close the door just as Jules stepped into her eye line, less than a foot away.

Before she had time to react, he was on her, clamping a hand over her mouth, dragging her back into the kitchen, kicking the back door shut. His arm was across her throat, pressing down, making it hard to breathe. He slammed her into the wall, her ribs taking the force, knocking the breath from her body.

He threw her to the floor, pushing up her skirt grabbing, grasping hands, tearing at her underwear. She used all of her force to kick and punch and try to get free and he slapped her, hard enough to make her ears ring. She fought against him, shouting, 'No, no, no!' as he ripped the delicate fabric down her thighs. His hand came up to clamp over her mouth, but she bit him, hard, bucking with all of her energy to get him off of her.

HIS HANDS WERE around her throat, squeezing, unremitting. She jammed the heel of her hand up, trying to slam it into his nose – she made contact, not hard but enough to make him release his grip.

She scrambled away from him, trying to grab her gun which had clattered to the floor, but he grabbed her ankle and pulled her back to him. Her body fell hard against the stone floor.

HE GRABBED her head between his hands and bounced it viciously off the stone. Dazed, she let her guard down for a split second – then he was in her, thrusting, grunting, tearing. He pinned her hands above her head. She was sobbing now, in anger, raging at him, at herself. She could feel the blood from the back of her head smearing across the floor, soaking her hair. He continued to force himself into her and she cried out with pain as he pushed her legs further apart. He pinned her arms to the floor, his breath heavy on her face. With effort, she brought her knee up and pushed with all her strength. With a frustrated yell, he pulled away, enough for her to kick him between the legs as hard as she could.

· · ·

HE JERKED AWAY, groaning in pain and she was up, scrambling away from him, clambering through the blood on the floor.

He rocked back, knees to chest, clasping his groin. 'Bitch!' She had darted into the hall, making for the front door but her feet, slick from the blood, slid out from beneath her. She skidded across the floor until her legs slammed into the base of the antique mirror. With a groan, it toppled forward.

She put her arm over her face as the glass smashed into her. The heavy frame made contact with her head with a sickening crunch and she slumped to the floor, unconscious.

JULES RECOVERED HIMSELF AND, limping, followed the sound of the shattering glass. She was so still, so vulnerable, lying there amongst the slivers of the mirror, some sticking into her skin, little pools of blood. A large gash along her hairline was spilling blood onto the floor beneath her. He bent over her, avoiding the shards around him, and placed two fingers against her throat, the delicate artery that pulsed against his fingertips. Alive. Good. He didn't want her dead, not yet, at least. He'd wait until she woke up. He wanted her awake for the next part, the part where she would beg him for her life...

THE FIFTH TIME Theo got her voicemail, he started to panic. He grabbed his jacket and strode out of the office, ignoring the surprised look of his secretary.

'I'm going home,' he barked back at her then he was at the elevator, punching the button up to the rooftop helipad.

He strapped himself into the little helicopter, thanking god he'd learned to pilot it a long time ago.. He cussed himself out of buying a house so remote and isolated now – what had he been thinking? Why had he thought to be away from the city, with the police and emergency services, would be safer? Fucking, fucking idiot. He prayed as he propelled the helicopter to its maximum speed.

· · ·

PLEASE, let her be okay, let her be safe...

A COUGH, a sharp noise in the quiet of the house. She started and gave a gasp of terror. Jules sat on the staircase, in his hands, a lethal shard of mirror glass. He turned it over and over; it glinted in the moonlight. She tried to get up but her body held no strength. She managed to pull herself into a sitting position, bracing herself against the wall. She could feel blood trickling down her face, it burned as it rolled into her eyes. Her would-be killer laughed at her struggles.

HE MOVED SUDDENLY, pulling her down, straddling her body. She cried out as the glass on the floor cut into her body. She could smell sex on him, stale sweat. Rape... Her head spun, pounding with pain, nausea rising up inside her. He showed her the glass shard and laughed.

'Who's the fairest of them all?' He laughed.

Her eyes whirled around, panicked, she sought out anything, anything that would help her. Her arms scraped around, feeling, anything to help, the glass slashing her skin.

But he pressed down hard on her, grabbing each hand and kneeling on them, hard, grinding them into the broken glass on the floor. She couldn't move, couldn't fight.

He's going to kill me, she thought, he's going to kill me and I'll never see Theo again. Oh God, Theo...

He tore open the bodice of her dress. Her eyes widened in terror as her assailant raised the shard of glass above his head. Time slowed down as she waited for the pain, for the weapon to be driven into her. As she waited to die. From somewhere, somewhere far away, maybe in her imagination, there was the sound of helicopter blades.

And then an explosion of pain as Jules began to stab her to death. Theo... oh god, Theo...

. . .

THEO WAITED, antsy while the chopper blades slowed and stopped. He unbelted and stepped out of the cabin and just listened. The weather had worsened, and all he could hear was the wind in the trees. The house was in darkness. Theo took a deep breath in. Was he overreacting? He had no proof she was in danger, any danger at all. Theo hesitated then walked towards the house and listened again. Nothing. He took a step onto the porch.

JULES LOOKED up at the sound of the chopper. Damn it, he would have to rush this and he wanted to enjoy every second. Jess had started to struggle was but was obviously still dazed and he easily pushed her down with one hand. Their eyes locked and Jules smiled at her tenderly. This is it. The end of everything.

He loved the way her lovely eyes opened wide, in horror, in terror. 'Goodbye, Jessica...' and he raised the weapon to kill her.

THEO PUT his key in the lock... and nothing happened. He tried again. The door wouldn't open. Had Jess put the deadbolt on? He cupped his hands around his eyes and gazed into the dark hallway. He saw something glittering on the wood floor but couldn't make out what it was. Then he heard a noise that made his heart freeze, his legs quiver. An anguished cry that was strangled off, a gasp, a noise of someone in agony. God, no, no...

JULES DROVE the shard of glass into Jess' belly, feeling the soft, vulnerable flesh give way under the weapon and Jess cried out in agony and tried to fight back, tearing her fingernails across his face, trying to gouge his eyes out. It just made him angrier, more vicious and, as he stabbed her again and again, he felt her becoming weaker. Dying. Jessica was dying and it was exactly as he had dreamed. She coughed a fountain of blood up and her body went limp. He was about to stab her for the fifth time when he heard the banging on the door. Storm's voice, panicked, desperate.

'Jess! Jess, let me in! Jess!'

Jules took one last moment to gaze at Jess, so beautiful, so damaged, so ruined. She was unconsciousness, the pain too much for her, her torn belly spilling blood in a dark pool around her, her thin dress soaking it up. She couldn't last much longer, she was losing too much blood. She's bleeding out. Jules smiled, then, as he heard Theo shout again and he took flight.

A sudden movement caught his eye. In the hallway. He got closer and saw someone running through the dark house. Jules. He'd know that profile anywhere. His stomach disappeared and he darted to the window. Whoever it was had gone out of the back. Theo sprinted around to the back door and his stomach dropped as he saw it swinging open. The figure he'd seen was nowhere. Theo walked into the kitchen, listening.

'Jess? Honey, it's me, it's Theo.'

The house was silent. Theo walked through the dark kitchen and into the hall. It took him a moment to realize what he was looking at, what he was hearing. Labored breathing. Gasps for air. Painful, rattle gurgles of a throat too full of blood. Blood. Too much blood. A woman's body, a woman who had been stabbed viciously, brutally, mercilessly, her clothes drenched. Ghastly, unimaginable stab wounds in soft flesh. Theo's mind could not make the connection between the woman and Jess. It couldn't be her. There was no way.

Because the broken and bloodied dying girl on the floor looked nothing like the women he loved. In a second, she was in his arms, his hands pressing down on the wounds in her belly, desperate to keep the blood inside her, keep her alive. He pulled his cell phone and called the emergency services, not taking his eyes from her face, amazed he could speak to the operator so calmly. All he could feel was abject terror. Jules had gotten to her. He, Theo, had failed to protect her, had broken his promise to her. She was dying and he didn't know how to stop it, didn't know how to do this. He couldn't take his eyes from the vicious stab wounds in her abdomen. So much hatred. So much violence. This couldn't be the way they ended, couldn't be the way she ended. Jules didn't get to win, he didn't get to win.

'PLEASE, Jess, stay with me...breathe, breathe...I love you so much.'

JESS CAME ROUND and wished that she was still unconscious. The pain of her wounds was nothing to the raw terror and hurt in Theo's voice. She concentrated on the feel of his arms holding her, trying to keep her alive. Jules had done what he'd always promised and she didn't know how to fight the pain, the blood loss. She stared up into those green eyes, those terrified, desperate green eyes so full of love for her that she tried to smile at him, to reassure him.

'Jessie, my Jessie, I've got you'

His voice was so tender and caring, after the violence of earlier, that she opened her eyes.

'I love you,' she whispered, 'I love you so much...'

'I love you, god, I love you,' Theo was sobbing now, 'Please hang on, help is coming, help is coming.'

She felt his arms holding her, tight, safe, comfort. She didn't know why he was crying. Her brain was hazy. Her eyes whirled, trying to focus on him. Nothing made sense. At the corners of her eyes, little black spots growing larger and larger. No, I want to see his face, his beautiful face... She could hear him talking to her but he was getting further away, so far away...

'No, no, sweetheart, stay with me, stay with me, oh God, no, no, please...'

The darkness came.

7

STAY WITH ME PART SEVEN

S irens.

She was so beautiful, her dark hair clouding around her shoulders as her robe slipped from her shoulders, revealing her heavenly body. Theo let out a fevered sigh as he saw that under her robe, she was wearing nothing but a harness, the supple leather straps crisscrossing her lush body, her dark red nipples hard and ready for him. She straddled him on the bed and he couldn't keep his eyes off of her.

FLASHING LIGHTS, voices shouting. In here, in here.... please...

HIS MOUTH SOUGHT her nipple greedily as his hands slipped between her legs to find her sex pulsing and wet. His cock, already rigid and engorged, strained to find her pussy. She lowered herself onto him, grinning and gasping as he clamped his hands on her hips and impaled her onto his swollen cock, ramming his hips upwards, wanting to take her, take her hard...

·   ·   ·

RUST AND SALT AND FEAR. Blood, her blood, everywhere. Please, Jess, breathe....

DON'T EVER STOP FUCKING me. Her lips were at his ear and he flipped her onto the floor, towering over her, taking control. He bit down on her nipples, buried his face in her pillowy breasts as he drove harder into her. Her legs were clamped tightly around him and she smiled up at him. I love you so much...

SHE'S DYING. They're telling me she's dying. She won't wake up.

SHE WON'T WAKE UP...

AMELIA WAS BREATHING hard as she ran down the hospital corridor. She nearly screamed when she saw the abject despair on Theo's face. For a long terrifying moment, she thought Jess was dead. But then he gave her a ghost of a smile. She hugged her stricken son.

'How is she?'

Theo shook his head. 'She's in surgery...Mom, it doesn't look good. She's lost so much blood.'

He sat down heavily on one of the chairs. Amelia was horrified.

'Oh my God. Theo.' She sat down beside him, appalled. 'I thought you said the mirror fell on her.'

THEO LOOKED AT HIS MOTHER. He'd told her the very minimum, knowing that if she knew the truth, she would panic and his mom's driving was erratic at the best. 'It did. But I think she crashed into it trying to get away from... she was stabbed, Mom. He knifed her in the belly, repeatedly, brutally. And he raped her.'

Amelia gazed at her son in disbelief. 'Who?' She asked, weakly, her face pale.

Theo's own face hardened. 'Her step-brother. He's tried to kill her before. Christ, Mom, this is just the latest in a lifetime of abuse and assault she's had to live with.'

'No, are you sure? I mean...' She searched Theo's face and saw the utter desolation in his eyes. He nodded.

'Yes. She was raped. There was so much blood, Mom. All over the kitchen, the hallway. When I saw her, I thought she was... she was so still, covered with blood. Someone had had their hands on her. There're bruises on her neck, finger marks, her dress had been ripped open. He stabbed her. Jesus, he really stabbed her...' He choked on his final words.

Amelia started to cry and Theo rubbed her back. He leaned back against the wall and closed his eyes, silent tears coursing down his face.

'MR. STORM?' The surgeon who stood in front of them had kind eyes but all Theo could see was regret in them. His heart clenched tightly in his chest. Theo introduced him to Amelia.

'Mr. Storm, Jessica is stable but still critical. She lost a lot of blood, as I'm sure you realize and we had to repair her liver and remove her spleen. Her abdominal injuries are...,' the doctor seemed to struggle, '...well, they're amongst the worst I've seen in my thirty-year career. The worst. The stabbing was brutal, merciless . Her assailant aimed to end her life in the most painful, savage way possible, of that I have no doubt. He or she used something other than a knife so the wounds were jagged, hard to repair cleanly, she will have scarring. We'll know more in the next few hours.'

Theo thought about the lethal shards of glass that had been scattered around her body. Jules had used one of them to stab her, he was sure. Nausea threatened to overwhelm him, and, the strain etched on his face, he cleared his throat. When he spoke, his voice cracked. 'Doc?'

. . .

THE DOCTOR NODDED. 'Yes, she was raped.' Theo slumped. 'I'm so sorry. We've sealed the evidence and sent it to the county.'

'Can we see her?'

The doctor hesitated. 'I think it's okay if you sit with her. She'll need friendly faces when she wakes up.' He studied Theo's desolate face. 'She will wake up, don't worry, but her recovery will take some considerable time. Now, I must go give my statement to the police, please excuse me.'

He smiled at them both and moved away. Theo stood to go into Jess's room when he saw Max approaching them. Max's face was drawn, angry, but he bent to kiss Amelia's cheek before rubbing his face.

'MAX?' Theo's voice was heavy with grief.

'We arrested Gachet. He's denying everything, of course. And Theo, considering what you told me happened, there's not a mark on him. No scratches, no bruises. Nothing. He let us do a strip search, take swabs. Willingly gave up his DNA.'

Theo shook his head. 'No, he did this, I know he did this. Does he have an alibi?'

'Says he was asleep at home. Yes, no-one can back that up but we can't prove otherwise. How's Jess?'

'Still unconscious.' Amelia said, strain evident in her voice. 'Doctor says she's stable but still critical. We just have to wait.'

'When she wakes up, she'll be able to tell us more. I don't know when she's come back from surgery but the doc's just been here.' Theo sat and made a growling noise. 'Dammit, I know Gachet did this.'

Mike gave them a sympathetic smile. 'Unless Jess formally identifies him as her attacker...'

'Her rapist. Her almost-murderer.' Theo spat. 'He wanted to murder her and nearly succeeded.' The weight of what he had said sank in. 'Oh Jesus.'

'I'm so sorry.' Mike put his hand on Theo's shoulder. 'I hope she can identify him. Any physical evidence?

'They're sending it to the police.'

'They're at the house too, they told me. But, Theo, until they've got something concrete –'

'They had to let him go.' Resigned.

Max looked at Theo and his mom, his face a mask of determination. 'We'll make this right, I swear to god, we will.'

SHE OPENED her eyes and stared at the blank ceiling tiles above her. Everything in her body screamed with pain but fresh air, precious, fresh air filled her lungs. She was alive. Jess drew in a few grateful breaths, taking in the medicinal scent of a hospital, hearing the beeps of machinery. She could feel heavy bandaging on her abdomen, the sting of the central line needle in her arm, the blood pressure monitor on her finger. Her body ached, but she managed to move her stiff neck, turning her head and saw him.

THEODORE STORM. *My love.* He was asleep, his head resting on the bed next to her hand. He looked older, tired, shattered but to her, he was the most beautiful sight in the world. She gingerly reached out to stroke his dark hair, feel his skin. He woke, startled by her touch and she smiled down at him. His eyes widened when he saw her awake. He stood, leaned over to her, took her face in his hands, as if not believing she was alive. His green eyes filled with tears.

'Oh god, Jessie, thank you, thank you for staying with me.' His tears fell onto her cheeks and he kissed her gently as if he couldn't believe she was still alive.

'Theo...' Her voice was soft, gruff but she kissed him back as hard as she could. 'I love you so much.'

'I love you, God, I love you, my Jessie.' Theo stroked her face, wiping away the tears with his thumbs. 'Jessie, I'm sorry he did this to you. I'll never leave you alone again.'

Jess frowned, her head fuzzy. 'Theo, I can't... I can't remember it. I don't what happened to me. Theo, why can't I remember?'

Theo stared at her in horror.

'So this really happens, not just in the movies?' Theo squeeze Jess's hand as the neurosurgeon shone a light into her eyes. She winced at the brightness.

Dr. Napier smiled. 'You've had a serious head injury and suffered a severe concussion, on top of your other injuries. Plus, and this isn't unusual, you've gone through just about the worst trauma a person can. Sometimes the brain just shuts out what it can't cope with.'

Jess nodded. 'Okay.' She looked over at Theo, perched on the side of her bed. He smiled and squeezed her hand. Jess tried to smile. 'When can I go home, doctor?'

'Jessica – can I call you Jess? – Jess, you're all hopped up on morphine at the moment so I doubt you can feel the extent of your injuries.' He sat on the edge of the bed and patted her hand. 'It's going to take a while. At the moment, your belly is still in trauma from the stabbing, from the surgery we had to perform. Your liver needs to heal itself, your body needs to adjust to your new reality. If all goes well, you might be able to go home in a month or so. On the understanding that you give yourself time to recover.' He added with a meaningful look at Theo.

Theo nodded and she knew she'd be under house arrest when she got home. A month. God. She looked up at the doctor.

'Thank you, really, for everything.' The doctor smiled at her and Theo.

'My pleasure. Call me if you need anything.'

Alone, Theo sat on the edge of the bed, his arms around his love. She leaned against him and they sat in silence for a few minutes.

He tightened his grip on her and buried his face in her hair. 'Jess?'

'Yes?'

He thought for a moment then moved so he could see her face. 'I want to ask you a question and it's going to be rough but I have to.

You can just nod or shake your head and when it's over, I'm gonna hold you and never let you go.' He smiled, a crooked, worried expression.

Jess took a deep breath and nodded. He took her hands.

'Jess. We don't ever have to go back to that place, you know, I can sell...'

'No,' she interrupted, 'no. That's our home, that's the place where we'll make our family. I know it in my bones.'

Theo was tense. 'I thought after you nearly died there. You were nearly murdered there.'

Jess pulled his lips to hers then smiled up at him, her eyes soft. 'It's also the place where I survived. Where you saved me. He doesn't get to take our home away from us.'

Theo kissed her then was silent for a long time. She could feel the question hovering in the air.

'Jess, it was Jules, wasn't it?'

She stared at him for a long moment, tears filling her eyes. Then, slowly, she nodded.

'I want to tell the police I'm positive, Theo, I do but I can't remember anything.' Her face crumpled and Theo kept his promise and held her while she sobbed.

THE HOSPITAL WAS QUIET, much later, the middle of the night when Jess woke. She saw Theo had gone down to get coffee, was relieved he was taking a break. The dark circles etched under his eyes, the pain in his eyes... it scared her.

A headache screeched around her skull, and she tried to sleep but the pain in her head was too much. She turned in the bed and gasped. Jules, silent, watchful, sat forward from the shadows. He smiled.

'HOW ARE YOU FEELING, JESSICA?' His voice was a caress.

'What are you doing here?' Her voice cracked and he smiled.

He raised his hands, shrugging. 'Well, there's nowhere else I'd rather be, Jessica. Nowhere.' Again that tone, intimate, tender. It scared her. She turned away, pretending to reach for the cup of water on her nightstand, wanting to grab the call button. She winced as the sudden movement jerked on the I.V. in her hand. Jules stood.

'Allow me.'

He leaned across her and she caught his scent. As she breathed it in, a jolt, a rush of nausea, of terror. She gasped, a torrent of memories crashing back. Jules's head snapped around and their eyes locked. In that moment, he realized she knew.

'Oh, Jessica, this would have been much easier if you'd just died when you were supposed to. Because now you've made it so much harder for everyone.'

He stroked her face but she jerked away from his touch, ready to scream for help. He clamped his hand over her mouth.

'Don't scream. You know why you've made it harder? Because it won't be just you I kill now, Jessica. I'll kill everyone you care about. Then I'll make Theo watch when I carve you up.'

Every cell in her body willed her to scream, scream for help, for Theo now, right now. But she believed Jules in that moment. In her eyes, in her broken, beaten mind, he had grown into a mythical creature, a daemon, an unstoppable force.

Come back, Theo, please, I need you.

JULES LEANED in and kissed her gently on the mouth. She tried to pull away and his face grew hard, his smile cold, his eyes dead.

'And then I'll kill him.'

And he smiled. He picked up the call button, he pressed it and placed it back on her nightstand.

'There now.' Without warning, he clamped his hand over her mouth and pressed down hard on her belly. The pain was searing and she moaned in agony.

Jules smiled, released her, leaned in and kissed her gently on the mouth. She tried to pull away and his face grew hard, his smile cold, his eyes dead.

'Get some sleep. I'll come and see you again. I'll always come to see you, Jess. I will finish what I started.'

The nurse came in. 'Do you want a sedative, honey?'

Jules smiled at her. 'I think she does. She was just saying she couldn't sleep.'

Jess couldn't speak. The nurse slipped a needle into her I.V. and she felt herself going under. Jules stroked her hair.

'Sleep now, sweetheart, I'll be here when you wake.'

As she closed her eyes, a tear dropped down her face.

WHEN THEY TOLD him at reception that Jess 's brother was in the hospital and asking where she was, his heart had stopped. He knew, he knew that it was Jules who was responsible for raping and stabbing her. Who else could it be? And now he was in the hospital

Jess. Oh God, Jess.

When he got to her room, he sighed in relief. She was alone. Asleep, she looked as young as when he'd first met her but the cuts, the bruises made his stomach twist with pain. He bent down and kissed her cheek.

Not wanting to disturb her, he went back to the corridor and sat down. Leaning his head against the wall, he closed his eyes and sighed.

'She seems fine.'

Theo opened his eyes and turned towards the voice. His voice. The bastard who stabbed her. Theo was off his chair, launching himself into Gachet.

'Motherfucker!'

JULES FOUGHT BACK but was no match for the bigger man's strength and skill. Theo twisted the man's arm behind his back and got him on the floor, kicking out the back of his knee. Jules's face banged against the hard floor and Theo was gratified to see blood, but then security got hold of him, ramming him against a wall.

'Okay, okay.' He yelled. They let him go. Jules was still on the floor, his nose pouring with blood.

'Get up.' Theo waved the security off. 'I'm cool, I'm cool.'

Jules got to his feet. 'What the fuck do you think you're doing?' He brushed himself down, wiped his bloody nose on his sleeve. A sly grin belied his apparent outrage. Theo shook his head, anger radiating from him.

'I know you're responsible for this, Gachet. I know.'

Jules smirked. 'Responsible for what, Mr. Storm? I was at home alone when Jess had her unfortunate accident.'

'It wasn't an accident. You know damn well it wasn't.' Theo glanced around, checking they were alone. 'You raped her and then you knifed her. You tried to murder her.'

Jules raised his eyebrows. 'Murder? That's a horrific accusation. And where's your proof?'

'Interesting you don't deny it.'

'Your proof, Storm?'

Theo paused and Jules leaped on his hesitation.

'I thought not. Careful, Storm, I think that counts as slander. Now, I would like to wait and see my sister, if that's all right with you.'

'Are you fucking kidding me?' Theo stepped in front of Jess's door. 'You're not going anywhere near her, not ever again.'

Jules smirked. 'I think you'll find, that as her only family, I count as next of kin. You can't stop me.'

It was Theo's turn to smile then. 'Oh but you see, as of earlier this evening, I am legally her next of kin. As her future husband, Jess wanted to give me power of attorney while she's in here. She had a lawyer come in to see her.'

Jules was silent for a long moment. 'Please tell Jess I hope she recovers soon. I look forward to concluding our business.' He grinned at Theo's anger, turned and strode down the corridor.

'Motherfucker.' Theo repeated to himself. He turned and went back into her room. She stirred as he bent down to kiss her and whispered his name, smiling even in her sleep.

'I love you,' he whispered, his eyes searching her face, drinking in every feature, her soft skin, her beautiful mouth. He leaned his forehead against hers. 'God, Jessie, I promise you, if it is the last thing I do, I will make this fucker suffer for what he's done to you. I promise. I promise.'

IT HAD BEEN the longest ten weeks of Jess's life but now, as Theo flew them back to the house on Whidbey, she felt a tense band tighten across her chest. She had insisted they do this. That they forge ahead with the life they had planned. Fuck Jules had become her mantra. But now, the panic was starting to build. What if she couldn't cope? What if she freaked out? Theo wouldn't need much persuasion to burn the house down if it scared her but she was desperate not to be run out of another home by Jules. He couldn't win this.

Theo reached over and took her hand. 'Okay, my love?' The soft, tender timbre of his voice was like opium flooding through her veins, soothing, loving and she grinned suddenly, and told him that.

Theo laughed and she realized how long it had been since she heard the sound. 'Opium, huh?'

'You have the 'voice crack',' she nodded, continuing the joke. Theo chuckled again.

'That makes no sense but thanks anyway. If you like, I give you some serious dirty talk with my 'crack' voice...'

He waggled his eyebrows suggestively but she knew he wasn't serious. She sighed. The lack of sex over the past couple of months was beginning to get to her but the doctor had told her – after repeated badgering – to take things easy.

And the last thing she wanted to with Theo was to 'take it easy'. She wanted him to fuck her senseless, to suck his cock, bite down on his nipples... She shook herself. *You are a nympho, Wood.* But she knew Theo was feeling it too. She caught him looking at her last night, his eyes raking over her body as they shared a bath. The red raw scars on her belly were a stark reminder of why they couldn't rush the sex thing and he'd traced them gently with his finger.

'Does it still hurt?'

SHE SHOOK HER HEAD. It wasn't a complete lie – it was just sometimes when she'd move awkwardly, the healing muscles inside her would screech and she'd curse softly. But, god, she wanted him so badly. She had felt, all this time in hospital that she had become this sexless thing. Someone who smelled of antiseptic and medication, someone as alluring as a bedpan. She'd told Theo that one night when she'd gotten upset, overtired and in pain. He had held her all too gently and told her she was the most beautiful thing in the world.

If only she could believe him. She looked over at him, saw the stress etched on his gorgeous face even when he was smiling, the smile never quite reached his eyes.

'We're nearly there,' he said, obviously sensed her scrutiny.

The tension in chest became almost crushing but she kept it inside as Theo expertly landed the helicopter and helped her out of the cabin.

THEO TOOK her hand and they walked slowly towards the house. His mother had been here, after the crime scene investigators and had cleaned up the blood. Jess's blood. Amelia hadn't said much to him but Seb, his usual exuberance missing, had told him that she'd gone home and immediately taken a long bath. The twins had heard her heart-broken, stricken sobbing through the silent house. His mother, Seb, and Tom had been frequent visitors to Jess's bedside when she was in hospital, and even his sister, Milly, had flown into meet her. Jess was their family now. It had helped him immeasurably.

Now, he unlocked the door and turned to Jess. He could feel her trembling and took her into his arms. 'Jessie...'

'It's okay,' she said, looking up into his eyes, 'I'm ready.'

· · ·

SHE WAS okay right up until she saw the blood on the floor. Her hand flexed, tightened in Theo's. As she took in the place where she nearly died – no, she thought, was almost murdered - she drew in a shaky breath and closed her eyes.

'Jess?'

She shook her head, put her hand up to silence him. She felt his arms go around her, his lips on her hair. They stood like that for what seemed an age. She opened her eyes finally.

'Okay.' She whispered. The wall looked bare without the huge mirror. Her stomach roiled when she remembered him, with that lethal shard of mirror raised above his head stab her to death. The indescribable agony when he'd plunged it into her belly. The smell of her own blood. She gagged.

'Honey? It's okay, it's okay.'

She nodded.

Theo stroked her face. 'Let's go.' He kissed her, 'We don't have to do this today. '

She smiled at him but shook her head. 'No. I want to. However hard it is. Until I do, I can't move forward. And I won't let him dictate my life in any way. In any way, Theo.'

He nodded, understanding. She took his hand and walked into the kitchen. Her legs shook. The bloodstains weren't so bad in here, the stone floor less porous than the wood of the hallway. Where Jules had stabbed her. Jess kept saying it in her head so that she could accept it. Jules stabbed me. Jules stabbed me. It worked. Every time she said it, she became less scared, angrier.

SHE NODDED AT THEO. 'Okay. I'm good.' He smiled at her but she could see he wasn't convinced. She put her arms around his neck.

'This was a place of horror. For one hour. One night. He doesn't get to sully all the good times we're going to have here. With you. Our family. With all of us together.' She kissed him and felt him respond. He ran his hands down her back, pulling her to him. She pressed her body into his, hearing his intake of breath. He picked her up and carried her into the living room, laid her on the couch. She took his face in her hands as he moved on top of her.

'You are the most wonderful man, Theo Storm. Have you missed this as much as me?'

He nodded, his smile filled with desire. She took his hand and guided it, under her dress, between her legs.

'Make this is a place of joy again, Theo. Please.'

He slid his hand into her panties and grinned down at her. 'My pleasure, ma'am.' He kissed her as she unzipped his pants and touched him. 'God, I love you.'

She laughed, gasping at his caress. 'I love you, Theo, so, so much.'

He started to unbutton her dress, kissing her from her neck, between her breasts. He pressed his lips to every scar, every bruise on her stomach. He hooked his fingers into the side of her panties and pulled them down. He smiled up at her.

'You're beautiful, baby.' Then his mouth was on her, his tongue caressing her. She moaned with pleasure.

'Theo.' she whispered,

'Yes, baby?' He looked up and saw she had tears in her eyes. 'What is it?' He moved up her body, concerned.

She kissed him. 'I want you,' she murmured, 'I want you inside me.'

Theo frowned. 'Jessie, I don't think...'

'Sssh....' She pushed him onto his back and straddled him, wincing slightly. Theo held her waist, still concerned.

'Jess, we should...'

'Sssh....' She moved lower and took his cock into her mouth, feeling it quiver and thicken as she sucked, tongued and teased it. She felt his fingers stroke through her long hair, massage her scalp, heard his moan of longing.

When his cock was rigid, pulsating and hard, she moved up and gently lowered herself onto him, closing her eyes as she felt him fill her entirely, moaning softly. Theo's hands clasped her hips as she began to rock gently, slowly, taking him in deeper, deeper, deeper...

. . .

THEO GAZED up at her as she moved. God, she was so beautiful that it hurt. His cock was being squeezed and massaged by her soft, wet cunt and his head swam with desire, longing, desperate love. His fingers bit into the tender flesh of hips as they fucked but he was aware of not hurting her still healing body. He slipped his hand between her legs and stroked her clit, feeling the small bud harden and pulse against his fingers and was gratified by her gasps of pleasure, the soft moans as she moved on top of him.

THEY MADE LOVE SLOWLY, gently, each experiencing a mellow climax that seemed to linger and afterward, they lay together naked, skin against skin and held each other and listened to the peace of the evening together.

Theo turned to kiss her temple. 'You okay, Jessie?' He felt her arms tighten around him, felt her press a kiss to his chest.

'I am good, very good,' she lifted her chin to kiss him, 'I love you, Theodore Storm. I feel like we're on the way to reclaiming our lives.'

Theo sighed and closed his eyes. He wanted to feel hopeful, wanted to feel happy in this moment but he slide his hand down to her belly and stroked it. He would never forget that night, the torn skin, the blood. 'Are you sure we didn't go too fast? Are you hurting?'

'No,' but when he raised his eyebrows at her, she smiled sheepishly, '...okay, I do ache a little but no more than a regular stomach ache.'

'ASPIRIN AND A HOT BATH THEN.' Theo started to get up but she moaned and pulled him back down beside her. He didn't protest – her skin was so soft, so warm next to his and she smelled so good. She burrowed into his chest. 'Theo?'

'What's up, beautiful?'

'I have to talk to you about something.'

He looked down at her. 'Oh yeah?'

She hesitated for a moment, her brown eyes wary then she took a breath in. 'I know about Kelly.'

For some reason, Theo wasn't shocked or surprised. He nodded. 'I somehow knew you did. Don't ask me how.'

'How come you never mentioned her?'

'Honestly? I have no idea. Possibly because we have so much else to think about since we met that there was no good time. Ollie tell you?'

She nodded. 'It's a big piece of your past, is all. I thought we said no secrets.'

'We did. I'm sorry, Jess, it was stupid and thoughtless of me. Kelly was troubled for a long time. Before I knew her even. I was too young to see the signs and we lost her.'

He sat up then and she moved to sit beside him, her hand resting on his chest. 'You know you can talk about it, you know? With me?'

He smiled. 'I do know, and I'm kind of glad you know. But I have to say something about that. I found her. I found her dead and it was awful, horrific, devastating. But, Jess, even that paled to what I felt when I found you that night. My heart was ripped out. I couldn't breathe, I couldn't think, it was as if everything human in me disappeared.'

Jess looked stricken and he realized that underneath the distress was something else: guilt. He cupped her face in his palms, made her look at him. 'None of this is your fault. None of it. It just is what it is. God, I hate that expression, but in this case, if I had to swap every-thing's that's happened for a life without you? Never.' He kissed her gently. 'I'm going make Jules's life a living hell, I swear I am. He doesn't get to do what he's done and get away with it.'

JESS HESITATED but then met his gaze. 'Do you love me?'

He looked confused. 'You know I do.'

'Then just promise me two things. One, you'll let me help you bring him down. Yes.' She added as Theo gave her an incredulous look. 'Don't let me be a victim. That's not what is going to happen.

You're already my white knight. That's a done deal. This is a partnership. Agreed?'

Theo nodded. 'I get it. Yes, agreed. With reservations.'

'Which are?'

'You never put yourself in harm's way. I never let you out of my sight. I'm the boss when it comes to anything less than legal. You agree to be naked at least seventy-five percent of the time. That last one depends on the situation.'

She laughed, grateful for his effort to lighten the atmosphere. 'Done, done, as much as possible. You're the boss and I will if you will.'

He coughed out a throaty laugh and she joined in.

'What was the other promise?'

Her smile faded. 'That you promise, promise, you won't put yourself in any danger. Promise me. Because if anything happened to you then he might as well get his way. I don't want to live in a world without you in it. I mean it, Theo'

Theo moaned at her words and she tightened her arms around him.

'Okay. You got it.'

She rested her face against his, feeling his stubble graze her skin. 'You and me now.' He buried his face in her hair and locked his arms around her.

'I'll never let him hurt you again. I'll never let anyone hurt you.'

Jess wanted to believe him, she knew he meant it with all his heart. But something in her that said that Jules would stop at nothing. Jess knew that at the end of all of this, someone would be dead. One thing was certain, she would never let that person be Theo.

Even if it cost her own life.

MAX ARRIVED with the dogs the next day and both Theo and Jess hugged him tightly. Jess was cooking, periodically disappearing into the kitchen from where they sat on the porch. When she had gone to check on the food, Theo looked over at Max. It seemed to him that they had both aged a million years in a few months. The loss, the grief, the horror they had been through had made Theo even more aware of how much Max was a brother to him – even if the guilt of Josh's murder would never leave him. As much as he tried to reassure Jess, Theo's own guilt kept him up at night: *Because I fell in love, Max lost his own love.* Max, knowing Theo's mind, had constantly reassured him but it didn't make Theo feel any better.

'So, Gachet has disappeared.' Max was the one who was in constant contact with the police whilst Jess recovered and he kept Theo updated with every detail.

Theo nodded. 'Doesn't surprise me. Well, we know now why he release Jess's inheritance. To fund his own escape.' They'd discovered Jess's account drained the day after she'd been released from the hospital, although no-one knew exactly how he'd done it. 'Jesus, how long has he planned to kill her?'

Max shrugged. 'I really don't want to think about that. The main thing is she's safe now.' He raised an eyebrow at the shadowy figures moving around the perimeter of the property. 'What's it like living in Fort Knox?'

Theo gave him a wry smile. 'Better than not sleeping.' He sighed and leaned back in his chair. 'So, we got any leads?'

'Not on Jules. His driver – or ex-driver is still in the city – why I'm not sure. The son-of-a-bitch may be here to spy for Jules. Pretty sure he knows more than he's telling the police anyways.'

Theo's face hardened. 'Maybe I should speak directly to him.' His words were heavy with meaning and when Max turned to look at him, he could see his own anger reflected in his friend's eyes.

'That might an idea,' Max said slowly. 'Then if he won't talk, then what? The police?'

There was a long silence. 'Oh, I think it's gone way past the police, don't you?' Theo felt a calm settle over him as he spoke the words and he watched Max nod once, firmly. 'Yeah, this is all us from now on. He's not going to know what hit him.'

．　．　．

JULES GACHET SAT BACK in his chair, admired the slim, brown legs of the woman that strolled past him. Paris was as beautiful as it had ever been but, even with the beautiful woman and delicious spring sunshine, he found it hard to concentrate.

She's alive. It haunted him, the fact that he'd failed. When he'd left her that night, broken and bleeding out, he'd felt sure she couldn't have possibly had a chance. None.

JULES SIGNALED to the waiter for another pastis. The fake passports Malcolm had procured for him long before his attempt to kill Jessica had more than proven their worth but yes, he was taking a risk coming here, back to the place of his birth. Soon he would go deep into the French countryside, change his name, appearance and lay low until the American police – and Jessica – thought he was gone forever. Malcolm was arranging things back in Seattle and when it was safe, he, Jules, would return and finish what he promised Jess he would. Kill her. Make Storm watch as he took her life, once and for all.

SPRING DRIFTED LAZILY into summer and Jess found herself swept along with the plans for the wedding. Despite her and Theo's wishes for a quick, small wedding, Theo's mother had other ideas and Jess couldn't bear to disappoint her. Amelia's kindness had no limit, it seemed, and neither did her creativity.

THE WEDDING WAS SET for early September at Amelia's sprawling estate on the island. Jess and Theo dutifully followed Amelia's arrangements for their wedding attire, telling each other that if it made Amelia happy, then it was worth it.

But they lived for the times when they were alone. As Jess got healthier, their sex life got back on track and even became a deeper thing, a closeness between them that seemed anchored in complete trust.

Jess, waiting for Theo to return home one Friday night, soaked in a long bath, feeling horny as hell and sexy for the first time in an age. Her scars were fading into pink lines and she traced the path of them. It still didn't feel real, but she remembered the agony all too well. She pushed that thought aside and got out of the bath, slowly drying herself and massaging lotion into her skin. She padded, nude, to the dressing room and was about to slip into her usual shorts and tee, when she saw it, peeking out of a box on the floor. The leather bondage harness they had only used once, the night before she was stabbed.

JESS STARTED to grin and pulled the harness out. The leather was so buttery soft, the fastenings cool steel. She slipped her robe off her shoulders and stepped into the harness, enjoying the feel of the leather as she strapped it onto her body. The inch-wide straps criss-crossed her breasts, framing them and swept between her legs and around her thighs, leaving her cunt, her buttocks exposed. Even putting it on made her so aroused she could feel herself getting wet, and grabbing her robe, she darted downstairs to prepare Theo's very special homecoming.

THEO LEFT the office just after eight, and, as had become his habit, flew the chopper back to the island. He hated the commute via car and ferry boat now – when he was done with work, he wanted to get to her now. Hell, all day at work, he thought about nothing but Jess, working from home, the safest place she could be. He called her a dozen times a day and she was always glad to hear his voice. My girl.

There was a storm brewing over the island as he arrived home and the sky was dark, heavy with rain. After landing, he checked in with his head of security and then headed into the house.

Theo opened the front door. The house was dimly lit and as he moved into the house, he saw candles guttering on the tables.

'Welcome home.'

HE TURNED to see Jess sitting halfway up the stairs and his breath caught in his lungs as he saw the harness crisscrossing her body. Her dark tumbled down to her shoulders and in the candlelight, her skin glowed. She smiled lazily at him and slowly, tantalizingly spread her legs wide. He could see she was already wet, the dark red folds of her sex glistening with her arousal, plump and ripe. His breath hitched and caught at the sight of her.

'I've been thinking about you all day, my love.'

Her smile widened and as he watched, her hand slipped between her legs and she began to masturbate for him. 'And I, you. Strip for me, Theo.'

HE GRINNED and pulled his clothes off, his cock already thickening and trembling. He fisted the root of it and began to stroke. Jess, moaning softly, nodded to a side table. An open bottle of champagne. Theo snagged it as he made his way up the stairs to her, putting it down by her head then grabbing both of her hands and binding them with his tie. Jess capitulated happily as Theo began to pour the champagne, first into the hollow of her throat then down her body. Jess arched her back as the liquid flowed over her body, down to her navel, snaking into her sex. Theo bent down and ran his tongue from her clit, over her belly. He bit down onto her nipples, teasing them into hard peaks and finally, taking a swig of champagne, covering her mouth with his and kissing her, their tongues caressing, the liquid dribbling down their faces. Jess dissolved into giggles as they both gasped for air and Theo swept her upstairs into their bedroom.

. . .

Jess had set up a video camera and a screen, and Theo raised his eyebrows. She kissed him. 'I want to watch us fuck,' she murmured, trailing her lips along his jaw, 'I want to see your cock plunging in and out of me again and again and again...'

He pushed her down onto the bed, his senses frenzied with desire, turned on by her whispers, her obvious lust for him. He hooked one of her ankles of his shoulders and angled the camera down onto her swollen cunt.

'Christ, Jessie, look how beautiful you are.' He spread her labia with his long fingers, rubbing her rock-hard clit with his thumb and smiled down at her. 'Do you want my cock, now, Jessie?'

She nodded, gasping as he placed the head of it against her and pushed in – stopping when he was an inch in. 'Are you ready, Jessie?'

She moaned with frustration and he laughed. He poured some champagne over his cock then drove himself into her as hard as he could. Jessie screamed and came almost at once and Theo, incredibly turned on, had to slow down to prolong her pleasure. 'Jessie, I love to fuck you, you know that? Your cunt is always ready for me, always hungry for me and I want to fill you, drive so deep into you. Look at us, my love.'

He turned her head so she could see the screen, the sight of his huge cock plowing into her, slower now, thick and rigid, the shaft pulsing with blood and arousal. They were both entranced by the sight of it, their bodies merging, moving as one. Theo watched her lovely face as she watched them. 'God, Jessie, how the hell did I exist before you?' He began to thrust hard and she looked back into his eyes, her legs clamped around his hips.

'I love you,' she was breathless as their fucking became almost delirious, overwhelming. She arched her back as she came violently, moaning so beautifully that he came too, shuddering as his cock pumped thick streams of cum deep inside of her. They barely took a breath before Jess, her hands still bound, made her way down his body and took his still ramrod cock in her mouth. She sucked him hard, drawing her mouth over the wide crest of his cock, hollowing her cheeks as she teased the head with her tongue, tracing patterns on the sensitive numb. Theo felt his entire body tense as she drove him towards a shattering climax.

AFTERWARD, they lay naked, limbs tangled, and drank the rest of the champagne straight from the bottle.

'We're all class,' Jess smirked up at him. Theo pressed his lips to hers.

'You could never be anything else and F.Y.I., being greeted by you in that get-up? Best welcome ever.'

She grinned. 'I found it today...you know we have a whole box of fun toys we haven't even used yet?'

Theo shook his head and sighed in mock-regret. 'What have I turned you into?'

She pulled his lips down for another kiss. 'Someone who loves and is loved, trusts and is trusted.'

'Mushy.'

'You bet your sweet ass. Now, Storm, fuck me again.'

LATER, he was about to fall asleep when his phone beeped. Theo stole a look at Jess, sleeping on her stomach, her head on the pillow turned towards him. For a second he watched as she breathed, the silky skin of her back glowing in the dim light of his reading lamp.

His phone beeped again. Max. *Call me now. Urgent. Keep it quiet.*

Theo eased out of bed and padded down to his study, closing the door behind him. Max answered on the first ring.

'We need to meet. Now. Tonight. Drive to the ferry terminal. Alan is waiting. '

'What the hell, Max?'

Max took a deep breath in. 'We've got Malcolm.'

HE HATED, hated, leaving Jess alone in the house, waking up the security guard outside the house to make sure he was alert but this could

mean the difference between Jess being safe for the rest of her life –
or not. If Malcolm knew where Gachet was...Theo and Max had
talked around the subject for so long and now it was within reach.
No, they wouldn't bring the police in. Theo wanted to end it. For
good. When Max asked him, point blank, if he would cross that line,
Theo had met his gaze evenly.

'For her? No question.'

Alan was waiting at the ferry terminal in a black-out sedan that
he didn't recognize. He slipped inside.

'Max says to stay inside until he opens the door. Plausible denia-
bility and all that.'

Shit. Max was taking a lot of the weight of this when maybe he
didn't need to. Now Alan was involved too. Theo's face must have
registered his frustration because Alan turned around in his seat.

'Boss, whatever you're thinking, we're grown men and we're just
as invested. We all love Miss Wood, you know.'

Theo smiled tightly and nodded. 'You're a good man, Alan.'

TWO HOURS LATER, Max opened the car door. As Theo got out, he saw
that they were in abandoned junk yard. Max nodded silently to an
empty barn and Theo followed him in. Inside, a bare lightbulb lit the
vast, echoing space. Malcolm was tied to a chair, his eyes wheeling
around in his head, a bloody welt above his eye. Max just shrugged
when Theo looked at him questioningly.

Malcolm focused on Theo. 'Well, look who it is. Mr. Billionaire.
How's the fiancé? Can she still fuck as well after her little accident?'

Theo's response was purely physical. His fist connected with
Malcolm's jaw so fast the other man's head snapped back. Spitting
blood, Malcolm cursed at him. Theo bent down and got in his face.

'Where is Julien Gachet?'

Malcolm merely smirked. Theo repeated the question, calmly but
with enough menace that the bound man's eyes became wary.

'How should I know? I'm not his keeper.'

Theo and Max just looked at each other and Malcolm found his smile again.

'Wherever he is, he's probably just working out how he's going to finish what he started.'

Max's head dipped just a little then Alan, unseen behind Malcolm, wrapped a chain around Malcolm's neck and began to squeeze. Shocked, Malcolm choked. 'Fuck you, fuck you all. That little whore's not worth jail time.'

Theo stepped towards him. 'You don't speak about her again. Do you understand me?'

Malcolm smirked. 'My pleasure. I don't waste my time on trashy little cunts like Jessica Wood.'

Theo launched himself at him, raining blows, wild, uncontrolled, frenzied blows. Max and Alan dragged him away. Malcolm's face was a bloody pulp, his nose, gushing blood, was bent at an impossible angle.

'You fucker, I'll kill you, I'll kill you...' he raged at Theo, held back now by his friends. Theo spat in the man's face.

'Tell me where he is!' Theo's voice was a roar, his whole body tensed to spring again. Max narrowed his eyes at Malcolm.

'Tell us or we'll let him have you.'

Malcolm started to laugh, his mouth a tangled mess of broken teeth and blood. 'He's going to kill her, you know. You can't stop him.'

Theo suddenly went very still. His friends, taken aback, let him go. Malcolm grinned at him. 'Don't blame him. If I had a chance to gut that fucking beautiful bitch, I'd do her myself.'

In one fluid movement, before anyone could stop him, Theo stepped towards the laughing man, and with a violent jerk of his hands, broke his neck.

8

RUN WITH ME PART EIGHT

J ess stirred as Theo slipped back in the bed and snuggled into his arms, her eyes still closed.

'Cold,' she complained at the touch of his cool skin. Theo wrapped his arms around her, needing her warmth, her hot blood to try to help the frozen heart of him.

He was a murderer. A killer.

The way Max had stared at him after he'd snapped Malcolm's neck was something he'd never forget. He knew it reflected his own emotions. When Malcolm had threatened Jess – again – he'd exploded, all the pain, the loss, the terror of losing her overwhelmed him. Only one course of action had seemed possible in that moment.

Afterward, he'd tried to calm himself, dragging lungfuls of air into his body. Alan stayed back, letting the two friends adjust. Max had put a tentative a hand on his shoulder.

'Theo...' The love in his friend's voice had broken the final wall and Theo bent over and sobbed.

'Jesus, Max.... what have I done?'

Max couldn't answer him, just hugged his friend. After Theo had calmed down, he turned back to Malcolm's body. 'No-one knows. No one except you, me and Alan. Let's keep it that way. We'll get rid of the body – no-one except Jules will miss this asshole anyway. He deserved what he got.'

Theo looked at Max, the hardness in his friend something he'd never seen. 'Max, I can't do that, I have to tell the police.'

'Not an option.' Alan spoke up and his voice was firm. 'Listen, I'll bring the car around.'

Max nodded. 'Good, Theo, you're going home. Alan and I will deal with this.'

Theo almost laughed. 'Are you kidding me? This is my responsibility.'

Max stared at him. 'Theo, if this had been Jules instead if Malcolm, would you be feeling this way?'

Theo slowly shook his head. 'I guess not. But still, we've no idea where Gachet is and I hate that.'

Max sighed. 'There's something else. If Malcolm was in contact with him, Julien will know something has happened. It could make him angrier, more vengeful.'

'I think 'vengeful' was over a long time ago. He's psychotic. He won't stop until he's killed Jess.'

Max rubbed his eyes, looked back at Malcolm's corpse. 'Look, go home to Jess. Remind yourself why this...' He kicked the dead man's leg. '...is no great loss to anyone. Yeah, Jules will know but it might just flush him out. Just make sure Jess is fully protected. If I've learned one thing about Jules, it is that he's a coward. He won't try to get to her through a damn army.'

Alan had driven Theo back to the office and Theo grabbed a pool car from the parking garage, drove to the ferry. He couldn't get Malcolm's dead face out of his head. He'd seen two women he loved, one dead, one dying, and both had seemed more human than the wide stare of the dead man. Maybe it was because, in his mind, Malcolm was merely an extension of Jules – and Jules was a monster.

Now, with Jess in his arms, the frozen heart of him began to thaw. She nuzzled his neck, pressing her lips against his throat.

'I'm sorry I had to go out, baby...' he murmured into her hair then as she opened her eyes wide and smiled at him, he kissed her , his lips firm against hers. She reached down to stroke his cock and he felt it jerk to life under her gentle touch. Adrenaline coursed through his veins then and he pushed her onto her back and covered her body with his hitching her legs around his hips. He took first one then the other nipple into his mouth teasing them until they peaked up, hard and sensitive. Jess sighed happily, pressing her groin against the hot length of his cock and then gave a surprised squeak as he rammed the entire length of it into her, clamping her hands roughly to the bed and grinding his mouth onto hers so ferociously he could taste blood. He just wanted to consume her, possess her, fucking nail her to the bed. His cock, ramrod hard and relentless, pounded into her and he could see by the excitement in her eyes that she was feeling it too.

They hadn't fucked like this since before she had been stabbed and the wild abandon of it absolved every other thought from his mind. This was what he lived for, being with her, looking at her as her lovely face shone with sweat, flushed a perfect scarlet, her pink mouth open and moaning for him, calling his name. Her sleek thighs moved against his waist, the soft flesh belying the strength of the muscles clamped around him. Her tight little cunt flexing and welcoming his cock, her gently undulating belly against his, her nipples brushing his chest. He breathed in every part of her, her clean, soap-and-gardenia perfume mixing with the heady scent of their lovemaking. His brains was a flash flood of emotion, love, rage, pain, hurt, desire, Jess, Jess, Jess....

She cried out as she came, her body vibrating and quivering, her legs wrapped around him pulling him deeper. Theo nearly growled with his need to keep driving himself into her ferociously. He never wanted to stop but when at last, he peaked with a carnal roar, his semen pumping violently into her, he collapsed down onto her and she wrapped her arm around his neck.

'Theo, Theo, Theo...' Her voice was a whisper, breathy and a balm to his bruised senses. She was the only thing that made any sense in his world, the only thing...

.   .   .

HALF A WORLD AWAY, Jules Gachet called Malcolm's cell for the twelfth time. Something was wrong. Something was very wrong.

JESS WOKE a little after eleven a.m. The sun streamed in through the window and soaked the bed in a blissful warmth. She stretched out her naked body and felt her muscles ache pleasantly. She had been thoroughly and expertly fucked last night and she felt glorious. Theo hadn't let her go, giving her orgasm after orgasm and exhausting her until she fell asleep wrapped in his arms.

Now she was alone in the bed and wondered where he'd gone. After brushing her teeth, she padded through the house, downstairs and eventually found him out on the deck, sipping coffee, an uneaten bagel in front of him.

She bent to kiss him and he pulled her onto his lap. He kissed her and she ran her hands through his hair, studying his face, the dark circles under his eyes and the strange look in his eyes. She frowned. 'What is it, Theo?'

Theo stared back at her, seeming to struggle what to say then he smiled ruefully. 'Nothing to worry about. Hey, how about we take a break? Get away from the city for a while. We both could do with that.'

Jess half-smiled but wasn't fooled by his change of demeanor. 'Okay, but why now? Haven't we got a lot of work on? What about the Freeman commission?'

'That's why I hire excellent staff,' he said lightly but she narrowed her eyes at him.

'I know you, Theo, what's going on?' Then she paled. 'Is... he... in the city? Is that why you're keen to get away?'

Theo shook his head. 'No, I promise, Jules is nowhere near here. If he steps back into the country, we'll know about it.'

She didn't entirely believe that. She knew how tricky Jules could be when he wanted, but she didn't want to argue with him. She snuggled into his chest so he couldn't see her eyes. 'Where were you thinking of going?'

'Wherever you want, beautiful.'

She kissed his neck. 'Anywhere?'

'Anywhere.'

'Mmm that's quite an offer, might take a bit of thinking... but I know where I'd like to go right now...' She slid her hands down the front of his pants and cupped his cock, grinning when she felt it respond. Theo chuckled and kissed her temple.

'I clearly did not exhaust you enough last night, you wanton hussy.'

She giggled and pressed her lips to his ear. 'You see those security guards over there by the fence?'

'Yeah, I see them,' he looked bemused. She smiled and her eyes were heavy with desire.

'Remember that time in the club, when we fucked in that booth...?'

Theo grinned, understanding. 'You are quite the exhibitionist, Miss Wood...' But his hand were sliding under her robe, and he slipped a finger inside her. 'Man, you're wet, baby.'

She drew in a shaky breath. 'I want your cock inside me, Theo.'

He wrapped his huge arms around her tiny waist and lifted her onto his rigid cock, both sighing as it sank deep into her. Theo caressed her clit, rocking her back and forth so his cock slid in and out, the friction making them both crazy. They locked eyes and when they heard the crackle of a radio, the monotone of a guard reporting back to his boss, they grinned at each other. This was such a rush, the imminent threat of discovery.

Jess nibbled at his ear. 'Come in me, Theo, I want to feel your seed inside me...' Her voice was a low whisper, but deep, gruff, the sound of it made the blood rush to his head and he did as she asked, grunting softly into her hair. Jess tensed her muscles around his cock, closing her eyes as a mellow climax shuddered through her body. They stayed connected for a few moments, reveling in their closeness and in the intimacy of their lovemaking.

·   ·   ·

UPSTAIRS THEY SHOWERED TOGETHER and as they dressed, Theo couldn't take his eyes from her delicious body, the curves of her, the way her breasts trembled as she towel-dried her hair. She grinned at him.

'Like what you see, sailor?'

'Hell yes. You didn't answer my question so let's do this... clear your mind and when I say go, name the first place you've always wanted to go to.'

She chuckled and nodded. 'Okay... ready.'

'Three... two... one... go.'

'The Maldives... oh, that was unexpected. I was going to suggest... oh, to hell with it, The Maldives, please. One of those little huts on the ocean.' She looked like an excited kid.

Theo grinned. 'You got it, beautiful.'

She hugged him, kissing him quickly. 'Think of all that private time.'

His hold on her tightened. 'We should take that box of toys you say we haven't used yet.'

'Oh, you are a genius, Theodore Storm.' She grinned then laughed as her stomach growled. 'Yep, I need food. Brunch? I could make some omelets?'

'Sounds good to me.'

When she'd disappeared downstairs, Theo sat on the edge of the bed and finally let himself drop the happy act. Not that Jess wasn't the best distraction but...Malcolm's face kept coming back to him.

The idea to go away had come to him when he'd awoken. Turning to stare at Jess's peaceful, sleeping face, he knew he wanted to wake up to that face forever, to have her look that relaxed, carefree forever. And the truth was that he wanted to run. Not from the police, he had no worries about that, but from worrying what Gachet would do next. Being a billionaire had its perks. He would tell Max and Alan to take a long vacation while they were away. He grinned wryly to himself. He knew Max would never leave the business while Theo was out of contact. When he and Jess returned then maybe he could persuade him to take a break. He owed Max. Big.

Jess called up to him and he went down to see her flipping a perfectly cooked omelet onto a plate. She looked so happy. Happier than he'd seen in a month now that he couldn't bear to ruin it. He, Max and Alan had vowed not to tell her about Malcolm but Theo had harbored doubts – he didn't want any secrets from Jess.

He just didn't want to see the look in her eye when she realized the man she loved was a murderer.

It had been two weeks now and no Malcolm. Jules had no doubt what had happened – Storm had gotten to him, and had probably killed him. Damn. This changed everything. He would have to go back to the States now, to do his own spying. He'd had it all planned: Malcolm would report on her every movement, see the weak spots in the protection that Storm had set up, and found the opportunity. Then if he could, Jules would return, kill her and Storm and then would flee down to South America. If not, Malcolm, a trained sniper, would take Jessica out with a bullet, Storm too. Quick, easy but not nearly the drawn out, agonizing death she deserved.

Now, he had to do it all himself. Fuck. Malcolm had put him in touch with some people who could get him travel documents, passports, but there was no-one he could talk to, no-one who would understand his passion for killing Jessica. Malcolm had understood.

The Parisian spring was leeching into summer and endless tourists filled the streets. Maybe it was time to go. Jules started to smile.

I'm coming for you, Jessica.

By the next day a blonde and bearded Jules – or rather Patrick Moreau according to the flawlessly produced passport – was on the way back to the States.

The flowing, delicate white dress Jess wore fell gently to the floor as Theo ran his fingers under the tiny straps and slid them down her slender arms. He cupped her full, ripe breasts as she tilted her head up for a kiss. His thumbs stroked a maddeningly erotic rhythm over her nipples as she slowly unbuttoned his shirt. The heat was tamed by a breeze from the ocean that swirled clear and blue underneath their private villa.

They had been in the Maldives less than two hours now but neither was tired from the journey. Jess had exclaimed over the beauty of the island paradise, the white sand and the crystal clear waters of the Indian Ocean. Their villa was bigger than she expected but then again, Theo would want the best and it showed. The bedroom was draped in fine white cottons and voiles, a ceiling fan keeping a decent breeze flowing through the villa. A large, private deck with an infinity pool, a little kitchen stocked with everything they could need.

Jess slid her hands under his shirt and pulled it off, her hands immediately going to his fly. She could feel his cock straining to be free, and she cupped it through his pants, feeling how hard, how hot it was, how it quivered under her touch. Theo buried his face in her neck.

'God, I want you so bad...' He slipped a hand into her panties, finding her already wet for him, slipping his finger deep inside her, caressing her clit with his thumb. Jess moaned and nearly his pants from him.

'I want to fuck in every room,' she murmured with a grin and Theo chuckled.

'You got it, beautiful, but let's start right here...' He tore her panties off and lifted her up, pressing her back against the wall of the villa. His cock nudged at her entrance and she groaned in frustration as he teased her with it. He laughed.

'Impatient girl. Jess, this holiday, we're going to do everything you've ever dreamed of and much more.'

She nipped at his ear. 'Put that cock in me now, soldier, fucking nail me to this wall. Now.'

Theo grinned. 'Whatever you say, Mistress.'

He plunged his diamond-hard cock into her soft, welcoming cunt so hard she screamed with pleasure, thrusting, slamming her back against the wall, his mouth grinding down on hers, her fingers tangled in his hair, pulling on it almost to the point of pain. They were animals, tearing, clawing, and biting at the other. Theo came quickly, unable to stop it, god she was amazing, and he felt his semen explode from him in a torrent, filling her. He rubbed her clit to bring her an orgasm then, withdrawing, quickly laid her on the bed, flat on her belly and parted her legs again. He could feel her slick with his creamy cum as he parted her butt cheeks and pushed into her ass. Jess gave a long, delirious moan as he moved in gentle but firm strokes, taking his time this time to enjoy the tightness of her, the extra friction on his prick. His hands massaged her round butt, the silky skin soft beneath his fingers. Her head was turned to the side on the pillow so he could watch her face flame with scarlet arousal, her mouth as she gasped for air, whispering his name over and over.

AFTERWARD, they lazed in the pool, watching as evening fell over the resort, candle light and flaming torches on the beach across the water. Jess rested her arms on the side of the pool and sighed happily. 'This is actual heaven,' she said and Theo smiled, kissing her temple.

'I'm glad you think so. You know that we can stay as long as you want. Forever would suit me.'

She half-smiled at him. 'I think your family and Max might object. Also your business colleagues.'

Theo shrugged. 'I could sell the business.'

Her eyebrows shot up. 'You're not serious.'

'Deadly.'

She pushed away from the side of the pool and face him, studying his eyes. 'Theo, you're being crazy. You'd get bored and that's no good for any relationship. You'd get so tired of me around all the time.'

It was his turn to look startled. 'Would never happen.'

She touched his arm. 'It's a lovely gesture but unrealistic. We need to build a life from what we have, not start over. We'd always be waiting for it to start. You have your work and when we get back, I want to start back at the Foundation full-time. We have the wedding soon too. Let's just enjoy this as the vacation we planned.'

He was quiet for a time then nodded. 'You're right.' He slipped his arms around her waist and pulled her to him, pressing his lips against her shoulder. Jess nuzzled his neck but a thread of anxiousness was spiraling through her stomach. She wasn't imagining it, the thing that had been bothering her ever since the morning they had decided to come here.

Theo was different. Changed. And it felt, despite everything he said, everything he did, like he was slipping away from her.

JULES HAD no trouble getting back into the country, the documents he held superbly and expensively forged. He stayed overnight in a city motel as he figured there was no need to draw attention to himself. The next day, he went out to Whidbey Island and rented a house two miles from Jess and Theo's home and dressing in his new persona, flannel and jeans, set out to explore the area. He found that he could walk to the perimeter of Storm's property unseen through the woods but as he neared the fence, he could see a security guard pacing around. Jules did a wide circuit of the house. One security guard? That was Storm's idea of protection? Jules was about to sneer when he realized: they weren't there. Shit. That meant he'd have to be on the island longer and every day brought him closer to discovery.

Later he drove into town to the small diner and ordered a big lunch. He was halfway through it when he heard his voice. That goddamn fag, Max. He turned halfway to see him walk in with a much older woman with silver hair. They sat immediately behind Jules, which amused him greatly, despite the risk of Max seeing him. They chatted a while of nothing much then the woman cleared her throat and spoke in a soft voice.

'You know, dear, you don't have to keep coming to the island. I can easily keep an eye on the house whilst they're away – unless,' and she chuckled, '...you're worried Theo has something he really doesn't want his mother to see.'

Max laughed. 'You are incorrigible, Amelia. What would that be?'

'Oh, I don't know, a sex dungeon?'

Max laughed loudly and Amelia joined in. 'Well, I know what you've been reading lately.' Max said. Jules heard the clink of a coffee cup being out down. 'But seriously,' Max continued, 'It's no trouble. I'd rather see things for myself, and it's a good excuse to see you.'

'Flatterer but I do like seeing you too. I don't see enough of Theo and Jess – don't get me wrong, they're always inviting me over – but I somehow feel that they'd rather be alone. They do seem wrapped up in each other, especially now, after the stabbing.'

Jules grinned into his cup of coffee. Yeah, talk more about that, you fools, if you only knew the man who stabbed your beloved Jess is right behind you.

Max shrugged. 'Understandable.'

Amelia gave a frustrated sigh. 'Max darling, be honest, do you think they're too...I don't want to use the word obsessed but...'

'No, I don't. I swear, Amelia, if you knew what being truly obsessed is... obsessed is what got Jess stabbed and nearly killed, obsessed is being raped over and over by your creep of a step-brother, obsessed is living in fear of your life for almost half your life. Theo and Jess have that kind of love that most of us are lucky to see. I had it, you had it once too.'

Amelia muttered her ascent but Jules, his fingers gripping his cup tightly, calmed himself at Max's words. Fucking bastard. What the hell did he know?

'When are they back?'

'Next week, Tuesday, I think. Jess says she wants to go back to work but we have a wedding to plan so I'm hoping to persuade her to stay home for a month or so.'

Max laughed. 'Good luck with that.'

LATER, as they left, Jules was outside waiting in his car. He watched as Amelia Storm got into her Mercedes and, leaving a reasonable distance, followed her across the island. After an hour, she pulled up to an impressive house. A man nodded to her and got into her car as Amelia ascended the stairs to the front door.

Jules watched the house for a while not knowing why he had followed the woman. She'd given him enough good information in the diner. Theo and Jess were away as he'd thought, and he would bet a million bucks that whatever Theo and his cronies had done to Malcolm, Jess didn't know about it.

Maybe it was time that she did.

There were dark clouds over the islands and at first Jess couldn't understand where they'd come from. She was standing on the deck of the villa and the breeze was cold against her bare skin, making her shiver.

'I can make you warm, baby...'

She turned at the sound of his voice, smiling but the joy turned to horror. Theo aimed a gun at her. Confusion.

'Theo? What are you doing...?'

The first bullet made a whooshing sound and smashed into her belly, right through her navel. She gasped at the pain, looking down to see blood start to pour from the wound when a second, an inch higher, hit her. 'No, no....'

Theo was laughing. 'I told you I'd make you warm, hot...' He shot her again, walking towards her. Jess wondered why she didn't fall or clutch at her wounds but she just stood there, taking one bullet after another. When Theo reached her, he pressed the cold muzzle against her skin, pulling the trigger so many time it was impossible...no gun would hold that many bullets....is this a dream? Am I dead? God, someone help me, wake me....

COLD. Something slimy passed over her skin. A fist was being jammed down her throat and she tried to cough, tried to gasp for air but the pressure in her chest, her lungs was unrelenting. She opened her eyes and saw blackness, a flicker of light but mostly dark, oily darkness. She realized what the slimy thing was, what the blackness was. Water.

She was drowning.

She struggled, tried to make her arms move, to propel her body upwards, out of the water but something seemed to be holding her down. Her mouth, her nose filled with water and now she began to panic, her lungs, her stomach filling with choking water. She pushed up desperately and managed to break the surface. The full moon was the only light in the dark night. The black spots in her eyes were back and they swept over her sight, blinding her again. She struggled, wrenched her body upwards but unconsciousness was threatening. She struggled but then one thought kept replaying itself in her mind.

Oblivion took her as, exhausted, shattered and broken, she finally stopped struggling and gave up.

SHE OPENED her eye to bright whiteness and a clean, antiseptic smell. Unfamiliar surroundings. A hospital. She moved her head and saw Theo at the window. Jess struggled into a sitting position before saying his name. He looked around, strain obvious in his eyes.

'How do you feel?' Clipped, distant.

'Theo, what am I doing here?'

Theo sat on the bed and sighed. 'You decided to go for a little midnight swim. I think you were sleepwalking, so do the docs, because I know, I know, you're not stupid enough to swim in the ocean alone at night.'

She raised her eyebrows at his harsh tone. 'Theo... of course not. Why the hell would you think that?'

His eyes were hard. 'And it wasn't... anything else?'

She was getting irritated now. 'Like what?' Then she realized and her whole body relaxed. 'God, Theo, no. It wasn't on purpose if that's what you mean.' She reached out to him but he drew away, not looking at her.

'You were just floating there. You'd given up. I thought... Jesus, Jess, I thought I'd lost you. Again.'

She slid out of bed and went to hold him, pulling his head onto her chest. 'Theo... never. I would never do that.' She tilted his head up so he could see her and tried to smile. 'Too many other people are trying to kill me, why would I do it myself? That's just poor time management.'

'Don't joke. I thought you were dead.'

'I'm sorry, I don't know what happened, I had a nightmare...'

She trailed off as the nightmare came screeching back. Theo. Shooting her. Theo. She shivered and then it was his turn to tighten his grip. 'What? What is it?'

She tried to swallow the stone that seemed lodged in her throat. 'Nothing. Stupid subconscious. Never gives me dreams about a three-some with you and Beyonce, does it?'

Theo smiled then. 'Nice to know who I can expect a threesome with.'

She nodded sagely. 'No woman would turn down Beyonce, straight or gay. It is writ.'

He laughed. "It is writ'?

She grinned and looked around the room. 'Where are we?'

'Medical centre on Male.'

Jess sighed. 'I honestly feel fine. Can we go?'

Theo hesitated. 'Maybe we should wait for the doctor.'

Jess flexed her shoulders in irritation. 'You know what, let's not. She slid out of the bed and grabbed the bag of her stuff Theo had obviously brought with him. She went into the little bathroom to dress, closing the door behind her. She couldn't figure why she was so irritated. She dressed quickly, avoiding her reflection in the mirror over the sink.

Scratch that, she did know. It was all the crap followed them everywhere. All she had done was slept-walked for Christ's sake and Theo was acting... god. She closed her eyes and drew in a deep breath. No. This was an accident. She didn't want the rest of their vacation to be tainted, like everything else, by fear, stress, a tense atmosphere.

She pulled open the door and smiled brightly at Theo. 'Ready when you are.'

Theo gazed at her for a long moment with an expression that she couldn't read them, eventually, held out his hand to her.

'Let's go home.'

JULES STOOD ON THE BRIDGE, staring down at Deception Pass, glinting with the last rays of the sun. He'd walked across the island in the hope it would alleviate some of his frustration at having to wait for Jessica to return home. His fingers, his hands, all of his limbs ached to be touching her, hurting her. He would sometimes, late at night, open his mouth as wide as it would go and scream, silently, into the darkness.

He looked down at the cold waters below. Sometimes he wanted to jump, no, no not even that that, fall, freefall into the depths, tumble. Let his limbs go weak, let the filthy water stream through his nostrils, his mouth, batter his eyes from their sockets. Dissolve. Even when he hit the bottom, to suck up the bed, bore into the earth. Disappear. So easy, so final. But then she would be left here, in the world and he could not let that happen. She would be with him soon and he would finally be at peace, bathing in her blood, watching her breathe her last breath. This time, she would not survive. And afterward, hell, he didn't care if he never escaped. He'd rather die alongside her. The thought was strangely freeing.

He flexed his hands. He needed to feel something, needed a release. Not here. He turned around and walked back to his house. The evening was falling as he changed clothes and drove down to the ferry terminal. He would spend the night in the city, find an alternative, a Jess-like victim and he would sate his thirst.

JESS WOKE up later than usual, fuzzy-headed. She got up, went into the bathroom to splash water on her face. Yesterday had been tense, strained. They'd barely spoken, retreating into their own spaces and for the first time they hadn't made love before falling asleep. She was still annoyed with him. She loathed it when he treated her like some precious little child who could not look after herself. Deep inside, she knew, and understood, why he behaved like that but it still irritated her. It was times like this when she cursed her lack of independence. She felt guilty at the thought. She shook her head and swung her legs over the side of the bed and sat there for a few minutes, rubbing the sleep from her eyes, trying to ignore a headache banging around the back of her skull. She grabbed her kimono from the bottom of the bed and wrapping it around herself, padded barefoot out of the bedroom.

She walked through the villa, peeking into each room until she found Theo, out on the deck. She stood and watched him for a while, his intense stare locked somewhere in the middle distance, his jaw flexing with tension. He wore the navy blue t-shirt she loved on him, khaki shorts. His dark short hair was damp; he must have been swimming. She walked silently behind him and ran her arms down his, kissing his temple.

'Hey handsome.'

He'd started a little when she'd touched him but now he pulled her onto his lap, smoothing his hands over her face, drawing her hair back away from it. She smiled and kissed him, felt his hands slip into her robe and onto her bare belly. His eyes, so often troubled nowadays, were softer, heavy with desire.

'You know, I kinda wish this wasn't our last day here,' he said, stroking his hands up and down her bare skin, 'I could get used to this.'

She silenced him with a kiss. Her mouth against his, her hands snaking down the front of his shorts to stroke his cock, her feather-light touch on the sensitive skin making Theo groan. She grinned and slid to her knees, taking his cock into her mouth, pushing his shorts away so she could fist her hand around the base of it, pulling gently, urging the blood to fill it as her tongue flicked around the ultra-sensitive tip. She was gratified by the sharp hiss Theo sucked through his teeth as she teased him, could taste the sharp salty tang of his pre-ejaculate on her tongue.

'Jesus, Jess...' He was breathless but she didn't relent, stroking and sucking until his cock was so ramrod hard, she felt him tangle his fingers in her hair, pulling at it as he groaned and bucked under her, his semen rushing in hot, long spurts into her welcoming mouth. She'd barely finished tonguing him when he lifted her and bent her backward over the table, knocking his coffee cup to the decking with a crash. Jess grinned up at him as he used his knee to spread her legs then rammed his cock deep into her cunt. Theo bit down on her neck, her shoulders, squeezing her breasts, biting down on the small pink nipples until she was panting and writhing beneath him.

'Tell me what you want, Jessie... tell me how you want it...'

'Hard... harder... more... fucking rip me in two, Theo.' She arched her body up and he picked her up, wrapping her legs around his waist, still impaled on his cock and carried her inside. They didn't make it to the bedroom, instead tumbling to the wooden floor.

Jess clawed and fought with him as he fucked her, both of them laughing and growling in equal measure. Plowing deep into her soft, warm wetness, Theo drove himself until he heard her cry of pain then her don't stop, don't stop.... please....

He pulled out and came on her belly, the thick white streams of cum streaking over her beautiful body. She shuddered and came as he massaged the sticky fluid into her skin, feeling her whole body vibrating with pleasure. Looking up, he saw the little box of toys they had brought with them. He caught Jess's eye and she smiled, nodded and he reached over and grabbed the box, pushing the top off.

'Hmm, what can I do you to you now, wife to be?'

Jess, her gorgeous body still undulating as she caught her breath, looked at him, a wicked smile playing around that lush, bruised mouth. 'What if we switch it up?' Without even looking, she stuck her hand into the box and pulled out the dildo - the strap-on-dildo.

Theo raised his eyebrows. 'You want to fuck me, baby girl?'

Jess grinned. 'Hell, yes. I do... get on your stomach, boy, I'm in charge now.'

'Fair's fair,' Theo said and kissed her before laying down flat on his belly, his trust in her absolute, no doubt in his mind. How many times had she trusted him to go there? It wasn't something he'd experienced with anyone else but then again, there were a lot of things he'd experienced with Jess that he never had before. He grinned and told her what he was thinking.

Jess laughed. 'You bet your sweet ass. In fact, you are betting your sweet ass.' Theo chuckled then sucked in a breath as she reached down between his legs and massaged his balls gently, pressing the tip of her middle finger deep against his perineum. 'Damn, Jessie.... before we go any further, can I persuade you to slip into that little leather harness?'

He felt her kiss his ear. 'You got it.' It took her less than thirty seconds and then he felt her weight on the back of his thighs again, her hand on his cock. She kissed the back of his neck then ran her tongue down the length of his spine to the top of his ass. He felt a warm liquid against his skin – oil, he guessed, because she moved her hands up and down his back, working his muscles. She was trying to relax him, he knew, and he leaned his head on his arms and closed his eyes, letting himself feel every sensation. Her hands worked up and down until, at last, one hand slipped into his crack, working massage oil into the deep crevice and caressing his cock and balls which pulsed and quivered under her touch. When, at last, he felt the tip of the dildo push into his anus, he was so relaxed that as she slid into him so slowly, so gently, all he felt was immense pleasure as the dildo massaged him and he felt Jess rocking gently above him, softly moaning, obviously enjoying it as much as he was.

He came with a slowly, shuddering groan, his cock, tight against the floor and his belly, pumping hard. Jess withdrew and, removing the strap-on, lay down, her belly against his back, her lips against the back of his neck. She linked her fingers with his and they lay together, closer than they'd ever felt before.

'Jessie,' he mumbled eventually,' Jessie.... you are my world, you know that.' He shifted onto his back and wound his arms around her, kissing her tenderly. She smiled down at him.

'And you are mine, Theodore Storm. Forever.' She stroked his face. 'Theo?'

'Yeah?'

'Whatever it is that's been bothering you lately... whatever it is... you know you can tell me, right?'

He gazed back at her. She knew him so well, he was stupid to thinks he wouldn't know something was up. Could he tell her about Malcolm? He looked into those lovely deep, warm eyes and couldn't bring himself to say the words.

'Jess... it's just been... overwhelming and I think I'm rocking back a little from it all. I love you so much, god, so much and I'm not saying I'd change a single thing about us...I wouldn't. But you, of all people know, it leaves scars.' He touched the scars on her belly but she grabbed his hand and kissed it.

'We'll get through this, you know. Me and you together, we can beat anything.'

'Never leave me.'

'Never. Hell, if and when I die – don't make that face – it'll be old age or illness and not some asshole who likes to slice and dice. Theo, I promise you, I'll fight to the end. And if you're really lucky, if I go first...I'll come back and ghost fuck you.' She crossed her eyes and stuck her tongue out at him and Theo started to laugh.

'You are a nutball, you know that?'

'Your nutball.'

Theo smiled and pressed his lips to hers. 'Damn right.'

HE'D COME across her in a shop Downtown She was arguing with the insolent-looking cashier. He'd helped her out. Followed her home. Arranged to bump into her. She'd been grateful, invited him in for a drink, looking at him with interest. So easy. An hour later, she had been slumped in her chair, looking at him again, this time in confusion as he removed her shirt. He knew she thought he was going to rape her, and looked down at her in disgust. Whore. He told her then, exactly what he was going to do to her, that she wasn't worthy. He wouldn't sully himself on her. She tried to move, tried to scream as he raised the knife. And then, there was only pain, resignation.

. . .

HE THREW a long swig of beer down his throat and looked around the room. It was a curious mix of the minimal and cluttered. One side of the huge room was stuffed with sofas, cushions, tables, books shoved in a jumble onto the shelves, the coffee table literature looked like it was actually read, rather than just for show. The space near the huge windows and the kitchen area, however, were sparse, clean lines. He nodded. It was a good place. She had taste. Pity.

The release Jules Gachet craved came later and later now. Glancing down, he took in skin, torn flesh. He realized he could not remember her name. He crouched down and listened carefully. No breath. No longer a presence, just a torn and twisted tangle of bloodied limbs. A pretty woman, he stared at her face, now peaceful, no longer etched with the terror he had inflicted on her. He could summon up no feeling for her, pity or otherwise. As he'd killed her, she had worn Jess's face, her screams were Jess's screams, her blood, Jess's blood. He relived the night he'd stabbed Jess, that wonderful, terrible night when he hadn't been able to complete his mission. The night that somehow, incredibly, Jessica had survived.

He stood, lit a cigarette, slumped into an old squashy armchair beside the girl's body. He imagined that in a few hours, homicide cops and crimes scenes officers, dressed head to toe in plastic moved around the room like ghosts, hoping to retrieve anything, any clue. Everything was sharper in his mind, sounds, sights, smells. The faint scent of honeysuckle pervading the air, the feel of the worn fabric of the chair through his light clothing. The girl's arm, flung above her head, the wrist curved around the chair leg, the fingers splayed, pointing accusing. He felt no guilt and yet still no release and he knew it was time

Olive skin, dark eyes.

As outside a shower streaked its way across the city, he thought only of her, his unending wait and how he would teach her, no, no teach them about loss. The longing grew stronger and stronger within him until his mouth opened, stretched wider and wider, and the rage flew from him, wrenching, twisting into a silent howl.

He almost staggered to the nearest bar, ordered a double on the rocks. His stomach was churning his excitement. He watched the people go back and forth past the windows of the bar and pitied them.

Every one of you, he wanted to scream out, every one of you will know my name.

'DARLINGS!' Amelia flew out of the house and gathered them into her arms. Theo grinned at Jess over his mother's shoulder. After traveling for nearly twenty-four hours, all either of them had talked about was getting home, going straight to bed – to sleep. Theo's mother clearly had other ideas.

'Let's look at you.' Amelia pushed them both away and looked over the critically. 'I expected you to have better tans...too busy screwing, eh?'

Jess snorted out a laugh as Theo cringed. 'Mom...god.' He glared in amusement at a giggling Jess. 'Don't encourage her.'

Jess shrugged as Amelia tucked a conspiratorial hand under her arm. 'She's right, though.'

Theo rolled his eyes as the two women cracked up and, leaving them to it, grabbed the suitcases and took them inside. Amelia and Jess followed him and greeted the two excited dogs.

Amelia made coffee and Jess and Theo dutifully sat with her while she chatted excitedly. 'Loves, I know this is not the time really, but I want to throw you an engagement party. Max agrees it would be a good thing.'

'How is Max?'

Amelia gave them a half-smile. 'He's doing better, I think. He seems.... what's the word? Fiercer. I don't know but he's rallying. About this party – '

'Mom,' She interrupted her with a hand on hers, 'We just flew halfway around the world. Can we please discuss this tomorrow?'

. . .

AFTER AMELIA LEFT, Jess and Theo, really dragging now, shared a decidedly chaste shower then fell gratefully into bed. They didn't even bother to push the two dogs off the bed where they'd snuggled in with them.

In the morning, Theo awoke, opening his eyes to see Jess's lovely face half-buried in the comforter. He brushed her lips with his, feather-light so to not wake her, but a lazy smile spread across her face. She opened those deep, warmth chocolate eyes, soft with sleep.

'Hey handsome.'

'I didn't mean to wake you.'

She made a cute noise and stretched, wriggling next to him and reaching for his cock. Theo grinned. Even half asleep, she knew how to turn him on.

'Morning breath?'

'Don't care.'

Theo pushed the grumbling dogs off the bed and covered her body with his, already rock-hard for her. He slipped a hand between her legs and stroked, feeling her dampen and swell for him. As he entered her, slowly, tenderly, he kissed her throat, felt her moan against his lips. This was one of their favorite times to make love when they were all soft and dreamy from sleep. Theo moved slowly at first as her legs wrapped around him, her limbs malleable, her eyes liquid silk as she smiled up at him, lifting her lips to his to kiss him.

After they'd come, Theo kissed her and slipped out of the bed into the shower. The jetlag was starting to hit and a headache was beginning to pound the back of his skull.

When he came out, rubbing his hair dry, Jess had obviously fallen back into a deep sleep and was sprawled diagonally across the bed. He dressed quickly and went downstairs. He grabbed a bagel from the pantry, a bottle of water from the refrigerator and went outside to the porch. The bright-white morning sun seared his eyes and he winced, sitting on the swing chair they had always had out there. He alternated gulps of water with air and felt a bit better. He thanked god it was Saturday and he could leave business to Monday. For the next two days, he wanted to settle back into a routine, hang out with

Jess and whichever family members decided to interrupt their weekend. Theo smiled to himself wryly – he knew his mom would be
back. Once she had a project in mind, there was no stopping her.
That she and Jess got along so well was something Theo treasured;
Amelia had like Kelly a lot and Kelly had been a sweet girl but she
didn't have the wicked sense of humor that his Mom and Jess shared.

'Sir?'

Theo looked up to see the head of his security team, Mike,
smiling at him.

'Welcome back, sir. Good holiday?'

Theo shook his hand.

'Wonderful, thanks. How have things been here?'

'Non-eventful, thank goodness. No sign of any intruders or snoop-
ers. I've put a report on your desk but it'll be a dull read.'

Theo smiled gratefully. 'Good, thanks, Mike.'

When Mike had gone back to his post, Theo leaned back and
closed his eyes. Jeez, this headache. He felt a wet nose pushing into
his hand. Monty or Stan? He looked down. His beloved spaniel was
pushing her head under his hand, wanting to be fussed. He picked
the wriggling dog up and settled her onto his lap. Stan trotted out of
the house and flopped down at his feet. The morning was almost
silent except for the breeze through the trees, the wash of water from
the beach at the end of the garden. Perfect he thought, ignoring the
leaden weight in his stomach. Almost perfect. He wondered if telling
Jess about Malcolm would ease that weight – then shook himself.
Why should she have to bear his guilt as well as everything else? He
could handle anything as long as he had Jess. Still, he reminded
himself to call Max and Alan later – he had a responsibility to them.

'Theo?' Jess's voice from inside the house.

'Out here.'

Her hair was wet from the shower, and in her simple white shirt
and Daisy Dukes, even as tired as she still obviously was, she looked
so gorgeous that he forgot anything else. He held out his hand and
pulled her onto his lap, burying his face in her neck, breathing in the
scent of her shampoo and soap. She smelled of home.

'I just got a text from your mom,' Jess kissed his forehead. 'She's going into town, wants me to go with her, do some wedding shopping.'

She rolled her eyes as Theo laughed. 'Good luck with that. Want Mike to drive you?'

She smiled. 'Your mom's picking me up. We'll be fine. Can you imagine going up against her? She's like a ninja.'

Theo chuckled. 'God, I love you, you absolute nut.'

She stroked his face. 'Damn. Why didn't I tell your mom to give an hour instead a half hour?'

JULES HAD BEEN BROWSING around a flea market on one of the islands when he found it, the small ornate weapon. The blade was old, dirty but salvageable, the handle metal, encrusted with amethyst and rose quartz. He'd nodded to the stall owner, watched him wrap it in growing excitement. Now, at home, he had cleaned, polished and sharpened the long thin blade. Holding it up, he bounced the light from it into his eyes. And smiled. He imagining it tearing through Jess's skin, slicing through the arteries and veins that held the precious blood inside of her.

He poured himself a cup of too strong black coffee, gulped it back, savoring the feel of the harsh taste on the back of his throat. He was impatient for all the things he had planned. He wanted them to happen right now. He thought of her, what she might be doing. Maybe fucking that bastard, all trembling honey-skinned limbs, perfect mouth, happy, alive, so far removed from him as was possible. Still belonging to someone else. He smirked: the new friendship he'd made would help with that. Theodore Storm's mamma. He'd struck up a conversation with her at the Farmer's Market, helped her with her groceries. Easy, too easy. With his hair bleached so it was almost white, his beard too and colored contacts, he looked nothing like the suave Frenchman everyone was looking for. Fools. He knew she would know him though. His Jessica.

• • •

WITH A FAMILIAR ACHE in his groin, he went and took a shower, jerking off with long, angry strokes. He forced himself to focus, made a conscious switch in his mind. He could not let anything interfere. The next days were to be his greatest achievement and for himself, well, he would receive the greatest prize for the moment the knife slid into her body, she would be his. As his orgasm shattered through him, he sobbed out his longing and his rage until he was utterly spent.

WHIDBEY ISLAND FARMER'S Market was busy, even for a Saturday morning, but Jess didn't care. The amount of fresh produce and arts and crafts meant that Jess and Amelia didn't even notice the time flying by. Amelia was impressed with Jess's knowledge of cookery and produce and in turn, Jess found herself enjoying the older woman's company. Afterward, they grabbed a bite to eat in a little bar Amelia used.

'So... a party,' She prompted Amelia then took a huge bite of her club BLT sandwich, moaning with delight as the juices from the tomato mixed with the mayonnaise, dripping from her fingers. Amelia smiled indulgently at her. She had become very fond of her future daughter-in-law, her humor, her intelligence, her love for Theo. And thank god, she actually enjoyed her food. Most of the friends Amelia dined with picked at a plate of asparagus. With Jess, Amelia could indulge once in a while.

'Yes, I thought it would be nice – and seeing as you're not letting me have my over-the-top society wedding, then I thought we could make the party a little formal, invite some names from the business world.'

Jess sighed inwardly but smiled her agreement. She knew entering Theo's society world would involve this kind of glad-handing and she couldn't complain. Up until now, he'd kept things low key. She couldn't let Amelia down.

'Of course, that sounds great.'

Amelia chuckled and Jess thought suddenly how Theo resembled her, the fine cheeks bones, the face that could go from haughtily aloof to crumpled and filled with laughter in an instant.

'Sat that like you mean it, kid. Seriously, though, you don't have to worry about anything, I'll arrange it all. All you have to do is turn up and look stunning, which shouldn't be too hard for you.'

Jess raised her eyebrows. 'Well, I don't know, I mean you can take the girl out of the trailer park...'

Amelia laughed but made a moue with her mouth. 'You do that a lot, Jessie, put yourself down. We Storms don't do that and you are one of us now.'

Jess flushed and grinned. 'You are too good to me, Amelia.'

'Mom.'

'Mom,' Jess said shyly and laughed. 'I'll have to get used to that.'

After lunch, they headed down to Amelia's favorite whole foods store and wandered leisurely through the aisles, chatting. Neither of them paid any attention to the blond man with the cap following them.

JULES GOT AS close as he could to them without her noticing. Every time Jessica half turned to speak to Amelia Storm, he would duck back into another aisle but so far, he'd been able to keep up with them. He enjoyed the secrecy, the thrill of discovery. The knife he'd bought at the flea market was in his pocket, newly sharpened. Even knowing it was there was making him hard.

'Hey, buddy.'

He turned, thankfully out of sight of the women, to face the boy who'd called him. The kid was seventeen at the most, insolently chewing gum. He stank of weed and dried spunk – typical teenager. Jules turned away but the kid grabbed his arm.

'Ain't I seen you somewhere?'

Jules smiled coolly. 'In the fresh produce aisle.'

The sarcasm didn't bother the kid who laughed as if Jules had made the funniest joke ever. As high as fuck.

'Nah, man. I mean, on the t.v.'

Fuck. 'Nope. Never been on t.v.'

'You sure?'

'Pretty sure, guy.'

The kid lost interest. 'Okay, well, sorry to bother you.'

Jules turned back, away from him – and straight into the eye-line of Amelia Storm. She smiled brightly.

'Clem! How lovely to see you again.'

'You too, Ms. Storm.' Ugh. Pretending to be subservient to this rich bitch made him want to throw up. His eyes darted quickly from side to side. Where the hell was Jessica? If she saw him now... he fingered the knife in his pocket.

No. It wasn't going to be rushed this time. 'Sorry, I can't stay and talk today, gotta run.'

He was flattered that she looked disappointed. 'Oh, I don't want to keep you then. I would have liked to introduce to my daughter-in-law, well, soon-to-be anyway but she seems to have wandered off...'

Jules tipped his cap to her and said goodbye, walking briskly towards the front of the store. As he strode down one of the empty aisles, he saw her. She turned into it, not even glancing up at him.

God. This was the first time he'd seen her since the night he'd stabbed her when she'd bled for him. He'd forgotten just how fucking beautiful she was, even in a simple sundress with no makeup. Her hair, a dark brown cloud, hung almost to her waist, was soft and messy. She took his breath away. He glanced around. No-one else was around.

A hand over her mouth, push her back against the wall, put the knife in her...

He recalled the feel of that first spurt of blood, her hot blood that had covered his hands that night. Her gasp of agony, of shock. He stared at her now. How the hell did you survive?

She looked up then and he stuck his face low into his collar, slouched down like an old man, and started to walk toward her. Everything in his body was telling him to do it, kill her now but he balled his fists up in his pocket. When he passed her, he slowed, pretending to study something on the other side of the aisle. He turned to make sure she wasn't looking at him then stepped immediately behind her. He breathed in, the fresh soapy scent of her skin filling his nostrils. Jesus, he was hard, so fucking hard, she smelled so good and...

'Jess?'

Jules turned and stalked off at the sound of Amelia Storm's voice. So close, so close... But at least, finally she was back. Jessica was home and now he could see the end of this all.

She was home.

JESS FELT FROZEN INSIDE. The guy in the store, harmless as he may have been, had creeped her out and when he'd stepped behind her, she could have sworn he was going to touch her. She heard his inhalation and her fists had balled, ready to fight. But then Amelia had called her and the guy had gone.

She felt sick. On the way home, Amelia hadn't noticed a thing but Theo, as soon as he'd seen her face had asked her what was wrong. She just shrugged, told him she had a headache and went upstairs. She sat on the edge of the bath now, nausea roiling around in her stomach. She tried to think why a lone creepy guy could make her feel this scared, this bad.

She knew, of course, she did. It was that he'd reminded her of Jules, that sneaky, stealthy way of his. Jesus. Was she that paranoid now? A wave of sickness hit her and she threw up into the toilet, retching again and again until she was dry heaving.

'WELL, goddamn Miss Wood, you're beautiful.' Amelia put on her best Southern-Belle accent as she opened the door to Jess and Theo on the night of their engagement party.

Jess had gone against all of her natural instincts and had poured herself into a long gold shift dress that clung to every curve. The color radiated against her olive skin, setting it aglow, and her tawny mane rippled down her back. Amelia hugged her proudly, her eyes shining. 'I knew you'd scrub up well, even if you are trailer trash.'

'Mom!' Theo was shocked but the two women dissolved into giggles.

'Told you that would get him,' Jess nudged her future mother-in-law and Theo sighed.

'Oh so this is how the rest of my life is going to be, my mom and my wife ganging up on me.'

'Yep, pretty much.'

'Live with it, son.' Amelia squeezed Jess's arm. 'You do look absolutely stunning, though.'

Jess's face flushed at Amelia's words. Theo's reaction had been similar, but far more physical and considering that Jess had just got redressed in five minutes flat, she was absurdly pleased with the result.

'Come on, circulate, there is a lot of people for you to meet.'

Two hours later, Jess was exhausted. All of Amelia's friends were utterly charming but she could see in their eyes, they were all curious. Not about her, but about what had happened to her. Sex and death sells she thought wryly, searching for Theo. He was nowhere to be seen and, excusing herself, she went to look for him.

Pushing open the door of the study, she heard Max's voice. She slipped inside quietly, not wanting to interrupt.

'Theo... you should tell her. You promised each other no more secrets. Jess is tougher than you think she is. God knows, hasn't she proved that? How many other people would have come back from such a violent past to be the person she is? She can handle this.'

'She shouldn't have to! Dammit, Max, how do I tell her what I've done, I can hardly believe it myself.'

'You did what you had to do, Theo.'

'Did I? I had a choice, Max.'

Max sighed then as he glanced up, he saw Jess, frozen. He paled and glanced at Theo.

'Theo...' He nodded towards Jess and Theo stood, his face a mask of distress.

'Sweetheart...' He came to her immediately but she backed away, his eyes full of pain.

'What did you do, Theo? Tell me.'

She gazed up at the man she loved and waited for him to break her heart...

9

LOVE WITH ME PART NINE

Seconds felt like hours.

Theo Storm watched Jess's face as she took in what he had told her. 'I killed Malcolm. I broke his neck. We covered it up'. Eleven words. Eleven words that could finally, inexorably rip them apart.

For the first time, he wished Jess's eyes weren't such a deep, deep brown. He couldn't read them. Jess turned to look at Max, who gave a short nod, unsmiling, obviously worried about her reaction. Jess turned back to Theo.

'I would have done the same.'

Theo had to grab the top of a chair to stop his legs collapsing with relief. Relief and astonishment. He saw Max's whole body slump. Jess reached out and put her hands on his face.

'I love you and I know you. Malcolm was a monster, as much as Jules is. He gave Jules an alibi for Josh's murder – that, or he was the one who killed him. I'm glad he's dead. I'm fucking over-the-moon he's dead. I wish you had told me sooner, is all, but I get why you didn't.'

He couldn't help himself then and pulled her into his arms and kissed her fiercely. Out of the corner of his eye, he saw Max put his hand on his heart, smile and then slip out. Jess started to giggle as the kiss went on and finally they broke apart.

'Dude, just sometimes, I do need oxygen.'

He grinned down at her, so lovely in the gold dress which clung to her soft curves, molded to her high, rounded breasts. 'Damn, Jess, how'd I get so lucky to find you?'

She answered him by pressing her body into his, cupping his cock through his trousers. At her touch, it responded immediately and then he was lifting her onto the desk, pushing the silk of her dress up to her waist as she unzipped his pants. She pulled his shirt open and teased his nipples with her tongue as he tugged her legs around his waist and plunged into her, lifting her easily into his arms. Jess shook her hair back from her face and grinned at him.

'You wanna fuck against the bookcase, big boy?'

God, he loved it when she was playful. He felt his cock thicken inside her, her soft vagina clenching around him, urging him on. He pressed her back against the books and thrust harder, finding the rhythm as they kissed, and bit, and sucked at each other. Jess dug her nails into his butt as she came, muffling her cries by burying her face in his neck. Theo came and came, his entire groin jerking hard as his semen pumped into her.

Catching their breath, they kissed tenderly but didn't speak. There was no need. Tidying themselves up, smoothing down their clothes, Jess giggling while she shoved a handful of tissue between her legs, they kissed again and nodded. 'Time to get back to the party, beautiful.'

He held the door open and as she passed, he ran a fingertip gently down her bare back. She shivered with pleasure and turned to smile at him. Something had changed in that room. A deeper connection had been forged.

Theo couldn't help but feel good about that.

THE PARTY HAD GONE on until the early hours and the sun was coming up when Theo and Jess finally made their way home. It was another hour until they made it to the bedroom and then they fell onto the bed, exhausted, exhilarated and slept, locked in each other's arms.

Jess moved through the house, ethereal and weightless in her wedding gown, her long hair tumbling to the center of her back. Every room was bathed in a soft, gold glow and she drifted through the house, calling for Theo. She wanted to see him, touch him, see his face when he saw her in the dress, and know she was his for all time...

Then he was there, at the end of the hallway, smiling at her. She moved toward him only to realize he wasn't smiling... it was a rictus, there were too many teeth and his face wasn't Theo's handsome face but a contorted parody of it.

'Come here, Jessica.' Jules. It was Jules. She tried to turn away but the Theo/Jules monster was pulling her to him, closer, closer, his hands were metal, his fingers knives and he slashed at her, spattering hot blood across the dress, cutting her open and the pain, the pain...

JESS WOKE UP, shaking. Theo slept beside her, his own face creased with stress. She moved closer to him and he stirred and locked his arms around her. She lay there, unable to sleep. A plan was forming in her mind. Something she in her life would never have dreamed she would have considered.

Killing another human being.

'HEY, MRS. STORM.'

Amelia turned and smiled. She really was a stunning woman, graceful, patrician. Her hair hung in a smooth bob around her face, a face untouched by a plastic surgeon.

'Clem! How many times have I asked you to call me Amelia? Good to see you.'

She kissed him on the cheek and Jules felt his junk tighten. Really, dude? They were standing at the edge of the harbor, watching the ferries slink in and out of the terminus. It was a clear Washington day and Mt. Rainier rose over the Evergreen state. The weather was warm as Jules and Amelia walked slowly back into town.

'I've got a lead on those champagnes you wanted for your son's wedding,' Jules mentioned casually and Amelia grasped his arm.

'Oh, you are kind. Clem, can I treat you to lunch? I'm so grateful for all your help, really, I can't believe how quickly the wedding day is coming.'

They walked down to a small family restaurant where Amelia had parked her car and they ordered a crab salad each. As they ate, Jules studied her with a smile on his face.

'So the wedding of the year is almost upon us, hey?'

Amelia rolled her eyes. 'For a wedding that the bride and groom wanted to be small and private. It's entirely my own fault. I love Jessie like a daughter and after everything they've been through, I just want it to be perfect.'

'I'm sure they'll love it, whatever you've planned. Tell me more about Jessica.' Go on, tell me how much better you know her than I do. I dare you.

Amelia smiled, a doting look on her voice, and she leaned forward conspiratorially. 'I can't tell you how right she is for Theo. I was beginning to despair that he'd ever find the right woman for him but as soon as I saw them together. She's had a very traumatic past, did you know? Her step-brother is a monster, there's no other word for it.' Her face had hardened.

Jules was suddenly aware he was clutching the table in anger. He released his hand and put it over hers. 'Tell me, Amelia. You know you can always confide in me.'

Amelia smiled and Jules could see something shut down in her. 'I don't want to talk about it all of a sudden. When I think of her tiny body in that hospital bed... would you excuse me, Clem? I need to go use the bathroom.'

After lunch, he walked her to her car. 'Thank you for lunch. Next time, my treat.'

She smiled at him. 'You're on. Look, I have to get to Theo's but I'll catch up with you soon.

'Look forward to it.' He weighted the words with meaning, and was gratified by her deep flush.'

She got into the car and tried the ignition. Nothing. He rearranged his face to register confusion. 'Pop the hood for me, Amelia.'

A minute later. 'Sorry, I can't see why it won't start. Why don't I give you a ride?'

Ten minutes later, he pulled the car into Theo's driveway.

'Thank you, Clem, you're a lifesaver. If I missed this delivery guy one more time, they'll give up and Jessie will have to get married naked.'

The familiar tug of his groin when he thought of Jessica's smooth skin, her curves. He tried to smile. 'No problem.'

The security guy gave him the once over but Jules could see that he didn't recognize him. Good. Amelia led the way into the house and Jules couldn't help the smile that spread over his face. Last time he had been here, Jess had been helpless under his knife as he stabbed her over and over. In the hallway, the wooden floorboards were still stained with her blood. Amelia must have seen him staring at the large stain.

'Jess won't let Theo replace the floorboards. She says it's a reminder of the night she survived. I don't get that, but it's not my house.'

From the set of her mouth, he could see that she disapproved. He touched her arm, stroked it gently. 'Don't think about it. She's fine now, right?'

Amelia sighed and went into the kitchen. He followed her and sat at the kitchen table while she made them coffee. He breathed in the scents of the room: wood, fresh air, newly laundered linen and faintly of Jess' gardenia perfume. He was almost giddy with glee at the thought that later, she'd be here, in this room, completely unaware he'd been here.

'Something funny?'

He shook his head. 'No, just, you know... it's a beautiful place.'

Amelia smiled, handing him a cup of coffee. 'Isn't it? Look, Clem, I'd like to invite you to the wedding, as my guest.'

He put his hands up. 'Oh, no, thank you, that's kind but I don't know anyone here, really I'd feel awkward.' And besides, there will be no wedding – not when the bride-to-be is found dead.

She argued with him for a moment but seeing his mind was set, gave up. He smiled. 'I'm sorry but how about, to make it up to you, I take you out sometime?'

Amelia's eyebrows shot up. 'Are you asking me out, Clem? Because I'm old enough to be your mother.'

He smiled his best, most perfect charming smile. 'Don't be ridiculous. And yes, I am asking you out.' The idea had come to him just then and he congratulated himself.

What could it hurt? Or rather whom?

Jess was in the middle of a humongous yawn when she suddenly noticed Theo, leaning against her office door, grinning that smile that made his eyes crinkle. Hurriedly she covered her mouth.

'Too late, I saw it.' He squatted down on the floor where she was sitting surrounded by papers. He looked through a couple. 'You know when we talked about taking it easy your first few days back?'

Jess smiled ruefully. 'I got immersed. They really did a great job whilst I was away. I'm not even sure they needed me to come back in, telling them what to do.' She looked a little tired. 'Maybe I should take a step back.'

Theo leaned over to kiss her, cup her cheek in his hand. 'You just need to get your confidence back. They were always going to run the day-to-day stuff smoothly, you put together a great team. It's the stuff that goes above and beyond that you're here for, the creative side, they what-else-can-we-do, the difference between this and other art foundations. That's your calling, Jessie.'

She shook her head, laughing. 'See? You always know exactly how to make everything alright. I love you.' She kissed him, wriggling across the floor so she could slide her arms into his jacket and pull it off. Theo gently pulled a spaghetti strap from her shoulder, kissing the silky skin there, trailing his lips across her collarbone to her throat, pressing his lips to the hollow. Jess sighed happily and Theo pushed her onto the floor, covering her body with his.

'Everyone's gone home, Jessie. It's past eight...' He used his finger to pull the strap down further, exposing her breast. His mouth covered her nipple, sucking and pulling at it as his tongue flicked and teased the small bud. She moaned softly, closing her eyes at his touch.

'That's it, Jessie,' he murmured, 'I'm in charge now, just relax.'

She felt him pull her dress down to her waist, his mouth warm and soft on her breasts, her stomach. She stroked his hair as his tongue traced a pattern, his lips against her belly, kissing her scars as his fingers pulled down her panties. God, she would never get tired of this man's mouth on her, his tongue tracing a pattern up and down her sex, flicking and lashing around her clit. He bit down gently on the swollen bud as she shivered through an orgasm, then another as he slid two fingers inside her, then a third until he was filling her, watching her face flush and change as he caressed her, his thumb stroking a maddening pattern across her clit. He kissed her deeply, feeling her breathless and excited, her mouth soft and warm, as pink as a berry, hungry for him. She tensed and sigh, coming again and again under his touch. Only after she'd come for the fifth time did he release her, allowing her to unzip his pants and reach for his cock. She wiggled down his body and he sucked in a breath as her mouth closed over the wide head, circling the sensitive tip until he was half-crazed then sucking and teasing it until it was engorged and so hard that all he could think about was getting inside of her.

Jess straddled him and he slid his hands between her legs and spread the soft peachy folds of her sex. She gripped his cock, sliding the tip up and down her wet sex before guiding him inside and lowering herself onto him, moaning as he filled her, the muscles of her cunt gripping and squeezing him as they moved. Jess thrust her hips against his and they both watched his cock slide in and out of her. She smiled down at him, her eyes sleepy with desire.

'Remember that time we fucked in that alley?'

Theo stroked her thighs. 'Of course, I do. How about the ferry?'

'The nightclub?'

They both laughed. 'God, I love you, Miss Wood,' Theo laced his fingers through hers.

'I can't wait to be your wife, Mr. Storm.'

IN ONE MOVEMENT he moved so she was beneath him, gazing up at him with adoring eyes as he trust his cock deep inside of her, feeling his climax build. Jess arched her back, pressing her belly onto his as she came, a beautiful pink blush sweeping up her golden body. There really was nothing to compare to Jessica Wood's beauty when she reached orgasm, Theo grinned to himself, as he came, his cock pumping hard spurts of come inside her. He loved that his seed would be inside her for a few days, that she would carry him with her. The fantasy he'd had months ago, about Jess pregnant with his child, came back to him. They'd never discussed kids – hell, he'd never wanted them until he'd met her. Now he couldn't think of anything better than a bunch of mini-Jess's running around.

After Jules is dead.

That thought came unbidden now but it obsessed him. What was he turning into? But he knew, he knew, Jess was thinking the same thing. There was a new fierceness to her, a resilience that he loved. She kept surprising him.

'What are you thinking, big guy? Your face has gone all... wookie.'

Theo bust out laughing. 'Wookie?'

She giggled. 'Sorry, I couldn't think of the right word.'

He was still laughing. 'So you went with Wookie?'

She snuggled deeper into his arms. 'Tell me.'

'I was thinking that I would anything to keep you safe. Forever safe, not just right now safe. Safe.'

'Wookie Safe.'

He chuckled. 'Wookie Safe.'

She kissed his jaw. 'I trust you completely, Theo. I trust in you, in us. Just know I'm in this too. I would do anything to keep you safe. Wookie safe.'

He looked down at her lovely face, so earnest, so strong. 'Always.'

'Always.'

AMELIA HAD TOLD the security guard that 'Clem' would be going in out of the property to deliver the wine and champagne for the wedding and to expect him. She couldn't have made it easier for him. The mini-cameras and microphones had been in their bedroom for good forty-eight hours now. Trouble was... Theo and Jessica hadn't been. He'd taken Amelia to lunch earlier and he discovered that they were away at a conference until tomorrow night.

Patience. Patience. This is the long game. But he was getting antsy. He needed blood on his hands.

THE GIRL HAD GIVEN the tiniest squeak before his hand went over her mouth. He dragged her into the trees, away from the tourist trails of the Gazzam Lake Preserve on Bainbridge Island. There were signs everywhere telling people not come here at night. Clearly these kids took no notice. He'd watched her separate from her friends, lag behind them as she checked her phone. Her black hair swung to her shoulders, her face sweet and plump. She was young, this one. She reminded him of the girl at the private school he'd been sent away to. Hannah. His first. He smiled at the memory. She'd complained about him to the faculty, asked them to make him stay away. He had stayed away, respected her wishes. Right up to the moment that he'd plunged his knife into her.

'Please don't..... don't...'

The girl he'd taken had now fainted. He pushed up her shirt and waited. She stirred and opened her eyes. She looked at the knife in terror, disbelief. His hand was still clamped on her face and she shook her head wildly to free her mouth, to scream, to beg him.

Jessica hadn't begged. He wanted her to plead with him to spare her. He needed her to do that.

Hannah had begged him just as he had shown her the blade and smiled tenderly at her.

And then she, like this girl, had bled for him.

MAX WAS WAITING for them in Jess's office as they arrived back, hand-in-hand, in the Seattle office. He hugged them both and shut the door behind them, chatting easily about their conference. He grinned at Jess.

'You, lady, are a star.'

She looked at Theo, who was equally confused. Max handed her a magazine, one of the top glossies. She saw her name on the cover and looked up in amazement. Max nodded.

'They've done a feature. A good one, Jess, before you make that face.'

'But I didn't give an interview or even have pictures taken...'

He took the magazine back and flipped to the centrefold. He held it up. The full page photo of Jess was of her laughing with Theo at some event they'd attended; the smaller photo was taken from her previous life at the college, working with Gerry. The headline read 'Fighting Back: The woman who tamed Theo Storm and survived a psychopath'

Jess took the magazine from Max and read the article, Theo leaning over her shoulder to read it. It was a puff-piece but a well-written one and very positive about Jess and the Stormfront Foundation. Still, Jess looked uncomfortable and Max leaned forward.

'I know you don't like this sort of thing, Jess, but in this case, I think it's a good thing. Your name is out there anyway, it has been since you and Theo met and with the attempted murder...it's time you controlled the narrative. You're the head of one of the largest arts foundations in the world. Yeah, okay, some are going to say it's because of Theo but no-one can argue you haven't made it a success.

If it hadn't been for the… well, your leave of absence, then we would be even bigger. This time next year, under your direction, we will be.'

Max's words brought tears to her eyes and, embarrassed, she looked at Theo who nodded. He moved to sit next to her, picked up her hand. 'Max's right. And from a security point of view, your visibility will make it even hard for anyone who wishes you harm to get near you.'

Jess nodded slowly. 'Okay. Okay then, well, what…?'

'We've been getting requests, interviews – print media and t.v., photoshoots.'

'Oh god.'

Both Theo and Max chuckled at her expression. 'Listen, my idea is this. A press junket. One big t.v. interview. One photo shoot and interview with one top magazine. That's it.'

Jess sighed. 'All they want to know will be how it felt to be stabbed by my rapey step-brother.'

Theo nodded. 'Because that's all they know. You give them a glimpse of you, Jess Wood, I promise it'll change the story.'

'I feel like you're both biased. I'm not that interesting.'

She couldn't help but giggle at the synchronized eye-rolling of the two men. 'Fine, fine, but you have to help me prepare.'

Max grinned and Theo kissed her cheek. 'I think a charity event would be appropriate to make the most of the publicity.'

'Now you're talking.' Jess leaned into Theo's big body. 'You sure the exposure will be okay? Security wise?'

Theo slid his arms around her waist and kissed her temple. 'Wookie safe, I promise.'

Max looked askance at them and Jess grinned. 'Long story.'

Max was collecting up his papers. 'Okay, I'll go start the ball rolling. See you two later.' He headed for the door then stopped, and turned back. 'And by the way, stop screwing in your office. You're corrupting the security staff.'

With a wide grin, he waved and disappeared while Jess buried her head in her hands and Theo started laughing. 'So much for your latent exhibitionism. To be fair, the security team are probably all in love with you anyways.' He pulled her, still blushing furiously, to her feet and kissed her softly.

She rubbed the tip of her nose against his. 'You're presuming they're straight, Mr. Storm, they could just as easy be enjoying your perfect body.' She pulled his shirt out of his pants and ran her hands underneath it. Theo grinned, his eyes crinkling at the corner, obviously enjoying the feel of her hands on his chest.

'I'm not sure this is quite what Max meant, but I'm okay with it,' he said, then pressed his lips against hers. She kissed him back then pulled away, closing his office door and locking it.

'Technically,' she said with a grin, 'This is my office and he didn't say anything about not screwing in here.' She closed the blinds, then in one easy fluid movement, peeled her dress off, over her head, shaking out her long dark hair. The dark red burgundy underwear she wore was glorious against her honey-colored skin.

Theo was at her side in two long strides, scooping her up into his arms and laying her on the desk. He freed his already ramrod hard cock as she wriggled out of her panties and reached for him. He hitched her legs around his waist and thrust into her hard as she gasped. She was already so wet for him that they moved together easily and he held her hands above her head as he fucked her, urged on her cries of pleasure. It was a quick, hard fuck and soon they were coming, and laughing and kissing, dressing quickly as they heard other people moving around in the hallway outside. Theo kissed her deeply then disappeared to his own office.

Jess sat at her desk, catching her breath, grinning to herself. She opened her laptop and logged onto her email system, glancing through the subject lines to see if anything was urgent. She might have missed it if she hadn't accidently clicked on the spam email above it. She deleted the spam and the next email showed up automatically. Her heart froze.

You look so beautiful when he's fucking you. Make the most of the time you have left, Jessica.

I'm coming for you.

. . .

THEY WERE BACK. Jules grinned to himself as he watched the footage taken from their bedroom. He wasn't disappointed, they screwed each other long into the night – not that he paid any attention to Theo Storm. All his attention was on Jessica as she fucked and was fucked, her beautiful, golden body all fluid limbs and soft curves. The camera he had installed was high definition and he enjoyed the fact he could still the see the vivid scars on her belly, the marks of his weapon. I did that. He closed his eyes, reliving the feeling of tearing through that tender flesh.

It was the way they were with each other after they'd made love that got him. Angered him. They were tender, intimate, fun-loving, best friends. Julien Gachet hadn't had any friends to share that kind of closeness with - certainly not women. To him, they were just something to fuck. But not Jessica. He found himself enraged by the obvious closeness, the trust between Jessica and Theo Storm. Why couldn't that have been him?

Because you raped and terrorized her. All that mattered to you was possession.

He shook himself. Jessica was his, despite what he could see was between her and Storm. She would die by his, Jules' hand, and soon. She would never become Mrs. Storm, he was determined.

He shut off the video and sat back in his chair. Going incognito was frustrating; he wanted Jessica to feel that fear of him every day, be cowed and cornered by him. To live in terror. Happiness ruined. He smiled to himself. He would have a little fun. Jules Gachet may not be a good businessman but he did know about computers.

Time to let Jessica know he was still waiting, still watching. Let he know he was still coming to kill her.

Amelia Storm looked over her glasses at her future daughter-in-law and frowned. Jess was quiet, staring blankly at the menu of the seafood place Amelia had chosen for lunch. Amelia could tell she was zoned out, her dark eyes sad and tired. The waiter arrived to take their order and Amelia put her hand over Jess' and the younger woman started then smiled ruefully.

'Sorry, I'm Ms. Space-cakes today.' Jess shifted in her chair and blinked. 'I'll just have a club sandwich, I think, please.'

Amelia ordered the same and the waiter, casting an admitting glance in Jess's direction, disappeared.

'What's up, Jessie?' Amelia kept her tone light, knowing that if something was worrying Jess, then it probably had to do with her asshole of a step-brother. Jess sighed and rubbed her eyes.

'Jules. He's been sending me messages. Threats. Nothing I haven't heard before but, stupidly, I was beginning to think he'd made his escape and was staying away. God, I'm so stupid.'

Her whole body slumped. Amelia studied her. 'Have you told Theo?'

Jess nodded. 'We have no secrets, not anymore. He's mad, of course, but Jules used an untraceable I.P. address to send the emails so...'

Amelia sipped her water. 'Have you ever talked about the night you were stabbed? To anyone? Theo, or a psychologist?'

Jess shook her head. 'No. I thought it would be better not to. I don't want Theo to see me like that, broken and dying. I mean, I know he found me but I want him to focus on the fact I survived. And no, I'm afraid I've gone for the head-in-the-sand method of coping.'

Amelia nodded. 'Understandable but I wonder, if you talked about it, if you named it, it would become less of a terror for you. You could talk to me, you know that.'

Jess chewed on her lip. 'Possibly. But would I say? Jules stabbed me, it was painful and terrifying and I thought I was dead. He was brutal, merciless. All I could do was lay there and take it, I was so concussed from the mirror hitting me. He used a piece of the mirror to stab me, I assume, because he knew it would be more painful.... see, that,' she broke off and pointed at Amelia's face, which had paled and turned green so sickened was she, 'That right there is why I don't talk about it, Amelia. It just horrible and sickening and it won't ever leave me. It might even happen again and I...'

'Stop. Stop.' Amelia held her hands up. 'It will not happen again,

Jessie. I won't permit it. Nor Theo nor any of us. You are loved, you are protected.' She cut her eyes at the huge bodyguard sitting a few chairs away. 'If he steps foot on the island, or even in Seattle, we will know.'

The waiter brought their food then and they thanked him, the strain in both of their voices obviously. They ate in silence for a time then Jess put her sandwich down.

'I'm sorry, Amelia, I shouldn't have told you all of that.'

'I think you needed to. I think you've been keeping it all in for too long to protect the rest of us. You are my daughter, Jess, and I love you. Let me carry some of the weight.'

Jess had tears in her eyes and she dashed them away impatiently. 'I love you too. And I'd love to change the subject now. What's happening with you?'

Amelia smiled. 'I think I'm seeing someone.'

Jess gaped at her. 'What? You kept that quiet. Who is it?'

Amelia grinned her wicked smile. 'He's a younger man. Yes, I'm a cougar or whatever they call it.'

Jess looked impressed, grinning at her friend. 'Have you...'

'Jessica Wood, you are a nymphomaniac. No, we haven't, we're just dating for now.'

'Will he be your plus one?'

'To the wedding?'

'No to the circus. Of course to the wedding.'

She rolled her eyes at Jess's wide grin. 'You are a pain in the butt, girl. I don't know. I mean, I enjoy Clem's company but...'

'His name is Clem?' There was a catch in Jess's voice and Amelia's eyebrows shot up.

'Problem?'

Jess shook her head. 'Sorry, it's just, it reminded me, Clement is Jules' middle name.'

Amelia patted her hand. 'And about a million other men's first name. Anyway, Clem is a blue-eyed blonde.'

'Does he live on the island?'

Amelia nodded. 'I actually ran into him a few weeks ago, the day we went to the farmer's market. I had hoped to introduce you but he said he had to go.'

'Next time.'

AMELIA DROPPED Jess off at home and she walked through the house, looking for Theo. He was in the garden playing with the dogs. Jess stood at the French windows watching them, smiling. Dressed in a simple vintage tee and jeans, Theo looked like a catalog model but acted like a kid, teasing the two barking dogs, throwing their toys for them to fetch.

Oh, you are my love, she thought, watching his athletic body as he twisted and ran with the animals. He looked up and saw her, and the biggest smile stretched across his face, it made her weak. He jogged over to her and kissed her hello.

'So much for spending the morning working,' she grinned at him. He shrugged good-naturedly.

'What's the use of being the big boss unless you can blow off work once in a while?'

He followed her inside, watched as she grabbed a pitcher of cold lemonade from the chiller. She smiled at him, pulling an errant leaf from his hair.

'Big kid. Talking of which, your mom has a new boyfriend.'

Theo nodded. 'She told me.'

'And you didn't mention him?'

Theo shrugged, pulling her to him. 'Seen it all before. I wouldn't say my mom's mercenary about her love life but she's not interested in candy and flowers. Very few people make the cut after the third date.'

'She seems pretty keen. Even mentioned double dating.'

He rolled his eyes. 'God, please no.' Jess laughed.

'I thinks she was kidding. Anyway...'

'Anyway?'

She slipped her arms around his waist and relaxed against his hard body. 'I'm actually really tired.'

'You sick?' His hand went automatically to her forehead but she shook her head.

'Nope, just tired. I think everything is catching up with me.'

He stroked his big hands down her back. 'Wanna go nap?'

Upstairs, she changed into her sweats and curled up on the bed. It wasn't more than a few minutes later when Theo and the dogs were snuggled up with her and she smiled to herself. *This right here is all that matters. Their family.*

She fell asleep smiling but the nightmares still returned. Ever since the messages had started to arrive, she'd had at least one a week and it was always the same.

You look so beautiful when he's fucking you.

Jules forcing his way into her bed, into her body.

Make the most of the time you have left, Jessica.

Knives. Cutting. Hurting. Killing.

I'm going to kill you, baby girl.

Blood. So much blood.

I'm going to stab you until the light in your eyes goes out. You won't survive the next time, Jessica.

I'm coming for you.

She'd learned how to wake herself from these nightmares without the screaming, without scaring Theo. Stan whimpered a little as she slid quietly out of bed and padded quickly to the bathroom down the hallway.

She just about made it before she threw up.

Sunday morning, Max came over from the mainland. Since Josh's death, he'd been more or less a homebody but seeing Theo, Jess and Amelia more than made up for it. He and Theo – already like brothers – had grown even closer and he loved Jess like a sister. There was not one part of him that blamed either Theo or Jess for what had happened – lord knows they'd been through enough themselves.

But he missed Josh. He missed the fun, the love, the sex. There had been no doubt in his mind that he and Josh would grow old together. None. And now...

Amelia prodded him. 'Hey, you still with me? I need you to decide some of this. Which champagne?'

They were at a little store which sold artisanal wines and champagnes. He looked over what Amelia was holding out to him.

'Amelia, how do I know? I know nothing about champagne.'

'Sacrilege.' The owner of the deep, resonant voice stepped out of the backroom. Tall, broad and with a wide gap-toothed grin, he greeted Amelia like an old friend. Amelia turned to Max.

'Max, this is my good friend, Seth. Seth, this is Max. He's single, and handsome and knows nothing about champagne. I have to go grab something from another store. I'll be back in ten.'

And just like that, she was gone. Max blinked at Seth. 'Did that just happen?'

Seth laughed, a deep rumble from the center of his big chest. 'I find, with Amelia, the best thing to do is just go with it.'

Max looked at this huge lumberjack of a man and a slow smile spread across his face. He was silent for a long moment then said. 'You know what? I think you're right.'

He saw Seth's shoulders slump with relief and realized he was just as nervous as Max – even if he had been in it with Amelia. Seth nodded.

'Good. So... you really know nothing about champagne?'

IT WAS PARANOIA. Plain, simple paranoia. She was at home, safe, guarded, enclosed. And yet she felt watched, observed. Hunted.

Jess reasoned with herself. Yeah, okay, Jules was still threatening her life but all the emails had gone to her work email, Theo's private security team and the detective had reported no sightings in Seattle. You're wigging, girl.

But the fatigue she was experiencing wasn't helping. She had no idea where it had come from and now, feeling too emotional, the paranoia was really starting to get to her. There was something else bugging her and it was Amelia. Well, not Amelia, but her new paramour. Clem. Amelia had tried, twice now, to arrange a double date but Clem had canceled both times, pleading work. Clem... Clement... Julien Clement Gachet... Oh wow, you really need to get out, girl.

She went to find Mike, Theo's head of security. She liked the man, he was no nonsense and commit to his role but he also had a great sense of humor. They had long chats about his wife and kids before and Jess counted on him as a friend.

'Hey Mikey,' she smiled at him now. 'Do you have some time, I could really do with going into town, getting some air?'

'Sure thing.'

She drove them into the town, parked next to the bookstore and was about to get out when she saw Amelia on the far side of the street, talking to a blonde man with a cap pulled low over his eyes.

Jess's skin prickled and itched. The guy was the same creep that had made her feel so uncomfortable in the store all those weeks ago. She tried to reason with herself: maybe he'd been about to say hello and was shy. Then why did he walk off when Amelia had called you?

It wasn't just that: his build, the shape of his body, the way he stood. He was dressed like a good old boy but that posture was too perfect, too studied.

'Jess?'

She'd forgotten that Mike was beside her in the car. She turned to him. 'Sorry, I was miles away.'

Mike nodded to Amelia. 'You want to go say hello?'

Jess looked across the street again, saw Amelia kiss the guy on the mouth. She looked so happy. Just go over, introduce yourself, put your fears to rest. It's not Jules, of course, it isn't. Amelia had seen photos of Jules, hell, the whole of America had. She shook her head.

'No, I think she's busy. I just want to go grab a book or two then go home. That okay?'

She could tell Mike didn't believe her. His eyes narrowed slightly, studying her, searching for anything he could help her with. She gave him a wan smile.

'Everything's cool, Mike, I'm just not feeling myself lately.'

Mike discreetly checked out the bookstore before nodding that it was safe. Jess got out of the car and went in. She felt a bit embarrassed at the fuss but no one in the bookstore seemed to care. They chatted with her, friendly and knowledgeable about the books she wanted. She wandered down the aisles, breathing in the smell of books and a calm settled over her. She was being paranoid.

She was nose-deep in an art history book when it happened. The feeling. She was being watched. She looked up in time to see the retreating figure of a man disappearing around the corner of the aisle. The cap he was wearing, she recognized immediately. She threw the book down and rushed after the guy.

'Hey... wait!'

But he was heading out of the door. She rushed after him, down the street.

'Hey! Clem!' She was screeching now but she didn't care about the stares people on the street were giving her. She had to know. Now.

'Clem' didn't turn at her call, just headed around the corner. Jess cursed to herself and anger roiled through her. 'Hey! Jules! Come and get me, you cowardly son-of-a-bitch.'

She was almost running when two strong arms curled around her. She struggled furiously.

'Jess! Calm down. Calm. Down.' Mike's arms were too strong and she gave up and slumped. Mike wrangled her back to the car and locked the doors.

'What the hell do you think you were doing? You never run off like that, I just.... god.' Mike had never raised his voice to her before and Jess suddenly came down from her frenzy and stared at him, ashamed, humbled. His face was red but his eyes were scared. The adrenaline left her body and then tears started to drop down her cheeks.

'Oh god, Mike, I'm so sorry... I just got it into my head that.... Jesus, Mike, I don't know what's happening to me, I'm so sorry....'

And she began to sob in earnest. Mike patted her hand awkwardly. When the sobs turned to gasps and sniffs, he made her look at him.

'Given everything you've gone through,' he started, his voice calm, reasonable,' It wouldn't be a surprise if you rocked back a little. Hell, a lot. No-one should ever have to go through what you did and god knows, Mr. Storm, his mother, me, we are all here for you, Jess. But look, I think you should talk to someone. A professional.' He sighed. 'I'm sorry if I'm overstepping but I think sometimes it helps to hear it from someone outside your family. Did you really think that guy was Jules?'

Jess was sucking in great lungfuls of breath. 'I don't know, Mike. It's like I'm losing all reason.' She wiped her eyes with the back of her hand. 'You're right, though. I should see someone.'

Mike was quiet for a moment. 'You want me to tell Mr. Storm about this?'

Jess shook her head. 'No, but I will. We promised no secrets.'

AT HOME, Jess called her doctor and made an appointment. Her brain felt like it was on a spin cycle, so much happening in such a short time. Her stomach roiled and the pain in her chest became an overwhelming, searing sadness.

Her cell phone beeped. A text.

I miss you. I love you. I'll be home soon. T x.

SHE WANTED TO FEEL SOOTHED, feel loved but she just felt cold and sick. She went around the house, locking all the doors and windows. She made some tea and took it to bed with her, locking her bedroom door. Blockade. Her whole body ached from tension but she felt hollow. She sat on the edge of the bed, numb. Should she report the incident to the police? What would she say? Amelia looked so happy.

Embarrassment flooded through as she realized that people on the island had witnessed her breakdown, would be talking about the crazy lady. Was that all her life would be remembered for? The lady who got stabbed and went crazy?

But Jules was still out there. He still wanted to kill her, and she knew, he wouldn't care if it was the last thing he did. She read the message from Theo again, trying to feel something but then she turned her phone off, put it in the drawer of the nightstand. She went over to the window, checked it was locked. When she got into bed, fully dressed, she slid her hand under the pillow, felt the cold, reassuring presence of the knife she had brought up from the kitchen. As soon as she turned out the light, the tears came and she sobbed until, exhausted, she fell asleep.

'She's different.' Theo's handsome face was wan, dark circles under his eyes. 'I really think she might be sick.'

He was sitting with Max in the bar down the street from the Stormfront building. It was late afternoon and Seattle was having a pretty comprehensive monsoon. Theo watched the rain lash against the windows of the bar. Jess was at her doctor's appointment and Theo tried not to feel hurt when she told him she needed to go alone. She had told him about the breakdown and he had seen the raw pain in her eyes. He wanted to try to reach her but she'd told him firmly that this was something she needed to do herself.

Max looked at him in sympathy. Theo made a frustrated sound. 'The thing is... what if she isn't paranoid? What if Jules is on the island, biding his time, waiting for that one second when she's not protected? She could be taken from me in a heartbeat and... Jesus, I'm sorry.'

He looked appalled but Max shook his head. 'It's okay. I understand that it's the part about having to live knowing the person you love could be killed any moment. Josh was a total shock. No-one expected it. In your situation, you're living with the fact this madman wants to murder Jess and is out there somewhere. I don't know how either of you live like that.'

Theo felt his body slump, both terrified and comforted by Max's words. 'It's hell. It's actual hell. Maybe it's payback from the universe for getting to love someone as amazing as Jess. In that case, I wouldn't change a thing except I wish it was me taking the physical brunt of it all. How...' His voice broke and he looked away from his friend. 'How could anyone do that to her? He ripped her apart, Max.'

Max put an arm around his shoulders. 'Maybe you should go get some help too.'

Theo shook his head. 'All I need is Jess. And you. And my mom, but don't tell her that.'

Max smirked. 'That'll cost you. But seriously, dude, anytime, you know that. We're doing everything we can to protect her. Did she really think your mom's new boyfriend was Jules?'

'She says not now. She thinks she was being paranoid.'

'Couldn't hurt to check it out.'

'Nope but then we don't want to upset my mom either. That's what Jess is worried about.'

Theo signaled for more drinks then looked at his friend, a wan smile on his face. 'Give me some good news, dude.'

He was surprised to see Max color, a shy smile on his face. 'I have a date.'

That floored Theo and a broad smile crossed his face. 'Dude... that's so cool. Where'd you meet him?'

Max colored some more then gave it up. 'Your mom introduced us.'

A beat then they busted up. 'Dude, god, I'm never letting you forget that my mom gets your dates for you, never.'

Ten minutes later, in the car, Theo was still laughing. God, it felt good to just laugh. He swung the car into the parking lot of the doctor's office. At the reception, the receptionist told him that Ms. Wood was still in with the doctor.

'She shouldn't be too long, have a seat.' She was beaming,

swinging from left to right on her chair, her eyes shining hopefully at him.

Theo nodded, gave her a tight smile and dropped into one of the overstuffed chairs. He picked up one of the glossy magazines, the gossipy kind who pander to the celebrities. In the 'Sightings' section, there was a picture of him and Jess, leaving a restaurant a month previously. God, look at her, he thought, so freaking beautiful....and she's mine. You're a lucky s.o.b., Storm. Jess was smiling at him in the picture, her long hair tucked into a messy bun at the nape of her neck, the dark red dress she was wearing playing up the red on her lips. He smiled down at the picture. How he'd love to see that smile again. He looked up as the doctor's office door opened and Jess came out. She looked tired – exhausted – and when she gave him a wan smile, his chest began to tighten with tension. Jess thanked the doctor then followed Theo out to the car. He waited and she put her hand on his, linked her fingers but didn't say anything.

Finally, he couldn't bear the tension. 'What did he say, Jess? Did he prescribe you something, arrange some counseling?'

She shook her head and in her eyes, there was some emotion he couldn't understand.

'No,' she said, her voice cracking, 'No, no, he didn't prescribe me anything. He said he couldn't risk it, Theo. Because he told me that I'm pregnant...'

10

FOREVER WITH ME PART TEN

T he woman in the exquisite designer suit leaned over and patted Jess's hand kindly. 'Don't worry, Jess, this will be easy.

Jess tried to smile at her, this legendary newswoman who was interviewing her and Theo to tell their story when she didn't know if there was any future. They'd barely spoken since that day. The day she'd told him she was pregnant.

He'd turned to her with joy and delight in his eyes only for the happiness to fade when he saw her cold face.

'You don't want it,' he stated in a dead, flat voice.

'I can't want it,' she'd replied, 'Not now. Not like this.'

His eyes had grown distant, cold. 'You're giving up. You promised me you wouldn't. You promised me, Jess.'

And a chasm had ripped between them.

At dinner the following night, the distance between them felt like a dead weight. Amelia looked between them, her serene face creased with worry. Eventually, the weight of claustrophobia bearing down on her, Jess escaped to the kitchen, dragging long breaths into her tight chest. She didn't hear Theo enter the kitchen behind her and as he slid his hands around her waist, she yelped in alarm and skittered away from him. She'd never forget the hurt in his eyes.

'I came to see if you were okay.' That dead voice again. 'I'll leave you alone.'

She reached out after him as he turned. 'No, wait...I...' But he stalked out.

SHE LOOKED AT THEO NOW, so still, so silent and upright beside her. He turned, aware of her scrutiny, and for a second, his green eyes were cold, accusing. Then his mouth hitched up a little and his eyes softened. He winked at her and Jess felt his hand cover hers. He leaned in and kissed her cheek.

'I love you,' he murmured, burying his face in her hair for a second. Jess felt tears prick her eyes.

'I love you, so much,' she whispered back and felt his fingers lace between hers, squeeze them. He stroked a finger down her face.

'Everything's going to be okay, Jessie, I promise.'

The floor manager called for silence then and Jess took a deep breath in. As the interviewer – Diane – began her introduction, Jess straightened her back as Diane introduced them. Theo's words gave her strength, gave her hope that it would be okay. She pressed a hand briefly to her belly, where their child still grew.

Because Jess desperately wanted this child – desperately. She just couldn't live with it being murdered along with her. She glanced back at Theo's handsome face. *Maybe you should tell him that. I will*, she decided, *after, when we are home, when all this was over.* As Diane asked her first question, Jess started to smile.

Max glanced at his watch and wondered for the millionth time how Theo and Jess were getting on. Seth rolled his eyes and handed him a champagne flute. 'Try this one.' They were sitting on the porch out the back of Seth's store. It was late afternoon, a sultry day, and too hot to sit inside. Seth listened out for the store's doorbell and customers but it had been quiet. The porch overlooked the Sound, and a cool breeze picked up from it, cooling hot skin.

'You trying to get me drunk?'

'Obviously. That and educate you, you philistine. Taste.'

Max grinned. He'd been dating Seth now for a few weeks and he knew he was falling for him. The big man, taller even than Theo, was a bundle of fun to be with, erudite, kind and made Max feel safe. Max tried not to compare him to Josh but both men shared the same easy-going nature coupled with a quiet strength. But whereas Josh had been model-handsome, Seth was a man of the land, a man who built houses before going into fine wines. He had Max his dream of one day owning a vineyard, building a ranch-style home for himself, his dogs and, if he wanted, Max. Max thought it sounded divine and told him so. Seth admitted he could see them both there but was worried about scaring Max off, maybe it was too soon to talk about that.

But Max wasn't scared. For the second time in his life, he knew it was right. 'I didn't think it was possible to find two great loves in one lifetime,' he'd told Seth simply and Seth had kissed him until both their heads spun.

He thought about that now and sighed. Seth nudged him.

'What are you thinking?'

'That I'm a lucky s.o.b. That I can love again after losing Josh. I didn't think that was possible. But here you are.' He grinned at Seth, who chuckled.

'Damn straight. But why the sigh?'

Max shifted in his chair. 'I am lucky... but if Theo lost Jess... he'd never even try to find love again. If Jules kills her, Theo would feel dead as well. I know him.'

Seth watched him carefully. 'Then we better make sure nothing happens to her. There's an army around her now, Max, she's not that scared little girl anymore.'

Max had told Seth everything, and when Seth had met Jess for the first time, he gathered her in a hug that conveyed more than friendship, it was a promise. Max had fallen in love with him at that moment. With one gesture, Seth had made himself family. He reached over to grab Seth's hand.

'I love you, big guy.'

Seth grinned shyly. 'Right back at cha.'

Max leaned back in his chair, closing his eyes, soaking up the late afternoon sun. Happiness. He'd missed it.

The store's doorbell rang and Seth levered himself out of his chair with a sigh. 'Business calls.'

A minute later, Max followed him into the building to use the bathroom. Washing his hands, he could hear Seth talking to a customer. Something about the man's voice seemed strangely familiar and Max frowned, trying to place it. He walked into the store just as the man, a tall blonde-haired guy, was walking out. Seth was writing something down and Max, trying to be nonchalant, peered over his shoulder. His eyebrows shot up.

'Order for the Storm/Wedding? Who was that guy?'

Seth grinned. 'Amelia's boyfriend, Clem. He's arranging the pickup for the wedding. Not long now, huh?'

Not long at all – two weeks and Theo and Jess would be married. Max couldn't shake the feeling. 'So who is this guy? Jess was pretty freaked out by him.'

'Is she okay?'

'She says it was just a panic attack.'

Seth studied him. 'You're not sure.'

Max scrubbed his hands over his face. 'I don't know. His voice sounded familiar is all.' He glanced at the invoice Seth was filling out. 'That his address?'

Seth made a face at him. 'You shouldn't be seeing that but yes. Why?' He looked at Max, frowning. 'You're not thinking of going over there?'

Max shook his head. 'Oh no. Just wondered how long he's been on the island.'

'Now you're sounding paranoid.'

Max sighed. 'Yeah I know, but it couldn't hurt to confirm or deny he's not who he says he is. Just to be on the safe side.'

Seth rolled his eyes. 'Look, next time he comes in, I'll call you.'

Sensing Seth wasn't happy about this line of thinking, Max agreed. But inside her was planning – if Seth wouldn't condone his snooping, he knew someone who would. The one person who had the most reason to make sure Amelia's boyfriend wasn't the man who was trying to kill Jess.

Jess herself.

THEO SLID a hand over Jess's belly as they were driven away from the television studio. She smiled at his dancing eyes, his obvious joy. It had been a complete spur of the moment thing: Diane, the interviewer, had been fair and persuasive, but her journalistic instincts had made for some uncomfortable questions. It was when she had asked Theo what his dream was and he'd replied.

'Me and Jess. The two of us, together, forever.'

It just seemed the right, the true thing to add... 'The three of us. Theo and I and our child.'

Theo had been stunned then his smile was breath-taking and she knew she'd done the right thing. Diane had congratulated them effusively and it was all Theo could do to stay in his seat and not take Jess in his arms. She could see his body relaxing and smiled at him. 'I love you,' she mouthed at him, not caring if the camera saw her.

Now, as Theo wrapped his arms around her, she leaned into him. 'I'm sorry I put you through the last few days,' she said, 'I really was scared. But today, I just realized... I'll never put the little bean in danger. I won't permit it. This is our family.'

Theo kissed her, his mouth rough on hers. 'Miss Wood, when we get home, I'm going to strip every last piece of clothing from your gorgeous body and fuck you all night long.'

She laughed, tangling her fingers in his short hair. 'Why wait until we get home? That's what a privacy screen is for.'

DEFTLY, she straddled him, rubbing her hand between his legs, feeling his cock stiffen against the movement of her fingers. Theo sighed happily as he unbuttoned her dress, scooping her plump breasts into his hands, taking her nipples in turn and sucking on them, drawing the tiny bud as it hardened. Theo slid his hands into the bodice of her dress, stroking the velvety smooth skin as he trailed his lips across her collarbone, to the hollow at the base of her throat.

'God, you are so beautiful,' he murmured as he felt her hand free his stiff cock from his trousers. Kissing him, she moved the crest against her damp sex, up and down until he was half-crazed with desire then guided him inside, rolling her hips along the length of him. They rocked together, oblivious to the movement of the car, their focus unshifting. Jess thrust herself hard onto him, wanting to take him as far she could, Theo sucking on her nipples, hands gripping her hips hard keeping her impaled on him.

'Fuck me, gorgeous,' he whispered and she grinned at him, slamming against him as her excitement built. His fingers dug into her flesh as she rode his cock, her muscles gripping him, hitting every sensitive point , driving him insane. She threw her head back and his lips moved to her throat, hungry to taste her skin, feel the pulse of her blood. He bit down on her shoulder as he neared his peak and he felt her cunt tightened around his cock, her thighs around his hips. She came to a shuddering climax a second before he shot into her, hard, groaning, grinding his hips up into her.

They caught their breath for a few moments before they reluctantly disconnected. Jess's face had that flush that he loved so much and to him, now, pregnant with his child, she had never looked so achingly lovely. He pulled her into the crook of his arms and she snuggled into him. She tilted her head up for a kiss.

'We should go tell your mom she's going to be a grandmother. I know the interview's not shown until Friday, but these days, it's bound to leak.'

He rested his forehead against hers. 'You're right. We should head over there but I may need to change first.'

She grinned. 'And that could take an hour...'

THREE HOURS LATER, Theo drove them both to his mother's house. Jess looked up at the impressive mansion.

'Can you believe in less than two weeks, we're getting married here?'

Theo took her hand as they walked up the stone steps. 'I can't wait.'

Amelia was, predictably, over the moon about the news. 'I have some news of a kind too,' she said, grinning. 'I think I've finally persuaded my friend Clem to be my plus one – I hope that's okay?'

She looked at Jess, her eyes searching the younger woman's reaction. Jess's heart gave a sickening thump but she kept her smile steady. 'Of course it is. Whatever makes you happy.'

Later, in bed, Theo's head on her chest, she listened to the steady rise and fall of his breathing as he slept. She had talked herself down from thinking Clem was Jules in disguise mostly. She still thought it strange that Amelia's new beau had avoided every effort to meet her and Theo – but, she reasoned, plenty of people were shy, or socially awkward and meeting the girlfriend's grown up, superstar son was bound to make anyone nervous.

Jess felt better, her fingers stroking gently into Theo's hair, she gazed down at him. 'I love you, funny face,' she whispered. Unconsciously, Theo's arms tightened around her and she closed her eyes, allowing sleep to wash over her. For the first time in weeks, she slept soundly without the nightmares that had plagued her.

MAX, however, couldn't get the plan out of his mind but it wasn't for a couple of days before he got Jess on her own. Thinking back, he pondered he probably have opened the conversation with something better than 'I think you're right about Clem.'

Jess's face had paled, turned green and she'd shot a look at Theo. They were in the garden and Theo was playing with the dogs. Seb and Tom were home from school and ganging up on their older brother as they teased and revved the dogs up into a frenzy. As fit as Theo was, the twenty-year age difference between him and the twins was beginning to show. Jess and Max were giggling at his exhausted demeanor and Max decided to broach the subject then and there.

Jess looked at him and he could see tears shining in her eyes. 'Max, don't.'

He immediately felt sorry, especially seeing how her hand fluttered protectively over the tiniest bump on her belly. 'I'm sorry, I shouldn't have blurted it out like that. What I mean is, there's something off about the guy. I'm not saying it's.... him... I'm just saying there's something about him we should maybe check out. You and me. I have his address on the island. You up for a little B&E?'

Jess studied him for a beat then a small smile crept over her face. 'Like Scooby Doo?'

Max laughed. 'Just like Scooby Doo. You can be Daphne. I'll be Freddy.'

Jess scoffed. 'If anything, you're Scooby.'

'That makes you Shaggy.'

'I can live with that.'

They chuckled then Jess nodded, her face suddenly serious. 'I would love to put my mind at rest once and for all. If he's Jules, I'll know immediately. I know him too well – even if it's him, there'll be some things he can't do without. He's too spoilt.'

'Good. Then we'll have to plan it for when... well, I don't think we should tell Theo.'

'Agreed. Well, he's got a meeting Monday evening. Come over and pick me up as if we're having dinner. I'll clear it with Mike.'

Max sat back in his chair, studying his friend. Even for her damage, maybe even because of it, Jess was a badass. She wanted this over. For a second, Max wondered if he'd done the right thing. Putting Jess in danger again? Theo would kill him if he knew.

This time, though, he would be prepared. Max thought of the little .22 he'd kept in his car ever since Josh was killed.

He was ready to use it if he needed to.

ON FRIDAY, Jess and Theo shut the world out and set up camp in the living room, switching on the big flat screen. Theo grinned when Jess cringed at the first sight of them on the screen.

'Camera loves you, beautiful,' he pulled her to him and kissed her temple.

'Who's looking at me when a god is sitting next to me?' She laughed as he rolled his eyes at her. The program went into an introductory package. Theo was studying Jess' face.

'Yeah, you're joking around but you, nervous?'

She nodded. 'Sure, I'm worried about the edit. Too many times people have twisted my words or make me seem frivolous, hysterical or worse, a liar.'

His arms tightened around her. 'Not this time.'

'You sure?'

'Yep. You know why? Because you are none of those things, Jessie. Not even close.'

She pressed her lips to his firmly. 'I love you.'

To her great relief, the interview was pretty much verbatim to what they had told Diane in the studio. There were more photos, video of Jess at work at the foundation and to her surprise and delight, interviews with both Gerry, her old boss at the college and the Dean, who spoke seriously about the painting Jules had destroyed and that he was sad that Jess had taken the blame for it.

'My regret is I made Jess a scapegoat when clearly, I should have supported her against the man who has hurt, terrorized and damaged Jess her whole life. I regret that decision greatly and would welcome Jess back as an associate anytime she would like.'

Jess flushed pleasantly at that but the glow faded quickly as the interview went into her relationship with Jules, and her stabbing. There was a brief clip of her being loaded into an ambulance, bloodied and broken, barely alive and worse, Theo, his beautiful face contorted with bottomless grief. She gasped, a brief intake of breath, a horrified sound and closed her eyes. Never again.

'Are you okay?' Theo's voice broke in the middle of his sentence and she hugged him as hard as she could.

'I'm so sorry, Theo...'

'It's not your fault.'

But she felt like it was. She could have been stronger with Jules at the start, told her Mom, her step-dad. Would they have believed her? Then, she would have never thought they would, but now, looking back, maybe she had misjudged them. Her step-father had sent Jules away to school for a reason. Jesus, what a fucking mess of a family.

JULES WATCHED the interview in a quiet bar in town. He stared at Jess's beautiful face, her smile, the way she looked at Storm, her voice – soft but with a new undercurrent of something else – strength. And then she'd said the words. The three of us... Theo and I and our child.

She was pregnant. Pregnant. With Storm's child.

Jules' fury knew no bounds. His jealousy rose up in him, a tide of vicious hate. He watched Jess as she smiled her happiness and he had never known such rage. Another betrayal. For this, he would make her suffer horribly before she herself died. Nodding to the barman, he brushed past the other customers and strode out purposefully into the street. Night was settling over the island, the rain unrelenting. He went home, found what he wanted and went to his car and drove out towards their house. Theo Storm's child.

He would make him watch while he slaughtered Jess and their baby.

AS THE INTERVIEW ENDED, Jess uncurled from the couch and went to the window. It was raining hard outside, thundering down, the lawn was already soaked. She felt Theo's arms slide around her waist, his mouth on the back of her neck.

'Theo...'

'Shhh.... it's just you and me now, Jessie.... all the pain is behind us...'

Even if he didn't mean it, his saying the words made her feel better. This was her family now. She turned in his arms and stared up into those intense green eyes she loved so much. Eighteen months and she'd lived and died a lifetime in those months.

She reached behind her and opened the French windows, pulling

Theo out with her onto the porch. Her face serious, she stepped out into the garden, the rain soaking her immediately and slowly stripped for him. Theo gave a hiss of feral excitement but she held up a hand, keeping him at bay. She was in charge now.

Naked, she walked towards him, pushing him back down onto the porch steps. She ran her hand between her legs and stroked herself.

'Theo?' Her voice was soft, sensual. 'What do you like?'

Theo seemed entranced by the rhythmic movement of her hand, the way the rain clung to her skin, golden-hued in the dim light. His hand moved to free his cock, thickening and straining against his pants and he fisted the root as he watched her masturbate, stroking and pulling at the quivering length.

'You...' he said, his voice a low growl, 'only you. I want to taste you.'

She stepped closer and he clamped his hands on her buttocks and buried his face in her sex. Jess bit down on her lip as his tongue delved deep inside her, tasting and biting down on her clitoris until it ached with desire. He brought her to the edge of orgasm before looking up at her, his smile lazy and languid. With a swift movement, he rolled her onto her back, pushing her legs as far apart as they could go and grinding his hips against hers, teasing her entrance with the wide crown, nudging in an inch and withdrawing until she was almost screaming with frustration and anticipation. He kissed her roughly.

'You want me?'

She nodded. 'God, yes, Theo... please.... now.'

'Tell me.'

'Fuck me, Theo, fuck me hard...'

'More.'

'Nail me to the ground, Theo, fucking fill me until I feel you everywhere.'

He grinned, still teasing her, feeling the hot, wet arousal of her cunt against his straining cock. He pressed a finger just above her clit. 'Will you feel me here?'

She nodded, enjoying the game, prolonging her arousal. He trailed his finger up to the bottom of her belly. 'Here?'

'God, yes...more...'

His finger circled her navel. 'Here?'

'Hell yes, god, Theo, please.... yes.....' She screamed as he drove his diamond-hard cock into her, pressing her legs open hard, his hand on her belly, he could feel his cock slamming into the very end of her. This was feral, animal sex and they were growling, biting and clawing at each other, not caring if they hurt each other, just need more, more, more...

Theo thrust with a fierce need to be inside her as deep as he could possibly be, his free hand plumping her breasts, taking each nipple into his mouth in turn, pulling and sucking until Jess was crying helplessly from desire. He pulled out before he came and ejaculated onto her soft belly, again and again, his semen mixing with the rain on her body. As he caught his breath, she slid down his body. Looking up, she smiled at him, sleepily sexy eyes shining. 'My turn to taste you, Theo... I'm going to milk you dry, handsome.' Then her lips parted over the crest of his cock and Theo closed his eyes as she took him into the warm hollow of her mouth, her tongue tracing a pattern over the tip, licking the salty taste of him, her hands at the root of him, pumping and stroking. She sucked at him hard, not relenting in her attack as he groaned and called her name into the gloom of the evening. He came again, almost violently, his semen gushing in a hot rush onto her tongue and she swallowed his seed down hungrily, the sight of her enjoying his taste made his cock tighten with desire, already semi-hard again after two orgasms.

'I need to fuck you again,' he growled and took her again, pressing her belly-first into the grass as he entered her from behind, her cunt slippery with her arousal. His fingers needed the tight round cheeks of her butt as he plowed into her, pulling them apart so he could see his cock driving into her. 'Christ, you make me so hard, beautiful...'

Jess's answering moan was long and shuddering and he felt his cock unbelievably thicken more until it almost hurt, sliding in and out of her silken dampness. He came quickly filling her and immediately plunged into her ass, wanting to possess her in every way this glorious night. Jess, helpless, her limbs liquefying under the assault on her senses, on her body, coming again and again. Theo reached under her body to stroke her hardened clit, feeling it jerk and pulse under his touch and Jess gave a shuddering cry a she came again.

Finally, slippery with rain, sweat and cum, they collapsed together onto the grass, gasping for air and laughing. Theo turned his head to smile at her.

'You think we'll ever get tired of doing that?'

Jess grinned, rolling onto her side and propping her head up on her hand. 'I hope not. I want to still be fucking in the rain when we're eighty.'

Theo stuck his hand out and she took it. 'Deal,' he said and pulled her on top of him again. She smoothed her palms over his face. 'Have you any idea how much I love you, Theodore Storm?'

He lifted his lips to hers. 'If it's the same as how much I love you, then hell, yes.'

Jess smiled at him and then shifted so she was straddling him, her hands wrapped around his stiffening cock. 'Ready to go again, soldier?'

HE WATCHED them roll naked on the grass and to his horror, his cock twitched up. He ignored it, instead fingering the cold metal of the pistol in his hand. God, he wanted to put a bullet into her as she fucked Theo Storm, see it smash into her soft abdomen, see the splash of her blood cover her lover as she bled out in his arms.

A fantasy, though – from this distance, he'd never hit her, he wasn't a good enough shot and it would blow his cover on the island. Besides, he wanted to be up close and personal when he killed her, wanted her blood on his hands again. Instead, he watched them fucking each other's brains out and jerked off, watching Jess's lovely body as she rocked her hips, riding Storm's cock until they were both coming.

After they dressed slowly, talking and laughing. Jules saw the security guard walk around the corner to speak to Theo. For a second, Jules tensed, wondering if they'd sensed his intrusion but when he saw the men smiling and laughing, he relaxed. Theo and Jess, hand-in-hand, followed him around to the front of the house. Jules watched them leave then turned his attention to the open French windows and smiled. Quickly, he shifted from his hiding place and darted across the lawn and into the house. The television set was still on, covering his movements as he snuck into the kitchen and down to the basement. He was in. He still didn't know what he intended to do but just knowing she was sleeping two floors above him, oblivious, made his cock harden.

So close, my Jessica, so close.

THEO WOKE up on Monday morning with a new sense of optimism. Somehow the interview had felt like a statement of intent – nothing can break us – and what followed, the amazing, sensual fucking in the rain...he had no words for that. He smiled as he shaved. A whole weekend of just being together, talking, having fun. It had been utterly perfect. Friday night's rain had disappeared and now it was glorious outside. He wondered idly if they could rent a boat, go out on the water, go whale-watching if the weather held to the next weekend.

'Theo?'

'Up here, baby.'

Jess came back up the stairs, pale, shaking, and immediately the tension in his chest returned.

'What is it?'

'I was just putting some laundry in the machine and could you come with me please and tell me I'm not crazy?' She whispered. The tone of her voice alarmed him.

He followed her back down into the basement. She stood in front of the basement's broken window and wordlessly, pointed at the floor. The bare lightbulb shone down onto the scrubbed floor-boards. Glints, sparkles of light. Glass. Broken glass lay on the floor and as he studied it, he realized with a shock that it had been arranged carefully, precisely. They looked at each other in confusion.

The glass was arranged into a single word.

Jess.

'Look, it's hardly threatening, is it? Maybe it was one of the twins fooling around.' Jess was getting annoyed. After her earlier unease, she'd talked herself down and thought Theo would see it more calmly but Theo's immediate reaction was to call the police, get Mike to increase security. Jess felt all the happiness, the security they'd built back up slip away.

'I still think we should call the police....'

'And tell them what?' She interrupted. 'Help, come quick, some-one's leaving words in our house?'

'Don't be facetious,' Theo muttered crossly. She put her hand on his arm.

'I'm sorry but...it's my fault, I shouldn't have reacted to it. I honestly think it's just a prank one of the boys played. That window has been broken for ages.'

'Mike would have spotted it.'

'From outside? Not likely, it's tiny and tucked away. Besides, you need to be a Lilliputian to fit through it so it's not a big security risk.' She tugged on his hand. 'Come on, let's forget about it. Work's calling.'

She went back upstairs but Theo stayed, staring at the glass. Maybe she was right; her name was hardly a threat, was it? He reminded himself to text Seb and Tom when he got to work. Theo bent down with the brush to sweep up the glass then stopped himself. Changing his mind, he went to get his camera and quickly snapped off a few shots of the glass. With the dustpan, he carefully scooped up the shards and dropped them into a bag. Instead of throwing them away, he stashed them in a cupboard. Fingerprints.

Paranoia. No way, he told himself crossly, after everything that's happened, nothing's too small. Satisfied, he went upstairs to finishing dressing.

MAX PICKED Jess up from work that night. Theo's meeting was going to run late into the evening and so it was easy for Max and Jess to find an excuse to go home together. As Max pulled his car from the ferry, Jess was getting a little excited about their less-than-legal excursion.

'What shall we do, wait till he goes out?'

Max shot her a look. 'Obviously, doofus.'

Jess grinned good-naturedly. 'Sorry, that was dumb, but all of this is new to me.'

They drove to two blocks away from Clem's house and parked. It was almost dark so they could slip along the street without being seen.

Clem's house was in darkness.

'Ready?' Max looked at Jess crouched next to him in the alleyway. His gaze drifted downwards to her black top and leggings. She raised her eyebrows at him, amused. Max smirked.

'Is that your special breaking and entering outfit?'

She looked down. 'It's the only black t-shirt I've got.'

'You look like Cat-woman without the mask.'

'Geek.'

'Doofus.'

The banter was making her less nervous and she was grateful to Max for making her feel better.

'I don't think he's in...let's give it a try, huh?'

They moved quickly, keeping to the shadows. At the door to the apartment, Jess reached up over the lintel. She shook her head. Max shrugged and reached into his pocket. Kneeling, he picked the lock.

'They teach you that at Pony?' Jess grinned at him.

'Nope. In high school. Came in handy when we used to break into my dad's liquor cabinet.'

Jess snorted. Max grinned and, flicking on his flashlight, led her in. They stood in the darkened living room. Jess looked around.

'I don't even know where to start.'

Max swept the flashlight over the room.

'Drawers, any drawers, boxes, stuff like that.'

'Got it.'

After five minutes, Jess hissed in frustration. 'Damn it. Nothing'

'Patience. Check the bedroom.'

Jess grimaced but did what he asked. She heard him thumping.

'What are you doing?'

'Checking for squeaky floorboards.'

She giggled and went to meet him. 'I don't think there's anything, Max. I know Jules, we'd at least find some exquisitely tailored suits, something that he couldn't live without, the big asshole. But there's nothing. This place is steeped in good-old-boy normalcy.'

Max nodded. 'Yep. The only thing I found is an old newspaper from when you were stabbed. But that could have been here forever.'

'Suddenly I feel bad,' Jess admitted. 'Poor guy. Let's get out of here.'

They were just about to leave when they heard a truck door slam. Max peeked around the corner.

Shit.' Max turned and pushed her back inside. 'Go, go.'

Max dragged her into the kitchen and into the pantry. The space was tight and she was pressed up against him. They listened to Clem enter, throw his keys down and went into the kitchen. Through the slats in the pantry door, they could see him grabbing a beer from the fridge. He leaned against the counter and drank.

Through her fear, Jess was aware of being pressed up against Max. The situation was almost comical. All the terror left her then. Jess felt laughter bubble up inside her and buried her face in his chest to muffle it. Her weight shifted and something moved on the shelf behind her. They froze.

Clem looked over towards the door and Jess stopped breathing. He had blonde hair and blue eyes but those eyes ... she shivered. She couldn't be sure it was Jules but they held all the malevolence of her reviled step-brother. She couldn't see what Amelia saw in this guy. She began to tremble. Clem opened a drawer, still looking towards the door, and pulled out a kitchen knife. Max reached around his back and slowly pulled out his gun. Jess bugged at him. Max winked at her and mouthed 'Don't worry.'

Clem reached over to the fruit bowl and picked up an apple, chopping it in two in one easy movement. He looked back over to the pantry door, took a step towards it.

Max slipped the safety off. Jess started to tremble and he kissed her forehead, never taking his eyes from Clem.

A loud knocking at the door. Clem hesitated for a beat, then strode over to the door and pulled it open

'Amelia! What a lovely surprise.'

Jess and Max gaped at each other. Amelia was walking into the kitchen with Clem'.

'I thought I'd just drop your invitation around.'

'Can I offer you a drink?'

'Oh no, really, I just stopped by on the off-chance. I'm actually just going to see Jess.'

Jess and Max froze as Clem glanced again at the pantry door. Jess could feel her heart beating out of her chest.

'Then how could I delay you?'

Amelia and Clem said goodbye and Clem stepped back into the kitchen. Jess and Max stopped breathing as he stood, planted square in his kitchen, staring at the closed pantry door. For a long, eerie, unsettling moment, his eyes seemed to drift in and out of focus. Jess stared at him.

It could be him. It could be him. The disguise was very good if it was Jules. The black hair that he'd prized was shaved almost to nothing and bleached a bright white. The beard – false or not – was bushy, huge, hipster-like and covered more than half of the bottom of his face. The eyes... too blue to be natural. Contacts, Jess thought now, with a growing terror building inside her.

A loud rapping at Clem's door made them all start.

'Clem? Let me in.'

Jess and Max gaped at each other. It was a woman from the bar on the island, Caroline. She was snippy redhead who had taken a dislike to Jess on sight. Amelia had told her, discreetly, that Caroline had grown up with Theo, had her sights set on him, even in the face of Theo's utter ambivalence. Clem strode over to the door and pulled it open. Caroline brushed past him into the room.

'Thanks for waiting for me.' Her tone was snippy.

'You said you'd be on the seven-thirty. I was there at seven-thirty. You were not. Do you want a drink?'

Caroline sat down in the living room. 'Yes. Scotch. What was so pressing you couldn't wait an extra thirty minutes?'

Jess and Max watched while Clem handed her a glass.

'Believe it or not, I'm not inclined nor am I obligated to wait around for you?'

Caroline grunted. 'I forgive you.'

Clem smiled without humour. 'What do you want, Caroline?'

'I want to know why you're fucking that old woman. Especially her.'

Jess could feel Max tense up, his hand flexing on his gun. She put her hands against his chest, cautioning him, calming him.

'Ah. How about we not talk about... that... for just this one night?'

Clem put his drink down and pulled Caroline to her feet. 'I think we can use this time better.' He kissed her and Caroline responded.

'I missed you, baby.' She crooned. Jess wrinkled her nose and made a gagging gesture which made Max grin.

Caroline held out her hand to Clem and led him into the living room. Max waited for a beat and pushed the pantry door open. Taking Jess's hand, they crept across the door to living room, eyes always on the couple there. They caught a glimpse of Clem's back, Caroline, on her knees before him. Max turned the handle of the back door and made Jess go out before him. They were almost at the bottom when they heard the door open above them.

'Go, go, go!' Max whispered and pushed Jess out of the door. Behind them, they could hear Clem's heavy footsteps. Max grabbed her hand and they raced through the night, ducking down the alleys behind the apartment until they reached their car, Max throwing it into gear and speeding off into the night.

. . .

JULES STOOD IN THE DOORWAY. He'd been sure someone was in the house and when the back door had opened, he had darted from the living room, leaving a frustrated Caroline shouting after him. Whoever it was, and he was pretty sure who it was, had disappeared from view just as he reached the door. He swore. It was the fag but he hadn't been alone. Surely Jess hadn't been with him? In his house, spying on him. Bitch.

'What the fuck are you doing?'

He turned. Caroline was standing at wrapped in a sheet. Stupid whore. She was becoming a problem, a risk factor. He would have to get rid of her before she blew his cover.

He smiled at her. 'Nothing, darling.' He moved to her side and kissed her.

He would have to make sure her body wasn't discovered until after Jess was dead. The wedding day was in less than a week.

Theo looked down at his love, her face so relaxed. He lived for these quiet moments, it was if they sunk into each other, the world outside could not touch them. He listened to her breathing as she slept, regular and peaceful. Her left hand rested on the pillow, the white gold band with the diamond on her ring finger. Theo smiled and sighed. They had decided to risk the bad luck ('Surely we've had enough') and spend the night before the wedding together in his mom's house. His mom had disapproved but had compromised by making him promise to go home to get ready so he wouldn't see Jess in her dress. In a few short hours they would be married, she would be his forever. He trailed a finger down her soft cheek, bent over to kiss the smooth pink skin. Jess stirred and murmured, still deep in sleep.

He showered quickly, then stood at the sink while he shaved.

Glancing in the mirror he saw, through the open door to their bedroom, that Jess was awake and watching him. She said nothing but a small smile played on her lips. He smiled back at her reflection and continued to get ready, glancing in the mirror every few seconds at her. She giggled as he raised an eyebrow at her.

When he was dressed he came back into the bedroom. 'You,' he bent down and kissed her, 'are a distraction.'

She cupped his face. 'Come back to bed.' She murmured and he laughed.

'Bad girl.' He considered her offer but then looked at the clock and grimaced. 'I'm kind of late already.' He laughed at her sulky face and sat on the edge of the bed. 'I have a very, very bossy best man. I feel sorry for Seth.'

Jess giggled. 'Can you believe it's today?'

'I cannot wait to call you Mrs. Storm.'

'Okay then, I suppose you can go to your mom's. She'll be here in an hour to lever me into my dress.'

He smiled tenderly and covered her belly with his big hand. 'You and the Bean.'

'Me and the Bean,' she agreed, happily.

She sat up and looked out of the window.

'God, what a beautiful day.' She grinned at him, excited, looking like a kid. He laughed.

'Yep, it's stunning out there.' He leaned over and kissed her again. 'Although it's nothing to what I can see right now.'

She moaned. 'How am I supposed to let you out of the door when you say things like that?' She pulled him down and he laughed.

'Woman, you're insatiable.'

'How late did you say you were?' She whispered as she pressed her body against his. He groaned, covered her mouth with his and started to take off his shirt.

'Not nearly late enough.'

He stripped the rest of his clothes off in a hurry and slid back into bed with her, kissing her, his tongue caressing hers, exploring her sweet mouth. Her legs twined around his body and he could feel the hot wetness of her sex against his thigh. God, would he ever get enough of her? His cock stood, ramrod straight against his belly and he teased her entrance with the tip of it, as his mouth found her nipple, sucking and biting down on it.

'I'm so wet for you,' she whispered in his ear, 'fill me, Theo, fuck me senseless, make me come.'

Jesus. His cock grew thicker, strained to get inside her and as he slid into her, her warm, wet softness enveloping the length of him, he thrust deep, to the root, to be as close to her as he could, skin-on-skin. Her thighs tightened around his hips, and their bodies moved as if they were desperate to sink into each other. Theo, with a brutal roll of hips driving himself into her, watched as her breasts swelled, her belly undulating with their movements, her face flush pink, her mouth open, gasping for air, her dark eyes shining and fixed onto his. So, so beautiful, Theo kissed her and she urged him deeper inside, tilting her hips to accommodate him. With a hand, he pressed her legs further apart, then scooping her buttocks up, slammed into her again and again until she was crying out with pleasure and pain. He came violently, his groin jerking, his cock pumping out hot, viscous semen deep inside her. He grinned, knowing his seed would still be inside her as she walked down the aisle, that she was his in every way. He felt her vibrating and quivering, crying out as she reached orgasm but he didn't let he recover, withdrawing his still hard cock and flipping her onto her back, parting her legs and pushing into her perfect ass, moving slowly as she moaned and writhed beneath him. They both came again and again and by the time Theo kissed her goodbye, they were so giddy and delirious with love, they could barely bear to part.

'See you at the end of the aisle, beautiful,' he murmured, his lips against her mouth.

'I love you.'

And then he was gone.

MAX WAS BUILDING himself up into a feverish state by the time Theo called to say he was on his way. Seth was trying to calm him down by distracting him but Max couldn't shake the feeling that something was wrong. Was it something he forgot to do? No... it's Jules. Max knew that today would be the day Jules would try to kill Jess again, maybe Theo too. What better way to get his revenge.

Paranoid, he told himself. Mike, Theo's head of security, was on everything – nobody on the island moved without Mike knowing about it. He went to look for him now and found him scanning a computer file.

'Hey dude, everything looking good?'

Mike looked up and smiled. 'All good. I'm heading over to Mrs. Storm's place now.'

HE DIDN'T SEE the truck until it was too late. Theo swore and swerved but the Mercedes slammed into it. Jules had moved it across the exit to the blind bend on the way to Amelia's house and they didn't have a chance. The car slid on the road and slipped down the embankment. It hit the tree side on. Theo's head smashed against the window and he was knocked senseless. The wiper blades kept moving while all else was silent.

Jules smiled as he stood at the road's edge looking down at the car. Time to call Jess and ask her once and for all, if she would give up her life for her lover's.

Jules was in no doubt of the answer.

MIKE ROUNDED the corner and slammed on the brakes. Theo's car was burning. 'Shit,' Mike leaped from the car and darted as close as he could. He couldn't see a body in the front seat. Yanking his phone from his pocket, he was about to dial 911 when he heard the tell-tale click of a safety being flicked off. He didn't have time to turn toward the noise before the bullet tore through his skull and silenced him forever.

JESS STEPPED into the dress that Amelia held and stood obediently as her almost-mother-in-law buttoned up the bodice. The dress, although deceptively simple, was light, flowing and of pure white.

Jess smirked to herself. Thanks to Theo, she was about as far from a virgin as someone could be.

Amelia stood back and looked at her, her eyes filling with tears. Jess's dark hair was soft waves, pulled over one shoulder. The dress itself had sleeves of the most delicate chiffon which belled out delicately at the wrist, the skirt ending just above Jess's knees. Against her honey skin, the white glowed, highlighting her subtle make-up and large brown eyes. Amelia sighed.

'You look beautiful, Jessie. I'm so proud to call you my daughter.'

Amelia's phone rang and she snagged it from the table as Jess turned and admired the dress in the mirror.

'Clem, darling, how lovely... what? Oh, that's a shame. Well, perhaps we'll see you at the reception this evening?'

Jess glanced at Amelia in the mirror. She and Max hadn't told her about Clem and Caroline and Amelia hadn't mentioned dating Clem so they decided to leave it. Amelia was smiling now.

'Yes, of course...' She put her hand over the mic. 'Clem wants to say congratulations.' She held the phone out to Jess, who took, a little bemused.

'Hello?'

'Keep smiling, it's very important you keep smiling. Say hello to me, Jessica.'

Terror screeched back into every fiber of her being. I knew it. I knew it. Jules.

'Hi, Clem, nice to speak to you.'

She realized her face was frozen in a false smile. 'Hello, Clem, nice to speak to you.'

'Good. There's a gun in my hand and the muzzle is currently against your fiancé's temple. There are five bullets in it. All five will be in his head very soon unless you go what I say. Tell me you understand.'

'I understand... Clem.'

'Keep smiling. Now, find a way to get out and drive home. If you're not here in ten minutes, Theo is dead. Then I'll come for you. It's entirely up to you whether he dies. Either way, this is the day you are going to die, Jessica. Say thank you, Jessica.'

'Thank you, Clem.' Her voice quivered just a little but Amelia, tidying the room, didn't seem to notice.

'Ten minutes, Jessica, and I'll let you say goodbye before I put my knife into you.'

The line went dead. Jess stood, holding the phone, frozen. Jules had Theo. She closed her eyes.

'Jess, honey, you okay?' Amelia sounded concerned. She tried to smile at the older woman.

'I'm fine. Just nerves. I might just get some fresh air.'

Downstairs she grabbed Amelia's car keys and ran. Theo, I'm coming... please, hang on...

SHE PUSHED OPEN the door slowly. The house was silent. She moved through the rooms silently, the gun in her hand. Jess was amazed she wasn't terrified – more like, she was mad. Real mad. This ended today. Jules wouldn't stop until one of them was dead so she had no doubt in her mind that she could kill him. She wanted to. He'd taken Theo, might have even killed him by now – she pushed that thought away. Her adrenaline coursed through her body.

'Jules?'

'In here.'

She turned at the sound of his voice and followed it to the main living room. Then all her fight left her as she saw Theo, tied to a chair, blood coursing down from a vicious head wound, his head slumped, his body crumpled. He looked dead.

Nonononononono.... she realized the frenzied screams were coming from her, and every plan she'd made left her brain in her grief. She started toward him then Jules grabbed her from behind. She felt a stinging pain in her neck and then she was falling....

. . .

THEO OPENED HIS EYES, for a second not understanding. Jess was in a chair opposite him, unconscious, her white dress – her wedding dress - cut open down past her navel. Oh god no. She'd come to help him and put herself into Jules' hands. Theo struggled again the cuffs Jules had used to bind him to the chair.

'I wouldn't bother.'

Jules' amused voice came from behind him and he heard the safety catch on a gun being clicked off, felt the cold metal of gun being pressed to his temple. Jules chuckled.

'When she wakes up for the last time, this all ends. You'll watch her die, Storm. You'll watch me stab her over and over until she's dead. But you won't have to mourn her for long. You'll be joining her very soon.'

The pressure of the gun lifted and Jules pulled up a chair between him and Jess. She stirred and Theo's heart jumped in fear. The one small hope was this – Jess didn't seem to be bound but he knew that was another one of Jules' games. He wanted Jess to allow him to kill her in the hope he'd let Theo go.

Jules went to check her and as she opened her eyes, he pressed the muzzle of his gun again her bare skin. 'Hello beauty.'

Jess's eyes rolled, dazed; when they found Theo's desperate ones, their gazes locked and she could see the devastation in them.

'I love you,' she whispered. Jules growled and cuffed her.

'Shut up, whore.'

Theo roared, trying to get up from his chair. In one flash, Jules whipped behind Jess, hooking the hand holding the gun around her neck, and with the other, pulling his knife from his pocket. He kissed Jess. 'Say goodbye, beautiful.' And he raised the knife.

Jess bit down on his other hand hard, as hard as she could and Jules roared in pain. Jess pushed back with all her might, knocking Jules over and the gun out of his hand, under the couch. She threw her body on top of Jules, fighting, kicking punching, ripping his shirt. The keys to Theo's cuffs fell out of his pocket and she grabbed them, throwing them in Theo's direction as Jules lashed at her with his knife. She ducked and scrambled to her feet as Jules fought to grab her. Jess paused briefly, one second when she met Theo's eyes.

He looked at her. Not understanding. Then realization. He shook his head. She winked at him. His face registered absolute horror.

'No, no. Jess, don't.'

Her gaze was intense. 'I love you. I will always love you no matter what.'

He shook his head violently, never taking his eyes from hers. 'Please don't...

She had tears in her eyes. 'I'm sorry, Theo. It has to be like this. I love you.'

Theo broke down. 'No, please... Jess...'

Her face was determined as Jules rose up between them. Her eyes alive with anger as she beckoned her killer towards her.

'Come on, Jules. Wanna kill me? Come on then, motherfucker, come get me.'

'No! Jess, please, no!' Theo was screaming now.

Jules in his frenzy didn't hesitate, he lunged for her, slashing the knife, catching her in a blow across her stomach.

'No!' Theo screamed as blood bloomed across her white dress, her honey skin. Jess ignored the searing pain and took off with Jules in pursuit. Theo, desperate, shuffled over to where Jess had thrown the keys.

'What the fuck are you doing, Jess?' But he knew. 'You stupid, stupid, brave, beautiful girl.' he sobbed as he managed to slide the key into the cuffs. She was leading Jules away from him, giving him time to free himself.

She was sacrificing herself to save him.

FIRST, she went to the front door but even from a distance she could see that Jules had dead-bolted it. By the time she could get it open, Jules would be on her. He was close, close enough she could hear his frenzied breathing. She darted up the stairs and nearly made it to the safety of a bedroom before he grabbed her. They tumbled to the floor together, Jess fighting with every ounce of strength she had left. Jules was grinning now, knowing his size and strength would beat her now, despite her struggles.

'I'm going to kill you now, Jess, nothing can stop me.'

He rammed his forearm against her throat and as she began to choke, he pulled a knife from his pocket. Jess, knowing that this was it, tried one last thing.

'I'm pregnant, Jules. I'm pregnant.'

He smiled. 'So I hear. Congratulations. But I don't care. I'm going to kill you anyway.'

It was over. Jess struggled but as she felt Jules's knife begin to slice into her belly, the searing pain nothing to the terror she felt for her unborn child. She could smell blood.

'No, Jess, no!'

A frenzied cry, close, so close, Theo was dragging Jules from her. Jess rolled onto her stomach, clamping a hand over her wounds, pushing the thought of the baby away. Please, little bean, hang on.

Theo was pounding on Jules, the two men locked in a death fight. 'Jess, get away, get out now!' Theo was screaming at her. Blood-loss was making her light-headed. Not again. She crawled to the stairs and almost tumbled down them. There was something she could do. Something Jules had missed in the fight. Something Theo had forgotten. Slowly, painfully, she crawled her way into the living room.

THEO, his immense strength almost leaving him when he saw Jules stab Jess – again – grappled with the other man, wanting more than anything to break this monster's neck, pound him into the dust. Jules, his knife gripped in his hand, swiped at Theo, one, twice before making contact. The knife tore through Theo's shirt, slicing into the skin of his chest and Theo jerked back, away from the knife. Jules caught him on the temple with the hilt of the knife, making Theo's already concussed head swirl. Jules took him out by the knees and Theo was on the ground. Vulnerable.

Jules laughed, raising the knife to plunge it into Theo's chest...

then his head exploded, his eyes bulging with surprise. Jules' body slumped to the side, blood gushing from the fatal head wound. Theo, still stunned, looked up to see his beautiful Jess, her hand clamped over the bloody wounds on her stomach, holding the gun she'd just used to kill Jules.

Dropping the gun, Jess stumbled towards Theo and he was up, grabbing her as she slumped into his arms. He scooped her up and went downstairs, cradling her in his arms.

'I'm okay,' she said weakly, 'it's not that deep, I'm okay, I'm okay.' Theo reached over to grab the phone, called 911.

In the distance he could hear sirens and almost collapsed with relief.

Theo and Jess, blood-soaked, exhausted, gazed at each other and started to smile, despite their injuries.

'It's over, my Jessie. All over.'

She started to laugh, tears rolling down her face. 'I know, my darling, I know.'

Theo grinned, kissing her tears away as the sirens got ever closer and now he could hear shouting. Max. His mom.

He heard them break down the door in their frenzy to get in.

'In here,' he hollered then pulled her lips to his again. 'Jessie....we're going to get out of here, and get all fixed up , and then it's just you, me and the Bean. For all time, Jessie.'

'For all time....'

THE END.

PREVIEW OF LUCKY BILLIONAIRE

PREVIEW OF LUCKY BILLIONAIRE

An Alpha Billionaire Romance

By Michelle Love

Blurb

Blake Chandler- 22 years old. *Has won five lotteries the previous year as he traveled across the country to spread his parent's ashes and purchased lottery tickets with money they left him and instructions to do. He won twenty billion, but after taxes he's down to a mere ten billion and is looking for financial advice. He lives in Lubbock, Texas, next door to Lexi's brother, Josh. Josh sets him up with Max Lane to help get his finances straight before he loses it all to taxes. Blake's physical appearance is; tall, 6'3" muscular, shoulder length blonde curls, symmetrical chiseled features, brown and blue hazel eyes. He's a sweet, happy-go-lucky guy. He makes fast friends with Max and Kip. (He's met Kip and Peyton in L.A. at the beach)*
Rachelle Stone- 20 years old, but turns 21 in the first book- In college at UCLA, in L.A. in the Culinary Arts Program. Her mother doesn't know who

her father is and has little to do with her. When she was three her mother placed her in a children's home. (The same one Max Lane was in, he was fifteen at the time) Her grandparents live in Round Rock, Texas and that's her only real family. She has abandonment issues. Her physical appearance is; Small frame, 5'2", deep black, straight hair that hangs to her small waist. Brilliant, deep blue eyes fringed in dark, thick lashes. Porcelain skin with hints of pink staining her high cheek bones and red, pouty lips. Her character is trying hard to be tough and keep most people at arms-length. Peyton is her best friend and after meeting Max again, she forms a little bond with him as an older brother figure.

ABOUT THE AUTHOR

Mrs. Love writes about smart, sexy women and the hot alpha billionaires who love them. She has found her own happily ever after with her dream husband and adorable 6 and 2 year old kids. Currently, Michelle is hard at work on the next book in the series, and trying to stay off the Internet.

"Thank you for supporting an indie author. Anything you can do, whether it be writing a review, or even simply telling a fellow reader that you enjoyed this. Thanks

❀ Created with Vellum